Praise for

INFINITY ALCHEMIST

'Richly built. This is magical.'
Booklist, starred review

'Callender's diverse cast of queer and polyamorous characters
provides some much-needed representation
to the YA fantasy genre.'
Aiden Thomas, author of *The Sunbearer Trials*

'Political intrigue, a fascinating magic system, and heart-
pounding action propel the plot and, combined with Ash's
unfurling relationships, result in a refreshingly
affirming and tender standout fantasy.'
Publishers Weekly, starred review

'A blast of heart-racing magic you won't want to miss.'
Andrew Joseph White, author of *Hell Followed With Us*

'This elaborate adventure leads to some surprising places –
readers will thrill to the high-stakes predicaments and
appreciate the characters' attempts to remain true to
themselves, no matter the cost.'
Horn Book

'Full of smart dialogue and moves with the kind of pace that
will keep readers drawn in, but it is the overriding feeling of
empathy throughout that elevates this resonant fantasy.'
BookPage

'Phenomenal.'
ReactorMag.com

T0372182

CHAOS KING

KACEN CALLENDER

faber

First published in the US by Tor Teen,
an imprint of Macmillan Publishing Group, LLC in 2025
First published in the UK in 2025
by Faber & Faber Limited
The Bindery, 51 Hatton Garden,
London, EC1N 8HN
faber.co.uk

Typeset in Adobe Jenson
Printed and bound by
CPI Group (UK) Ltd, Croydon, CR0 4YY

A CIP record for this book is available from the British Library

ISBN 978–0–571–38386–3

MIX
Paper | Supporting
responsible forestry
FSC® C013604

Printed and bound in the UK on FSC® certified paper in line with our continuing
commitment to ethical business practices, sustainability and the environment.
For further information see faber.co.uk/environmental-policy

Our authorised representative in the EU for product safety is
Easy Access System Europe, Mustamäe tee 50, 10621 Tallinn, Estonia
gpsr.requests@easproject.com

1 3 5 7 9 10 8 6 4 2

THE EIGHT HOUSES
OF NEW ANGLIA

HEAD HOUSE OF ALEXANDER: Leaders

HOUSE OF KENDRICK: Redguards

HOUSE OF LUNE: Diviners

HOUSE OF ADELAIDE: Healers

HOUSE OF GALAHAD: Merchants

HOUSE OF ALDER: Keepers

HOUSE OF VAL: Scientists

HOUSE OF THORNE: Engineers

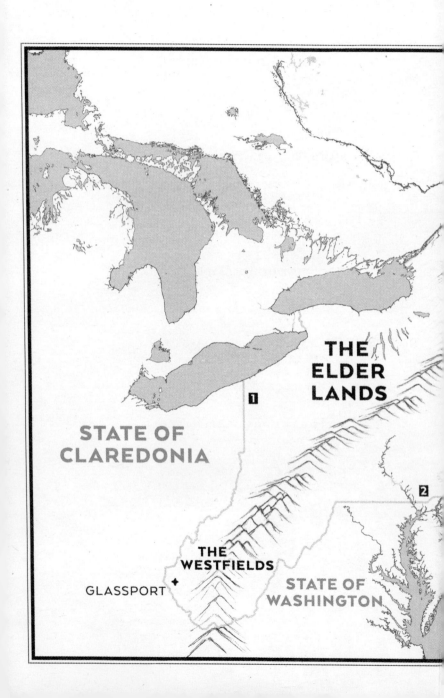

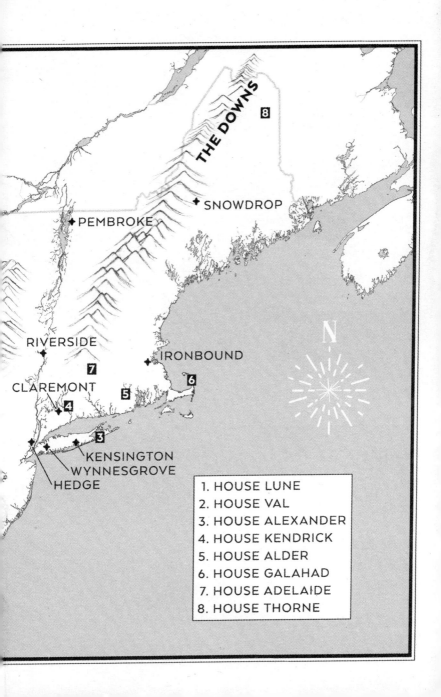

THE DOWNS

◆ SNOWDROP

◆ PEMBROKE

RIVERSIDE

7

IRONBOUND

CLAREMONT

5

4

6

N

3

KENSINGTON
WYNNESGROVE
HEDGE

1. HOUSE LUNE
2. HOUSE VAL
3. HOUSE ALEXANDER
4. HOUSE KENDRICK
5. HOUSE ALDER
6. HOUSE GALAHAD
7. HOUSE ADELAIDE
8. HOUSE THORNE

CHAOS
KING

1

"Y ou are his children," he said. "Hear me when I say that you are
perfect and beloved creations."

Flickering torches made shadows dance on red clay walls.
There were no windows. The floor was dirt. So many crowded
into the room that there was hardly any space to move or breathe.
The rumors had spread through the Elder lands: *He has returned.*

"You who have waited with faith and have fought in our Creator's name," the man said. "You are the worthy."

Marlowe's hood shadowed her face. She stood against a wall
near the archway at the back of the room, an old habit in case
of a needed quick escape. She tried to appear relaxed, but tension gripped her limbs. Her heart thrummed. She tried to catch
a glimpse of the man, but she could hardly see through the crowd.
She saw only a lock of hair, the threads of linen clothes. People
around her stood on their toes, craning their necks. Others cried,
tears streaming. It was as the prophecy foretold, someone whispered. The world had burned, and now he had come to save them.

"But there is work to be done still."

Marlowe wasn't sure why she suddenly found it difficult to
breathe, as if the air itself had become too thick.

"There are some," the man continued, "who hope to tempt you
onto a path that leads away from the Creator's will."

The person in front of Marlowe probably wasn't conscious of
it, the fact that he had moved just a little to the left, nor the person before him that she had shifted to the right. The movement
rippled forward, a sudden parting of the crowd—and there, at
the very front of the room, the man sat in Marlowe's view. He

was surprisingly young, Marlowe thought vaguely, maybe only in his thirties, with pale skin and eyes so light that, from afar, they appeared white. His gaze settled on her.

"There are those," the man said, as if speaking only to Marlowe now, "who steal from the Creator's power."

Marlowe swallowed, then pulled at the edges of her hood and turned away, pushing through the crowd that surrounded the exit. The man's voice followed. "Children, hear me now: This is the Creator's will."

She slipped through the bodies that waited, ignoring the glances and frowns. She burst out of the crowd and into the dark hall, and still she could hear the man, the one who called himself Sinclair Lune. "Before I can take you to sanctuary, you must fulfill the wishes of the Creator. You must eliminate his enemies.

"You must kill those who call themselves 'alchemists.'"

2

The city burned. Buildings cracked and crumbled. Bodies hung by their necks from the railway tracks, fires crackling beneath. Black smoke gushed into the sky until it blocked the sun. White dust rained, coating Ash's skin and stinging his eyes as he ran. He couldn't breathe, his throat clogged, and the bodies—people lay strewn in the street, mangled corpses stained red with eyes wide open, mouths parted in surprise. Ash slowed to a stop as he realized who the bodies belonged to. It was his father, again and again at his feet, knife sticking from his ribs—

Ash spun around. A black orb, as large as the moon itself, was crashing to the earth. Its gravitational pull tore apart the towers that still stood, wind whipping debris into its path. Ash heard an echo—heard his name—and when he blinked, his mother stood in front of him, eyes wide with panic as she screamed—

Ash shot up in bed. He wheezed, heart slamming against his chest and echoing in his ears. He was alone. A lazy breeze shifted the curtains of an open window that yellow sunlight poured through. A bird tweeted, and another replied. A nightmare. It'd only been another nightmare.

Ash wished he could let out a breath of relief. Instead, he put his face in his hands, gulping down air. The dreams had been so bad recently that he was afraid to fall asleep. Sometimes it was the destruction of Kensington, the embers of buildings and smoke pouring from flames. Sometimes it was his father, dead on the bridge.

Worst of all was his mother. Ash had rarely dreamed of her before. He'd hoped she would visit him in his sleep after she'd died so that he wouldn't feel so damn alone—he'd heard that energies of the dead would sometimes do that, visit their loved ones with messages, but she'd never come. Now, she appeared almost every single night. Now, his mother would always shout his name.

"Ash?"

He looked up, startled. Callum hesitated on the threshold. Ash realized what he must've looked like in that moment: skin graying, eyes tight.

The other boy dipped his head to enter the room. His dark brown skin looked especially beautiful in the early morning light. Ash's heart fell, just a little, as he saw that Callum was already dressed in his red button-down and black slacks.

"Are you all right?" Callum asked. He'd probably felt Ash's panic from the other room. Callum paused, then seemed to think better of it. No, of course, Ash wasn't all right.

Ash threw off the sheets, damp with sweat. His loose sleeping shirt and pants were wet and cold, too. "Just another nightmare."

Callum padded across the room and sat on the edge of the bed beside Ash, the mattress sinking under his weight. He rested a hand on Ash's thigh, thumb brushing his skin. Ash sighed as pale blue light pooled over him. Whether Callum extended energy purposefully or not, he'd always had a way of calming Ash.

"Have you given my offer any more thought?" the older boy asked quietly.

Ash chewed the inside of his cheek. He knew that Callum was only trying to help, this insistence that Ash see a healer. House Adelaide didn't only heal physical ailments. *They can help with emotional troubles, too.* Ash wasn't sure why it annoyed him, Callum's determination to bring up the topic again and again.

"I'm fine," Ash said, swinging his feet to the floor.

Callum took a breath and seemed about to argue, but then only sighed. "I have something for you."

"A gift?"

Ash watched as Callum went to the dresser and pulled out a drawer. He returned with a pair of red cuff links. "I thought you could wear them tonight," he said.

Callum pressed the pair into Ash's open palm, cold against his skin. "Thank you," Ash said, "but these are House Kendrick's colors."

"Wearing red could be a sign of your loyalty to me, too, not just my House." The smile on his face seemed exhausted to Ash. "I've made a pot of oatmeal, if you'd like any. I'll be leaving soon," he added.

"Ramsay, too?"

"In a little while, I think."

Ash rubbed a hand over his face, closing his fingers around the cuff links. "I'll join you in a second. And Callum?" Ash held up his fist. "Really. Thank you."

Callum gave Ash's shoulder a quick squeeze.

Ash watched Callum's retreat, then put the cuff links on the nightstand and stripped off the wet shirt he'd slept in and dropped it to add to the collection of clothes tangled across the floor. Callum had given up on scolding Ash and Ramsay about the mess. "We're not living in redguard barracks," Ramsay had said dismissively. "There's no point in folding clothes that'll only need to be worn again." Ash, admittedly, was just lazy.

Ash tugged open the bottom drawer of a faded blue dresser—he'd offered to take the lowest, seeing that he was the smallest of the three—and pulled out his binder to wrap around his chest, tying up the sides. He pulled on a dry cotton shirt and pants, then slipped out into the hall. The Riverside cottage was small. The kitchen shared the same space as the sitting room, and the rustic furniture was just a tad too big for the space. Still, it was comfortable. Cozy. The walls had been painted a pale sage green, and the open windows let in the scent of freshly fallen rain. That with the breeze and golden sunlight . . . It all felt distinctly like *home*. The first few weeks after Ash, Ramsay, and Callum had moved in had been filled with soft sheets and laughter. It never ceased to amaze Ash how quickly things could change.

Ramsay leaned back in a chair at the table, pulling off her round spectacles. Purple circles rimmed her eyes. "There you are," she said. "I thought you might've been trying to avoid Callum's porridge. Not that I can blame you."

Callum turned to the table with a mug of tea. He scratched out his chair and fell heavily into it. It was a wonder the chairs never collapsed under his weight. "I could always not cook breakfast for you, if you like."

Ramsay gave the sheepish grin that Ash had started to learn was Callum's weak spot. "Sorry. I shouldn't tease so early in the morning."

"It's all right. I'm just feeling a bit touchy right now, I think." Callum tapped the surface of the table. "This tea is for you, Ash."

It was lavender, Ash's favorite. He pulled out the third and last chair and sat, watching the steam swirl. Source, there'd been years when Ash dreamed of a moment like this: sharing morning tea with the people he loved and who loved him, free from the loneliness that'd consumed him for years after his mother had died. "Thank you."

Callum put a hand on Ash's, idly playing with his fingers. Ash wondered if Callum had told Ramsay about his state, a quick whispered conversation about him. "The oatmeal isn't that bad, is it?" Callum asked.

"No, no," Ramsay said. "I just hate porridge. The texture, the *moistness* . . ."

"Just when you think you know everything there is to know about a person," Callum murmured. "It's a breakfast I had every day at McKinley."

"It makes sense, given the stress you're under," Ramsay said. "You feeling more sensitive, I mean."

Callum leaned his elbows on the table and rubbed his palms

over his face. "It can't be helped." That had become his go-to line, over the past few months. Quite a lot couldn't be helped, it seemed. "This position—Creator, I knew it wouldn't be easy, but it's been especially difficult as of late."

Ash frowned. "Have there been more attacks?"

"A mob in Glassport attacked a twelve-year-old girl accused of tier-three alchemy," Callum said mechanically, as if reading off a report. Tier three would've required a license for the performance of alchemy that was considered *unnatural*—not that having a license mattered much, those days. "She and her mother were both killed. Another throng of Lune followers strung up a man in Ironbound, too."

"Source," Ramsay said beneath her breath.

"Twenty-three total killings of anyone even thought to be practicing alchemy for this month alone."

Ash's temples pounded, headache growing. He gripped the mug in his hands.

Callum continued. "I've suggested more anti-mob patrols, more education about alchemy to show the public that it isn't a threat, but it's like Edric *wants* innocents to be murdered. He refuses to approve anything I propose."

"It's never easy to change scared minds," Ramsay said. "Not to mention your brother is a fucking twat."

Edric still blamed Callum for their family's death; after all, Callum had helped Ash escape, sparking a thread of events that ended in the city's destruction. Ash sometimes worried that Edric's hatred for Callum ran so deeply that the older brother would find a way to have the youngest Kendrick killed, ordering an execution or claiming that Callum's death had been an unfortunate accident during training. House Kendrick had always been the most brutal, as the house that maintained order and oversaw punishment. Winslow Kendrick, Callum's father, had been the perfect symbol of cold, unempathetic discipline. He would have undoubtedly ordered the execution of his own son—would have killed Callum with his own hands, even—had he survived Gresham Hain's massacre.

Callum's fists clenched as he glared at the surface of the table. "I need to at least try."

"A redguard commander trying his best help alchemists, of all people," Ramsay said lightly. "I wonder how that one will end."

Ash had known about the growing number of attacks against alchemists, of course. He'd seen the reports in newspapers and heard the accounts that both Callum and Ramsay brought home on the rare occasions that they returned.

The two had promised to come back to Ash whenever they could, but recently it'd fallen on Ash to find Ramsay in the Downs or Callum in Kensington (where the city burned and the smell of charred bodies filled Ash's lungs, and he couldn't find the words to explain why he hadn't visited Callum as much in the past few months, only twice in comparison to the dozens of times he'd sought Ramsay's side—).

Ash had tried to pretend he didn't see the surprise in their eyes whenever he came, as if they'd forgotten about him entirely; tried not to feel like a burden when promised he would be joined for bed as soon as a meeting was over and papers were signed. Ash liked that his partners had easy access to their shared home. He didn't like that they were just as quick to leave as they were slow to return.

Callum cleared his throat. Ash didn't miss Ramsay's head-shake.

"Ash," Callum said, still holding Ramsay's gaze. "I—well, I've actually been thinking for a while now . . ."

Ash frowned. "What is it?"

Callum took a breath. "Ramsay and I—"

Ash's heart fell. He'd never spoken his fear aloud, that the two would realize their love for each other didn't include him anymore.

"Not now," Ramsay said beneath her breath.

Callum ignored Ramsay and soldiered on. "We've both been thinking that maybe—well, maybe it would best if you didn't leave the cottage anymore."

Silence prickled the room. Ash looked from Callum, who sat straight in his seat, to Ramsay, who had leaned away, arms crossed, eyes focused anywhere but on him.

"What?" Ash said.

"Callum thinks it more than I do."

"But you do agree," Callum said to her. "It's too dangerous, and without either of us here to protect you—"

"I didn't realize I needed protection."

Ramsay stared hard at the table's surface. "You're the son of a man who decimated an entire city—who killed hundreds of thousands of people."

"I hadn't forgotten," Ash said. He surprised even himself with the chill in his voice. His heart tightened when he saw Ramsay's gaze drop with a pinch of hurt in her brow.

Callum had entered his commander mode, without expression or emotion in his tone. He reminded Ash a little too much of the other boy's late father sometimes. "Attacks on anyone even suspected of alchemy are on the rise. What do you think will happen to you if word gets out that you're Gresham Hain's son?"

The mere mention of his dead father's name sent a bolt of energy through Ash.

"You wouldn't only be killed," Callum said. "You'd be tortured, paraded through the streets by Lune followers—"

"That's *enough*, Callum," Ramsay said.

"Is it?" Callum asked her. "I'm not sure. I really don't think Ash understands—"

"I'm not your prisoner," Ash snapped. "You don't get to order me around anymore."

Callum flinched as if he'd been slapped. Ramsay's gaze flitted between the two of them, breath sucked in.

Pressure swelled in Ash's throat. He swallowed. "Sorry," he said.

Callum took in his own breath and stood. "I should get going. I'm going to be late."

Ash was stiff when Callum leaned forward to kiss his cheek.

Callum hesitated, then murmured, "Happy birthday, Ash."

Ash had asked the two not to make a big deal of him turning nineteen. They both had their own stresses, after all, and Ash had never been the type to celebrate. It was enough for him that they'd come back home again.

Callum kissed Ramsay's cheek, too, then thudded across the room to the door. He murmured a password and turned the knob. Ash could see the inside of the mahogany Kensington town house office where Callum now spent most of his days.

"I'll see you both tonight." He paused. "Please," he added. "Just think about it. At least until the attacks slow down."

"Sure," Ash said, knowing his energy said otherwise.

Callum closed the door behind him. Silence filled the room. Ash hated how quiet the cottage could be sometimes.

Ramsay was watching Ash closely, he realized. "What?"

He half expected a lecture—*Callum's only looking out for you; we both want what's best for you*—so was surprised when Ramsay shrugged. "Your energy feels a little . . . subdued."

Maybe Ash could try to understand the concern Callum and Ramsay both showed him. He looked at the nearly untouched tea. It'd become cold now. "I was just thinking."

"That's what scares me," she teased.

He bit his lip but didn't pause long, especially now that Callum was gone. "I had another nightmare," he said.

Ramsay clenched her jaw, then pushed back her chair to stand. "Oh?"

"My mom came to me again," Ash said. He lowered his voice, as if afraid Callum could still hear them through the closed door, though he was hundreds of miles away now. Callum would only worry over Ash more if he knew. "She has a message for me, Ramsay. I know she does."

Ramsay walked to the counter with her back to Ash. "We've already tried, haven't we?"

"Yes, but—but maybe we're doing something wrong, or . . ."

They'd harmonized their vibrations, gone to the higher realms with the intention of meeting Ash's mother as they had met Ramsay's parents once before. But each of the times they made their attempt, the two only appeared in Ash's old Hedge apartment, where his mother had died, higher realms showing an abandoned space with boarded windows and flickering versions of the home that had been taken over by strangers and endless fields, as if Hedge had never existed at all. Ash's mom never came.

"We could try again—"

Ramsay turned to face him, leaning against the countertop. "Ash," she said, exasperation clear. "We've made six attempts already. The chances of anything changing—"

"Maybe she's been waiting for the right time."

"Time doesn't exist in the higher realms," Ramsay said. Ash looked away, frustrated, but Ramsay continued. "If she really had a message for you, she would've come."

"What if something or—or someone is keeping her from reaching me?" Ash said. "What if she needs my help?"

"Do you really think someone in the physical realm is stopping your mother's energy from meeting with you?" She spoke in the logical, know-it-all tone that had once infuriated Ash and was close to doing so again. "If she hasn't come, the reason is her own. Maybe she's already returned to Source." Ramsay hesitated, then added softly, "Maybe she doesn't want to be found."

Ash's frustration bubbled in his chest. "Then why does she keep coming to me in my dreams every night?"

Ramsay seemed unwilling to speak her theory out loud.

It didn't matter. Ash picked up on enough of her energy. "It isn't just a dream," he said.

"How can you be so sure?"

"So, what?" Ash said. "You think I'm having a nightmare with my mother shouting my name every time I fall asleep?"

"No," Ramsay said. "I think it's possibly your subconscious. Maybe there's something you're trying to hide from yourself, and your subconscious wants you to pay attention to whatever it is you've buried."

Ash shook his head, unable to look at Ramsay.

Her voice was gentler now, at least. "How much of your desire to meet your mother is fueled by this question of your nightmares," she said, "and how much is fueled by your desire to distract yourself?"

Ash thought of the black orb, as large as the moon, falling to the surface of the Earth. "It isn't my anxiety."

"I know that you turned Callum's offer down, but—"

"Why do you two act like I'm the only one affected by the attacks?"

Ramsay was quiet enough that guilt pinched Ash. He knew as well as anyone that the past nine months had been difficult for Ramsay and Callum, too. They'd each learned to handle their grief in different ways, and wasn't it also true that Ash at least didn't have to worry about commandeering a force of redguards, nor leading an entire House while teaching and finishing his own studies on top of everything else? Ash knew that the two only wanted to help him. He just wasn't sure he appreciated being coddled and locked away, as if he were something fragile that would eventually shatter, glass shards cutting Ramsay and Callum, too.

Ramsay sighed and turned to the stove and the pot of oatmeal. "Are you going to eat any of this?"

Ash rubbed his temple. "I'm not hungry."

"Put it in the refrigerator, will you? I'll eat it later." Ash watched as Ramsay picked up her leather messenger bag from beside the sofa. "Did you wait for Callum to leave to bring this up?" she asked.

Ash hesitated.

"I don't like lying to him."

"We're not lying."

"Only omitting the truth."

Ash had told himself that he didn't want Callum to worry more than he already did, that the older boy had enough to handle and didn't need to hold Ash's struggles, too. But, well, maybe there was a little more to why Ash kept this a secret from Callum, something Ash couldn't quite yet place. He swallowed. "Why does he need to know?" Ash asked. "He doesn't need to know everything we do in our daily lives, does he?"

"No," Ramsay agreed, "but attempting to contact the dead isn't exactly a stroll to Market Square."

She walked over to Ash and kissed the corner of his mouth.

"Are you leaving already?" he asked.

"Don't sulk," she said with the touch of a smirk.

"You and Callum are almost never here," he said. "Even less together."

Ramsay hesitated, but only for a moment. "Come with me to Lancaster," she suggested. It wasn't the first time she had. "Go to the headmaster and request that your application be reviewed again. I'm sure you'd be accepted if you reapplied, no matter the fact that you burned down the college. And my office," she muttered. She'd lost priceless texts and endless papers of her work and research on Source geometry.

Ramsay sighed, putting that all aside. "The college would be honored to have you, especially after tonight."

Source, Ash didn't want to think about *tonight*. "Lancaster wouldn't be honored," Ash said. "They'd feel obligated to accept me with smiles while sharpening their blades behind their backs. They'd look for the first reason to get rid of me."

Ramsay, at least, did not attempt to argue with that.

"Besides," Ash continued, "I don't want to put myself back in a position where I have to kiss anyone's ass again. I'm happier in Riverside."

Ramsay bit her lip, and in the silence, Ash was sure she felt the energy of his lie. Ash wasn't happy. He loved the peace of the cottage and his garden, taking walks along the river and into the woods, avoiding the village and the people who stared. But while he had his peace, Ash hadn't felt this lonely in years. Not since the death of his mother, in fact.

And the jealousy, too—there was envy smoldering inside him, knowing that Ramsay and Callum lived with purpose, not questioning for a moment their role in the great universal field of energy. Ash felt lost. Now what? He had no goals, no grand plans, no evidence that, after he'd died and reconnected fully to Source, he should have returned. He wouldn't admit this, certainly not to Ramsay nor Callum, but sometimes he wished he hadn't been brought back to life at all. He dreamed of the endless peace he'd felt with Source—the infinite power and love and serenity. There was nothing on earth that could grant him that peace again.

Ramsay didn't seem aware of the extent of Ash's feelings, at least. "All right. If that's what you truly want." She paused, as if remembering something, and reached into her bag as she crossed the room and dangled a silver necklace from a finger. At the end was a vial only as big as a jewel. The vial was in a familiar shape: a hexagonal pyramid, two bottoms twisted together. Ash reached out and fiddled with it. One end could be pulled from the other.

"I saw it and thought of you," Ramsay said simply, though red colored her cheeks. It was the same symbol that'd connected them both, the day they met. Ash thanked her, letting her pull the necklace on over his head. "Think of the vial as being filled with my love for you."

Ash snorted while Ramsay smirked, turning for the door. She muttered the password she'd created to her new office in Lancaster College, *wedelia*, and paused long enough for Ash to catch a glimpse of the mess of papers and texts spread across her desk. "Please don't try to get out of the gala tonight by pretending to be sick or—I don't know—leaving the state. Our dear Callum will have an aneurysm, and neither of us will hear the end of it if you do."

She left the cabin with a wave, the door shutting firmly behind her. Ash groaned and let his head fall back, fingers reaching for his necklace. He held it up, staring at the ceiling, warped by the container's glass. Source knew he hadn't survived his father just to live an unfulfilling life like this.

But maybe there was a new goal Ash could discover, a new purpose in his life. Even if Ramsay didn't want to help him, Ash decided then he would find a way to speak with his mother again—no matter what it took.

3

The cottage was on the edge of town, closer to the woods and the rushing namesake river that carved its way down from the northern lakes and the eastern mountain ranges. Riverside was nothing like the sprawling cities Ash had been used to. The town was surrounded by farmland and fields and had a collection of wooden houses with gardens and chickens kept behind rickety fences. There was one sinking brick-paved road that led to the heart of the Market Square, which was really more a circle of shops: the baker and the tailor, the blacksmith and the carpenter, along with the inn and the Great House, where Ash's tribunal had been held six months before.

It was nearing midday. A chill had recently fallen, air thick with mist and grass covered with dewdrops that wet Ash's boots. A burly man chopped wood with a *thwack* in front of the carpenter's shop. He reminded Ash of his former best friend, Tobin, he thought with a pang. Ash ducked his head as he approached, not that this helped. Riverside hadn't been *welcoming*, exactly. Survivors had streamed into the town for months before many moved on to Ironbound or returned to Hedge and the ruins of Kensington to rebuild. Still, some stayed in tents in the fields beside the town, and Riverside's patience with strangers had dwindled.

The man paused to stare at Ash as he hurried past, energy screaming, *Distrust, dislike, he should go back to wherever he came from.* It was fortunate word hadn't spread about Ash's identity. If he, Ramsay, or Callum were recognizable to anyone in the town, it was only because they'd been imprisoned in the inn before their tribunal. No one had any way of knowing the three had been accused of aiding in Gresham Hain's attacks, nor that Ash was his son, unless one of the House Heads made a habit of idly gossiping with locals in the streets. Ash remembered Callum's earlier warning and wondered just how long that luck would last.

Ash reached the bookshop, a pretty little cursive sign reading OPEN hanging in the window. The bell jingled when Ash pushed open the door, heavier than it looked, and slipped inside. The space smelled of freshly opened books and dust. A woman read at a round table. Neat shelves of carefully curated titles lined the walls. Ash browsed, his boots tapping the glossy hardwood floors, until he slowed to a stop. He squinted, leaning forward and biting a thumb in concentration. It was a small section with barely ten titles, easily overlooked, but he'd been surprised, relieved, to see that the bookstore carried titles on alchemy at all. There were even some that focused on his latest interest, the one possibility he'd started to wonder about again and again . . .

"It's good to see you."

Ash jumped and whirled around. Mr. Brown stood in front of him as if he'd materialized. He was a kind, tiny man, smaller than even Ash, which was certainly saying something. He was balding and had round spectacles and pale skin with a red nose and cheeks. "Sorry, lad, I didn't mean to startle you."

Ash grinned and rubbed the back of his neck, embarrassed. "That's okay. I probably should've sensed you coming."

Ash's favorite thing about Mr. Brown was that he held no judgment whenever he found Ash browsing the alchemy section—none that Ash could feel, anyway. Mr. Brown wore the darker green colors of House Alder and was a man dedicated to the pursuit and keeping of knowledge, no matter his personal opinions.

"Have you finished the last book you bought already?" Mr. Brown asked.

"Yes," Ash said, turning back to inspect the shelves. He'd hidden the text beneath the bed a month before, not that there'd been much chance that Callum or Ramsay would find it since the two were almost never home. "It referred to one title called *Communicating with Plasma Particles*. I was hoping you might have it."

Mr. Brown chuckled at that, which Ash didn't take as a good sign. "Ah, that's a very old text indeed. Popular before even my time."

"It isn't out of print, is it?"

"I'm afraid so," Mr. Brown said, adjusting his glasses. "It was considered groundbreaking at the time it was published, you see," he continued, "and would more likely be found in a museum or a personal archive."

"Is there any way to find a copy that can be borrowed?"

"You sound rather anxious to read this book."

Ash heard his mother's scream, her eyes wild with fear. "I'd hate for my research to be limited."

Mr. Brown studied Ash closely. "*Communicating with Plasma Particles* was groundbreaking, in part, for being one of the first studies on the potential of bringing passed energies back to the physical realm."

Ash clenched his jaw. He knew this well.

Mr. Brown continued. "Still, some believe that the dead are meant to stay dead. That requesting their presence in our physical world is an affront to Source, or to the Creator, whichever you believe, though I suppose it could be said that the two are one and the same." He turned back to the shelves. "Perhaps there is some truth in this. Not all things are meant to be within our grasp, Mr. Woods."

Ash nodded, pretending to consider the man's advice. He'd already made up his mind to do whatever it took to speak to his mother again, and Ash was well acquainted with doing everything in his power to obtain a book. If there was even just one more copy of *Communicating with Plasma Particles* in the state, he would find it.

"Are those manipulation books?"

Manipulation. It was a word that contained so much energetic disgust that Ash winced. He turned to the woman who sat at the table. She had pale hair and was around Ash's age, maybe younger, which surprised him. He'd always thought hatred for alchemists tended to be a habit of the older generations.

Mr. Brown raised his brows. "These are texts on the science of alchemy, yes."

"Why does your shop carry books that teach how to steal energy from the Creator?"

It was how Lune followers had always positioned alchemy, but the view had become more popular in the past months. "Alchemy does not steal from the Creator," Mr. Brown stated with an even tone. "Rather, alchemy sees each being as a fractal of the Creator—of Source itself."

"It's evil," the woman said, watching Ash still. "It's sinful."

Even if the townspeople didn't know that Ash was Gresham Hain's son, they'd without a doubt suspect that he was a practicing alchemist now. "How is it *sinful?*" Ash said. "It can't be evil if we're a part of Source, too."

"It's sinful because you're killers," she spat, louder now.

The words Ash fumbled for were stuck in his throat. "I'm not a killer." Ash had never killed anyone, and besides that: "We're all alchemists. Everyone uses alchemy to breathe and think and feel, whether they know it or not—"

She stood suddenly, chair scraping back. "You're going to lose a lot of loyal customers, Mr. Brown, if you continue to sell manipulation books."

Ash felt rooted to the spot as the door opened and closed again, bell jingling in the silence that followed.

"I'm sorry," Ash said. It always took his breath away, how much hatred strangers could have for him.

Mr. Brown's smile was unshaken. "You have nothing to apologize for, lad."

"If I hadn't been looking at alchemy texts—"

"You can't be blamed for the ignorance she was taught," Mr. Brown said. "No, I suppose what interests me most are the patterns we humans are caught in, these cycles that seem to repeat again and again. I wonder if there's a new pattern we can begin to form instead."

With that, the bookseller raised a parting hand and started his slow walk to the back room. "Please let me know if you need any more assistance."

⁂

Hours passed, and Ash realized Ramsay knew him better than he wanted to admit, as he'd wondered to himself, more than once, how he might be able to get away with skipping the gala altogether.

It was evening, owls hooting in the distance. He pushed the cuff links from Callum into the shirt's buttonholes at his wrists and frowned at himself in the mirror that leaned against the bedroom wall. Ash was thinner than usual, he realized, with purplish bags beneath his eyes. His brown curls were tangled, no matter how many times he tried to comb his fingers through the strands. He wore a black suit that clung so tightly to his frame that he could hardly move. What if he needed to run? He wouldn't make it very far. On top of it all, he hadn't been able to figure out the bow tie, so he left the strip of silk hanging around the back of his neck.

Callum had dropped the suit off weeks ago, when it was first announced that Ash was to be honored for *saving Kensington*, though he didn't think he'd really done much saving. Every high-ranking House member had been invited. Ash sorely wished he'd refused, especially when the gala would be held in the manor of House Alexander itself. Ash hadn't returned to the city for months now (black smoke gushing into the sky, stinging his eyes and clogging his throat, screams)—

He released a slow, shaking breath. Maybe Callum had a point after all. A healer of emotions? It seemed intrusive, but it might've been worth considering, if only to stop the nightmares that found Ash even when he wasn't asleep.

Ash sighed, attempted to adjust his collar one last time, and walked down the hall and through the sitting room, orange fireplace embers dimly glowing. He stopped at the front door. The invitation had been sent with a password written just for his use as the special guest and honoree—temporary, of course; he would never be given *permanent* access to House Alexander.

"Baneberry." Ash put his hand on the knob, twisted it, and pushed open the door.

Ash blinked at the bright light of the hall he stepped into, closing the gilded door behind him. The corridor had bare golden wallpaper with shimmering floral patterns and white marble floors that reflected in the bright domed ceiling lights like snow. There were no paintings nor any rugs. Maybe the manor's staff was still decorating—House Alexander had only just been rebuilt, after all. The air itself was colder than Ash expected, as if alchemy had been used to chill the halls. Ash shivered as he took a step, wondering where he should go next, when he heard a familiar voice.

"There you are." Ash turned to see Callum walking toward him.

"I didn't know you were meeting me," Ash said.

"You're the guest of honor," Callum answered simply. "You should have an escort."

"And Ramsay?"

"Already waiting in the ballroom," Callum said. "The Houses can be . . . *traditional* about some things."

It wouldn't have been acceptable for Ash to have two escorts, then. Source, the elite and their *social rules* irritated Ash to no end.

"You're late." Callum reached for the silk hanging around Ash's neck. "I was worried you decided to run."

Ash wondered if Callum had been ordered to be Ash's escort

or if he'd volunteered in case he needed to drag Ash through the door himself. "Run, and risk your wrath? Never."

Callum's grin quirked. "Lift your chin."

Ash swallowed and did as asked. He stared over Callum's shoulder as the older boy's fingers worked the bow tie. Callum's fingers moved swiftly and confidently. Heat built in Ash, warming his neck. Even worse, he knew that Callum could sense Ash's energy. He'd always had a particular talent for sensing emotions.

Callum finished, hands brushing over Ash's shoulders. "You look handsome," he said.

Ash sighed. Callum was clearly trying to make amends for that morning. "You do, too."

And he did, in his tailored black suit, red vest beneath showing his loyalty to his family name. Ash often wondered how Callum felt wearing the Kendrick colors when it'd once taken him so much to leave his family for the life he'd wanted instead.

They were quiet as they walked, discomfort of not knowing what to say caught in Ash's throat. He apparently wasn't the only one.

"Ash—" Callum began.

A thin older man with a pointed white beard and mustache turned the corner, saw them, and quickly approached, his shoes tapping the tile. He wore a golden suit, the official color of House Alexander. He was sweating and looked choked by the collar buttoned up to his neck. "You're very late," he hissed, then turned swiftly on his heel, apparently expecting that the two would follow. Ash almost suggested the man count his blessings that he'd come at all.

Their footsteps echoed in the otherwise-empty corridor, slower in comparison to the hustling steps of the scribe who guided Ash and Callum around one corner and another of near-identical halls, finally pausing outside a set of large golden doors. The man cleared his throat, took a breath, and pushed them open.

The three stepped inside to stand at the top of a staircase that

swooped down into a ballroom. The doors had been magnifi-
cent at muffling sound, apparently. The laughter and chatter and
stringed music assaulted Ash's ears, and the energy of the dozens
of people in the room, all eyes turning up to him, made Ash falter.
The room fell silent, music slowing to a stop.

The man beside him spoke. "I present to you," he said, voice
booming, "Ashen Woods—"

"Ash," he corrected numbly.

"—escorted by Commander Callum Kendrick."

It seemed there were stage directions Ash had not been given.
He looked at Callum, who only smiled and mouthed, *You'll be
fine*. Callum then bowed to Ash, turned, and walked down the
staircase to join the crowd, leaving Ash behind. Even with the lingering discomfort between the two, Ash much preferred to have
Callum by his side.

It was amusing, in a way: Just months before, most of the guests
had called for Ash's arrest and execution. Now, they honored and
celebrated him. Ash recognized some of the Heads of Houses in
the crowd, each of whom had been among the jury at his tribunal.
Charlotte Adelaide's brown eyes seemed kinder than the judg-
mental stares that surrounded her, at least. Edric Kendrick was
a shorter, stockier version of Callum, which made the burning
hatred in his narrowed gaze that much more difficult to bear.

One man stepped forward, walking up the stairs with his arms
spread wide. "Mr. Woods," he said. "Welcome to House Alexander."

If the others had been the jury, then this man had been the
judge. Lord Easton Alexander was the youngest ruler in the history of the state of New Anglia at twenty-two years old, but he
held himself with the confidence of a young lord who had been
trained all his life for the role. He was several heads taller than
Ash, his chin raised with a touch of arrogance. His dark hair and
brown eyes were handsome, but his face was too symmetrical for
Ash's tastes.

Lord Alexander placed one large palm on Ash's shoulder. It took Ash everything in his body to not shrug it off. "It's an absolute privilege to have you as my guest."

The young lord had certainly perfected his charming performance. That's all this was, Ash knew: a performance in which Ash was the star, except that he hadn't been given any lines to memorize nor directions on where to stand; and besides that, Ash had never been particularly fond of acting. "Thank you for inviting me," he managed to say, words heavy on his tongue.

"The pleasure is mine," Lord Alexander said, not to Ash apparently, but to the entire gala as he spun his gleaming smile to his guests. "It's my greatest honor to take this moment to celebrate you. These are tense times, no doubt. The backlash against alchemy continues to grow with every passing day due to Gresham Hain's actions."

Actions was quite the euphemism for *massacre*, Ash thought.

Lord Alexander kept a hand firmly planted on Ash's shoulder, steering him closer to the edge of the staircase and the watching audience below. "It took one alchemist to undo the generations of trust built toward the field of science," Alexander said. "But perhaps we have not done enough to recognize that it also took another alchemist to save our state."

So this was why he'd been invited: Lord Alexander wanted to use Ash as a game piece. Surely not all alchemists could be so bad, if Ash had been the one to save them all. Maybe Ash should've been grateful. Even if he was being used, it was to help House Alexander combat anti-alchemist sentiment. Still, Ash didn't like to be *used*.

"Ashen Woods," Lord Alexander said. "To show my appreciation, I would like to officially offer you the title of *Sir Woods, Hero of Kensington*."

Ash forced a tight, quivering smile as polite claps filled the air.

❋

As soon as Lord Alexander's speech ended, Ash was descended on by hungry House members with their perfume and ruffles and lace. He'd craned his head this way and that, trying to catch Ramsay's or Callum's eyes to beg them for rescue, but they'd been swept away in their own conversations. Ramsay's energy had shifted, quietly exerting that his gender had changed, as it sometimes did. He frowned with concentration as he nodded, listening to Lord Val, who whispered urgently, fist landing in palm. Callum spoke to Charlotte Adelaide with a shine in his eyes that Ash hadn't seen himself in some time.

"Such a pleasure to meet you," said a woman who'd introduced herself as a second cousin of Lady Galahad, wearing the bright green of her House's colors—Source, she wouldn't let go of Ash's hand. "Have you considered which House you would like to join? I heard Lord Alexander gave you free entry to any of the eight."

Ash finally slipped his hand free. "No, I haven't."

"It would do you well to carefully consider the appropriate House for you," another older gentleman said. "Not all Houses will be to your benefit, no matter their skill in pleasantries."

The lady's smile did not falter. "There will, of course, be some Houses that would rather use you as a trophy piece."

"I'm not joining a House," Ash told them before anything more could be said.

The group that had formed around him gaped.

"Whyever not?" Lady Galahad asked.

Because he would rather be buried alive than have to deal with conversations like this on a daily basis. Before he could speak, Ash was interrupted by a pleasant low voice. "Why indeed?"

Heads lowered with deference as Lord Alexander stepped into the circle. After his speech he'd immediately been surrounded by members who'd wanted their audience with him. Ash had been grateful. He could feel Lord Alexander's hungry gaze fastened to his back.

Alexander continued, genteel smile planted on his face. "It's a question I've asked Sir Woods myself, to no avail."

Expressions flickered across the faces in front of Ash—surprise, envy, dislike for someone who would spit in the face of such a grand opportunity. "I don't owe an explanation," Ash said with a clipped tone. "I've said no. That should be enough."

Affronted murmurs followed—Ash was certainly bold, to speak to Lord Alexander that way—but the lord himself didn't seem to mind.

"Yes, of course," Alexander said, "but I can still hope to be humored. Especially now that you're the Hero of Kensington, it would do you well, wouldn't it? To join our society."

Lord Alexander reminded Ash of a predator eyeing its meal before taking a bite. There was no physical evidence that Ash shouldn't trust a man like Easton Alexander. He'd pardoned Ash when there were calls for his execution, protected him and now even honored him . . . and yet, whenever Ash was in Alexander's presence, he couldn't ignore the distinct feeling that he should get as far away from the man as possible.

"Perhaps the young sir will reconsider," Lady Galahad said with an appropriate level of politeness, well-mannered nods all around.

Ash didn't bother to reply as he murmured some excuse that was unknown to even him, pushing out of the crowd that had circled him, feeling the heat of lingering stares. He caught sight of Ramsay and Callum—they were speaking to each other near the windows now, heads ducked low together, Ramsay playing with the end of Callum's sleeve; perhaps Ash could convince them to leave early with him—

He didn't make it far. He felt a pull on his elbow and turned to see that Lord Alexander had followed. "A word, please, Sir Woods."

Ash wondered if he'd be able to get away with outright refusing. "Well, I—"

Lord Alexander's smile seemed just a little more cutting. "I'll only take a moment."

Alexander led Ash out of the hall and into an empty corridor. He didn't bother to fill the silence with false pleasantries, at least, the only sound in the hall their echoing footsteps. They reached a door that Alexander pushed open to a simple office: a golden oak desk, shelves that didn't yet hold any books, a window that looked out at the twinkling lights of Kensington. The rubble had been cleared for the most part, towers of the city surrounded by scaffolding. Though alchemists had been persecuted in the past months, it had been the assistance of alchemy that helped the rebuilding of the city, too, energy used to clear rubble and put blocks of concrete and brick into place.

"Please," Alexander said, gesturing dismissively to a chair before the desk. "Sit."

"I'd prefer to stand."

Lord Alexander watched Ash with narrowed eyes. He held the same smugness that all House heirs did, Ash found—but unlike Ramsay, it wasn't sardonic and self-deprecating, and unlike Callum, it wasn't naïve and ignorant to its own existence. Alexander knew precisely who he was and seemed to believe he was worthy of the arrogance that tilted his head and chilled his gaze. He seemed to expect a minimum show of respect that might be akin to kissing his damned feet.

"You seem to refuse a lot."

Ash knew this was in reference to his denial of Lord Alexander's other continuous offer. He shrugged. "Only anything that would make me want to stab needles into my eyeballs."

Alexander was surprised into quiet for a moment before he chuckled. "Would working for me really be that painful?"

Ash decided this was a rhetorical question.

The lord stood at his window for a moment, looking out at the city he owned. "You do realize that this is a highly coveted position, correct? Dozens have sent letters hoping for a chance at the opportunity, and I've received a number of recommendations as well."

"It sounds like you have plenty of people to choose from, then."

Lord Alexander's gaze slid to Ash. "I would rather work with you."

Ash crossed his arms, fingers tight. "There are more qualified people who have a head for politics. There's no point in having me be your advisor, not really." He met Lord Alexander's stare. "Unless there's another reason you're trying to hide."

Alexander's eyes glimmered.

Ash tilted his head. "I'm an alchemist. No, not only that—I'm the son of the alchemist who nearly destroyed our state, who killed your father along with hundreds of thousands of people. You don't want me to work with you. You want to send a message."

"You're clever," Alexander said. "But you've made a mistake in deciding that it's one or the other. Why not both because you're Gresham Hain's son and because you're the right person for the job?"

"My only talent is in alchemy."

"Yes," Alexander agreed. "Exactly."

"You specifically want an alchemist as your advisor?"

The lord didn't reply. There had to be more to Alexander's motives, one of the *hidden-agenda* variety. "Sorry, but I'm not in the mood to become your pawn," Ash said. "My answer is the same. No."

Alexander's chin rose as he inspected Ash for a moment. "You certainly are fearless," he said. "Not many would dare to deny my request once, let alone three times."

Ash had died—been killed by his own father—and come back to life. He knew what waited outside this physical body, this physical realm. The world seemed little more than a playground, now, life just a dream. What else did he have to fear? Ash ignored the clench in his chest, the distant sound of screams that echoed in his mind even then—

There was a muffled thud. The floor shook and the desk rattled. Ash flinched and looked up at Lord Alexander. The man's brows pinched. The screams were louder now, Ash realized, and not just in his head.

Footsteps echoed outside the door before it slammed open. Edric stormed into the office and shoved past Ash to get to Lord Alexander's side.

"What happened?" Alexander said.

"An attack," Edric replied shortly. "I need to get you to safety."

Another explosion, louder now. The walls and ceiling shook. Faded screams filled the air.

Ash snapped out of his shock. "Was Callum still with Ramsay in the ballroom?" Ash shouted, breath caught in his chest, but Edric had already pulled Lord Alexander through the door. Ash followed to the threshold, heart pounding, and watched the retreating backs of Edric and Lord Alexander—looked in the other direction to the people who had streamed into the hall, already hazy with gray smoke. Ash covered his mouth with his elbow as he raced down the corridor, weaving past people who cried, others screaming, searching each face that pushed in the opposite direction.

He skidded to a stop at the ballroom's open doors. The lights were off. Smoke clogged the air, stinging Ash's eyes. A crater in the opposite wall showed the night sky and the maze of city streets below. A tangle of bodies and chunks of stone were strewn across the marble floor. Ash's heart seized as he rushed inside, nearly tripping down the stairs—his eyes darted from one body to the next, the explosion's crater was where he'd last seen Ramsay and Callum standing—

Figures melted out of the shadows and stepped into the ruins. Ash's body acted before he fully processed what he saw, diving behind a pillar. His spine dug into stone, head tilted back as he breathed hard and listened to the tapping footsteps, a crunch of shattered glass. One spoke a muffled order, voice garbled: "Find him."

Ash peered around the pillar and counted four—no, five. Each wore a gas mask that hid their face. Heavy energy rolled from them in waves of light that emanated from their skin. They were high-practicing alchemists, that much was clear. The alchemists got to work, strolling over to where the fallen lay, one kneeling to inspect the faces, another kicking a body over. One guest groaned. Another called for help in a broken voice. Someone lay on their stomach in front of the crater, chunks of stone crumbled across legs, black hair haloed around his head. Ash's heart stopped. Ramsay wasn't moving.

One of the alchemists slowed to a stop at Ramsay's side. He held up a hand, palm emitting a faint white glow. "He's here."

The leader looked up from where they crouched. "Take care of it."

The glow brightened as it condensed into a marble of light. It floated for one moment, hovering over Ramsay, vibrating as it aimed—

Ash's body moved before he could think. He jumped out, energy shooting through him before it blasted from his outstretched hand. A gust of wind flung the ball of light and its owner through the air and out of the crater, only the echo of the alchemist's scream remaining. The leader stood, fist raised. Ash froze. He was suspended in midair. Pressure grew beneath his skin as he realized he couldn't move—couldn't *breathe*—

Footsteps crunched in the otherwise-silent room. The stranger stepped into Ash's view. He could see his own reflection in the shine of the mask's goggles. The alchemist tilted their head. "Ash Woods. Interesting."

Ash's frozen eyes watered. His gaze was unfocused as he watched the alchemist who'd been thrown from the room fly back inside, landing on their feet beside Ramsay. Ash's vision blurred. Fear and rage blended into heat. It grew beneath his skin, frozen body quivering.

A garbled voice spoke behind Ash, near the door. "We need to hurry."

The leader still did not look away from Ash. Their head tipped down, gaze falling, as Ash's fingers twitched. "Change of plans."

"But Thorne is—"

The alchemist didn't respond. A finger rose and touched Ash's forehead. Pain splintered through his skull before his vision burned to black.

4

Ash—wake up!"

Ash jolted. His brows tugged together. His head pounded. He blinked open his eyes with a groan. His hands were tied behind the back of the chair he sat in, ankles strapped to the legs. He was in a sitting room that might've belonged to any of the House manors: The walls were a pale blue with gilt-lined panels. The sofa opposite him had faint floral patterns. An open window framed by lace let in a cool night breeze. The air smelled sour, like something was rotting.

He gritted his teeth and tried to untangle his wrists. The rope's rough threads scratched his skin. He closed his eyes, breathed in and out again—tried to imagine the particles of the rope itself to convince it to come undone, but his breath was short, panic thudding through his chest—

A door clicked open. Ash looked up as a person stepped into the room. She was unfamiliar to Ash, an older pale-skinned woman with graying yellow hair and steely eyes. She wore the same black coveralls and leather boots she'd worn in the attack, though her gas mask was gone now. Others filed into the room as well, all wearing similar uniforms. The last of the group stepped into the room, closing the door behind her.

Ash's mouth fell open. *"Marlowe?"*

Marlowe had the same light-brown skin and red hair, though it was cut shorter, to her ears now. She leaned against a far wall, staring hard at the floor.

Ash's heart pounded at the sight of her, the onslaught of memories of her. He had last seen Marlowe when she'd killed his father on the bridge. She'd helped Ash, saved the state—and now she stood by and watched as he was held captive. Ash swallowed a dry lump and looked from Marlowe to the woman who sat in front of him, who seemed to be studying every expression that ticked across his face.

"What the hell is this?" Ash rasped. He only remembered being frozen in the air, Ramsay still unconscious on the floor. "Where's Ramsay?" And Callum—Ash hadn't even seen him in the hall nor the ballroom ruins—

"I can assure you that Ramsay Thorne is alive," the woman said.

Ash would believe her when he saw Ramsay for himself. "Where is he now?"

"My name is Elena," she said, as if this were an introduction over tea. "That is Hendrix, Finley, and Riles." She pointed out the three others who stood about the room, watching quietly. Ash didn't bother to look at any of them as he glared at their ring-leader. "You already know Marlowe," she added.

Marlowe shifted on her feet.

"So, this is what you've been up to, then?" Ash said. "Why'd you bother to save the city if you were just going to attack House Alexander and help destroy it again?" He knew it would do no good, provoking his captors—but, well, Ash also found he didn't particularly care.

Elena's mouth pressed into a line. "I wouldn't be so quick to judge. Marlowe convinced me that you'd be more useful to us alive."

Her meaning sank in. Ash was used to the idea that Lune followers hated him for being an alchemist, that they would want him dead for being Hain's son. It hadn't quite occurred to him that other alchemists might just feel the same, too.

"Should I be grateful?" Ash said, though he felt choked by his words.

"I don't usually tell others how to feel," Elena said.

"I guess that means you didn't want to argue for Ramsay's life also, then," Ash said to Marlowe. "I didn't think you were the type to hold grudges."

At this, Marlowe looked at the ceiling in frustration. "It isn't personal."

"How is attacking Ramsay—trying to *kill* him—not personal?" Ash shouted.

The others in the room watched Ash, the echo of his words fading. Elena crossed one leg over the other. "Ramsay Thorne is a threat," she said simply.

"What?" Ash shook his head. "Why would he be a threat?"

"He's designing a blueprint for House Val that's been commissioned by Edric Kendrick."

Ash stiffened. Ramsay had mentioned he was working on various inventions, but he hadn't said his work was ultimately for the redguards. Still, that didn't matter. "How does that justify *killing* him?"

Elena continued as if Ash hadn't spoken at all. "The weapon Thorne is designing would give too much power to House Kendrick," she said, "along with House Alexander."

"Kill Edric Kendrick, then," Ash said before he could think better of it. He wondered how Callum would feel, knowing Ash had suggested these alchemists kill his brother instead.

"We had multiple targets tonight," Elena admitted, "though Thorne was prioritized."

Ash glared. "What is it?"

"I'm sorry?" Elena asked.

"What's the weapon worth killing Ramsay over?"

She hesitated.

"You fuckers don't even know what the invention is—"

"We do know," Elena interrupted. "I'm just not sure you need to—not yet."

Ash looked at the others now, eyeing each—the older man who looked like he'd had a past life as a dockworker, if the tattoos were anything to judge by, and the youngest of the group who didn't look a day older than thirteen. Ash's gaze settled on the last, the boy with red hair who looked to be around Callum's age. His face had been hidden, but he had the same lanky height as the one Ash had shot through the manor's blasted wall.

"Was it you?" Ash said. The other boy's eyes narrowed. "Are you the one who tried to kill Ramsay?"

"I should remind you that you're our prisoner," Elena said, "and though I've been convinced to keep you alive for now, that can always change."

Ash gritted his teeth. The boy glared at Ash as if he preferred the latter option.

"Why am I here, then?" Ash said, stare still on the boy, before he pulled it back to Elena. "Why don't you just kill me, like you keep threatening to do?" No, it wasn't very smart of him at all, to provoke these people like this.

She leaned forward, elbows on her knees. "I'd heard a lot about you, Mr. Woods—but meeting you, *feeling* your energy . . ." Her voice quieted. "It's often said that inspiration comes from Source once the right threads connect."

Ash's hands clenched behind his back, fingers digging into his palms. "What threads?"

"You should know more than any of us that physical reality is a lot like a dream," Elena said. Ash's breath stilled. "And this dream, just like the ones that find us when we sleep, is ripe with symbols and metaphors. We had the intention of killing Ramsay Thorne. You stopped Thorne's death and threw yourself at us instead."

"So, what—you think that was Source's way of telling you to kidnap me? Keep me prisoner? You're delusional."

Gray strands fell into Elena's face as her head lowered, gaze on her boots. "I knew that if we killed Thorne, you would refuse to help us."

"If you think I'd have anything to do with you—"

"You might, once you've heard me out."

A muscle in Ash's jaw jumped. He didn't have much of a choice but to listen.

Elena seemed to take her time, thinking over her words carefully. "I planned to have you killed because your position with House Alexander will ultimately be used to harm alchemists."

Uncertainty tugged at Ash's brows. He knew Alexander wanted to use Ash as a game piece, yes—and though it annoyed him, Ash saw only the benefit of Alexander being on the side of alchemy.

"You don't even see it, do you?" Elena asked. "How you've become a toy."

Anger gripped Ash's fists. "I'm not a *toy*."

"The good, benevolent little alchemist," Elena continued, "doing exactly as he's told. *Honored* by the Houses—"

"*That's* why you wanted to kill me? Because I was honored?"

"Showing that alchemy can be good, too—"

"I didn't even want to go to the fucking gala in the first place!"

"As long as you're controlled."

Ash fell silent, jaw clenched.

Elena lifted her chin. "Marlowe convinced me that your death would be spun, and you'd only be turned into a martyr for Alexander," she said. "But tonight, I realized you could be useful in other ways, too."

Ash's voice was hoarse now. "Like I already told you: I'm not a toy, especially not one that can be exchanged from one pair of hands to the next."

"But you are Gresham Hain's son."

Ash swallowed at the mention of his father's name.

"Hain has become a symbol of freedom among some circles."

"He was a piece of shit."

"Your father fought for the evolution of alchemy."

"My father was a mass murderer."

"Maybe his actions weren't morally correct," Elena said, "but his intentions were. You are his heir. This could be your chance to help create the change he wanted."

Ash shook his head. "By attacking galas? Killing House members?"

"It may come to that at times, yes," Elena confessed. "I won't pretend otherwise. But if you agree to work with us, I can promise you that Ramsay Thorne will not be touched. We'll find another way to disrupt his work, but he will no longer be a target."

Ash knew better than to trust the promise of someone who had tried to kill a person he loved, who had captured and held him prisoner.

"This is a critical moment in the battle for alchemists' rights," Elena said. "You could be a key piece in deciding our future."

Ash's gaze flitted to the others who watched: the older man who frowned at the floor, the younger child whose eyes glinted as they met Ash's stare, and the one who had attacked Ramsay, too, gaze narrowed as though hoping for the chance to kill Ash himself. Marlowe stared forward at nothing, but her stillness suggested she was intently listening.

"*Our future*," Ash echoed. "If you believe in alchemists' rights like Hain did, then you must believe in alchemy being used to kill anyone who disagrees with you." But even then, the words didn't feel true on his tongue. He knew that wasn't all his father had believed.

"And what, exactly, do you think is happening in this state right now?" Elena asked him. "Alchemy is only a tool. Others are using the tools at their disposal to control, oppress, and kill alchemists as we speak. Can you really blame any of us for wanting to live?"

"So, it's us or them? Is that it?"

But Elena didn't answer him.

It was possible this merry little band was waiting only on Ash's answer before they decided what they would do with him. If he said no, Elena might simply have him killed then and there before moving on to finish the attempt on Ramsay's life. Ash tried to sense the vibration behind Elena's words, but he felt nothing.

"Why should I trust you?" he asked.

"How about this?" Elena said. "In a show of good faith, I'll let you go."

Ash squinted in disbelief, but even then he felt the ropes around his wrists loosening. He ripped his hands away, curling them into fists, heat growing. Elena must've felt his wave of energy and the oncoming attack, but she didn't move. "I have no desire to force you to help us," she said. "It would just do more harm, and besides, that wouldn't make me any better than Alexander."

Ash hesitated. He looked to the others—to Marlowe, who still wouldn't meet his eyes.

"Take time to think," Elena said. "Decide what you'll do."

The ropes around Ash's legs had slackened, too. He wasn't going to help them, he already knew he never would—but attacking the group now didn't seem like the greatest plan, either, when he was so outnumbered and they were all clearly so powerful. Besides, as much as he hated to admit it, Ash would have a hard time attacking Marlowe as well. His anger toward her didn't erase everything they'd survived together.

"And if I say no?" Ash asked. "Will you try to kill Ramsay again?"

Elena's blank expression didn't change.

"Pretending I have a choice, then," Ash said. "Maybe you're more similar to Alexander than you think."

Elena stood from the sofa. The room around Ash blurred, the air itself shimmering. The blue-and-gold walls faded, dissolving into stone. Ash's seat became a rickety wooden chair, the sofa across from him a splintering crate. The House manor's sitting room had been nothing but an abandoned warehouse. Ash felt a wave of nausea. He'd heard of illusion alchemy, of course. The changing of another's perception of reality was tier four, but he'd never witnessed it to this extent on such a large scale.

"Marlowe will take you back," Elena said, her back already to him. She pressed a hand to the wall. Tendrils of smoke unfurled from her palm and down to the floor, spreading toward Ash like fog. "I look forward to hearing your answer, Sir Woods."

The others followed Elena through the black hole that had appeared in the wall, the youngest glancing over their shoulder at Ash again, each of them vanishing as if stepping from one dimension to the next. The smoke faded. Only Marlowe remained.

They were both silent for one long moment before Marlowe took a step, foot crunching on bits of stone. "Ash—"

"I felt sorry for you, once," he said. "I thought my dad had taken advantage of you—forced you to work for him."

She stopped, mouth open and breath held.

"But he's not alive anymore," Ash told her. "What's your excuse now?"

"You don't understand," she said, voice quiet. "You've been hidden away in a bubble among the Houses. You don't see how bad things have gotten for alchemists—how much worse they'll get, if we don't—"

"Thanks, I guess," he said, cutting her off, "for arguing for my life. But it's going to be a little harder for me to forgive you, for trying to kill Ramsay, too."

Marlowe's mouth snapped shut. She took a breath, then nodded. "I understand."

Ash began to walk toward the warehouse's doors—he had no idea if he was still in Kensington or if he would step outside to find himself in Glassport. He only knew he couldn't stand to be near Marlowe for another second.

She called after him. "There's something I need to warn you about."

"It's not backstabbers, is it?" he threw over his shoulder.

"There's a man," Marlowe said, "claiming to be the reincarnation of Sinclair Lune."

Ash stopped, unsure if he'd heard Marlowe correctly. Sinclair

Lune, the original founder of House Lune hundreds of years before, had been influential for his praise of Source as the Creator. His teachings had been used by the generations that followed, claiming Lune's philosophies were evidence that alchemy was sinful.

House Lune had been the first to be destroyed by Gresham Hain, its manor and leaders razed to the ground. Ash never gave much of a shit about Sinclair Lune, but if the House's founder had really come back . . .

Marlowe spoke. "Elena is keeping a watch on him for now, but he's quickly gaining a following." Ash turned to her, quiet. "He could have the numbers to take control from House Alexander altogether—to authorize the execution of any alchemist in the state. I don't know about you," she added, "but that's not a world I'd like to see."

A chill spread across Ash's skin. He'd witnessed another world like that, once—one where the redguards wore uniforms of white, where practicing alchemy had been an executable offense and a different Callum had been willing to kill Ash for it.

He swallowed. "Is it really him?" Ash asked. "Sinclair Lune, I mean."

"I don't know. For now, all we can do is watch and wait for instructions from Elena."

"I'd have thought your new friends would be eager to kill him, too."

"An alchemist, killing the reincarnation of Sinclair Lune?" Marlowe shook her head. "That'd do more damage than anything else."

She walked to his side. "I know you're angry with me, Ash, and you have every right to be—but I hope we can work together. We might just need each other's help, to survive a world like this." She offered her palm. "Here. I'll take you back to Kensington."

He clenched his fist, then took her hand.

5

With a stomach-turning lurch, Ash blinked open his eyes. He stood with Marlowe in the shadow of a brick alleyway, black puddle shining on the cobblestone beneath his feet. The full moon hung heavy in the sky. The charred scent of smoke lingered. Ash stepped out onto the sidewalk to see that he was only blocks away from the manor of House Alexander. The hole on the second floor was a scar in the white stone façade. Sweat chilled on Ash's skin at the sight. It only solidified how horrific the attack had been.

"When you've made your decision, call my name," Marlowe whispered. "I'll have a web spread."

"The same web you used to spy on me, you mean? When you were stalking and trying to kill me?"

She ignored him. "I'll be listening out for you. Do you understand, Ash?"

He took a heavy breath. "Yes. Understood."

She nodded, and without another word, Marlowe took a step back into nothingness, and air sucked in on itself as she disappeared.

Ash raced out of the alley, turning the corner for the manor and slipping on wet stone as he ran to the reds who lined the gates.

One saw Ash coming and shouted, hand on the hilt of her sword. "Stop—"

Another red held up his hand. "That's Sir Woods."

The golden gates were opened for Ash, and he was escorted by two reds through the courtyard and the manor's front doors. Ash hurried ahead of the guards as he raced down the halls, ignoring their call for him to wait. He followed the muffled voices as he turned a hall and came to the center of the manor and its grand staircase. People had gathered, some with bruises and drops of blood staining their clothes. Ahead Ash saw a red turn the corner—ran without thinking until he'd thrown himself at Callum.

"*Ash*," Callum said, gathering Ash closer, holding him so tightly, it was difficult to breathe. "Creator—where were you?" he demanded, pushing Ash back again at arm's length, eyes sweeping over him as if searching for wounds. Ash took the opportunity to look over Callum, too, but there was no sign of injury, only dust and spots of blood that appeared to belong to someone else. "No one could find you."

Ash shook his head, unsure of what to say. Only one thing mattered, now that he knew Callum was all right. "Where's Ramsay?"

Callum stiffened. "This way."

Ash followed Callum through the maze of golden halls, the corridors emptying the longer they walked. Callum explained that it'd been only luck on his part, that he'd stepped out of the ballroom to search for Ash minutes after he'd left with Lord Alexander. "I thought you might've wanted an excuse to end the meeting," Callum said. "I assumed he'd taken you to his master office. I was on the third floor for the first explosion."

Ash's chest hurt as he realized how easily Callum could have been caught in the blast, too—that Ash could've lost him and Ramsay both. Suddenly, that morning's argument seemed so small. He reached for Callum's hand as they hurried down the hall, chest warmed when the other boy's fingers squeezed his own.

A door ahead of them opened, and Charlotte Adelaide stepped outside, brows rising as she saw them approach. Her brown hair matched her warm brown eyes. The soft blue gown she wore had rusted drops of blood along the front. "Thank the Creator you're all right," she said to Ash. Ash had never spoken a word to Charlotte outside of the tribunal, so was surprised by how genuinely relieved she seemed. "We were all so worried. Ramsay almost re-fused treatment until you were found."

Ash's heart dropped into his stomach when he looked through the open door. The small chamber had only one bed and dresser. It might've once been meant for visiting guests, but it'd become a temporary care room. Ramsay was asleep on the mattress, shirt-less, bandages wrapped around his arms and chest.

"He'll be fine," Callum said before Ash could ask.

Charlotte nodded her agreement. "His leg was broken, and his ribs were fractured, but bones are easy to mend."

Ash stepped closer to the bedside, a flood welling in his chest. Ramsay's face was paler than usual, green bruises patched along his cheek. His brows scrunched in his sleep. His chest rose and fell steadily. Ash grew cold at the thought of how close he'd been to never seeing Ramsay breathe again. His hands balled into fists. Elena wanted him to help her? Ridiculous, when it was because of her that Ramsay was like this.

Callum's hand fell on Ash's shoulder. "We should let him rest."

The door closed again, and Charlotte excused herself to check on other patients. Ash and Callum stood together in the hall, silent and unmoving for one long moment, before Callum raised his hand and rubbed Ash's arm. "Where were you, Ash?" he said, voice soft. "What happened?"

Ash bit his lip. It was strange, to be so angry at Marlowe and simultaneously feel guilty for betraying her. "I think I need to speak with Lord Alexander."

⁂

The conference room was where the Heads of Houses met. The chamber itself was surprisingly small, most of the space taken by a marble table with a pinkish hue, so large that it was over half the length of the Riverside cottage. The lights were too bright, espe-cially after the dimness of the warehouse and the dark alleyway.

Ash sat on one side of the table, facing Callum and Edric, who sat on the other. Ash would've much preferred for the older Kendrick brother to not be present but knew that the Head of House Kendrick was closely involved with Lord Alexander, especially for matters such as these. He considered himself lucky that Callum had been allowed to stay, too. Lord Alexander waited at the head of the table. It didn't feel like a questioning, at least, though Ash knew it technically was.

Ash had changed out of the forsaken suit, cuff links from Callum handed to the older boy for safekeeping, and put on a comfortable sweater and a loose pair of slacks, brought by an attendant. He'd been given a glass of water, which he drank nearly half of in one gulp.

"You say that you were abducted," Edric said. His expression was blank, but his tone suggested he didn't believe Ash for one moment. "And where were you taken?"

"I don't know," Ash said. He'd already described the illusion alchemy of the manor. Uncertainty squeezed Ash's stomach. He knew it was the right thing, to share what information he could about Elena and the rest—but there was just the smallest part of him, too, that wondered if he was ultimately harming all alchemists by handing Edric Kendrick of all people this information. "The warehouse looked like it could've been in any city."

Callum sat straight, hands clasped together on the table's surface. He'd seemed silently surprised to hear that Marlowe had been a member of the group as well, but maybe because he was in front of Alexander and his brother, he said nothing on the matter. "Did they call themselves anything?" he asked. "Did they refer to one another using a specific name?"

Ash shook his head, running through the scattered memories. "Only as alchemists."

"Was there any mention of how many members were in the group?"

"There were only five," Ash said.

"Five who participated in the attack," Callum let him know. He looked at Lord Alexander. "They fit the profile."

"Unless this is another new faction that's sprung up," Alexander said.

Edric shook his head once. "That's unlikely, given how organized they were. They knew when the gala would be and where it would be held. They moved efficiently to find their target to avoid a skirmish with redguards. They knew what they were doing."

"Who are *they*?" Ash asked Callum. The older boy had come home with stories of attacks on alchemists, but he'd never mentioned any concern about alchemists possibly attacking the Houses, too.

Guilt flashed in Callum's eyes. He glanced at Lord Alexander and his brother as if for permission before answering. "There've been whispers of radical alchemist groups springing up across the state," he said, "but it's unclear if they're all chapters under the same leader or if they're separate parties with similar beliefs." He paused. "Some claim to be followers of Gresham Hain."

Ash's fists tightened in his lap. "What do they want?"

"To do away with the tier laws, mostly," Lord Alexander said. "To have the ability to practice alchemy without a license. To protest, I suppose, the widespread killing of alchemists."

Ash bit his lip. Source knew he sympathized. Of course he believed it was justifiable for anyone to defend their right to live, and beyond that, he'd always agreed with his father, to an extent—had resented the idea that he could only practice his alchemy now that he'd been given permission on a piece of paper by the elite.

"It's curious that they let you live," Edric said, tapping the table surface.

Ash stared at him for one long moment. "If you think I'd be part of a group that would try to kill Ramsay—"

"Thorne survived," Edric noted.

"I didn't have anything to do with this!" Ash looked at Callum for help.

Callum stared forward without any expression. "Ash has been at the cottage in Riverside for months. He wouldn't have had any way to communicate with extremists."

Ash's brows tugged together. He would've liked to see his boyfriend assert a bit more passionately that Ash would never participate in an attack on the Houses.

"He could've left the cottage at any time," Edric said, tone level. "Let's not forget, this wouldn't be his first offense."

"The college was an accident," Ash snapped.

"Yes, as you've claimed."

"You can't seriously think—" Ash began, breath hitched. "Callum, you know I would never hurt anyone, let alone Ramsay."

"Commander Kendrick is under my order," Edric said. "It doesn't matter what he thinks." He turned his gaze to Lord Alexander. "I recommend that Sir Ashen Woods be incarcerated until we learn more information about the group that attacked the manor and that he alleges captured him."

Callum balled his hands into fists on the surface of the table but said nothing.

Lord Alexander let out a breath with a hum. "It wouldn't reflect well on the Houses, to arrest the boy the same night we've honored him as the Hero of Kensington." His eyes slid to Edric. "Though I suppose for some that might be more convenient than for others."

Edric didn't falter, but Ash noticed the slightest flare in his nostrils.

"On the other hand," Lord Alexander continued, "I can understand the concern. It's a little too convenient, isn't it? That they allowed Sir Woods to live."

Callum still wouldn't look at Ash, but Ash saw the other boy's chest rise without an exhale. "Permission to speak, my lord."

"Permission granted."

Callum hesitated. "Perhaps we could find a compromise."

Ash clenched his jaw. Callum always had been one for concessions. It'd helped at times, especially when Ash and Ramsay bickered over little nothings. But wasn't it also true that some things—such as Ash's *freedom*—should not have been a point to bargain over?

"Go on," Alexander said.

Callum at least had the courtesy to glance at Ash now, brows pulled together. *I'm sorry*, his expression seemed to say. "If there's concern over Sir Woods's innocence, then perhaps it would be best for him to stay sheltered in place until further notice, in a location where he can be easily watched."

Air sucked out of Ash's lungs. He couldn't have heard Callum correctly. "You want to put me under house arrest?"

"Our town house, for example."

"Are you fucking kidding me, Callum?"

"Guards could be assigned to keep close watch."

"No," Edric said. "The last time that allowance was made, you helped Woods escape, ultimately leading to Gresham Hain's attack."

Ash shook his head, eyes stinging. Source, maybe it would've been better to stay quiet about what had happened—but then, if it'd been found that he'd kept his meeting with radical alchemists that night a secret, he'd be in a much worse off position.

Edric sat perfectly still. "I suggest that Sir Woods be detained in the Kensington dungeons until his story can be verified, lest we risk another attack and assassination attempt."

Ash's head fell back as he squeezed his eyes together. "Fuck this."

"Ash," Callum warned beneath his breath.

"It may be true that you're going a little easy on Sir Woods," Lord Alexander let Callum know. "I've heard rumor that you both share a home with Head Thorne. Is that true?"

Heat built in Ash's cheeks. Callum only blinked rapidly, jaw clenched.

"But, let's be frank," the lord continued. "Had he been anyone else, you'd be at least a little suspicious, too. The son of the man who inspired this attack, captured for one night and then released?"

Ash shook his head, at a loss for words. This all felt like one large, orchestrated prank.

Lord Alexander paused, seeming to consider everything that had been said, before he finally spoke his decision. "Commander Kendrick is being lenient, yes, but I ultimately agree."

Ash never had liked Lord Alexander, but in that moment, he decided he might just hate the man. Tears of frustration pricked his eyes. "Bullshit."

"However," Lord Alexander said, as if there'd been no interruption at all, "rather than the Kendrick town house, I would like for Sir Woods to stay here, in my manor, instead."

"This is fucking bullshit."

"It's for your own safety as well," Callum said. "It's for the best, Ash."

"You don't get to decide what's best for me."

Lord Alexander placed both palms on the surface of the table. "Sir Woods will remain under watch and may not leave this manor without my express permission."

Callum nodded. "Understood, my lord."

Ash's stare snapped to Callum's—one last plea, one more chance for Callum to speak on Ash's behalf—but Callum only swallowed, gaze dropping.

"Thank you for your perspectives," Alexander said to the Kendrick brothers. "Dismissed."

Callum and Edric got to their feet without hesitation and bowed, fists to their chests. They turned, footsteps echoing across the conference room. Ash listened to the distant thud of the door closing behind them. Ash scratched his chair back, too, already thinking of how he would get the hell out of the manor—maybe he'd hide in the Downs, though he was sure reds would be sent to look for him there—

"One moment, Sir Woods," Alexander said.

Ash ignored him. He couldn't stand to be near the man a moment more.

"I think you'll like to hear me out. Listening might just be your only option for freedom."

Ash hated that he paused. He spun around. "First, you imprison me. Then, you blackmail me. I'm not in the mood for your bullshit games, *my lord*."

Alexander didn't respond as he stood as well. He took his time as he walked across the room to the back wall. Ash's brows tugged in confusion as he watched Lord Alexander press his palm against the panel, unmoving and unspeaking—until the wall jolted. It shook before it slid slowly, revealing an opening and a room within. Ash only stepped forward when Lord Alexander looked over his shoulder at him, expecting he follow.

The office walls and floor were stone, as if it'd once been a part of a small dungeon cell or a storage closet. There was only enough space for shelves of books and two large leather chairs that faced each other, a round glass side table between them. Alexander turned on the gas of a wall lamp that flickered dimly. "This room has a protective barrier," he said, as if continuing a casual conversation. "No one can enter this space without my palm print. The wonders of alchemy never cease to amaze me."

The door slid shut behind Ash. "Why don't you just learn it yourself?"

"I've tried. I have no natural talent, unfortunately."

Ash eyed the space, uncertain. Alexander didn't seem like the type to invite another person into a small hidden room just to kill them, but then, Ash supposed he didn't know the young lord very well.

"This is my refuge," Lord Alexander said, falling into one of the chairs. "In case of attack, I'm brought here."

Ash chose a spot against the wall opposite him, arms stiff at his sides. "You'd have to trust someone to let them know where you hide."

"I do trust you."

"Really? Not many put the people they trust under house arrest."

"I was also considering your safety in the matter."

"I don't believe you," Ash said. "I think you want to keep me close. That's how you'll keep control of me—of your *symbol* of alchemy, right?"

"Sounds like someone's been talking to radicals," Lord Alexander said lightly.

Ash pressed his mouth into a line.

Lord Alexander examined Ash, hands perched on the armrests of his chair as if it were a throne. "I want to make you an offer."

"Yeah?" Ash said, suddenly tired. He wanted to check in on Ramsay again—wanted to rest, far away from everyone who seemed to want something from him. "What's that?"

"You won't be allowed to leave this manor without my permission," Alexander said, "but I will grant you access to come and go as you please—as long as you're willing to help me in return."

"Another request to be your advisor? I've already said no."

Alexander peered at Ash. "You always refuse, but I've never quite shared the details of the job description."

Ash frowned. He'd assumed becoming the lord's advisor would mean a position similar to his father's former role—sitting in on meetings, whispering his opinions in the House Head's ear—but now Lord Alexander seemed to suggest there was more. Ash, despite himself, was curious. That'd always been one of the traits that seemed to get him into trouble the most.

He hoped he wouldn't come to regret his next question. "What're the details?"

Alexander leaned his cheek against a forefinger, unable to hide the briefest of smiles. "You'll officially become my advisor on paper, that goes without saying—but the title will mostly be in place to ward off suspicion," he said. "After tonight, I'm certain my instinct was correct: You're the right person for this job. Half the work has already been done. You've even been invited to join them."

A laugh of disbelief bubbled in Ash's chest. "You want me to work with the radical alchemists?"

"I want you to keep an eye on them," Alexander said. "Pretend to join their ranks. Bring me information on what they plan next."

Guilt at the thought of meeting with Marlowe, lying to her and using her, splintered through Ash. Though Marlowe had betrayed him, he wasn't sure he could do the same. "Don't you think they'll already be suspicious that you sent me?"

"Yes, I'm sure they will. But if the information we have on this particular group is at all accurate, then there will also be an initiation—a chance to earn their trust."

"And if I fail? I'm not the best actor, you know."

"Then you'll likely be killed," Alexander said.

"Ah, well, that sounds like a wonderful opportunity. When do I begin?"

"Besides," Alexander added, ignoring Ash's sarcasm. "I have a feeling that at least a small part of you wouldn't be acting."

Ash hesitated, heart beating harder. "What do you mean?"

"I've gotten the sense, I suppose, that you might not disagree with all of your father's ideologies."

Ash's mouth twitched. "Then why risk sending me at all?" he asked. "If I agree with the group, then I could end up really joining them."

"Because the information you provide would be worth any risk," Alexander said. "Besides, I've learned over the years not to underestimate the loyalty of romantic partners. I doubt you'd betray Callum Kendrick and Ramsay Thorne anytime soon."

Ash looked away from the lord—stared around at the room he could only assume was a secret to everyone else in the state except maybe Edric. "You've claimed to want to help alchemists," Ash said. "How does spying on a group of them fit into that plan?"

Alexander dropped his hand from his face and leaned back in

his seat. "We were lucky tonight, that no one was killed—but that might not be the case if this group attacks again. What do you imagine the response will be?" Lord Alexander asked him. "The actions of a few will harm the many. They'd give fuel to Head Kendrick and the others under my rule who see alchemists as a threat. Alchemy could be outlawed altogether, seen only as a tool of extremists—or thieves of the Creator, depending on who you ask."

Ash frowned at the floor. Yes, he could see that possible future. It sometimes seemed like the path New Anglia was already on.

"I've heard Source continuously seeks balance as it expands," Lord Alexander said. "There are currently two sides—those fighting for alchemy and those fighting against it—pulling further and further apart. Perhaps this is only an opportunity," Alexander said. "A chance to find balance within our state. *You* could help to create that balance, Sir Woods. Seek out the group. Warn me of their plans."

Ash pushed away from the wall. "Isn't it funny that in the search for balance, there's always one side that's expected to compromise more?"

"I'll give you time to consider."

Alexander stood, walked to Ash's side, and placed his palm against stone again. "Another thing," the older said as the wall began to open. "Don't tell anyone about my offer—not even Commander Kendrick and Head Thorne. You'd be surprised by how easily information spreads among the Houses, and if Head Kendrick were to learn what I've asked of you, well . . ."

The wall had fully opened, but neither Ash nor Lord Alexander moved. "It would undo the work I've done on behalf of alchemists. Think on my offer," Alexander said, walking ahead and leaving Ash in the room's shadows. "You have a day and a night to decide."

6

Ash left his meeting with Lord Alexander expecting to see Callum waiting for him in the hall, but instead two reds stood stationed outside the door, the older boy nowhere to be found. Maybe it was for the best. Ash wouldn't be able to look at Callum without anger burning through him.

Ash was taken to the guest quarters in the east wing. The quarters were on the top floor and had their own suite, with a washroom and a balcony that overlooked the central courtyard. The sparkling white tile and golden floral wallpaper might've impressed Ash, once, but he found the lack of decoration to be cold and sorely missed the dim embers of the cottage's fireplace.

"Your things will be delivered in the morning," an attendant said. The door closed, and Ash was left standing in the center of the silent room with nothing but his thoughts. That made him most anxious of all.

He padded across the chambers and sat on the edge of the bed, mattress too firm for his tastes, and stared at his hands, fingers trembling. He realized, vaguely, that he was in shock. The adrenaline of the night had slowed, and too much had taken place for his mind to catch up with. The only emotion that lingered was the sting of Callum's betrayal, slowly turning to a dull ache. His body was heavy with exhaustion, but Ash already knew he wouldn't be able to let himself sleep. He didn't know which nightmare would find him. The burning city, the black moon, his dead father, his mother's screams?

"Fuck this." Ash abruptly stood and left his suite, heavy door slamming shut behind him. He hurried through the empty corridors, footfalls tapping as he made his way down the sets of stairs. The first floor was abandoned and silent, an odd sight after seeing the halls crowded with survivors of the gala's attack.

Ash reached the room where Ramsay had been resting and knocked on the door to no response. He tried pushing it open with a creak. The room was empty, sheets stripped from the bed. He frowned—the worst possibility crossed his mind, but only for a moment; he would've been told if something had happened to Ramsay. The only other likelihood took him back down the hall and up the stairs, to the portal door he'd used to arrive earlier that night.

Ash was technically under house arrest now and knew he needed Alexander's permission to leave the manor, regardless of whether he agreed to be the lord's little spy or not; but, then again, Ash simply didn't give a shit. He would take whatever punishment Alexander gave him. There was only one place Ash could think Ramsay would've gone. Hand on the doorknob, he murmured the password Ramsay had decided to keep, this time an intentional reminder of what they couldn't allow to happen again. "Snowdrop."

The door opened to a welcome, familiar sight, even with the biting cold that settled on Ash's skin. He closed the door behind him and stepped into Ramsay's office. It was in its usual mess, desk holding piles of papers and texts, towers even taller than when Ramsay had been only a graduate apprentice of Lancaster. The wallpaper was the same water-stained emerald green, the hardwood floors scuffed. Lamps lit the room.

"Ramsay?" Ash called. He walked into the chilly stone halls that had once been so easy to get lost in, first popping his head into the main chambers where he'd spent a number of nights intertwined in the bedsheets, and then the sitting room and library and kitchen, but to no avail. He hadn't considered that Ramsay might not even be home. Maybe he'd gone to the Kendrick town house in Kensington. Ash's heart squeezed at the thought that

Ramsay would've gone to Callum, both abandoning Ash to his prison.

He sat at Ramsay's old mahogany desk, in the hard wooden chair, and folded over, head in his arms. His eyes were heavy, his body drained whether he wanted to let himself sleep or not. He began to drift, dreams searching for him—sweat prickled at the thought of hearing the screams and seeing the flames—

The office door opened, and voices filled the room, the only warning Ash had before Ramsay stepped inside. Ash eyed her quickly, but her broken bones appeared healed, as Charlotte had promised. Her brow furrowed as she nodded, listening to Lord Val. The Head of House Val was a much older man and always had such a serious, grim expression that Ash couldn't help but feel like he'd done something terribly wrong whenever in his presence. The man had become a mentor and manager of sorts to Ramsay, giving assignments and offering guidance on the slow but steady rebuilding of House Thorne.

"It won't do any good, you see, to supply the proposal without—"

Lord Val stopped speaking as he looked up, prompting Ramsay to do the same. Her eyes widened in surprise, eyebrows raised. "Ash."

Ash felt like he was interrupting—no, not only that. He felt like Ramsay didn't want him there. "Sorry. I should've asked before—"

"No, no," Ramsay said quickly. She looked between Ash and Lord Val as if unsure what to do.

"I should leave," Ash said.

Val seemed to silently agree. He'd never approved of the boy who had destroyed half of Lancaster College, even after he was officially pardoned of all his crimes. He pursed his lips. "We don't have much time, Lady Thorne."

"Understood. I'll have the full report on its properties delivered to you by tomorrow evening." It amazed Ash how easily Ramsay's tongue-in-cheek tone changed into the sort that seemed coldly appropriate for a House Head.

Lord Val nodded gruffly and went to the office door, excusing himself, and murmured a password before disappearing into a brightly lit white hall, door closing behind him.

Ash hesitated, unmoving even when Ramsay went to his side and pressed a kiss to his cheek. "Callum said you were meeting with Lord Alexander privately, or I would've come to see you."

"I'm sorry," he said again, ignoring the flare in his chest at the mention of Callum. "I didn't mean to interrupt."

"Lord Val and I were almost finished anyway." She quirked a smile, sitting on the edge of her desk. "And your company is much preferred."

Ash wanted to believe her. "How're you feeling?"

Ramsay's green bruises were bright against her skin. "Better," she said. "But never mind me—how are you?" she asked, eyes sweeping over Ash. "What *happened*? Callum said you'd have a story to share, but that I should wait to hear it from you directly."

Ash took a breath. He could already hear Ramsay's insistence that Ash have nothing to do with Marlowe, even at Lord Alexander's request—that she and any friend of hers could not be trusted, especially after tonight. "It's a long story."

"I'm not particularly tired."

"I am," Ash said.

She nodded her understanding. "All right. I'll be patient." She sighed, pushing herself from the desk and crossing the room to fall into one of the leather chairs before the fireplace. "How long have you been here?"

Ash checked the clock hung on the wall. It was five in the morning. "A couple of hours." He must've fallen asleep after all. He stood from the desk to sit in the chair beside Ramsay's, pulling his feet up and resting his cheek on his knees. He was reminded of the nights he'd spent with her there, harmonizing their vibrations together. It was amusing to think about how much he'd disliked her, once.

"Should you even be on your feet?" Ash said. He realized he sounded like Callum and Ramsay both when they worried over him. "Pretty sure the Adelaide healers would advise against meeting with House Heads when your ribs are cracked."

"My ribs are healed." Ramsay closed her eyes and pressed a finger to her temple. "And Lord Val and I were concerned with how close we were to losing my work tonight. I was transferring notes."

"You should be resting."

Ramsay only waved a hand dismissively. They sat together for a moment more, listening to the crackle of the fire, Ramsay staring aimlessly, as if already lost in thought. She scratched a cheek. "Callum will give you an earful if he finds out you're here, by the way."

"Did Callum tell you I'm not allowed to leave House Alexander?"

Ramsay nodded slowly. "Not that it's stopped you from leaving the first chance you had, apparently."

"I'm under *house arrest*."

"Callum says it's for your safety."

"It's bullshit, and you know that."

"He'll give *me* an earful for letting you stay."

"I don't care."

"That's obvious."

"It feels like you two are always ganging up on me these days. Like you're not on my side."

Ramsay paused. She stood and took her time bending over him, hands on the armrests, with a smile that tugged. "We're only worried about you."

He was caged in. "I'm not a child for you two to take care of. I'm nineteen now."

She gave one nod. "You're right." Her stare was challenging, smirk growing. "Will you forgive me?"

Ash's cheeks heated. "I don't want to."

"I'm sure you don't."

"I'm still upset."

She grinned. "Yes, evidently you are."

Ash sighed. Ramsay had apparently found Ash's weaknesses, too. "Fine. Yes. I forgive you."

Ramsay leaned forward, waiting for Ash to close the distance. It was only meant to be a quick kiss, Ash thought—but Ramsay lingered even after they parted, lips barely touching, before she pushed forward again—and for a moment, Ash truly did forget all about his frustration, kiss deepening until he felt lost in her energy.

"I've missed you," Ramsay murmured, foreheads pressed together.

They'd seen each other just hours ago, but Ash knew what she meant. His heart seized as he remembered how close he'd been to losing her that night—how he might lose her, still, if he didn't agree to become Elena's pawn. "Me, too," he said.

＊

Morning was a greeting of wind whistling through stone walls and light bouncing off the white mountainsides. Cold air drifted through the room. Ash shivered under the sheets. Source, he hated the Downs.

Ramsay was waiting for him in the kitchen, sipping tea at a small table, more comfortable than the formal dining room. Stacks of papers surrounded her, round spectacles sliding to the end of her nose. "I thought you planned to wake up after the day already ended," she said as she scribbled across a sheet of paper.

"You're one to talk," Ash mumbled, pulling out a chair beside her, blankets wrapped around him. "Have you eaten yet?"

"You know I hate eating in the morning."

Ash bent over, arm acting as a pillow for his head. "Do you think Callum's noticed I'm gone?"

"Without question," Ramsay said. They were quiet, but only for a moment. Ramsay nudged Ash's leg with her knee. "Will you tell me what happened last night now? I've been patient enough, I think."

Ash hesitated. He'd planned to tell Ramsay everything—the full truth, from the interrogation with the rebels to being asked to spy on them by Alexander . . . but the lord's words echoed in Ash's mind now. He'd said that, if Edric found out, it would undo the work Alexander had done for alchemists, even if Ash didn't know the details of why or how. And, after all, Ramsay never had liked keeping secrets from Callum.

He bit his lip and began his story, though Ash did skim over the details of seeing Ramsay in the wreckage, the fear that she had died. Ramsay slid off her glasses as she listened, frowning in concentration as Ash described waking up for the interrogation and the conversation he'd had with Elena—her proposal that Ash join their group.

"Marlowe was there," he said.

Ramsay stilled. "*Marlowe*—as in your father's spy, the girl who tried to kill you multiple times, *that Marlowe?*" When Ash nodded, she said, "Source, she's like a forsaken gnat that just won't leave, isn't she?"

"There's more," Ash said. Ramsay blinked, brows raised, when Ash said Ramsay had been the main target of the attack.

"An assassination attempt?" she said, bewildered.

"They've promised not to target you again."

"Oh, yes, I'll gladly take the word of my would-be *murderers*." Despite her sarcasm, her face had paled. She pressed her lips into a line. "Did they say why?" she asked more quietly.

"Elena mentioned an invention," Ash said, eyes flicking up to watch Ramsay's response. Her vibration muddled, but only for a moment, before it returned to its rigid pace. "She said it'd been commissioned by House Kendrick."

Ramsay's pinched brows suggested she was already in deep thought as she stared at her tea. Steam had stopped rising a while ago now.

"Why didn't you say you were making an invention for Edric?" Ash asked her. "You mentioned you were working with Lord Val, but . . ."

Ramsay stood from the table, mug in hand, and gave a fleeting smile. "That's classified, technically."

Ash knew when Ramsay only wanted to push away a subject. "I'm serious."

She sighed, back still to him, as she stopped at the sink. "Why would an invention commissioned by House Kendrick be a problem?"

Ash turned in his seat to watch her. "Why *wouldn't* it be? House Kendrick is actively working to suppress alchemists. Anything they ask for can't be good."

She put the mug down with a clink. "That's our boyfriend's House, in case you've forgotten."

"Callum isn't in charge. He means well, of course he does, and he wants to help—but there isn't anything he can do for us as long as Edric is the Head." Ash asked again, "What is the invention?"

Ramsay took a breath and turned to face him as she leaned back against the wooden counter. "It's called a firelock. It's a weapon of sorts," she said, "but it'll help redguards and alchemists alike."

"How can you be so sure it'll help us?"

"How can you be so sure it won't?" Ash tried to interrupt, but Ramsay continued, hand raised. "I understand the concern, Ash, especially if this *group* wanted to kill me for it, but I promise you there isn't anything to worry about." She hesitated, then added, "The firelock is nothing like what my parents have invented in the past. Okay?"

Ash's jaw muscle jumped, ashamed that she had felt his silent question, his main concern, but what else could he say? He nodded. "Okay."

Ramsay tilted her head ever so slightly. "And what about you?"

Ash's gaze flitted up to meet hers. "What about me?"

Ramsay's arms were crossed as she moved her lower jaw back

and forth for a moment. Ash considered it a gift, that she'd taken the time to learn how to choose her words more carefully, thanks to Callum. "You were with a group that describes themselves as alchemist liberalists."

"Yes? And?" Even though Ramsay had tried to soften her implication, Ash felt the flint of anger. "I'm not my father, Ramsay."

She held up both palms. "Source, I never said you were. I just want to . . . caution you, I suppose. Patterns like these often show themselves in Source geometry."

"Another lecture?"

"Parallels are often drawn."

"You've stopped giving me lessons, remember?"

"Children turn into the parents they swore never to become."

"Are you saying I'll turn into a power-hungry maniac who kills hundreds of thousands of people?" Ash asked.

Ramsay took a deep, slow breath, and said, "No. That's not what I'm trying to say at all."

Maybe Ash could benefit more from Callum's influence, too. He bit his lip, guilt piercing him. "Sorry."

"Just—please, be careful with the extremist ideology you hear. Be discerning."

Ash hesitated. He hated the lie he decided to tell then, but maybe it really was for the best that he kept some things from Ramsay, too. "It isn't like I'm going to be hanging around the rebels much anyway," he said, forcing a quick laugh with a spike of frenzied energy so that Ramsay wouldn't be able to sense the truth behind his lie.

She squinted, but only nodded. "I suppose that's true," she said.

※

It was easy to find Lord Alexander in his main office, surrounded by scribes and attendants. The lord took one look at Ash and immediately waved a hand at everyone else in the room. "Dismissed."

The scribes and attendants filed out, glancing at Ash as they passed. Ash waited until only he stood in the center of the office, the door shutting behind him. He sorely hoped he wouldn't regret the next words out of his mouth—but Ramsay's voice had carved into him. Ash would prove to her—to all of New Anglia—that he wasn't following in his father's footsteps.

"I accept."

7

The sky was covered by black clouds that threatened rain. Fog drifted from the docks and through the maze of brick row houses. Worn boots and tattered heels clacked across stone. People moved quickly, heads low. One man staggered, eyes darting to every person he passed. He looked over his shoulder, face pale.

The candlelight had been put out. Embers from the fireplace glowed. Her mother had whispered to stay quiet. Fists thudded against the door, vibrations echoing through the walls. The girl hid beneath her bed, biting back her cries.

A boy ran through the stalks that sliced his skin, gasping for air, blood seeping from his side. The others laughed. They were close behind.

The rain began to fall. It started slowly before it was unsheathed, slapping the cobblestone and pavement and gushing over rooftop gutters. People splashed by, holding umbrellas or dripping newspapers over their heads. The man limped into an alley, back against the wall with a shuddering breath.

The knocks became heavy thuds. They would break down the door before long. Her mother begged them to leave. "She meant no harm!"

The boy tripped, stumbled—scrambled to his feet again, sobbing now—

People wearing soaked robes of white marched. The crowds parted, gazes falling. The man gasped—stepped deeper into the alleyway's shadows, but too late. One Lune follower held up a hand.

The door splintered. Her mother was thrown aside. "She's just a child—"

The boy's screams echoed across the fields.

The man quivered—stepped away, but he had nowhere to run. The Lune followers pulled him from the alley, grasps strong. One follower stepped forward to share his verdict. "You're an alchemist," he said.

"Please—please, I haven't hurt anyone—"

"You've come for revenge—"

"I've done nothing wrong—"

"—come to finish the work of Gresham Hain."

The silence that followed crawled through the air.

The house's charred skeleton remained.

The boy's screams abruptly ended. Stalks swayed in the night breeze.

※

It was easier than Ash anticipated, to call out to Marlowe. He closed his eyes and thought her name as if blasting it into a foghorn, imagining his voice spreading across the dimensions through New Anglia. It was as if she'd waited just to hear his voice. Smoke began to unfurl from his wall immediately, the outline of Marlowe waiting on the other side.

"Source," she said, "you didn't have to shout my name that loudly. A simple thought would do."

Ash hesitated, staring at the pool of ink that waited for him in the wall. It looked like a round, black, reflectionless mirror.

"Come on," Marlowe said, tone impatient. "It isn't anything to be scared of."

"Forgive me for not trusting everything that comes out of your mouth."

He took a deep breath and held it as he stepped into the darkness.

A blast of cold hit him hard enough that air was sucked from his lungs. He gasped, felt like he'd plunged into a lake of ice— Source, he was drowning—

His foot landed on the other side, as if stepping over a threshold. He wheezed, stumbling forward, caught only by Marlowe's hand that gripped his elbow. "It can be hard, the first few times," she said. "But you get used to it."

Ash turned to look at the inky shadows, but they'd already started to soak back into the walls until they were gone. "What *was* that?" he said, throat raw. He knew that life was limitless—that when he died again, he would only continue to live on in a different form—but this? It was the closest he'd felt to the concept of non-existence.

"Too much to explain now," Marlowe said. "Let's go. Elena is waiting."

They'd stepped into what appeared to be a bedroom. The window was boarded up, only a sliver of white light shining through. A single twin mattress was on the floor beside a stack of books. Ash recognized his father's on top, the one that had gained Hain notoriety decades before. It was surprising, that Marlowe would keep a reminder of the man at all.

An open window let in a chilled fall breeze. Outside was a line of row houses, many with shattered or boarded-up windows, along with scattered abandoned shops. It all looked familiar to Ash, though he wanted to be sure. "Where are we?"

"Ironbound," Marlowe said.

"Is this where you're living now?"

Marlowe opened the door. "Yes."

Ash wouldn't have been surprised to learn the town house had been abandoned, before Marlowe's new friends found it and decided to make it their home. The pale floral wallpaper had yellow water stains; the hardwood floorboards were so scuffed that some parts were more white than brown. There was a distinct smell of mold that scratched Ash's throat.

He followed only a few steps behind Marlowe as she walked down the hall. Several doors to rooms were open. One muscley man walked to the threshold to watch Marlowe and Ash pass.

Another leaned against the frame, arms crossed as they stared Ash down. Ash recognized the child who had been at the attack on the gala; they looked up with wide eyes from a book they read on a chair. Though no one said a word, it felt as if the air had thickened. Ash's eyes stung with the pressure of so much energy directed at him.

"What is this place?" he asked Marlowe beneath his breath. Another stood in the threshold, raising her chin as she inspected Ash. "A base of some kind?"

"Careful," Marlowe said with a glance over her shoulder. "Your questions might be mistaken for prying."

"Is it wrong to be curious?" he asked, swallowing the air that'd built in his lungs. "I think I'm allowed to want to know more about the place I've been dragged off to."

"And you will, with time." She added, "Besides, you haven't been dragged anywhere. You voluntarily called for me, didn't you?" She hesitated, but only for a moment. "Why did I find you in Alexander's manor? Have you moved into the mansion now?"

"Careful," he said. "You might be mistaken for prying."

They came to a creaking wooden staircase that led down to the first floor. There was an ornate fireplace with unlit, charred wood stacked atop black soot and two sofas that faced each other, color worn and the stitching coming undone. The place looked like a town house that might've belonged in Kensington but had been forgotten. But then, after his last interaction with this group, Ash wasn't sure he could even trust what he saw in front of him.

Riles, the lanky one who'd tried to kill Ramsay, leaned against the wall beside the fireplace. He stared at Ash in a way that reminded him of the bullies he and Tobin used to handle in the Hedge streets, the sort who was just a little more bark than bite. A young woman, younger than even Ash perhaps, sat on one sofa; but despite her age, her hair was graying, pulled back into one long braid.

"Ash," she said. "I'm glad you could join us."

Ash hesitated, glancing at Marlowe, who only took a spot against the far wall opposite Riles. It appeared to be an intentional position, as if the two stood on guard, ready to attack if necessary.

"Do I know you?" he asked, gaze falling back to the girl in front of him.

"I would think so." Her smile was practiced. "I'm the one who invited you here."

Ash's brows rose—but maybe he shouldn't have been surprised. She'd managed to change an entire room's appearance, after all; why not herself, too? Elena only gestured at the sofa opposite her.

Ash sat slowly, muscles tense as if subconsciously preparing to run. "How did you manage to change your body's physical appearance?" he asked. He'd attempted to make changes to his own numerous times, but the body's structure was too complicated to permanently alter, or so Ash had thought.

"I haven't," Elena said. Ash blinked as the air in front of Elena blurred, heat shimmering. "I've only altered your mind's perception of me."

More illusion alchemy, then. She'd have to be powerful indeed to continuously affect Ash's mind from one moment to the next; it seemed second nature to her, like breathing or blinking. Ash wasn't sure if it was wise to speak his next thought aloud, but: "You could have any face you like. You could be anyone, claiming to be a woman named Elena, couldn't you?"

"Is that what you think?" she asked with a puff of a laugh. "What? Do you believe I'm secretly an agent of Alexander's, sent to trick you into some sort of game?"

He hesitated. Was Elena playing with him? Maybe she already knew that was exactly why Ash was in front of her—that *he'd* been sent by the lord to watch the group, to warn Lord Alexander of any oncoming attacks. The anxiety of getting caught thrummed with every heartbeat. *She already knows. She already knows.*

"Maybe not of Alexander's," Ash admitted, glad when his voice didn't crack. "But Alexander isn't the only House that could use a talent like yours."

"You have a lot of nerve, questioning anyone's motives," Riles muttered.

Ash ignored him. He wasn't sure he could acknowledge the boy without the desire to set his skin on fire. "What is this place?" he asked Elena, eager to get away from the topic of spies.

Riles spoke again. "Don't answer that."

"You don't give me orders," Elena said lightly. "But he's right. I can't tell you—not yet. You came here to me, Sir Woods. Why?"

"I thought I was invited."

"Did you come out of curiosity? Boredom?" Elena shrugged with a pleasant smile. "Or did you come because you understand that alchemists deserve more than what this world offers? That *you* deserve more, too?"

Her words ignited Ash's veins. His chest burned. Source knew this was a thought he'd had again and again, anger curling inside him at the realization that he'd never been given the same acceptance nor equal footing as others—that there was more he was owed. Once, he'd been preoccupied with the anger that he wasn't as seen nor respected as others, simply because he was a boy from Hedge. He thought he'd overcome those feelings by now, but they still smoldered. Yes, he was entitled to freedom—to *existence*—without the hatred of strangers. Without fearing for his life.

Riles spoke behind him before Ash could answer. "Or were you sent to us?" Footsteps thudded on the hardwood floor, falling closer until Riles stood in the corner of Ash's eye. "Told to accept our offer?"

Shit. The question wasn't a surprise. Ash already knew it would be hard to convince them. This didn't do much to calm down the buzzing in his chest. "If you don't trust that I'm here to help you, then why waste time?" Ash asked with more bravado than he felt. "Might as well kill me now and get it over with."

"Oh, believe me, I'd gladly—"

"Riles," Elena said, holding up a hand. He fell silent. "Answer my question, please, Sir Woods."

He took a long moment to reply. Ash didn't usually have the patience for political games like these, but too much was at risk now. His time surviving the Hedge streets as a child came in handy. One of his first lessons had been that a believable lie needed an ounce of truth. "I don't agree with all of my father's ideologies," he admitted. "I don't think that the answer to change means blowing up buildings—assassinating innocent people." His cheeks warmed at the memory of a discussion he'd had with Ramsay, once, as she'd given him his first lesson. "I don't believe that's the true definition of power."

"But you do *want* power."

"I want freedom," Ash said.

"The path to freedom isn't always bloodless."

"Maybe it could be, if—"

"He's been around that red of his too much," Riles muttered.

Enough. Ash turned to face Riles, choked with the effort not to scream. "Don't fucking talk about Callum—"

"Source, now we have to deal with his tantrums, too?" But Riles was smiling now, pointed teeth gleaming. It seemed he'd finally gotten the reaction he'd wanted out of Ash. He gestured at the younger boy, turning to Elena. "Do you see how he jumps to the defense of a redguard commander? And this is who you want to trust?"

"We've been through this already," Marlowe said from across the room.

"I'm not on House Kendrick's side," Ash snapped. "I just don't think anyone needs to *kill*. We could—I don't know," he said, words falling short and voice now smaller. He sounded like Callum even to his own ears. "We could find a compromise."

Riles snorted. Marlowe's gaze fell. Elena's chin rose as she inspected Ash. "Do you expect peace to come from compromise?"

"How else would we find it?"

"Historically speaking, peace has only ever come from war."

"It's not true peace, then," Ash said, breathless. It felt impossible to explain what he'd experienced once he'd died and returned to Source. "Peace is unconditional. It's unchanging. This? This space that's in between killing and war and—"

"And yet," Elena interrupted, "even war is a part of Source. Isn't that true?" she asked him. "Everything in existence is woven into the threads of the universe. These killings, the deaths and murders of innocents—they, too, are Source."

His father had said something similar to him, once. "No," Ash said, thinking of the blackened city, fire plumes rising to the night sky. "It's unwanted pain that we've caused."

"And so *our* pain is wanted?" Elena asked. "Why are the murders of innocents caused by House Lune acceptable, but the deaths of those who kill us are not?"

Ash had stopped breathing. His gaze dropped as he sucked in a shallow breath. He realized, then, that he had no answer to give her.

Elena stood. She crossed the narrow space and rested a hand on Ash's shoulder. He looked up, and the image of her face blurred before its mask returned. "Listen to me," she told him. "I know that you were brought to me by Source for a reason. I'm not enough to lead a rebellion against the Houses. Who am I? An unknown woman from Ironbound. I'm not the figure that can unite all practicing alchemists, who can inspire us to fight back. But *you* . . ."

Ash's throat stuck when he swallowed. He looked to Marlowe, air filling his chest when he saw the intensity of her gaze—her hope, even. Ash didn't owe anything to Marlowe, not really, and yet he felt he had a responsibility to her, for the years of freedom she'd lost because of his father. Maybe, in a way, Ash owed all alchemists if he truly wanted to atone.

Only Riles snorted, shaking his head. "You rest the future of our freedom on a spy's shoulders."

"We haven't given him a chance," Marlowe said to Riles, then to Elena: "Give him a job. A mission. Let him prove to us that he's on the right side of this."

"Something even marginally convincing, please," Riles said. "It can't be some secret he's brought from House Alexander that was most likely given to him by the lord himself."

Elena nodded, considering Ash. "I believe I have just the thing."

Ash's fingers fidgeted. He'd been warned he'd be tested, hadn't he? "What do you want me to do?"

"You're quite loyal to Ramsay Thorne and Callum Kendrick," Elena said.

"I'm not going to hurt them. I refuse—"

"No, of course not," Elena said. "But House Kendrick works closely with the college that trains young redguards—McKinley, correct?" Ash frowned in confusion, but Elena only went on. "Thorne's prototype is to be tested at the college, given to the students as training weapons. You don't have to hurt Thorne nor Kendrick to work against them. You could help us destroy those prototypes, before they're unleashed on alchemists next."

Ash choked out his next words, already fearing the answer. "And how would you want me to do that?"

Elena's smile was grimmer in the moment, at least. "You will help us with our attack on McKinley College."

8

The attack would be in one week, Elena let him know. Ash would be expected to return to the base, where they'd travel to McKinley together. "Use the week to prepare yourself," Elena told Ash. "Stock up on food, sleep—energy. It won't do us any good if you become a hinderance instead of an aid."

Ash knew that warning Callum wouldn't help, if Elena and her group arrived to a swarm of waiting redguards. Maybe that didn't matter. Maybe he could give up on his role as Alexander's spy now, rather than let the college be attacked.

And if there was something else the group plotted? Elena had said that this time, the target was only the firelocks, not human lives—but what if there was eventually a plan to kill hundreds, even thousands, and it'd been within Ash's power to stop it? No—Ash realized he needed to wait, even as guilt ate away at him inside. Ramsay and especially Callum wouldn't be happy if they learned he helped attack McKinley, but he hoped they could understand.

"Come on," Marlowe said. "I'll show you around."

"Sure that's a good idea?" Ash asked. "I mean, I could be a spy, right?"

"You probably shouldn't say that, even if it's meant to be a joke," Marlowe said.

She walked him down a creaking hall where there was another line of doors, some open and some closed. Ash wondered if the base had once been an inn; that would be helpful information to share with Lord Alexander, if the man wanted to figure out the base's location. Marlowe gestured into some of the doors that were open. "This is Ralph; that's Judith." An older man looked up from a book he read at his desk, the blank stare he gave Ash unreadable. "This is Otto, our resident healer."

"How many of you are there?" he whispered as they continued on.

Marlowe was quiet for a moment, as if she wasn't sure if she wanted to answer that question. "There are twelve of us here right now," she eventually said, "but we don't all live here permanently. Some come and go. We get visitors from other chapters. Only five are really on the official *team*, I guess you could say."

"There're other chapters?" Ash asked.

"Elena should really be the one to tell you all this."

Ash decided it was best not to push.

Marlowe opened a door to what looked like an office that had been turned into a library. It was musty, dust floating in the dim light. Ash curiously glanced at the titles on the shelves, all with cracked covers and yellowing pages. His eyes did a sweep for the one title that remained lodged in the back of his mind, a habit he seemed unable to break, disappointed but unsurprised when he didn't see it.

"Have you ever heard of a book called *Communicating with Plasma Particles*?" he asked Marlowe.

She'd already picked up a copy of a book that seemed focused on the healing of physical ailments. She barely glanced up as she turned the page. "No. Why?"

"It's nothing."

Marlowe slid the book back onto the shelf. "Come on."

The tour ended in a kitchen that seemed to be more of a communal space. Chipped red tiles covered the floor, and countertops lined the smoke-stained walls. A swollen wooden bench took up most of the space. The coziness of the room reminded Ash of the cottage he'd left behind. He'd been lonely, bored, listless, and searching for a new goal to focus on; ironic, that now he almost longed for that solitude and its peace. But maybe two things could be true at once. Maybe there was just the smallest part of him, too, that had always craved some sort of adventure in his life again.

"Would you like to stay a while?" Marlowe asked. "Have something to eat? We don't have much, but . . ."

"Should you really be inviting a spy to stay for lunch?"

"I told you, Ash, that isn't very funny."

Marlowe opened the fridge and pulled out stale bread and grabbed a bowl for grapes. It was the only sort of meal Ash ate up until a year before, and the lunch felt nostalgic.

Marlowe sighed as she picked at the bread.

"You must be used to meals fancier than this," Ash said. He hadn't known much about Marlowe, except that she'd lived in a Kensington town house funded by his father. He'd adopted her and paid for her training, her clothes, everything.

"Yes," Marlowe admitted. "The others laugh at me for it, but I miss—well—*food*, real food." She gave him an envious glance. "You're living in Lord Alexander's manor now. Your meals must be incredible."

Ash shrugged. "Haven't actually eaten there yet. I just moved in."

"Oh? What made you decide to join House Alexander?"

"It wasn't my choice," Ash said. The topic was a dangerous one, but he could find a way to tell a part of the truth, at least. "Lord Alexander forced me to become his advisor."

"Advisor," Marlowe repeated with some surprise. "That's the same position your father had. And you were forced into it, you said?"

"A part of the reason I'm here now, I admit," Ash told her, glad that his tone sounded as bitter as he felt. "I don't like being made to do anything."

"Revenge against Lord Alexander, then."

"Maybe a small part of my motivation, if I'll be completely honest," Ash said, glad that the lies were coming so easily, "though not my only one." He tore his bread into smaller pieces. "Elena's made a few good points, I guess you could say."

"They were your father's points, originally."

Ash chewed and swallowed. "I won't kill anyone," he added after a moment had passed.

Marlowe understood what he meant. "There won't be any need to," she said. "We'll focus our attack only on the prototypes: Get in, find them, destroy them, and get out."

"Is the group always so—impulsive?" For a moment, Ash wished that Ramsay were there; he could already see the look she would've given him, her bemused expression suggesting it was very ironic indeed for him to ask a question like that.

"Not usually. This was a mission we were planning for at least one month from now," Marlowe said. "A week won't be enough time to fully prepare. I'm surprised Elena gave the go-ahead at all. We still haven't gathered enough information about the weapons' locations."

"Haven't you attempted a remote viewing?" It was how Marlowe had spent so much of the previous year spying on him, after all.

"McKinley has decades-old barriers and protections against remote viewings in place. House Kendrick claims to want to limit alchemy, but has no misgivings using alchemy themselves."

"They'd like to limit its use to a select few, maybe," Ash said. He wasn't sure if he said this just to convince Marlowe of his loyalty.

"We do know, at least, that there's a curfew on the campus. Students who still live in the college's dorms won't be roaming after dark. It'll be an easy chance for us to sneak in."

"There won't be a battle, then."

"No, there won't." Marlowe ate quietly for a moment. "I'm glad you came, Ash. I know life among the Houses can be . . . appealing."

Ash had to bite back a laugh. "Appealing? For whom? I admit, I wanted to join the Houses, once, before I knew what they were like. But I've never been interested in kissing ass."

"I know," Marlowe said. "That's what I've always respected about you."

Ash looked up, surprised. "You respect me, do you?"

"When I was ordered to spy on you, follow you—kill you," she said, "I—it's hard to explain, but I don't think I was my full self. I don't think I had a concept of who I was, then, if I ever even knew."

Ash's gaze dropped to the table's surface. His father had done that to her. Even though it hadn't been his fault, Ash wondered if it was a shame he'd inherited.

"And now I'm experiencing freedom for the first time—getting to know who I am, not who others expect me to be, and yes, I respect you. I regret attacking you."

"You've more than made up for it," Ash mumbled. He was embarrassed to admit it out loud, but he respected Marlowe quite a lot, too. He cleared his throat of its tension. "How did you find Elena, anyway?"

"She found me," Marlowe said. "I was in Ironbound. I had nowhere to go—no money, no food, a lot like any of the survivors who had traveled north. I was accused of practicing alchemy to steal on the street."

"And did you?" Ash asked. "Steal, I mean."

"A pear, yes," she said. "I hadn't eaten in days. I was desperate."

"I'm not judging you." Ash would've done the same.

Marlowe tore off another piece of bread. "A group had formed, screaming that I was a practicing alchemist, I was a sinner, I deserved to die—and I was too weak to attempt to materialize away from them. I could barely run. No one looked like they would help me, but then a hand grabbed my own, and suddenly everyone screamed that I'd vanished, and next thing I knew, Elena had pulled me into an alley. She'd used illusion alchemy to make it look like we disappeared. She made sure I wasn't injured. She gave me food and water and offered a place for me to live. She saved my life."

"And now you're working for her because you feel like you owe her?"

"No," Marlowe said. "I'm working with her because she believes in what I believe, too. Your father was right," Marlowe told Ash, "even if he was cruel."

"'Cruel' doesn't quite cover it."

"No," Marlowe admitted. "Maybe it doesn't."

Their shared silence didn't last long. Quick footsteps were the only warning before someone leaped into the seat opposite Ash. The child Ash had seen at the gala and in the bedroom above leaned forward on the table, on their elbows. They couldn't have been any older than thirteen. "Your name is Ash," they said.

Ash nodded, glancing at Marlowe, who only sat back in her seat with a small smile. "Ah—yes, my name is Ash."

"You're the boy Elena wanted to kill."

"Source, that's enough, Finley."

Ash blinked. "I—yes, I guess I am."

"I didn't think you should be killed, for the record," Finley said.

"Thank you?"

Finley only grinned. Their stare was intense with energy, enough that Ash could feel heat prickling his skin. It'd be un-nerving for most, maybe, if they couldn't tell why their hairs were standing up on end, but Ash felt the immensity of the child's power. Usually, a person had a thin line of light energy emitting from their physical body—a constant sign that each human be-ing was merely a fractal of Source; but with Finley, Ash could see practically a halo of light around their head, glimmers of gold streaming above them, as if Ash were outright witnessing the thread that connected the child to Source itself.

The level of power drove Ash's curiosity. "Just how old are you?"

"I'm twelve. Where're you from?" Finley asked without even a pause.

Ash raised a brow and looked at a bemused Marlowe. "Hedge."

"Really? I'm from Hedge," they said. "Where in Hedge?"

"The row houses near the docks—"

"Oh, I know those. I lived in the tenements—you know, the ones by the railways?"

Ash knew exactly where Finley meant. Tobin used to live in the same. The thought pierced Ash's heart as he nodded. "Yeah, I know those, too."

"We probably passed each other in the streets every day without even realizing it. Isn't that funny? But, well, I guess Source can be funny sometimes."

Ash knew that well, too. Finley's intensity was on the edge of intimidating, which was funny, because they were only a child—yet Ash couldn't help but be curious also. "How did you end up here, then?"

"I was almost killed for practicing alchemy. I was showing my friend a trick." Finley clapped their hands together and pulled them apart to show a ball of light hovering between them. Ash's brows rose. He couldn't perform alchemy like that until he was seventeen. "Hendrix saved me. When he found out my parents were killed by Gresham Hain, he brought me here."

Ash's heart sank. He swallowed the shame that stuck in his throat. "I'm sorry."

Finley dropped their hands, the ball of light disappearing. "What're you sorry for? You didn't kill them, and besides, I'm not the only one who's lost my parents."

Ash realized all three of them were orphans; Marlowe had been raised on the House Lune estate without ever knowing her family, too. It was a morbid trait to bond over, but still, there was something to be said, the deeper understanding Ash felt he had for Marlowe and Finley both. Finley had that confident grin that implied they knew they could do anything they wanted to, if they tried hard enough. Finley reminded Ash quite a lot of himself.

"I like you," Finley told him. "You shift genders, too."

Marlowe raised a brow. "So, what? You don't like me because I don't?"

"I do like you," Finley said honestly. "I just like Ash more."

Ash laughed at the look on Marlowe's face. "Don't be jealous. When did you realize you shifted genders?" he asked Finley.

"Always," Finley said. "I have dreams of beings who aren't on Earth and don't see gender the way that we do. Gender is just energy manifested into bodies, but our energy isn't our body, is it? So, that means I'm infinite, just like Source. That's what I realized, ever since I was a kid."

"You're still a kid," Marlowe reminded them.

"If I'm still a kid, then you are, too."

"Other beings?" Ash said, curious.

"Well, Source is infinite existence. Do you really think the universe would just stop with us humans? How boring would that be?"

Ash knew Finley was right, though he wished he could see these other beings for himself, too. But, after all, his energy had only come from Source to visit Earth, so that he could experience a physical life as a boy named Ash; maybe he didn't need to concern himself with all the other manifestations of existence in the universe, too.

"Finley?" a voice called. The former dockworker covered in tattoos—Hendrix, Ash remembered—appeared at the doorway for the kitchen. "Come on, Finley. What'd I tell you?"

Finley groaned. "Why do I need to learn to read? We're in the middle of a revolution."

"It's because we're fighting for our freedom that you need to learn," Hendrix said. He nodded at Marlowe, gaze hesitating on Ash. Ash wondered if he was as welcome as Marlowe seemed to think. "The kid isn't bothering you, are they?"

Ash shook his head. "No. Not at all."

"See? Ash likes that I'm here."

"All right. Let's go."

Finley dragged their feet as they went to Hendrix's side. Ash and Marlowe watched them until both left the kitchen. It felt like there'd been a vacuum suck of energy, losing Finley's presence.

"We don't like having them fight," Marlowe said, as if she could hear Ash's thoughts. "We try to contain them to missions where we're certain there won't be any confrontations with guards."

"But you can't plan for surprises," Ash said.

"No," Marlowe agreed. She hesitated, then said, "Unfortunately, we need their help. You saw their energy field. They're the most powerful one here."

"I don't think their life is worth the risk. They're just a kid."

"You don't get to decide if it's worth the risk or not," Marlowe said. "Besides, if we don't fight now, they might end up losing their life anyway, the way things are going." She pushed out from the table. "Come on. I should get you back to Kensington."

Marlowe led Ash up the stairs and down the hall. She stared hard at her feet as they walked. Something was clearly on her mind, so Ash waited to hear what she had to say.

"Are you angry, Ash?" she asked him as they reached her room.

He knew, somehow, exactly what she meant. Maybe they were more connected than he realized. "Yes," he said. "Source, of course I am." How could he not be angry, in a world where humans justified killing others? Where so many believed that some deserved to be hated for simply existing?

"I think if I could choose, I wouldn't be angry at all."

Ash agreed. "I'm jealous of people who aren't. They seem so at peace."

"They're only at peace because they're ignorant. It isn't even within their imagination, the amount of hurt a single person can survive," she said.

Ash's stomach tightened. He didn't know everything that his father had done to Marlowe. He sorely hoped it wasn't what his father had done to his mother, too, even if it was the reason Ash was alive.

"I wonder what it must be like, to be born into a world that's for them," Marlowe whispered.

"I've wondered the same," Ash admitted. He'd once questioned what his life might've looked like if he'd been born into the Houses instead, respected as human instead of looked down upon—but then he'd had the chance to see his lives in the parallel realms, and he'd still been so unhappy, so unfulfilled . . .

"Not many understand anger, I think," Marlowe said. "They see it as a negative—an energy that blocks Source. But you . . . you've managed to funnel your anger. To turn it into power. I envy that."

Ash's face grew hot. He rubbed the back of his neck. "You don't have anything to envy. You're one of the most powerful alchemists I know." Marlowe might've even been more powerful than Ramsay, and that was certainly saying something.

They walked into her room and paused in front of the same wall Ash had come through. "Ash," Marlowe said after a moment. "I don't think I ever apologized. For—well, trying to kill you."

Laughter escaped him before he could stop it. "It's all right. You more than made up for it by killing Hain."

The small smile that'd grown on Marlowe's face faded.

Ash pressed his mouth into a line, wishing he'd thought better than to bring up his father. "I'm sorry. I shouldn't have—"

She shook her head. "It's all right." She put a hand to the wall, smoke unfurling to the floor. "He wasn't the first I've had to kill, and he won't be the last."

9

It seemed at some point an attendant had brought a bag of Ash's clothes from the cottage, as he'd been promised. He'd never had much, just a few stained shirts and slacks that had suited Hedge, though Callum had tried to hire a tailor to thread Ash a new wardrobe. "Why?" Ash had groaned. "My clothes are just fine." He supposed Callum's newest argument would be that Ash needed clothes that better suited the Alexander manor.

Ash spent the better part of the day struggling to fill his time. He read a text he'd already practically memorized, a book teaching various techniques of alteration alchemy. He walked around the manor and even the new gardens, sorely missing the one he'd left behind in Riverside.

He was offered an invitation to dine with Lord Alexander and his other guests that evening, but he declined, opting to eat a bowl of soup alone in his room instead. When there was another knock on his door, Ash expected Lord Alexander, seeking an update from his little spy—and was surprised to see Charlotte Adelaide standing at the threshold instead. The last Ash had seen her, she was in a gown stained with blood. Now she wore a powder-blue blouse and skirts. There was rouge on her cheeks and lips, and her brown hair had been freshly curled. This was who Callum had been expected to marry, once. She was very pretty, Ash had to admit, in that *upper-Kensington-society* sort of way. Ash realized he was still in the sweater he'd slept in and cotton shorts that left his legs feeling especially bare.

"Ash," she said with the kind of warmth he'd assume a person would save for a friend—but then, Ash knew it was common for

House Adelaide members to believe every being was worthy of love and friendship. "I hope it's all right I came. I wanted to check in on you—see how you're doing."

"I'm fine." He realized too late how curt his tone sounded. He didn't mean to be rude.

Charlotte's smile faltered, but only for a moment. "I'd heard you officially accepted Lord Alexander's position as advisor. I hope it's all right I came by," she said again.

Ash bit his lip. Charlotte had likely saved Ramsay's life, and he'd forever be grateful to her, but he also wasn't sure why, exactly, she was there. "Thank you again," he said, "for—"

She shook her head with a smile. "No worries at all. I just ran into Ramsay at dinner. I thought I'd pay you a visit."

"Ramsay was here?" Well, there wasn't any particular rule that Ramsay should need to stop by Ash's room now, every time she came to House Alexander.

"Yes. She suggested I come see you." Charlotte hesitated, then added, "Callum told me that he'd asked you to pay House Adelaide a visit, to see if we might be able to help you. It seems you've been having reoccurring dreams."

Ash closed his eyes, silently cursing Callum and Ramsay both. He looked at Charlotte again with a nod and strained smile. "Yes, but I'm fine."

"Nightmares like the ones Callum described—they can reflect the state of your subconscious, and—"

"I said that I'm fine," Ash told her, firmly enough now that Charlotte clamped her mouth shut. He felt a pang of guilt.

"You've said that you're fine three times now," Charlotte said after a long pause, "and I have to admit, I haven't believed you once."

Ash's breath was short, he realized—his pulse deepening at the reminder of the nightmares that stalked him. "I don't need you to believe me for it to be true."

She nodded—paused, then said, "You know, Ash, I've often found that sometimes, the most difficult part of healing is knowing when we need help at all. It can be easy to accept pain when that's all we've ever known."

It struck Ash, then, how good of a match she and Callum would've made. They were both so insistent on saving others, whether their aid was wanted or not. "I don't need your help," he let her know. "Nothing is wrong with me."

"I never thought there was," Charlotte said. She released the smallest puff of a sigh that seemed resigned to Ash, polite smile lingering. "Well, I'm always here if you change your mind."

⁕

Hardly a day had passed before Ash was called on by Lord Alexander. The pointy-mustached scribe in his golden frock, the same who had greeted Ash and Callum the night of the gala, glared down his long nose at Ash and turned on his heel, eyeing Ash's choice of a plain button-up and slacks. "Follow me."

It didn't surprise Ash that Alexander had requested a meeting; Ash expected the lord would want an update. No, what did surprise Ash was when he was led down the halls, away from the man's private office, and to the grand doors of the same conference room where he'd been questioned.

"Wait—what is this?"

The scribe raised an angular brow, hand on the door's handle and ready to push it open. "The Heads of Houses meeting, of course."

Ash froze. He'd somehow managed to forget that his new role as advisor meant—well—*advising* Lord Alexander, even if it was more of a puppet role. "I've already missed the last meeting," Ash said, trying on his sheepish grin. "Couldn't I just skip this one, too?"

The scribe's face soured. "Head Alexander expects your attendance. Your last absence was noted. Don't worry," the man said. "I'm sure our lord chose you, out of thousands of qualified applicants, for a reason."

The scribe pushed open the door. Ash swallowed at the sudden onslaught of heads turning, eyes sweeping from the top of his head and to the bottoms of his shoes. The Heads of the Houses sat in their respective chairs, Ramsay's stare focused on the surface of the table. Ash internally groaned at the thought of being watched by Ramsay as he was expected to sound *intelligent* and *knowledgeable*.

Alexander sat at the top of the table, facing them all. "Sir Woods," he said with the twitch of a smile. "Welcome. We were waiting for you." The scribe beside Ash bowed and stepped back, slamming the doors shut behind him. Ash was trapped. "Please, sit."

Chairs had been lined up along the wall behind the Heads as well, seated in many a mixture of scribes and assistants. Callum sat behind his brother. Ash took a sharp breath. "Um—where?"

A stupid question, perhaps. There were shared smirks around the table. Head Val outright rolled his eyes.

Alexander tilted his head. "The seat behind me is saved for my advisor."

Heat filled Ash's cheeks as stares followed him across the room, not all of them unfriendly, at least. Charlotte offered a pleasant smile and nod. A pang stung Ash's chest when Callum's soft gaze found him, too. Ash was still angry with Callum for requesting that he be locked away, but even then, the familiar calming energy reached for him, wanting to soothe Ash—to let him know he was safe, even in a room where half its occupants preferred him dead. Ramsay's brows pinched, still unwilling to look Ash's way. The last Ash had seen her, she'd suggested Ash might follow in his father's footsteps. The friction of their argument hung like gauze between them, the words cutting deeper into Ash with every breath.

Ash tried to sit still, stopping his knee from bouncing as a scribe read the minutes of the previous meeting. Edric stared forward at a spot on the wall in front of him, but Ash felt the heated, pointed energy of the man's hatred. Lord Val gave Ash the usual contemptuous stare, eyeing him before looking away with an impatient huff. And could Ash really blame him? He was nineteen years old. He clearly was not the right fit to advise Lord Alexander on the politics of New Anglia. It felt as if Ash had been invited to perform a speech for the entire room, but that he hadn't been given any notice to prepare nor lines to memorize.

There was a general update from each Head on the state of their House: the number of new members, a tally of taxes collected. Ash was surprised when Ramsay sat straight in her seat and announced that twenty-six new members had been accepted into House Thorne. "Most are graduating seniors of Lancaster," she said. "They're all excited to assist in the exploration of potential inventions. Three have already submitted proposals."

"Excellent indeed," Alexander said. "And I assume Lord Val has been a great help."

"Yes. He's been vital in House Thorne's rebuilding."

Lord Val inclined his head in acknowledgment.

"Very good," Alexander said. "The next agenda item?"

"The Alchemist Liberation Party."

Ash's breath shuddered in his throat. He kept his gaze fastened to the back of Lord Alexander's head, feeling the glance Callum sent his way. It was too easy for the other boy to sense Ash's emotions.

"We've learned that the party is behind the attack on the gala of Sir Woods's honoring," Edric said. "The ALP has already attacked a number of House Kendrick stations across the state and are to blame for several killings of redguards as well. The extremist group is increasing in power and its number of members. Their dismantling has become a priority."

Ash managed to keep his breath and expression still. *Dismantling*, for House Kendrick, likely meant the execution of all its members.

"Do we know *why* the alchemists attacked the gala?" Lady Alder asked. She was a prim woman, thin and pale.

"An assassination attempt, apparently," Edric said, "on Lady Thorne's life."

Murmurs followed the news. Ramsay shifted in discomfort, but only for a moment. "Luckily for me, their success rate doesn't seem to be particularly high."

Edric continued. "The group covers their bases well, but they're not completely infallible. I believe House Kendrick will be able to investigate and find at least one chapter of the party within a few months' time."

With Ash's help, this would certainly be possible. Ash only clenched his jaw as the lord nodded. "Very good. Next agenda point?"

※

Ash was glad to escape the conference room once the meeting had ended. He felt lucky that Alexander hadn't turned to him once, asking Ash to offer an opinion or advice on any of the day's topics. The embarrassment and the searing judgment of the House Heads would've jumbled his thoughts and words and made it impossible to speak.

He considered returning to his chambers, but the thought of being trapped inside his room for even another minute prompted Ash to explore the manor instead. It occurred to him, suddenly, that he might be able to succeed in another goal of his as well. Most House manors had personal archived collections. The texts at House Kendrick would likely be on war strategy or accounts of battles from the Great War, and would be much different from the books kept at a place like House Val or Adelaide, for example; but Ash was curious to see what might be kept in the manor of the Head of all the Houses. He needed only to find the archives first.

Ash went down one hall and another, glancing into open doors, but most were closed, and he didn't want to risk opening a door to see a guest of Alexander changing into their dinner clothes.

Ash was just thinking he might need to give up on this particular venture when he came to the third floor and remembered Callum had mentioned the lord's primary office was in this corridor.

The office was easy to recognize. The grand gilt-lined double doors were closed and locked when Ash fiddled with the knob. He took a breath, wrapped a hand around it, and imagined a push of energy clicking it open.

The office was dark. A desk stood in the center of the room, and an empty fireplace was built into the far wall. The room itself was the size of a suite, and, yes—there was an archway into another adjoining room, through which Ash could see shelves of texts. Ash was certain he'd need permission to freely enter, but then, he also didn't much care. The lord could consider it compensation for having Ash locked up in the manor in the first place.

The archive was smaller than Ash expected, maybe only about the same size as Ramsay's library in the Downs. It was two floors, at least, with roses carved into the wooden shelves. A tight knot inside Ash unwound. Even with all Ash had experienced lately— being trapped within a manor, forced into working as a spy and haunted by nightmares—it seemed that the energy of books still offered Ash peace. He let a finger drift across the leather-bound covers, eyes skimming the golden-embossed titles. Based on the titles alone, there were quite a few texts on the history of New Anglia and the families that had warred for control over the state. There were few texts on alchemy, but still, it couldn't hurt Ash to search for the one he needed most.

It appeared the texts were alphabetical. He climbed the stairs to the top floor and stood on his toes before kneeling to the bottom shelf. There was no sign of *Communicating with Plasma Particles*. He bit back his disappointment.

"Having trouble finding what you're looking for?"

Ash jumped to his feet and spun around. Lord Alexander leaned against the staircase's banister behind Ash, arms crossed, with the barest of smiles. Shit.

"It shouldn't surprise me, I suppose, that you've managed to find a way into my archives. I was warned you have a tendency for stealing books."

Perhaps Ash's first words should have been an apology for breaking into Alexander's office. But, well, he hadn't quite forgiven the man who had imprisoned him in the first place. "Don't you have something more important to do?" Ash decided on instead. "Running New Anglia, for example."

Lord Alexander's smile twitched. "It continues to strike me how fearless you are, Sir Woods," he said. "I can't remember the last time someone attempted to give me a direct order."

"Glad I can keep you on your toes."

"But, yes," Alexander added. "You're right. *Running New Anglia* is precisely why I was looking for you."

Business, then, and not just a chance for the lord to display his power over Ash. He turned back to the shelves. "I'm surprised you didn't ask for a report sooner."

"There's quite a lot to juggle as Head of the state, as I'm sure you can imagine. You don't feel neglected, do you?"

Ash decided it was best to ignore that question. "There isn't much to say," he told the lord, opening a text and pretending to skim, though the words blurred on the page. "I met with the group, as you asked."

"Go on."

Ash snapped the book shut again. He'd already decided not to tell Alexander about the plan to attack McKinley, but now he questioned his own judgment.

"Well? Surely you have something useful to share."

Ash swallowed and slipped the title back onto the shelf. "No. They don't trust me yet."

Alexander hummed, eyes narrowed. "Disappointing."

Ash forced himself to meet the man's eye, glad that Alexander had no talent for alchemy nor reading minds. "But I'm working to earn their trust now. I haven't been given the test you'd mentioned—"

"I find it a little suspect, I must admit, that you haven't learned anything at all. Not even the location of a base?"

Ash swallowed. He had to give the lord something. "I heard names."

"Do tell."

Ash couldn't hesitate, no matter how much the pressure in his chest swelled. "Elena. Riles." The lord's eyes narrowed. "Hendrix." Ash blinked. "Marlowe."

"No surnames? Only given?"

He nodded.

The lord silently watched Ash for one long moment. "Marlowe. That isn't a particularly common name, is it?"

Ash shrugged tense shoulders. His neck muscles ached.

"That was the name of Gresham Hain's assistant. She followed your father everywhere he went." Lord Alexander eyed Ash with a smile. Ash blinked one, two, three too many times. "It wouldn't hurt, to release a copy of her image," the lord said. "Have red-guard patrols keep an eye out for her."

Ash forced a nod of agreement.

"And you didn't hear any discussions? Plans?"

Ash sucked in a breath. "I overheard the leader speaking about weapons," he said, glad when the lie fell from his mouth without pause. "She sounded worried."

"Only weapons? Nothing else?"

Ash met the lord's eye and shook his head. Alexander pushed from the railing, preparing to leave. "Well, that's somewhat help-ful, at least," he said.

Alexander turned on his heel to leave, then paused by the door. "What book were you looking for?" he asked.

"I didn't say I was looking for a specific book, did I?"

"You don't strike me as the *break into my personal archives to idly browse* type."

Ash chewed on his lip. Maybe Lord Alexander would help to point him in the right direction. When he said the name of the title, Alexander's brows tugged, though his face was otherwise unreadable.

"Have you heard of it?" Ash asked, swallowing the desperation in his tone.

The lord was quiet, face still, as though calculating a response. Source, it felt like every movement and conversation was a game with him. "I haven't," Alexander eventually said, "but I'm certain a keeper of knowledge would have a text. The archives at Lady Alder's estate are especially extensive. Perhaps you'd find a copy there."

Ash swallowed. Mr. Brown had said the same. "Are the Alder archives open to the public?"

"Only members of her House are allowed an invite, I'm afraid." Lord Alexander smiled. "But I could always ask that she allow you entry."

Ash's fist twitched. "What do you want in return?"

The man didn't bother to seem embarrassed about the exchange. "Another piece of helpful information about the group," Alexander said. "The invitation can act as motivation. That seems a fair enough trade, does it not?"

Ash nodded his agreement. What other choice did he have, really? But as Ash left Lord Alexander's archives and padded down the hall to his chambers, he could still feel his mother's fingertips brush his cheek. He couldn't wait, not anymore; and he was already well acquainted with what it might take to sneak out of a manor and steal a book.

10

Ash waited until it was late enough that he was sure he wouldn't run into anyone as he escaped. He climbed from his balcony, a rope created by alchemy assisting him down to the cobblestone and again over the courtyard's walls, out of the sight of the posted redguards. He slipped away into the bitter night, cloak's hood up. Maybe it had been impulsive of him, to leave the manor in search of a book. As much as he hated his house arrest, Callum might've had a point about safety. What if someone recognized Ash and attacked him? Ash would defend himself with alchemy, and someone could get hurt or even killed—

Kensington Station was among the first public sites to be rebuilt. The floors and pillars were a marble that shined white, but the building's cerulean ceiling hadn't been restored. The station itself was nearly abandoned, only a few passengers waiting on benches and giving one another a wide berth. Ash went to a teller, head low and eyes averted. He held up a pouch of coin Callum had given him weeks before. "One ticket to Prudence, please."

It'd be a short trip in comparison to the journeys Ash had gone on across the state. He took a public seat rather than a private room—it'd been all he could afford, and besides, there wasn't anyone around to see him anyway. He stared out the window at the darkening sky and the gray ocean in the distance, the faint twinkling lights of towns and villages. Farther west, he was likely passing the Claremont manor at that very moment.

The train rushed through a town. Ash flinched. The windows of each house were blackened with smoke. Tree branches dangled the bodies of fly-covered corpses. Painted across a wall read JUDG-MENT OF THE CREATOR. The town ended, and there were only fields and coastline again.

✳

House Alder was surrounded by the small town of Prudence. The station was nothing more than a platform, Ash the only person stepping onto the creaking wood as the train whistled and rumbled away. The cobblestone road sank into ditches of mud. The houses that dotted the land had peeling paint and dead gardens. An unseen dog barked. No one was outside at this late hour, the sky a deep color, signaling that the sun would rise in another hour or so. The last time Ash had traveled at all like this, he'd had a protective Callum and a reasonable Ramsay at his side. He realized how dependent he'd been on them both. But he was determined to depend on himself now. He took a steely breath and approached the manor that stood in the center of the town.

It was a relic, a small stone house that looked at least a century old, with wings and a courtyard hidden behind a closed iron gate. The walls were at least ten feet high. Source, Ash wished he'd learned demolition alchemy. That'd certainly be one easy way inside.

Luckily, there were no guards waiting. There was little reason for anyone to attack House Alder. Ash walked along the perimeter, searching for a way in—and there, just on the back end of the manor, was a dead tree. It was a good ten feet away from a wall, and the nearest window on the third floor was several feet away from even that, but it was the only option Ash could see. And, luckily for him, the window was open.

Ash gritted his teeth as he climbed, wishing he'd taken Callum's offer for more physical training. He panted as he reached a top branch. It wavered and shuddered beneath his feet. He waited for his heart to stop beating quite so hard, for air to fill his lungs. He closed his eyes, and he imagined a plank of light made of particles, pulled from the air itself, energy dancing along his skin. He opened his eyes, and the plank waited at his feet.

He couldn't hesitate. The plank would vanish altogether. He jumped onto it and ran, the surface disappearing into bursts of light with every step, stumbling as his concentration lost hold and the plank faded—he leaped into the air, hands grazing the wall, cuts scratching into his fingers and palms—

He grabbed hold of a stone that jutted out. He let out a shout as he managed to pull himself up, grasped the edge of the window-pane, and yanked himself inside, tumbling to the ground.

Ash lay on his back for several minutes, waiting for his heartbeat and breath to slow, before he sat up. He knew enough about Source and the workings of the universe to be unsurprised that he was in exactly the room he'd wanted to find. The library's archives were draped in blue shadow. The wooden alder shelves must've been generations old, with carvings of clusters of flowers as if growing from trees, rows of books creating a cramped maze in an otherwise unoccupied room. He lit the tip of his index finger so that it glowed as dimly as a firefly while he walked down the aisle, the velvetlike carpet muffling his footsteps, lighting the spines of the thick textured books that lined the wooden shelves.

There was a thud. Ash spun around, breath caught in his throat. A text had fallen from a shelf. His eyes darted back and forth, but no one else was there. His gaze landed on the book. He felt like its pages were calling to him—pulling him closer with a magnetic energy. The gold-embossed title glinted in the light.

It was the one he'd come for. Ash squinted with suspicion. Yes, Source did always deliver what was wanted and desired, but surely *this* was too good to be true, too much of a coincidence— and why would the book suddenly reveal itself? Maybe there was an unseen energy in the aisle, tossing the book to the ground for him, knowing it was the text he'd come to find. Maybe it was a silly, childish hope, to wonder if his mother's energy was there with him at that very moment.

Ash inched closer, bending to pick it up—but the second his fingers grazed the leather, the title disappeared. The cover went blank. A high-pitched scream blasted, piercing through the quiet. Ash yelled with a grimace, clapping his hands over his ears. It felt like the siren would split his head open.

He turned away from the book, ready to run—but he stopped. Ash *needed* the text. He might not ever have a chance to return to this library again.

Fuck it. There was no point in sneaking around anymore. Ash focused energy to his hands. They both began to glow so brightly, he might as well have been holding two miniature suns. The library's aisles lit up. Ash closed his eyes, imagining what it would feel like to finally have the text he needed, the rough texture of the leather-bound cover, its pages yellowed with age—

"Bring me what I'm looking for," he commanded.

The text—the *real* text—flew off the top shelf about ten feet above him and zipped into his outstretched palm. The book looked forgotten, cover worn and scuffed, pages yellowed, just as Ash had imagined. He stuffed the book into his satchel and clenched his hands into fists. The lights went out, and the library became even darker than it had been before. The bridge hadn't lasted Ash jumping to the window, and he wouldn't be able to create another one to the tree itself. He'd have to take a chance to run out the front door, then. The book on the floor still screamed its high-pitched warning. Ash gave it a good kick as he ran for the door, sending it skidding across the carpet. Sensing the invisible energetic barrier that went up, ready to catch him like a spider's web, he threw out a hand and concentrated all his energy on his fingers. The barrier snapped like a rubber band, and Ash burst through.

The hall was stuffy: green wallpaper and golden-framed portraits of dead pale-skinned scholars on display. There were shouts and footsteps, but Ash didn't know which direction they came from. He ran to a window and tried to pull it up, but it was jammed shut. Someone turned the corner.

The guard of House Alder was a lot younger than Ash was expecting, wearing his faded green scholar robes. The boy, only a few years older than Ash, might've been an apprentice or a scribe, working extra night shifts as a watchdog over the archives of texts. He was also, apparently, a licensed alchemist. He held up a palm, glowing yellow light that made Ash wince from its brightness.

"Who the hell are you?" the boy demanded, voice tight with fear. "What're you doing here? You can't—wait, are those books? Are you stealing books from the archives? The *private, restricted* library of Lady Alder's collection, no less—"

Ash rolled his eyes and let a bolt of energy charge through his arm as he brought his elbow back, paused, and smashed it through the glass window. Splinters shattered. Ash leaped up onto the windowsill before the guard could take another step. A stone courtyard waited three stories below.

"Hold on!" the boy shouted. "You're too high—a fall like that—"

Ash jumped. For a second, he felt like he was floating. He'd never jumped from anything so high before. Exhilaration blasted through him. But then he began to drop. Perhaps Ash hadn't thought this through enough.

Chilled air rushed around him. The three stories were going by a lot faster than he expected, and suddenly, he couldn't think of the right words to break his landing, the right image to create that would save his life. Panic spread.

This is how I die—shit, this is how I die—

It would certainly be a pathetic end, Ash realized—surviving his father and the attack on Kensington, just to die falling from a window. Ramsay would be livid.

He squeezed his eyes shut—the ground was inches from him—but the crunching thud of his body never came. Warm energy cascaded around Ash, and the stones felt as soft as grass when he hit them. He rolled, wishing he were more elegant as he ended up sprawled on his back with a groan. His satchel slipped from his shoulder and slid across the stones. He looked up, and a woman stood across the courtyard.

Ash sighed and slumped back as he listened to the footfalls, eyes closed. He felt when the figure stood over him.

"Sir Ashen Woods," the woman said. "I wish I could say this was a pleasant surprise."

"It's Ash," he muttered. There wasn't much point in attempting to escape now. He couldn't very well *attack* Lady Alder, not if he hoped to keep his life and his freedom—and besides that, he didn't particularly want to fight her, anyway. She was an aging woman, well into her seventies. The idea of attempting to strike her didn't sit well.

Lady Alder sighed as she stood over him. "I'm assuming that's a book from my archives?"

Ash didn't reply as he stared blankly at the night sky. She'd assumed right.

"Haven't you had your fill of stealing books yet?" she asked, squinting down at him.

He again did not reply as he wondered just how furious Callum would be with him. A stern hours-long lecture, perhaps, while Ash struggled to nod as if he were listening.

Lady Alder seemed to take a long moment to decide what Ash's fate would be, before she took a few steps away, across the courtyard, and picked up the satchel.

"Would you like some tea, Sir Woods?" she asked.

It was clear Ash didn't have much of a choice. "Sure."

※

The estate itself was nothing more than one large library, from what Ash could see. Small doorless archways lined the halls, showing where scholars remained even then despite the hour, bent over wooden tables and studying texts by candlelight. From what Ash knew of the House, once pledged, an apprentice would choose a topic to spend the rest of their life studying and researching, perhaps hoping to become a professor of that field, or a researcher, or maybe a knowledge keeper like a librarian or bookseller. To have moved into the main manor of House Alder would suggest these were very dedicated students indeed.

Lady Alder called on an attendant who stood in the hall, asking that tea be brought to her private parlor. The attendant didn't seem surprised by the late visitor. Maybe Lady Alder often entertained guests long after midnight. The room itself was also surprisingly small and lacked decoration. There were only two threadbare beige cabriole sofas that might have been prized possessions of the House generations before, when it'd still held wealth. But even Ash, who tried to stay away from House politics, knew that House Alder had become unstable in recent years, without as many pledges to the pursuit of knowledge.

"Sir Woods," she began. "The *Hero of Kensington*." Source, Ash hated that title. "It doesn't seem to me that you're very heroic at all, if you're acting like this."

"Acting like what, exactly?" Ash said.

She smiled. "Not only stealing from me, but breaking the order that you remain within the walls of House Alexander. It's almost as if you're purposefully rebelling against our fine society, pushing the grace you've already been shown to its limits."

Ash wasn't in the mood for Lady Alder's reprimanding speech. He would've preferred that she simply had Ash tied up and called on the reds. "This *fine society* was never meant for someone like me anyway," Ash told her.

"No, maybe not," she said, eyeing him. "But I have a feeling that you're not the type to find much of any happiness, no matter what sort of society you're in or where you find yourself. You might just discover that the problem leads with *you*, then," Lady Alder continued, "and not where you are or the people you're surrounded by."

There was a flicker in his chest at her words, a flicker that he decidedly stomped back down into its shadows. "Bullshit," Ash said, and was impressed that the severe Lady Alder didn't flinch at his language. "It's easier to find peace in a place where people aren't actively hating me, attacking me, trying to kill me."

"Perhaps that's true," Lady Alder said. "But isn't it an even greater victory, then? To find true peace, despite the odds, and not because of them."

Ash wasn't sure that he liked the challenge in Lady Alder's voice. He wanted to argue with her—easy for her to say, she was *from* the very society that gave her peace and gave him hell in turn—but he forced himself to pause. The lines around her eyes and mouth were deeply engraved. She looked like she'd aged dozens of years in just the past few months alone since Ash last saw her in the tribunal in Riverside. Grief could do that to a person, Ash knew. He understood what it was like to lose a mother, but he couldn't fathom what it must be like for Lady Alder to have lost her son. Most of the citizens of New Anglia had lost someone they loved—entire lines had been wiped out, friends and family killed in the attacks by Ash's father. Ash blinked, gaze dropping, as he tried and failed to smother the shame that smoldered inside him.

The attendant arrived with tea. Cups were placed gently on the table between Lady Alder and Ash, before the attendant left once again.

The elder woman didn't pick up her teacup, but instead reached for the satchel that waited on the seat beside her. She picked up the book Ash had stolen, eyeing the title with little apparent interest.

"I understand the desire," Lady Alder said, "to find a way to commune with the dead. But our collections of history and text have long shown that once the energy leaves the body after physical death, it cannot return to our realm—not in the way that we are so used to, anyway. The dead are only bursts of energy without a shell. To capture that energy—to make it stay here, for our own desires, whatever they may be . . . This text will only confirm what's already known: You will destroy yourself, attempting to force your loved one back into this physical world. You will fail."

Ash disagreed. "Just because it hasn't been done successfully before doesn't mean it can't be done at all."

Lady Alder seemed tired, suddenly, too tired to entertain a little thief. "Your delusions are fueled by grief," she said. "But if it grants you peace, then here." She handed the book to Ash. "Take it."

She stood, a small gesture dismissing him. Ash had a number of enemies in this state, people who didn't believe he should've been allowed to live. Lady Alder could've easily taken this moment to use him as a political chip in the games of Kensington. He was lucky that she didn't seem to hold enough ambition to care. Maybe surviving the attacks, and the death of her son, was enough.

"I don't suppose you could keep this between us?" Ash asked, attempting a charming grin that didn't falter, even under Lady Alder's expressionless stare.

"Good night, Sir Woods," she said. "I'll allow you to use my portal door back to Kensington."

11

What were you *thinking?*"

Callum stood by the fireplace in Ash's chambers, orange light flickering against his brown skin. Callum seemed taller to Ash then, somehow—and certainly bigger, with the amount of physical work and training he'd been doing as a commander of the reds.

It'd only taken a few hours before word spread of Ash's little nighttime getaway. The last time Ash had been yelled at by Callum like this, he'd visited the older boy in Kensington and had gotten into an argument with Edric over the freedom of alchemists. Ash had flicked an ember of energy at him—it'd been small, miniscule, barely a particle, and certainly *nothing* that deserved the backlash of shouts and promises of execution and Callum's never-ending lecture on not attacking the Head of a House.

Ash had pretended to at least seem sorry then, but now he could tell there was no use—Callum wouldn't be so easily swayed by Ash's big-eyed apologies. And besides that, Ash couldn't ignore his annoyance with Callum, too.

"It's as if you're purposefully testing the patience of the Houses," Callum said, "and Lord Alexander as well. How many pardons do you think you'll get?"

Ash shrugged. "I don't know. Let's find out, shall we?"

Callum shook his head. "You don't have to prove how difficult you are, you know," he said. "Everyone's well aware of your dislike for House Kendrick and the redguards. These little rebellions don't need to be added onto it all."

What annoyed Ash more than anything else was that Callum

hadn't even bothered to *ask* him why he'd stolen from Lady Alder's private collection or even to consider that maybe Ash was the one who needed help.

"And just one week after your honoring, too," Callum said. "Couldn't you have at least waited a month after Lord Alexander publicly thanked you?"

"You were more than willing to disobey your own family's laws, once."

"That was different, you know that it was," Callum said.

"Was it?" Ash asked, sarcasm dripping. "Breaking out a prisoner, aiding a fugitive—"

"I was *helping* you," Callum said. "Same as I'm trying to do now."

"Right, yes, by keeping me locked away like your father did. Very helpful, thank you."

Callum's fists were shaking. "The in-shelter order is for your own safety."

"You're sounding a little defensive, Kendrick."

Usually, Callum would handle such arguments with a gentle breath and a suggestion that they continue the conversation at another time when both were calm. This, apparently, was not one of those moments. "Don't do that, Ash," Callum said. "Don't push me."

Ash stared at the crackling fire.

"Relations between the Houses are strained enough as it is," Callum said. "Stealing from Lady Alder's records? You're lucky she's in a forgiving mood. She could've used this as a chance to gain more favor with Alexander."

"I don't care about House politics," Ash said. Maybe he was purposefully testing Callum's patience, too.

A vein throbbed in Callum's neck. "You might not care about House politics, but I hope that you care enough about *me* to stop making my work more difficult."

"You're in charge of managing House relationships now?" Ash asked, blinking innocently.

Callum stared at Ash, and in the silence—oh, yes, there it was: the painful splinter that they had done their best to ignore. "It doesn't look particularly good for me, to be a commander of the redguards and be unable to control my own boyfriend."

This didn't surprise Ash to hear so much—more that Callum had actually said it out loud. "Oh, so I'm to be *controlled* now?"

The other boy took a tight breath and released it. "That was the wrong choice of words. No, of course not *controlled*, but—"

"But it's true, isn't it?" Ash asked, fire biting through him now as he glared up at Callum. "You just want me to be controlled and kept out of sight."

"That isn't true at all."

"No?"

"Tensions are too high to risk sparking a riot," Callum told him. "If you were recognized in Kensington, the people could begin to distrust Alexander and the Houses for giving you sanctuary."

Ash swallowed, arms crossed. Callum never quite said it, same as anyone else in House Alexander's manor, but Ash sensed that the state of New Anglia was closer to war than anyone wanted to admit.

"People are desperate, Ash—so many have lost their families, their homes. They wouldn't have anything to lose. The people could demand your execution. We'd be forced to make a difficult decision."

"Is it really just a choice between me and peace?" Ash said. "Maybe there's another option you're not thinking of—one where you don't choose the redguards over me."

Callum sighed, running a hand over his short curls. Both were quiet as they listened to the logs splitting in the fire. Ash wasn't sure, exactly, when things had gotten so tense between them. It'd been a slow building over the months, and it didn't help that Callum and Ramsay were rarely home. There hadn't been an opportunity to sit down and speak, to reconnect. Ash's anxious thoughts caught up with him. What if he and Callum had never really loved each other? They'd only been brought together because of Ramsay, after all. If she weren't a part of their relationship, would Ash and Callum even be together?

"I need to get back to the town house," Callum murmured.

"This was just a quick pop over to yell at me, then?" Ash muttered.

Callum at least looked sorry at this. "I wish I could stay longer. My brother—"

Ash didn't want to hear about Edric and the forsaken Kendrick redguards. "I'll see you later, then."

Callum rubbed the back of his neck. "The state needs me to play my role as a Kendrick," he said, voice soft. "You understand that, don't you?"

Ash didn't want to admit it, but a part of him did understand. He understood that New Anglia would fall apart without the foundation it had been built on. Callum, returning to his family's roots, was a part of that foundation. Ash was worried, just a little, when he wondered if maybe that's what New Anglia needed: to fall apart, and begin again.

"Yes," he finally relented. "I understand."

"I love you, Ash," Callum said.

Ash wasn't sure if it was only his imagination, that it sounded like the other boy was trying to remind himself of this fact as well. "I love you, too."

※

Maybe it was only luck that Ash's room hadn't been searched, the gift from Lady Alder taken away as punishment. The moment Callum left, door closed behind him, Ash scrambled for the book he'd hidden under his mattress, flipped it open, and began to read.

There are many plausible techniques to bring back the dead, the text stated. *I, dear reader, only say "plausible" in the sense that these techniques are only theorized, and should not in any way be attempted.*

Ash's heart slowed as he skimmed. He sat on the edge of his bed, his finger tracing the lines.

To force an energy from another dimension into this physical realm is a great violation of that energy's autonomy.

But Ash's mother had come to him willingly, again and again, in his dreams. She had a message for him, Ash was certain of that. Wasn't it his responsibility, then, to do what he could to find her, to speak to her?

In addition, the techniques listed in this script are only theorized, with no factual evidence that they will at all be successful. Attempting to "bring back the dead," as some say colloquially, may have disastrous consequences.

Ash nearly closed the book. Frustration itched at his insides, fingers gripping the pages so tightly, he thought they might tear.

If you, dear reader, are understanding of this author's warning, then please: read on.

※

Ash was used to reading all night; he'd studied stolen alchemist texts until dawn many times, when he'd thought there was a chance he could attend Lancaster College, once. This wasn't so different. Still, the text was dense in its language, with complex instructions that Ash had to read and reread several times before he fully understood.

He sat up in his bed, legs crossed beneath him. The first chapter suggested it would be possible to reanimate a physical body in order to bring his mother back. If the person was recently dead, and the body had not started to decompose, the energy could be tied back to that body forcibly; but that was really only if the victim had died minutes ago. Ash's mother had been dead for years now.

Another possibility is the use of alteration alchemy: Using earth, for that is essentially the makeup of the human body's physical design, one can envision the structure of the departed. Ash leaned forward, breath held. He was most proficient at creation alchemy, one step above alteration; any technique using alteration would be within his grasp.

However, one must have a clear and concise understanding of each molecular pattern and formation. To forget, say, a strand of the deoxyribonucleic acid molecule could easily translate into the departed missing an eyeball, a tongue, or the ability to breathe.

Ash groaned as he fell back onto the mattress, nearly slapping the cover of the book shut. He didn't know his mother's physical makeup. Even if he'd wanted to uncover her body from the cemetery in Hedge, which he certainly did not want to do, Ash wasn't sure he'd have the tools or the wits to unravel her entire sequence.

Source, it made sense now why Ramsay had decided to focus on traveling to the higher realms to meet his parents; even if he had managed to find a copy of *Communicating with Plasma Particles*, its methods seemed impossible.

The sun had started to rise, pink lighting the sky. Ash was relieved at the thought that he wouldn't have to go to sleep and deal with the nightmares that threatened to strangle him. He closed the book and slipped it beneath his mattress. He'd keep reading the next night, and the next, until he found the right method. There was a way, Ash was certain of it, to speak with his mother again, and hear the message she had for him.

12

Ash's neck ached as he tried his best to sit still for the Head of House meeting. Eyes wouldn't leave him; whispers had followed him all morning in the halls, too. "The boy is a hoodlum!" Ash had overheard one of the lords whispering. "I don't understand why Lord Alexander trusts him so."

Ash tried to escape the meeting the moment the doors opened, but he didn't make it too far before his name was called. He turned, Callum following closely behind. Callum raised his fingers to touch Ash's elbow, but he hesitated, glancing about at the others who streamed from the meeting room. "Can I have a moment?"

Ash wanted to say no. Source, he wanted to say yes. He took a sharp breath and nodded, unsurprised when Callum met Ramsay's eye and motioned with his head for her to join them. Ash bit back his curiosity as the three walked down one hall and another, until Callum found an empty parlor. The walls shined like velvet, and there was a window that looked out onto the courtyard below.

Ramsay plopped into one of the couches that faced each other, legs and arms crossed. "Well, let's get this over with."

"Get what over with?" Ash asked, heart pounding now as he sat against the sofa's arm.

"Isn't it obvious?" Ramsay asked, a dismissive hand waving about.

Callum leaned against a desk in the corner of the room. "This isn't a joke, Ramsay."

"Did I ever suggest it was?"

"You've both meant so much to me."

Ash worried his heart might stop. He'd feared the three would break apart, but for it to happen because of one argument? "I don't understand . . ."

Callum pushed away from the desk and stood tall, hands on hips. "We should go on a date."

Ash blinked. "What?"

"The three of us, together. We should go out."

"Again: What?"

Callum nodded, entirely serious. "We're pulling apart more now with every passing day—the stress of our jobs, and with your new position as advisor, Ash . . ."

Ash, brows raised, turned to Ramsay, who snorted at Ash's expression.

Callum didn't seem to notice nor care. "I thought about what you said, Ash. 'Just a pop over to yell at me.' You were right. We've all been busy, and it's only going to get worse from here. I want to put more energy into reconnecting with you both."

As the surprise faded, Ash's heart lightened with relief. Yes, Callum could be unbearably sweet at times, but at least he wasn't breaking up with Ash and Ramsay.

Callum hesitated, scuffing a boot on the carpet. "I'll be the first to admit I've been more distant than I should."

Ramsay sighed, head falling back as she stared at the ceiling. "It's understandable, isn't it? You, a commander now. Me, Head of House Thorne. Ash, advisor to Lord Alexander himself."

Ash bit his lip, taking a breath. Callum glanced at him as Ash thrust forward a spike of energy to hide the thought that nearly slipped through his mind: *Not only am I an advisor, but I'm the lord's spy.*

Ramsay didn't seem to notice. "We're bound to drift," she said. "As long as we manage to find our ways to one another again, right?"

"And how is that going to happen if we don't leave breadcrumbs along the way?"

"You're so poetic, Kendrick," Ramsay muttered.

"I do try."

This was only another cruel irony of Source, as far as Ash was concerned. He'd wanted both Callum's and Ramsay's presence only weeks before—would've been overjoyed at Callum's suggestion, then. But now? Ash would have to focus on holding a wall against Callum, nervous that he and Ramsay would realize Ash was hiding something from them.

Ash nodded. "Ramsay's right. This is just a busy time in our lives. Relationships are like Source geometry, aren't they?" His voice quieted when he looked up. Both Ramsay and Callum stared at Ash, Ramsay with a raised brow. Ash's face heated. "Ebbing and flowing, I mean . . ."

Ramsay outright laughed. "What's with you two today?" She sat straight up, ankle crossed over a knee. "Listen, Callum. I appreciate the gesture—truly, I do—but we can't be under one another's feet all day, every day."

"I'm not asking for every minute of your life," Callum said. "Just an evening would do. We could spend time together now."

"Now?" Ash echoed.

Callum nodded. "We'll only have more work piled on us, more excuses to find. We might as well, right?"

Ramsay hesitated. "I have papers to grade, reports to sign, research to complete—"

"And two boyfriends who love you," Callum said. Ramsay released a sigh as she rolled her eyes, but he continued. "Don't you think I'm busy, too? I'm assisting my brother with the investigation of the alchemist extremists—"

Ash forced himself to breathe.

"—and I have a squadron to lead. We need to prioritize one another, or what did we even fight for? What was the point of it all—of me losing my family—if we drift from one another now?"

His words silenced any vibrations of humor in the room.

Ramsay looked to the ceiling, unblinking. Ash swallowed. His father had done that to Callum, after all.

Callum's voice was quiet. "I won't try to force either of you, of course. But you're the two most important people in my life. The work I do now—it's all for you," he said.

Ash tucked his lips into his mouth, quiet. He couldn't help but think this was only a lie Callum told himself, but weren't there lies Ash had told himself, too?

"It wouldn't make much sense," Callum said, "to lose the two of you now, after everything that's happened."

Silence followed, but only for a moment. "Source, do you have to be so romantic?" Ramsay sighed. "Fine. I'll come."

Callum looked at Ash with raised brows, hope gleaming in his eyes. The mission to attack McKinley was at the end of the week. Ash would need to do his best to think of any and all else. He couldn't risk Callum finding out now.

Ash nodded, forcing a grin, glad when it didn't tremble. "Sure. Me, too."

Callum smiled, standing taller as if a weight had been pulled. "I know just the place."

✳

The fact that Callum knew where Ash would want to go more than any other place in New Anglia reminded him just why he loved Callum Kendrick so much. Callum had explained that he'd requested special permission for Ash's leave from Lord Alexander before the day's House meeting had even begun. "He said as long as I stayed by your side, it would be fine."

The three stepped through the portal door and into the cramped cottage. Source, it'd only been a few days since Ash had been home, but dust had still managed to gather, floating through the air.

"Did you want to come here only because it's safer?" Ash asked as Ramsay stretched and plopped onto the sofa, where she'd always loved to spread out most.

"Guilty," Callum said with a shrug. "But it's also where we're happy. This is the home we've made for ourselves."

The older boy's thoughtfulness still managed to surprise Ash, somehow. The depth of his empathy had always seemed at odds with his family name.

"So?" Ramsay said, absent-mindedly performing a touch of alchemy as she twirled a finger so that light swirled in the air around it. "Will we spend the evening pretending to be happily married, playing wife and husband and husband, and ignoring the fact that alchemist extremists are attacking redguards while Lune followers are killing anyone even suspected of alchemy?"

"You can be so cynical sometimes," Callum said beneath his breath.

"If that's another way of saying *realistic*, then yes, I agree."

"I'd thought maybe we could eat dinner here," Callum said, already opening cabinets and cupboards and pulling out bowls and whisks, "before taking a walk along the river, then going to the bookstore." Another pair of Ash's favorite activities.

Ramsay's curiosity was piqued, at least. "What's for dinner?" she asked.

"Eggy bread," Callum told her, smiling to himself as Ramsay sat up. They were all well aware of Ramsay's addiction to sugar. "With berries and cream or syrup. I haven't decided on which yet."

"Why not both?" Ramsay suggested hopefully.

"Isn't there anything you'd like to do?" Ash asked Callum.

"Having the chance to make both of you happy is enough."

Ash wanted to argue. Callum was too used to sacrificing himself to show his love, without giving Ash the chance to show his love in return. There'd been a time when he and Callum had agreed to see how their feelings for each other would develop. Ash wasn't sure, exactly, when those feelings had developed into *more*; when it'd become a simple, unspoken fact that their love for each other had grown.

Ash offered to whisk the eggs and flour while Ramsay helped by picking out the best of the strawberries, eating those that were less than perfect. It wasn't long before the scent of cinnamon filled the air and the three had a casual conversation that, for once, had absolutely nothing to do with Lune followers or redguards or alchemists.

"I think you would've liked her a lot, at Pembroke," Callum said as the table was set. He didn't bother to scold Ramsay and Ash as they both took bites of the eggy bread before they even put the plates down.

"Are you sure about that?" Ash said. "Really, positively sure?"

If Ramsay had been anything like how she'd acted at Lancaster the first time Ash had met her, he was quite positive he wouldn't have been able to stand her. The pair wouldn't have gotten along at all, if Ash had been another student at the school.

"I was—let's say an *acquired* taste," Ramsay said.

"That isn't true," Callum said.

"I went out of my way to treat you like slime floating on the top of a lake, Callum."

"That was only because of our family names," Callum said, stretching his arms over his head. "I wasn't exactly kind to you, either."

"But you were practically the prince of Pembroke," Ramsay argued. "No one liked me."

"That's not true, either. You and I had the same friends," Callum said, "before . . ."

No need to go into the *before*. Ramsay shrugged. "That's only because I was a House heir and because you and I eventually became best friends. If I hadn't, I would've been ignored by all of you."

Callum leaned back in his chair as he chewed on both this and his food. "Ah, well," he finally relented. "I suppose I was a bit of a prick, too."

Ash nodded emphatically and laughed as he dodged a blueberry Callum tossed at his head. "When you think about it, I'm the only one who wasn't a complete asshole to either of you when we first met."

Ramsay and Callum looked at him, then at each other, and then laughed.

Ash sat straighter in his seat, heated now but still grinning. "What? Why is that funny?"

"You broke into my office and illegally performed alchemy the first day I met you," Ramsay said.

"Yes, and you ended up using that as a reason to blackmail me into working with you, so I think we're pretty even, don't you?"

"You refused to do anything I told you," Callum said, "even though you were my scribe."

"You can't blame me for that, can you?" Ash said. "I wasn't happy being your prisoner."

Their laughter died down. They ate slowly for a moment, forks and knives clanking against plates. The three had done well, avoiding the topics that would turn the day sour, but now they were on the edge of the question that had been on Ash's mind for some time. He told himself to push it aside—there would be another chance, a time when they weren't all enjoying one another so much. But then, Ash also couldn't help but wonder when he might be able to have a conversation with Callum like this again.

"Why did you return to the redguards?" Ash asked.

Callum looked up, surprised, as Ramsay's fork paused midway in the air. "What do you mean?" he asked.

"You wanted to escape the redguards—your family. You planned to leave Kensington with Ramsay altogether, to escape New Anglia."

"Yes," Callum agreed. "That was before my father was killed."

Ash thought for a moment that maybe he should drop the conversation and change the topic, and Ramsay's widened eyes seemed to agree, but he still pushed on. "You wanted to be a healer."

"There're many things I wanted," Callum said, exasperated,

putting his utensils down. "The circumstances have changed. House Kendrick needs me. My brother—I know you aren't a fan of him, Ash, and neither are you, Ramsay, but he is still my brother," he added when Ash scoffed and Ramsay rolled her eyes. "I can't just abandon them on a whim."

"Your life, and what you want for it, isn't a whim," Ash argued, and continued on when Callum stood from the table to clear his plate. "You constantly sacrifice yourself—your own needs and desires—for the happiness of someone else," Ash said. "What about you? Don't you deserve to be happy, too?"

"I am happy," Callum said, back to Ash. He said it with such stillness and softness that Ash had no reason to think he spoke anything but the truth. "When I've managed to change House Kendrick from the inside, then I can retire. I can explore what else I'd like to do."

He turned to face Ash once more. "Until then, I have everything I need. You, Ramsay, the chance to make the change I want to see in New Anglia: This is enough."

Maybe that was a fundamental difference between Ash and Callum, after all. While Callum could be sated, Ash always felt hungry for more.

Ramsay abruptly stood, too, picking up her empty plate and taking it to the sink. "You mentioned a walk and a trip to the bookstore?" she said.

13

The three walked through the forest that the cottage stood on the edge of, where lichen and moss grew across the bark of trees and a golden haze shimmered through swaying leaves. Callum lumbered ahead, as if this were a scouting mission rather than a leisurely stroll. Ramsay shook her head. "It's always amazed me how fast Callum can be."

Ash *breathed*. "Doesn't the air smell fresher out here?"

Ramsay groaned as she stepped in a wet patch of dirt. "I honestly don't understand the fun of being in nature willingly."

"Really? But we spent so much time traveling through the Derry Hills, the Westfields . . ."

"Yes," Ramsay said. "That's why I said '*willingly*.' Nature is beautiful and nice to look at and all," she added, waving a hand about, "but it's best appreciated from the comfort of a home, through a closed glass window."

Ash snorted as he stepped over a fallen branch. "I've always thought the earth powered my alchemy."

Ramsay paused, as if considering the possibility, then shrugged. "Perhaps. Some have theorized that our bodies are really only animated earth, so maybe our bodies can be revitalized by the earth itself, too."

Callum had marched ahead so far and fast that he'd already reached the clearing that was their goal and was little more than a dot in the distance. He paused, looking back at Ash and Ramsay, as if he'd only just realized they weren't right behind him, and waved. Ramsay raised a half-hearted hand. "Source, he's just too fast." She nudged Ash's shoulder. "I'm glad the two of you are getting on better now, at least. I'm not the best at facilitating arguments. That's usually Callum's role between you and me."

"Callum and I are only getting along better because of him," Ash admitted.

"You're trying your best, too."

How disappointed would Ramsay be, if she learned that Ash's *best* included betraying both her and Callum—all of New Anglia—no matter what excuses Ash used? Source, maybe he shouldn't have decided to keep the attack on McKinley to himself. Elena's group was going to destroy Ramsay's inventions, her work, and Ash had decided to keep quiet about it. He stared hard at the grass beneath his boots, struggling to swallow the shame that stuck in his throat.

Once Ash and Ramsay finally caught up to Callum, the three sat in the clearing, bellies full and eyes heavy. They lazed in the grass, Callum's head in Ramsay's lap as she pulled at his short curls. Ash rested on top of Callum, head nestled against his chest. He thought he might fall asleep like this, until he heard a telltale sound and glanced up to watch Ramsay leaning over as she kissed Callum's cheek, the corner of his mouth, his lips. Ash felt a flash of envy, which made both look up at him as if they'd sensed his energy.

"I thought we'd moved past the jealousy," Ramsay teased.

Ash's cheeks heated. He hated that he was the youngest of them and often felt the most immature when it came to their relationship.

Callum sat up. "Jealousy is a natural emotion," he said. "It's not something that Ash can help, and it's not something to shame."

Ash supposed that was right. He couldn't help it if he felt jealous. It was his actions that mattered most. He leaned back on his hands. "Maybe it would help if I got more used to the sight."

Ramsay quirked an impressed brow, while Callum frowned in confusion—until Ramsay placed a palm to his cheek and turned his face to her so that she could kiss him again. Callum seemed to understand, then, as they pressed against each other, his hands rising to her shoulders, thumbs brushing her jaw. Ramsay parted her mouth and opened her eyes to look at Ash. His breath got slow as he watched. He was used to seeing Callum and Ramsay share small, quick kisses; there'd been an unspoken rule between them that they wouldn't share a bed with one another while one of the three was missing. Usually, if their touch got more involved, Ash was included, too.

Impatience to join made his fingers fidget, but Ash forced himself to look—to really watch. Callum lowered Ramsay to the dirt, his hands guiding her on top of him as she straddled and leaned down to kiss him again. Ash wondered if this was how they had been at Pembroke, too, Ramsay being more the type to take charge. It fascinated him, how each of their roles and personalities shifted depending on the equation.

Ramsay gasped as Callum sat up, pulling her hair back to kiss her neck and jaw. "Will you really only watch, Ash?"

Ash hadn't thought they would go much further than this, though as he paid more attention to the hunger in their energy, he should've realized sooner just how their *walk* would end. They'd spent days at a time in bed together, before their responsibilities pulled them apart.

He nodded. "I want to see."

Callum seemed too invested in Ramsay's neck and unbuttoning her shirt to notice much of anything else, so Ash was surprised when he murmured, "We'll see how long that lasts."

"Is that a challenge?" Ash asked, hoarse.

Callum kissed Ramsay's collarbone, her flat chest, and laid her down as his mouth moved over her rib cage and lower still. "You enjoy sex with us too much to just sit this out."

"Really?" Ash feared that Callum might be right, but he was also competitive. "Do you want to bet?"

Callum unbuttoned Ramsay's pants. "Depends on what we're betting."

Ash considered it for a moment. "A book. Whoever wins has to buy the other a book, any they'd like."

"Deal."

✳

Ash sighed as he walked into the bookshop, the bell jingling. Callum followed closely behind, hands in his pockets as he glanced around the shelves. "Any I'd like, you said?" Callum asked.

Ramsay laughed under her breath as she stepped away, browsing titles against a far wall.

Callum slipped the nearest text off a shelf, inspecting the cover. "I haven't always enjoyed reading. That was always more your interest, and Ramsay's," he said as he slid the book back into its place. "What do you recommend?"

"There's a book I've been eyeing about the history of alchemy," Ash said. The depictions of early humans and their fumbling sciences had been fascinating when Ash flipped through the pages. "Oh—even better, I think I saw a book about healing, too." He headed for the small alchemist section, but paused when he noticed Callum stiffen. "You can work for your family and simultaneously feed your curiosity about healing, can't you?" Ash asked.

Callum seemed surprised by the idea, but then took a few steps to join Ash's side, holding out a large palm for the book Ash placed in it. "I guess the desire to learn healing is so strong, and the thought that I won't be able to for some time so painful, that I . . ." He flipped open the book's cover. "It's felt easier to avoid the topic of healing altogether."

"I worked long days and managed to study every night, once," Ash said. "You could do the same. Who knows? Maybe after you've helped alchemists as a commander, you could know just enough healing to work for House Adelaide instead."

"He'd need to graduate from Lancaster first," Ramsay said as she passed by.

Ash could've thrown the book after her. "Maybe they'll have a special apprentice position, just for you."

"Working under Charlotte Adelaide, maybe?" Ramsay said with the smallest smile.

Callum cleared his throat and slid the book back onto its shelf. "Thank you, Ash, but I think I'll find something else."

Ash looked between the two. Clearly Ramsay had also noticed the chemistry Callum had with Charlotte. Ramsay must've remembered, too, that Callum and Charlotte had practically been betrothed, once. Ash had hoped their connection had just been an old friendship, but now he wasn't so sure. He walked to Ramsay's side as she bent over the alchemist section, murmuring that it was quite small.

"What was that about Charlotte?" Ash whispered.

Ramsay glanced up at him. "Those two have been making eyes at each other for months now. I'm sure you've seen."

Ash blinked at Ramsay. He hadn't expected her to be so straightforward about it or act like it wasn't an issue whatsoever. "But we agreed to be in a relationship together—the three of us, no one else involved."

"Come now, Ash," Ramsay said as she stood straight with a sigh. "We three are together because we've recognized love can't be limited. It isn't fair to deny Callum if he has feelings for Charlotte, too." She shrugged. "Besides, from what I can tell, it's really just the remnants of an old crush."

Ash hesitated. "Is there anyone else you like also?"

"I've started to notice how handsome Lord Val can be in a particular light." Ash's mouth fell open as Ramsay snorted. "No, Ash, I have not found anyone else I *like*."

Ash turned to the alchemist section himself, relieved despite himself. He was surprised by Ramsay's next question.

"What about you?"

"What about me?"

Ramsay stared only at the titles in front of her. "Lord Alexander has taken a particular interest in you as of late, from what I can see."

Ash had to suppress a gag. "*Lord Alexander?*"

"What?" She shrugged. "He's handsome."

"Not my type."

"He's not much older than Callum."

"He's an *asshole.*"

"Careful," Ramsay said with the touch of a smile. "That's our Head of New Anglia you're talking about."

Callum approached behind them, resting a hand on Ash's shoulder. "What was that about Lord Alexander?"

Ramsay and Ash only exchanged glances, Ash widening his eyes with a clear message of *don't you dare*. Ramsay bit back a smirk. "Nothing," she said.

Before Callum could say anything else, Ash felt a familiar steady energy and turned to see Mr. Brown shuffle in from the back rooms. He held a box that seemed almost as tall as him, nearly stumbling under its weight. Ash hurried over and caught the box for him with gathering energy that helped it float as if it were a feather, landing on the countertop.

"Oh," Mr. Brown said. "Thank you. I didn't realize I had any customers."

"It's good to see you," Ash said, and meant it.

"And you," Mr. Brown replied. "It's been some time. Did you have any luck finding the book you were looking for?" Ash wanted to frantically wave his hands and signal, *No, please don't say anything else*, but Mr. Brown didn't catch on to the desperate gleam in his eye. "*Communicating with Plasma Particles*, was it? I put in a request to have a copy delivered, even though it's out of print, just to see if one might come for you, but nothing yet."

Ash noticed Callum and Ramsay's stillness as they glanced at him with curiosity. Surely they'd both be able to put two and two together, and realize this was the book Ash had wanted from Lady Alder's archives. He didn't need either looking into the text further.

He made sure to keep his smile planted to his face as he answered. "Thank you," he said. "No luck so far."

"Probably for the best," Mr. Brown said. He shuffled across the floor to the counter and the register. "Is there anything you need help with?"

"I'd just like this," Callum said, holding out the cookbook. Ramsay peeked at the cover and its illustrated cakes with interest. Ash dug into his pockets for his pouch of coin. It wasn't lost on him that this was the very coin Callum had given him as an allowance, but Callum was at least kind enough not to mention that.

"Friends of yours?" Mr. Brown asked as he smiled at Callum and Ramsay. Ramsay had stuck her head into the bookshop once, but there was no real reason for her to visit regularly. Giddings Library in Lancaster College had been untouched by Ash's explosion, and she had access to practically any text she could ever want or need.

"Um—yes," Ash said, and when Ramsay and Callum gave him blank stares, he sighed. "Well, more like partners."

Mr. Brown nodded, but didn't give any indication that he thought there was something wrong with the fact that Ash had two partners rather than just one. Ash quite liked House Alder members. Their vow to the pursuit of knowledge generally meant existing with curiosity for others rather than judgment.

"It was nice meeting you," Mr. Brown said to Ramsay and Callum. "I hope to see you again soon."

✳

The sun was quickly setting. The sky was a mixture of reds and pinks, the brightest of stars already shining beside a half-moon. The three were quiet on the walk up the path, across the cobblestone of Market Square, and through the field. Ash wanted to say a number of things: to apologize for the arguments they'd had recently, to thank Callum for asking that they all spend the afternoon and evening together, to admit that it wasn't only Callum's and Ramsay's fault that they'd begun to drift—Ash had played his part, too—

Callum stopped. Ash looked up, and Ramsay paused beside him. A group stood in front of them under the purpling sky. Seven people, Ash counted, mostly men, though a girl was with them. She was the same who had called Ash a manipulator in Mr. Brown's bookshop.

"Can we help you?" Callum called. He didn't move, but blue light shined from his skin and tensed muscles.

The girl pointed at Ash. "That's him. He's the one who looked at those manipulation books."

Ramsay put a hand in front of Ash while Callum stepped in front of them both. Ash might've been annoyed at their overprotectiveness, once, but he was grateful now. His breath was tight. He'd seen nightmares begin like this.

"It isn't illegal to read texts on alchemy," Callum said. His voice was calm, but his body was stiff.

"It should be," one of the men replied. "It should be illegal to have texts on manipulation at all."

"We don't want any trouble," Callum said, holding out two hands. "We just want to go home."

"Problem is," the man said, stepping forward before all the rest, "the books aren't the only issue." Ash had seen him before, chopping wood. He was tall enough, big enough with bulging muscle, that he could easily give Callum a hard time in a fight.

"What other issue is there?" Ramsay asked, anger spiking her tone.

"You're the three who were on trial."

Air caught in Ash's lungs.

"Heard a nasty rumor," the man said, "that a manipulator who worked closely with *Sir Hain* was here in Riverside."

Callum shook his head. "You heard wrong. None of us worked with Gresham Hain."

"And that's why he was on trial," the man continued as if Callum hadn't spoken at all. "Which of you is it? Which one of you helped that man destroy Kensington?"

"None of us," Ash said. "We didn't—"

Ramsay's hand tightened on Ash's arm.

"Since you were the one looking at manipulation books," the man said, "I'm willing to bet you're the manipulator who helped Hain destroy Kensington, too."

"He isn't the only *manipulator* here," Ramsay said, ice in her voice.

"No—Ramsay, stop," Callum said. He held up a hand at the group before him. "My name is Callum Kendrick. I'm the son of the late Winslow Kendrick—"

The group had been watching him, blinking, then began to erupt into slow laughs, even as Callum continued.

"—and currently commander of the redguards, Seventeenth Squadron. We have no desire to fight you. Let us pass, and—"

"See, we *do* want to fight you," the man said, stepping forward. Ash had somehow, horrifyingly, missed the dagger he'd yanked out of his boot.

Ramsay moved first. Even as Callum shouted at her to stop, she sent a white burst of light sailing toward the man, upending him and flying him through the air. He landed hard on his back, screams rising from the others in the group. They spun toward Callum, but he wasn't wearing a uniform, hadn't brought a weapon. He balled his hands into fists and knocked one into the gut of the first man who came at him. Ash spread out his fingers, energy crackling. An invisible wall of air pushed forward, throwing Callum's assailant to the ground.

"We haven't hurt anyone!" Ash shouted. "We haven't done anything—"

Another rushed at Ash as Ramsay pushed him out of the way with a hot burst of light. Ash rolled as the man slashed the air where he'd been seconds before. Ash pulled himself to his feet—took a breath, hands heating and ready—

The smell of smoke stole his attention. One of the men had moved closer to the cottage without anyone's notice. He'd lit a stick with a match, it seemed, and pressed its fire against a cottage wall.

Ash's eyes widened. "No—"

He raised his hands, trying to imagine water gushing forward, but the flames had caught and started to spread, jumping from one panel of wood to the next. Ramsay blasted ice at the fire, stopping it in part, but a wind caught the fire, and it exploded back in strength.

All three were at a loss for words as they stood, frozen, and watched their home burn. The fire's heat seared Ash's skin, not unlike when the heat of the firestorm his father had unleashed on Kensington found him, the smell of smoke and charred bodies filling the air and Ash's lungs. This time, the clenched fist around his heart didn't let go.

The group of townspeople had watched for a moment, too, as if seeing the destruction of the home sated their bloodlust. One by one, they began to leave. The girl stood behind Ash. "You get it now, right?" she said. "You're not wanted here in Riverside. Leave, and don't come back again."

When she was gone, too, Ash nearly sank to the ground. He was held up only by Callum, who murmured to him. "Come on. It's going to be all right. Come on."

They stumbled along the field, away from the cottage that creaked and swayed in the fire that had consumed it, mirage shimmering in the heat and smoke that poured into the sky. They stopped, fire's orange light flickering against their skin as they watched, helpless. The roof collapsed with an explosion of sparks. The fire had caught onto the ground, spreading to the nearby forest, where Ash and Ramsay and Callum had rested in one another's arms just hours before. A siren sounded, a bell ringing in the village.

"Shit," Ramsay said, voice tearing. "Fucking hell, we didn't do *anything* to deserve—"

"*Ramsay*," Callum said.

She looked at him, then at Ash, who was shaking. Ash raised his hands, watching his fingers tremble. He couldn't breathe. Ramsay cursed under her breath and hurried to Ash's other side, clutching his palms, as Callum rubbed his back.

"Deep breath," Ramsay said. "Remember what I taught you? In through the nose—yes, like that—slowly release through the mouth . . ."

It was embarrassing, the tears that stung Ash's eyes. He wasn't the only of them who had lost their home.

Callum shook his head as if he'd heard this thought, and maybe he had. "The cottage was all of ours," he said, "but it was your home more than mine or Ramsay's. You don't have to be ashamed of grieving."

Townspeople had pulled barrels of water from the river and to the fire.

"We should help them," Ash mumbled.

"No," Callum said without any space for disagreement. "It's not safe for us. The same people who attacked could try again. We could be blamed for the fire and imprisoned."

Ash didn't have the energy to argue. He breathed with Ramsay for a minute more, until she asked, "Are you all right to move?" He nodded, so she said, "Okay. Keep breathing."

There was no portal door to use, no easy way to get back to Kensington. They walked away from the flames and silhouettes of people in the distance until the sound of their shouts faded. Ash's feet sank into the dirt and grass as the sky became black. The only light for their path glowed from Ramsay's hands.

The three eventually made it to the train station, a small platform creaking in the breeze. They waited with no way of knowing when the next train would arrive. They sat on the splintered wood, huddled together against the misty cold. Callum pulled Ash closer, and Ash leaned against his shoulder, then chest, then lap as the hours passed. Ash listened to the breeze.

Callum and Ramsay murmured to each other every now and then.

"I had a meeting scheduled with Lord Val in the morning," Ramsay said. "I hope he doesn't send out a search party."

"I'll need to file an official report with Edric," Callum said. "Even less reason for the people of Riverside to welcome us in the future, I suppose."

They must have thought Ash was asleep, but he was too afraid to let himself drift. He tried not to let himself think nor feel. He was numb following the loss of the cottage, except for the remnants of his anxiety. The dread was like the fire that had consumed his home, heat building in his chest and embers rising into his throat every time he closed his eyes and saw the flames. He wanted to scream.

The sky lightened to gray, birds singing. The train whistled in the distance, then slowed to a stop. The car they chose was nearly empty. The three sat around a table, Ash beside the window. Callum handed over coin for their tickets once the conductor passed.

Ash stared out the window at the landscape that rolled past. He felt Callum's worry emanating from his skin beside him—but there was another energy, too. "I wish you had let me handle it," Callum murmured after a long while.

Ramsay's eyes were closed as she spoke. "What? Do you think we would've been saved by you, just because you're a red?"

"We already knew they were hostile toward alchemists. Clearly practicing alchemy against them would not help."

"Careful, Kendrick," Ramsay said, peeking open an eye. "You might sound like you're blaming the victim."

Callum took a quick breath. "I'm sorry. I don't mean—" He paused, then tried again. "You both could've trusted me to handle it. That's all I mean to say."

Ash didn't respond as he rested his head against the window's cold glass, staring out at the dark gray clouds that hung low in the sky.

14

The three were exhausted and damp from an early morning drizzle by the time they reached House Alexander's manor. Lord Val had, apparently, just been minutes from reporting Ramsay as missing, claiming she had never been late once in the months he had known her. Callum reported the incident to Edric, as he'd promised he would; even if Edric wasn't happy with his younger brother, he would not let it stand that a group of citizens had threatened a commander of House Kendrick. Apparently a squadron of reds would go to Riverside to "handle the situation."

"Nothing you need to worry yourselves about," Callum said.

Ramsay had a class to teach. "Not even enough time for a shower," she said. She kissed them both before she headed for the door they'd entered through, murmuring the password for Lancaster College.

Callum walked Ash back to his room. Maybe he noticed Ash's frown and decided it was as good a time as any. Maybe he had planned to give Ash the book then anyway, before they went another stretch of time without seeing or hearing from each other again.

Ash stared at the title in his hands: *A Succinct History of the Sciences.*

Callum rubbed the back of his neck. "Since you mentioned you'd been eyeing it."

Ash flipped it open. A note had been scribbled onto the first blank page. Ash usually hated to see books marred, but the *XO Callum* in chicken scratch made his chest warm. Callum must've sneaked a copy to the register, along with his cookbook, and hidden it for the rest of the night. Ash's face warmed. "You're unbearably sweet sometimes," he said, despite any lingering anger. "You know that, right?"

"Yeah. I know."

＊

The end of the week came, the day Ash had dreaded. He stayed in his room, practicing his breath to ease the pressure building in his chest. He half hoped that Marlowe, Elena, and all the rest would have changed their minds about Ash joining their mission. Marlowe hadn't reached out to him in the five days that had passed, after all, and anything could've happened since they'd last met. But as the hours crept on and evening came, it wasn't long before tendrils of smoke unfurled from Ash's bedroom wall, an energy beckoning him in.

He stepped out of his room with a blast of cold slithering through his veins and into the worn sitting room of the rebel safe house. The rest of the group was already standing there, waiting for Ash's arrival, it seemed. It was the same five who had attacked the gala, all dressed in the same black coveralls. Ash had done his best, wearing a dark loose-fitting pant and shirt, but it was another reminder that he didn't belong with this group. And if he didn't perform well? Would they simply decide they didn't want Ash joining them after all, or would they decide he was too dangerous to let live—to kill him, as Elena had originally wanted to do?

Finley bounced between their heels and toes, arms folded behind their back. The older man named Hendrix reminded Ash of redguards, from his stance; he'd clearly been trained to fight with his fists as well as alchemy, at the very least. "Good evening," the older man said, to which Ash nodded. Ash was happy to see that Riles was on the same page, when it came to pretending that the other didn't exist.

Elena, the original, older version Ash was used to seeing,

strolled into the room. "Sorry I'm late." She tossed Ash a gas mask.

He caught it, watching the others as they began to strap on their own masks, too. He could see the benefits of the mask: Keep identities hidden, while also protecting the fundamental necessity of any alchemist—breath. He pulled the buckle on around the back of his head. The goggles tinted the world a dark emerald green. He was surprised to see that a brighter green with a yellow tinge glowed from each of the people in the room.

"Heat sensors," Marlowe said beside him, voice muffled.

"They'll be particularly useful when finding the firelock prototypes," Elena said. "Orders: Hendrix with Finley. Riles with me. Marlowe, stick with Ash. You've all seen the map of McKinley before except for Ash, but I believe you spent some time there, correct?"

Ash could've done without the reminder of being Callum's prisoner. "Only about a week."

"It's more likely that the firelocks are hidden away, rather than kept out in the open or in a room with easy access, so let's focus on the underground storage halls. Riles and I, Marlowe and Ash—we'll enter the staircases from the cafeteria. Hendrix and Finley, keep a lookout while searching the storage rooms beneath the classrooms, to be on the safe side. Understood?"

"Understood," all the rest said as one.

Elena stepped to one of the walls. Ash frowned as he watched—it looked like she had every intention of simply walking headfirst into the panels—but he realized a shadow he'd thought was Elena's had started to melt from the wood where she'd placed a palm. It drifted to the floor, pooling like fog. It was the same alchemy that the group had used to enter the gala—that Ash and Marlowe had used to arrive at the safe house, too. *What the hell is that?* Ash had studied as many properties of alchemic sciences as he could, and never had he heard of an alchemy like this. It wasn't anything like a portal door, and even when he'd once attempted to materialize and failed, he hadn't experienced the shadow's dread, tearing breath out of his chest.

He knew what to expect this time, at least, as he stepped into the shadows, too, with the frigid ice that coated his skin and sank into his lungs. He took another step, out of a stone wall. The others were ahead of him, Marlowe walking behind.

It was odd to return to Callum's school, like stepping into a distant memory Ash would've preferred to forget. The cafeteria looked different at night, blue shadows filling the hall and falling across the empty tables. McKinley had been a few streets away from the blast zone where buildings and people had been razed to the ground; it'd taken minimal damage, and students had returned within a month. It'd been over half a year, but the space hadn't changed from the last time Ash had come here, when he was forced to follow Callum everywhere the older boy went.

The room was silent. Ash's breath echoed in the mask, pulse thudding in his ears. Elena held up two palms. Hendrix and Finley tapped across the hall, Riles and Elena in the other direction.

"Let's go," Marlowe whispered.

Ash followed her. There was a door on the opposite end of the cafeteria that she hurried toward. She put a hand on the knob and twisted. It was locked. She clutched the knob, unmoving for a moment. Ash watched as the golden light that filled her grew brighter in her chest before it extended down her arm and to her hand—glowed around the knob, until Ash heard a click.

She pushed the door open to a tight concrete stairwell. "The storage rooms aren't far from here."

"Wouldn't the firelocks be kept closer to the classrooms?" Ash whispered. They walked down, the rough concrete walls on either side practically brushing Ash's shoulders.

"If the number of prototypes that were delivered is correct, then the storage by the classrooms wouldn't be large enough. They'd need space for stacks of cartons."

"How many are there?" Ash asked as they got to the last step.

They stood in a narrow stone hall. "*What* are they?" He'd heard the word *firelock* several times now, but no description of the weapon Ramsay created had ever been given to him. Even if Elena said she and the others knew, none had bothered to offer an explanation.

"Wait," Marlowe said. She paused. Even behind the mask, Ash could feel her frown. Marlowe turned to look at him. "Did you hear—"

A blast rocked the hall. Fire tore toward Ash. His arm was yanked back. He fell on top of Marlowe on the stairs. He threw his hands up, envisioning a bubble of glass, able to withstand heat—

The shock wave ended. The staircase was charred, but it stood. A glob of melted glass hit Ash's shoulder. He grimaced and gritted his teeth against a cry, but Marlowe immediately clutched the burn with a cooling hand until the pain faded.

"There was another explosion right before this one," Marlowe said. Elena and Riles had probably been hit first with a similar attack. "Shit."

His chest heaved. "Callum never mentioned security was like this."

"We would've found out if it were," Marlowe said. "This was a preemptive attack."

"How would they have known we were coming?" Marlowe didn't respond. "You don't think *I*—it wouldn't have been smart of me, to betray you all so obviously—"

"No," she said. "I don't think it was you."

If the reds knew the group had come, then they'd undoubtedly do their best to kill each and every single one of them. Ash thought of Finley and Hendrix, close to the classrooms and the student barracks. He hurried up the stairs, but Marlowe snatched his arm. "Stay still. Stay quiet," she whispered.

"But—"

"Anyone above might be banking on us being dead. Wait and listen."

Ash could hardly hear anything with the echoing thump of

his heart racing. He swallowed, paused. For a moment, he didn't hear anything—but there it was, the soft tap of footsteps. Someone above was trying to be quiet. Ash's hands still trembled—it'd taken a lot to make the protective shield—but he'd do it again, if it meant his and Marlowe's lives.

Whispered voices above. "No sign of them."

"They wouldn't have survived on the stairs."

"Check anyway."

Marlowe waved a hand and kept the palm facing forward. The air around Ash shimmered. He looked down at his own body, and nothing was there. Marlowe's breath was held beside him. She began to tremble. It seemed she'd learned illusion alchemy from Elena, altering the perception of anyone nearby, but Source knew how long it would hold—from the looks of Marlowe's quivering hand, not long.

The door above clicked and creaked open. A guard peered down the staircase. Ash's heart fell as he saw the maroon school uniform of McKinley. He would've thought, hoped, that if McKinley knew of an oncoming attack, they would've evacuated their students—but then again, this was also the top school of redguards in New Anglia. From Ash's time here, he wouldn't have been surprised if the college's professors claimed it was the students' duty to fight, deciding to use this attack as a training opportunity. The students would've only happily obliged.

The student on top of the staircase was familiar, Ash realized—one of the very who'd been in Callum's class. Callum would've been a senior with the boy, if he hadn't been promoted to commander; he would've been in this very school, one of the reds sent to attack, capture, and possibly even kill Ash and everyone else in the group. Marlowe's one hand fell as she raised the other. Ash's body flickered back into view. The student's eyes widened, mouth open to shout a warning. A white light glowed from Marlowe's hand, sharpening into a daggerlike point, aiming up the staircase and at the student's neck—

Ash grabbed her wrist. The light-arrow shot into the wall beside the student and ricocheted into embers. "Here!" the student screamed, voice breaking. "Two are here!"

"What the hell are you doing?" Marlowe yelled, but there wasn't time for Ash to answer. Another student had run into view. They threw a black ball the size of a fist down the hall, bouncing off the wall and down the stairs. A flash exploded, overtaking Ash's goggles—everything was a bright green, and even with the mask on, he could smell the haze of smoke—

Something firm gripped his arm. He lurched. He fell to one knee, almost sick. He looked up to see Marlowe striding toward a door. She'd materialized them out of the stairs and into what looked like an empty classroom, tables neatly lined up and notes from an earlier class still scrawled across the chalkboard. Marlowe usually needed to know the inside of a space before materializing there. Ash knew it was luck they hadn't ended up in the middle of a wall.

"Hurry up," Marlowe snapped. "We have to find the others."

Ash jumped to his feet and ripped off his mask. "You said we wouldn't kill anyone!"

She spun to him. "It was our life or theirs! The mission isn't to kill anyone, but I sure as hell will protect myself if—"

"He was just a student!" Ash yelled.

A flash of light reflected in the hall outside. It looked like an echo of alchemy. There were rapid popping sounds in quick succession, small explosions one right after the other. Ash and Marlowe were in a classroom, which meant they were closer to the barracks than Elena or Riles had been, assuming they'd survived the first attack—which meant Finley and Hendrix were likely fighting for their lives nearby. Ash yanked the mask back on and pushed past Marlowe to hurry into the hall, ignoring her when she called after him.

He raced down one corridor and the other, searching for anything that looked remotely familiar, until he saw the archway that led into the courtyard where the students ran drills—and there, he saw Hendrix on one knee, mask cracked in half, bleeding from his forehead. Finley stood on their own beside him, a wall of light standing against dozens of flashes; but the wall was flickering, Finley's arms trembling—

Ash threw a shield up and raced into the courtyard. He saw the surprised expressions of the line of students that faced him. Each wore their maroon uniform, and all seemed as old as Ash, maybe younger. They pointed metal sticks at him—weapons Ash recognized. He'd seen them once before, in what had felt like a nightmare.

"Ash," Finley gasped. "They knew we were coming—"

"I know," Ash said. The weapons—firelocks—appeared to be powered by alchemy. A built-in flint sparked fire, shooting rock-like projectiles at a fast-enough pace that they could do damage, even kill. Ash closed his eyes and took a slow inhale, allowing his shield to grow. Finley's arms dropped in relief. The shield covered the three, but it was as thin as a pane of glass. Ash couldn't be certain it would survive a round of blasts.

Hendrix groaned in pain beside them. A hole was in the man's shoulder and another in his thigh, both gushing blood. He rasped, "Take Finley—"

A commander stood beside the line of students that faced them. It was Rake, the same professor who had led the students' drills. Anger ripped through Ash's gut at the thought that *this* was just another drill for the students, an attempted execution of alchemists, never mind that the group included a *child*. Rake almost seemed bored as she eyed Ash with contempt, unfazed that he had joined their fight.

Rake opened her mouth to speak an order, interrupted when Ash shouted. "Stop!" he said, voice muffled by his mask. "Please—we didn't come here to fight—"

"And yet you, a group of alchemists, have invaded McKinley College."

"We're not invading—we don't want to hurt anyone—"

But their lives did not matter, not to her. "Redguards do not negotiate." She raised a hand and faced her students. "Again."

The students, just about ten of them, fiddled with the weapons. Ash gasped as they held the firelocks up and aimed at Ash, Finley, and Hendrix. Finley took a step back. Ash took a breath, trying not to let the panic tear through his chest and lungs. The firelocks went off. Explosions hit the shield. It cracked with each blast and shattered. Several of the projectiles zipped through. One hit the wall above Hendrix's head, brick blasting into dust. Ash grimaced, breath tightening—movement caught his eye. Marlowe had hidden in the archway to the courtyard. She peeked out now, looking from the students to Ash and back.

Rake raised yet another hand. "Again."

The students concentrated on clicking open a barrel in the weapons and dropping what looked like marbles of stone inside. Marlowe took the pause as an opportunity to race into the courtyard, too, stopping at Ash's side.

"You really shouldn't run off on your own like that," she muttered, but Ash was too focused on building another shield. Light spread, but there were too many gaps, holes where the projectiles would shoot through and into their skin, their bones—

Rake only raised a brow at Marlowe. "Helpful of you to join us. It's much easier to kill you all here and now."

Marlowe ignored the woman and put a hand on Ash's shoulder. He felt a rush of her energy tingle down his arm and into his chest. "You all right?" she said. "Can you try to put up a stronger shield now?"

He nodded, calling back to the days when he'd trained his breath with Ramsay, inhaling and exhaling slow and steady. Another shield materialized like frost growing over air, a wall of ice solidifying. Marlowe's energy flickered gold behind his eyelids. He focused on his breath enough that the set of explosions that rained against his shield sounded far away now. He opened his eyes. Only one projectile had cracked through the corner, blasting off a chunk.

"Good, Ash," Marlowe said, her voice trembling. She was giving too much energy to him. "Keep breathing. Hendrix, can you stand?"

"Leave me here to fight them off," he said through gritted teeth. "Get back to Elena, I can buy you time—"

"This isn't the time to be a martyr," Marlowe said. "Get up."

The man groaned in pain, but he got to his feet.

"Finley," Marlowe said, placing another hand on their shoulder, also sharing her energy with them now, "can you cover us?"

Finley's limbs were stiff with fear. "Yes." This was the first time the child had ever been in combat. They raised another shield that flickered, but it was better than nothing.

"Ready?" Marlowe said. "Let's go."

They ran. Rake's gaze followed, eyes narrowed on her prey as she held up a fist and shouted orders. "You five, block the exits. The rest, follow. Do not hesitate to kill . . ."

Her voice chased Ash and the others into the hall, Hendrix limping. He was losing too much blood. He wouldn't last long.

Marlowe could materialize, but Ash didn't think she could handle taking them all to safety at once. There were no portal doors to rely on, and they wouldn't make it far if they ran out into the streets to escape, especially with Hendrix's injuries.

"Do the thing!" Ash yelled at Marlowe. "The thing with the wall, to get us back to the warehouse—"

"I'm not leaving without Elena and Riles!" Marlowe shouted. She turned to Hendrix. "Did you see them, when—"

"No," Hendrix said through gritted teeth, face twisted in pain. "We heard the explosions beneath us and tried to get back to the cafeteria, but the reds—"

The halls were long, with too many turns, and all the mahogany walls and hardwood floors looked the same, with no indication that they weren't simply running in circles. The echo of boots on stone followed, shouts of voices near; and the students knew their own school much more than anyone in the group did, no matter how much they'd studied McKinley's blueprints.

"Wait," Finley said to Ash. "You're going too fast—"

He slowed just as two students ran into the hall in front of them.

"Shit," Marlowe said, voice hoarse. She was giving more energy than Ash and Finley both now. A sweat had broken out over her skin, hand on Ash's shoulder trembling.

Ash glanced behind him in time to see the three students slow to a stop. Even in this the reds had been meticulous, able to see the weaker member holding the shield would be faster taken down by three students instead of two.

"Finley, Ash, I have to let you go," Marlowe said, the only warning before she dropped her hands. The weight of the shield Ash tried to hold almost brought him to his knees. Marlowe spun around with a gust of hot wind flying toward the three reds who sprinted at them, but one jumped over the wind and rolled, while another ducked; the blast only sent one flying back. Without Marlowe's energy, Finley's shield shook before it fell. One red produced a dagger, cutting the air where Marlowe's neck had been a second before. She shoved the red back, and Hendrix stuck out his good leg, tripping the student while the other soared with a leap—Ash realized too late that *he* was the target—

A blade scratched his shoulder. He yelled out and stumbled back as he envisioned a vine weaving together and around his assailant's leg—it yanked, throwing the student into the air and across the hall. His focus had dropped, his shield with it. The two students in front of him held up their weapons. Two pops went off. One hit the stone beside Ash's head, blast ricocheting. His ear rang, cheek burned. Beside him, Finley jolted.

"No—"

Marlowe grabbed Finley before they could fall. She pressed a palm to Finley's stomach. Their eyes were wide, color quickly draining from their face as their mouth silently opened and closed. Blood was quickly spreading from their abdomen, soaking their uniform, but Ash couldn't see where the wound was. He held up both hands now, straining for any last drop of energy he could find, but the shields that rose were weak. The two students behind him were joined by the third, each holding blades. The two in front had reloaded their firelocks and took their time raising both. He hadn't considered the possibility, really, that he might die. Ash had thought he'd be relieved when given the opportunity to return to Source and its everlasting peace; but instead, now, he could only think that he hadn't told Callum and Ramsay goodbye.

Before the students could pull the triggers, a shimmering force crashed into them. They were thrown into the wall. Elena and Riles raced around the corner, Riles with his hands glowing, even with the cut above his brow and the blood that leaked into his eye. Elena took one look at them all and raised a hand. A wall of stone grew from the floor and snapped shut, cutting the three students off behind them. She raised a fist at the two students who'd fallen. As if her fist had gripped them by their collars, they were both yanked into the air with cries. One was knocked into the wall. Her head dropped, and she slumped in the air, unconscious.

"Who told you?" Elena yelled, but the other student only groaned, hands grasping at the invisible fingers that choked him. "How did you know we were coming?" she demanded.

The red only spat on the floor. "Fucking—manipul—"

He couldn't get the word out, but Ash felt the surge of hatred in his voice anyway. Riles's hands were still glowing when he bent and snatched one of the knives that had fallen from a student's hands. He marched to the student—

"Riles—*no*—"

Riles stopped. He looked at Ash, face still. "*No?*" he repeated.

Ash stood to one shaky foot, then the other. "They're defenseless."

"These fuckers tried to *kill* us," Riles said, voice so cold that the words trembled in the air. "Look at Hendrix—at *Finley*—"

Ash swallowed and looked down. Marlowe had gotten to work on the wound in Finley's stomach, shirt soaked with blood and torn in half. It looked like the firelock had gotten Finley right beneath the ribs. Their breath was shallow and quick, eyes glassy. Marlowe's eyes were shut as she focused energy and seemed to ignore the world around her entirely; it was the few precious seconds that could mean saving Finley's life.

"This piece of shit," Riles said, eyes filled with tears now, "*deserves* to die."

Ash looked at the student. The hatred had melted into fear, even if the boy tried to wear a brave face. His lip quivered. Ash wondered if he was fighting the urge to beg for his life. Ash wondered who would mourn, once they learned he had died.

Ash struggled to find the words to explain the tangle of feeling and thought that clogged his throat. "We wouldn't be any different," he managed to say.

Finley huffed behind him. It reminded Ash of the sounds his mother had made the night she passed.

"The child doesn't have long," Hendrix warned.

"Let him live," Ash whispered. Riles's glare cut into him. Heat glowed around the older boy's eyes. Ash wasn't sure if it was his imagination, that his own skin began to burn.

"Enough," Elena said. She pressed a hand to the wall. Shadows spewed, and the hall fell into darkness.

15

Finley was carried to the kitchen and put atop the table. "Clear the room," Elena ordered.

Marlowe had managed to keep Finley alive, but she wasn't a trained healer. Otto got to work as Finley lay sprawled across the table where they'd eaten and laughed just days ago. Their face was pale, eyes squeezed closed. The door snapped shut in Ash's face.

Ash sat in the hall with his back to the wall, knees up and arms resting on top. He listened to Riles yell from the sitting room, just a hall away.

"Finley was dying at his feet, and that bastard was worried about saving a red's life!"

There was a low grumbling voice—Hendrix, though Ash couldn't hear what the man said in response.

"Fuck that! We don't have any proof that he *wasn't* sent to us," Riles shouted in return. "The reds knew we were coming. Someone warned them."

Marlowe spoke now, voice soft but firm. "The reds attacked Ash, too."

"It was a fucking act! He's defended the reds—*chosen* their lives over ours. How can we trust that he's not on their side?"

Ash shook his head and dropped it back against the wall. He hadn't wanted *either* to die. Why was he expected to choose one life's importance over another? He couldn't. He refused. Maybe it was because he had returned to Source—remembered the power's immense, unending love for every life that threaded together to create existence itself—

There was silence. Ash only assumed Elena spoke to them in

a voice too low for him to hear now. He was numb, a weight of tangled emotions heavy in his stomach. He felt like he was going to be sick. Shit. It was supposed to be easy—a quick in and out, no one hurt nor killed . . .

"Ash?"

He looked up to see Marlowe standing over him. He hadn't heard her come nor sensed her presence. He hadn't realized he was so out of it.

"Elena wants to speak with you," she said.

Ash wanted to know only so that he could prepare himself: "Is she going to kill me?"

Marlowe didn't answer his question. He got to his feet shakily and followed her into the room. Hendrix was on a sofa, leg propped up beside him. A white bandage stained with rusted brown was wrapped around his leg, another tied around his shoulder. Marlowe had done what she could, but the older man would still need proper help from Otto as well.

Riles stood in front of the fireplace, Elena in the center of the room. She'd returned to the younger version of herself now. Ash wondered how much energy it took her, to constantly keep up the illusion, but it was only a vague thought, one that helped him avoid the important topic at hand.

"I didn't betray you," Ash said, voice hoarse.

Elena didn't respond. She squinted for a breath.

"I *didn't*," Ash said again.

"This is the first time our attack was anticipated," Elena said. "We've been on seven missions across New Anglia so far. Don't you think it's a little suspicious, then, that the one and only time we were ambushed, you happened to have joined our team?"

He nodded. "Yes—yes, I can see how it doesn't look good, but—"

Riles scoffed, turning away.

"I wouldn't do anything to hurt you—any of you," Ash said.

"Bullshit. You made your allegiance clear today," Riles said.

"Because I didn't want you to *kill* a *kid*?" Ash shouted.

"That kid is no younger than you—than me," Riles yelled, spinning to face Ash. "He was older than Finley."

"Why does that mean we get to take his life?"

"This is *war*, Woods—or did you forget that? People die in war. *Kids* die in war." Ash shook his head, but Riles continued. "They're the necessary sacrifices to make change."

"You don't get to decide if someone's death is necessary," Ash said. "You don't get to decide if someone else should be sacrificed for your cause!"

"My cause?" Riles said. "Or our cause?"

Ash hesitated, words sucked away.

"You see?" Riles said, seemingly calmer now as he gestured a hand at Ash. "He doesn't even consider himself to be on our side. Just because he's Hain's son doesn't mean he's the right leader for this revolution," he said to Elena.

Marlowe only watched, arms crossed as she leaned against a wall. Ash felt a twitch of betrayal, that she didn't speak on his behalf—argue that he not be *killed*—but then, another part of him couldn't blame her. If she also believed he'd had something to do with this attack, that he was responsible for Finley almost dying, he could understand how she wouldn't be able to forgive him.

"We should kill him now," Riles said. "Dump his body by the docks, before he gets us all killed instead."

"I wouldn't do that," Ash said again, voice weaker now. "I wouldn't do anything to hurt any of you." But that was a lie, wasn't it? He hadn't betrayed them today, but if the group let him go, the moment he was released, he was supposed to go to Alexander and tell the man their secrets.

Silence followed. Everyone but Riles watched Ash, as if trying to see inside him—to see where the lies might be hidden. Ash swallowed, his throat sticking.

Marlowe hadn't said a word for the duration of the conversation, but she spoke now. "Ash was with me."

"So what?" Riles snapped.

"We were alone from the moment we arrived at McKinley. If the goal was to kill us, he could have turned on me at any time, but he didn't. And besides that," Marlowe added, voice rising when Riles tried to interrupt, "the reds tried to kill Ash, just the same as they tried to kill us. It wasn't an *act*, as you claim. He's lucky to be alive. Would they really have done that to their informant, their spy?"

Riles worked his jaw back and forth, clearly trying to come up with an explanation and argument.

"You've been against Ash from the moment he stepped foot here," Marlowe said. "No," she amended. "The second he attacked you at the gala."

To this, Riles didn't respond as he glared at nothing.

Hendrix groaned as he used both hands to lift and shift his leg. It looked like he'd started bleeding again. The skin around his eyes was green. "Is it possible that some sort of alchemic surveillance was placed on Ash without his knowledge?" the man rasped. Ash hadn't considered the possibility, but it didn't seem outside the scope of something Lord Alexander would be willing to do.

"The barriers would've protected against that," Elena said.

"The bastard's figured out a way around the barriers, then," Riles said. "He figured out a way to trick you. You're just too foolish to see it."

Marlowe ignored him. "Let him live," she said. She pushed away from the wall to join Elena in the center of the room. "I trust Ash with my life. I believe him when he says he wants to help us."

Ash ignored the tug of guilt, the vibration he hoped wasn't strong enough for anyone to pick up on in the room. He spoke to cover it. "I can share information with you," he said. "I live in House Alexander's manor." Riles snorted in disbelief, but Ash went on. "I attend Head of House meetings as Alexander's advisor. I have access to reports you might need."

Elena seemed to consider this in the silence that followed.

Marlowe added, "Ash is a powerful alchemist, one of the most powerful I know—and we need someone like him on our side. We need someone like him to unite us." She lowered her voice. "And besides that, we also need all the help we can get."

Elena took a deep breath and exhaled a hum, arms crossed. "How about it, then?" she finally said. "Would you like to officially join us?"

Ash might as well have been split in two. Relief filled him, of course—relief that he wouldn't be killed, that Marlowe and Elena at least believed in him; and there was, of course, the other part that drowned in shame. Riles shook his head and left the room, slamming the door shut behind him.

"Don't mind him," Elena said, without taking her eyes off Ash. "He'll sulk for another week or so, but he'll get over it eventually."

Ash bowed his head, hoping it looked like he lowered it in deference rather than guilt. "I'd like to help however I can."

Elena eyed Ash for one long moment, before she stepped to the wall and placed a hand against its panel. "Good," she said. "I'll reach out to you when we're ready."

※

By the time Ash returned to Alexander's manor, the sky was red with the rising sun. Despite the early hour, there was a storm of boots and shouts in the hall outside his chambers. He tore off his filthy clothes and paused, looking around his room, before he stuffed it all in his closet. He washed furiously in the bath, scrubbing grime and specks of blood from his skin, before he dressed in his sleeping clothes, pulling on a sweater to better hide his chest. When he opened the door, it was just to find a surprised Ramsay in front of him, fist raised to knock. Ash could barely meet her eye, and not only out of guilt. The firelocks that had been shot at Ash all night, that had blown holes in Hendrix and almost killed Finley . . .

"Source, Ash, where've you been?"

He blinked, hoping his face seemed sleepy and confused enough. "What's wrong?" he asked, but even the question made bile rise.

"An attack on McKinley." Ramsay frowned. Ash hoped it wasn't with suspicion. "We should go see Callum."

It was pathetic, Ash decided, that he was too afraid to face Callum now. "Lord Alexander—I'm still under house arrest, technically—"

"What?" Ramsay said. "Fuck Alexander." She looked at Ash as if she thought he'd been taken over by a mysterious energy, and she didn't recognize who was standing in front of her. "And fuck the house arrest. Come on. Callum needs us."

How, exactly, could Ash argue with that? He nodded, throat dry. "Okay."

✳

Ramsay led Ash through one of the manor's portal doors and into the Kendrick town house. The office was dark, mahogany-paneled walls and desk doing nothing to help lighten the space. Callum sat behind his desk, elbows on knees, when Ramsay and Ash found him. He looked up but said nothing. Ramsay moved to him, taking his hands, then wrapped her arms around Callum. His shoulders sank. He buried his face into Ramsay's neck with relief, shaking as he cried.

Ash hesitated by the door's threshold. It still felt sometimes that Ramsay and Callum knew what the other needed best and that he was only intruding; and now more than ever, Ash wasn't sure he belonged in this space, knowing he was a part of the reason Callum was hurting.

Callum breathed in and swallowed, pulling away as he wiped his face with his shoulder. "Creator, I shouldn't—"

"What?" Ramsay said with a half grin, though only concern filled her eyes. "Be human? Cry?"

"I'm a commander now."

"I didn't realize becoming a commander meant ignoring your own emotions."

But of course it did. It was why Callum had struggled so much, once, with the role he was expected to play under the Kendrick name. He had too many feelings for a family that only saw emotion as weakness.

"Crying isn't helping," Callum said, taking a shaky breath.

"You're the one who always insists we acknowledge our emotions," Ramsay said, tone teasing but worry creasing her brows.

"If I acknowledge emotion now, I also need to acknowledge my anger, and that—" Callum swallowed, cutting himself off.

"Anger is just another feeling, isn't it?" Ramsay asked. "And it's only appropriate, given what's happened."

"It won't undo the attack. It won't bring Sophie back."

Ash might as well have been punched in the gut. He took a step forward, hating that Ramsay and Callum both looked up, blinking as if they'd forgotten he was there. "Someone died?"

Callum gave a quick nod. "Sophie Galahad. Head trauma."

The girl who had been thrown into the wall by Elena, knocked unconscious . . . Ash swallowed the sick that threatened to rise. "Source. I'm sorry, Callum." He wished the older boy could know that Ash's apology wasn't only a condolence.

"She was in the class below me." Callum's brows rose as he stared at nothing. "We were always told by the professors to understand that we were training for battle, ultimately—that even as students, we had to understand the risk . . ."

Ramsay's hand was still on his shoulder. "You should rest. Do you want to come to the Downs with me? I can make you breakfast— well, I can attempt to, anyway."

Callum shook his head. "No—thank you, but I can't. I only had a moment to collect myself. Edric is at McKinley now and expects me back. I'm likely going to oversee the investigation," he added.

"The investigation?" Ash repeated, heart slowing as it pounded harder.

"Yes," Callum said. "To find the people who did this."

The older boy had continued talking, though his words had an odd echo in Ash's ears. *"Likely connected to the same group that attacked the gala . . . The same that kidnapped you, Ash . . ."*

His breath was shallow. What would Callum think, to find that Ash had been with the people who had attacked Callum's former school—killed a student, an old friend? Even the explanation that Ash had only been acting as Lord Alexander's spy felt more like an excuse.

"I have to go," Callum said. He leaned in to kiss Ramsay's cheek, then walked to Ash, still waiting at the threshold, and put a hand on the boy's shoulder with a kiss on his cheek, too. "You should be at House Alexander," he reminded Ash, though he at least didn't have his usual chiding tone.

Ash gave his sheepish grin, the corners of his mouth quivering. "It's Ramsay's fault. She told me to come."

Ramsay rolled her eyes. "With good reason."

"As long as you return," Callum said, squeezing Ash's shoulder. Ash usually welcomed Callum's warmth, the swaddling energy that felt so calm and protective. Now, only shame burned Ash's skin. He didn't deserve Callum's affection, not after this.

Once they were alone in Callum's office, Ramsay sighed, face in her hands. "Source, it feels like everything we fought to keep together is falling apart."

"That's one of the laws of the universe, isn't it?" Ash said. He sat heavily in one of the chairs in front of Callum's desk, knees suddenly weak. He meant to sound lighthearted, but his voice came out rougher—more bitter—than he expected. There was a clenching in his chest. He was angry, he realized—at both himself and at Source. "If a manifestation is meant to happen, nothing we can do will stop it."

"And what is that manifestation, exactly?" Ramsay asked. "Destruction? Chaos?"

Ramsay approached the door, hand on the knob, and pulled

it shut with a click. Ash expected Ramsay to murmur any of the portal door passwords, but she paused for one long moment. "Ash," Ramsay finally said. "Where were you tonight?"

Ash stopped his knee from bouncing. He forgot to breathe. "What do you mean?"

Ramsay's back was still, hand unmoving. "I'd gone to your chambers in House Alexander earlier, when I first heard about the attack. You weren't there. I searched the manor, looked in the Downs . . . It was only because I decided to check your room again that I found you at all."

"I'm sorry. I didn't hear you knock." Ramsay raised her chin with a silent vibration. She didn't believe Ash, that was clear. He kept going anyway. "I must've been asleep."

Ash and Ramsay had argued and fought with each other enough that Ash might've been confident, once, that the two would find their way back to each other again, even if she did learn the truth; but this? Ramsay and Callum would never forgive Ash if they found out what he'd done. And after tonight, Ash was having a difficult time seeing just how he'd learn to forgive Ramsay, too.

16

Ash could barely sleep in the days that passed; he couldn't, not when the trails of nightmares stalked him. He didn't dare mention this fear to either Callum or Ramsay. The two would only begin to insist that he call on House Adelaide again. He opted to stay locked away in his room instead, asking that meals be brought to his door, and spent every moment of his free time reading through the text hidden beneath his bed. If there was a time to find his mother—to discover a way to speak to her again—it was then. He needed her guidance, needed to know what message it was she wanted to share; and, even if it was difficult to admit, Ash wanted her comfort, too. His mother had always had a way of knowing exactly what he'd needed to hear, when she was still alive. He was convinced that whatever it was she needed to tell him would be the cure for the anxiety that stole his breath.

Draw the diagramed Source geometry pattern detailed below and light a flame with the intention that the departed return. Their energy may seem like a mirage, but they will be tied to the candle, and thus, the physical plane, until the flame goes out.

Ash thought on his intention until the candle was nothing more than melted wax and a wisp of smoke.

Find a living volunteer who is proficient in reaching the higher realms; with their energy tied to those planes, their body can be filled with the energy of the departed as well, and for a time, they will be taken over by the dead if the below steps are followed most closely. (Be aware of the risk that two conscious energies will be too much for the average body, and the volunteer may pass as well.)

Ash would never have risked another's life; and anyway, it was nearly impossible to find someone who'd be able to reach the higher realms on their own. Even Ramsay had needed his help in this.

Travel to a point along the timeline of Source's thread to find your loved one still alive, before they have passed; though your departed will not be the same as the one you have known, they will in essence hold the same energy of Source.

Ash nearly tore the page in frustration. There was no feasible way he could travel to the past on his own, and besides that, his living mother wouldn't know what message she needed to share with him.

Breathe with the pattern detailed here, each night before you sleep: six breaths in quick succession, a slow exhale of two seconds, and repeat. Think only of your intention to meet with the departed repeatedly.

Ash narrowed his eyes as he read.

If the departed wishes to contact you as well, and simultaneously holds this same intention within their energy, then the dreamworld theoretically could be a shared dimension where both parties can meet.

Ash felt a tingling of heat over his skin. Was it not true that his mother reached for him every night in his dreams?

He read the instructions again and again, then spent the rest of the day attempting to force himself to sleep—but it was no use. He tried to concentrate on the breathing pattern and his intention, but within moments of drifting into dreams, Ash would remember that he was trying to sleep, wake up with a jolt, and be forced to start all over again.

Ash decided to limit his attempts to night, to better match his body's natural sleeping patterns. He did his best to tire himself out during the day. He went for walks around the manor, exploring various rooms and offices and their shelves; he even began to take his meals in the dining hall, surrounded by Alexander's guests and visitors from other Houses, many of whom would strike up conversations with him. The dining hall was smaller than Ash expected, with a darker gold wallpaper and shining wooden floors.

The walnut table stretched across the floor, seating thirty guests easily, Ash would've guessed.

Lady Alder invited Ash to sit with her one afternoon. "Have you enjoyed the book you stole?" she asked, pleasantly enough.

He took a breath with a sheepish grin. "A lot, yes."

"Good. At least it's found some purpose in its older years."

At night, Ash's eyes felt heavy as he sank into his pillow. But when he did manage to fall asleep, only nightmares found him. A man screamed that his child had hurt no one. A girl cried as she clutched the hand of her dead mother. A boy was stabbed in a pub. He wasn't any older than Ash, but an argument had grown, his killer insisting that the boy was an alchemist—

The black orb was closer now. It sank into the crumbled earth, debris floating through clouds of smoke. A familiar scream found him—

Ash opened his eyes to the sun. He couldn't remember if he'd met his mother at all.

※

Ash was very late by the time he pulled himself from the bath and dressed for the Head of House meeting. An attendant pushed open the golden doors with a dirty look, and Ash ducked his head as he tried to sneak to his seat at the other end of the room, though many pairs of eyes followed him. Callum shook his head while Ramsay released the puff of a sigh.

"Lord Alexander," Head Val said as Ash slipped into his chair. "It might be helpful to speak with your advisor and suggest that he arrive to these meetings on time. It's most distracting for him to come through those doors when the meeting is already underway."

Charlotte tilted her head with a smile. "Is it really so distracting?" she asked. "I would've thought it within our ability to maintain focus, even when a pair of doors opens and closes."

Val huffed but said nothing else.

Lord Alexander hadn't bothered to acknowledge Ash, hadn't

even looked at him when Ash walked through the doors. He was surprised the lord hadn't sought him out in the days since the attack on McKinley, but he certainly wouldn't demand Alexander's attention. He considered himself lucky that the man hadn't decided to question Ash's involvement.

"If you're all finished," Alexander said with a clipped tone. Silence fell. "What is the next agenda point?" he asked his scribe.

The scribe sat straight in his seat. "The continued investigation of the extremist group known as the Alchemist Liberation Party."

Ash's heart stuttered as Callum stood without hesitation. Source, maybe he would've been better off staying in his room, pretending he'd forgotten about the meeting altogether.

Callum emulated his brother's expressionless tone. "The Alchemist Liberation Party has been confirmed as the group behind the attack at the gala honoring Sir Woods," he said, then paused and cleared his throat, before adding, "as well as the attack on McKinley."

Ash tightened his fists. When he glanced up, he met Ramsay's expressionless stare. She blinked and dropped her gaze.

"We're searching for a base of operations now," Callum said. "I hope to lead a contingent against that base once it's found. Our hope is to take as many prisoners as possible for interrogation," he said, "though, of course, the redguards will have to take lives if deemed necessary."

Ash struggled to look up from his shoes. His breath was caught in his chest. He wanted to shout that no one in the safe house was worthy of killing, that there was a *child* who lived there and was currently recovering from a wound caused by Ramsay's weapons. He clenched his jaw and swallowed his tongue, stiff in his chair. He jolted when Alexander spoke.

"What do you say, Sir Woods?" he asked.

Ash blinked at the back of the man's head. Everyone at the table turned to look at him. Ash was Lord Alexander's advisor, but of the meetings he had attended, this was the first time the man had asked for his opinion. "What do you mean?"

Alexander glanced over his shoulder at Ash, eyes sparkling with a humor that Ash didn't understand. "What do you think of this planned attack by House Kendrick? Will it only incite further violence from these alchemists? Perhaps some would seek revenge."

"If our attack does incite violence, then it'll be our responsibility to do what is necessary to quell the radicals," Edric said.

"Anyone accused of practicing alchemy, whether guilty or innocent, has been tortured," Alexander replied, "many killed. Practicing alchemists are starting to fight back in turn. I'm certain the various chapters of the ALP will not sit silently if their base of operations is attacked by the Houses. I think it's only fair that we pause to consider the consequences."

Ash's hands were clenched so tightly that they trembled. He tried to speak, but it only came out as a whisper. He tried again, voice louder. "Attacking an alchemist base will only make it clear to any practicing alchemist that the Houses have aligned themselves with the Lune followers."

Quiet fell in the room. Many of the stares in his direction were cold.

"If you truly do want to earn the trust of alchemists, then maybe an attack is not . . ." Ash swallowed his own words at the confused and surprised expression on Callum's face.

"And so, what?" Edric said. "According to you, we should allow an extremist group to run rampant—to attack and kill anyone they like?"

"No, of course not," Ash said, annoyance pricking his tone. "But maybe making an attempt at contact first—actually trying to speak to them, ask what they want—"

"We don't negotiate with extremists."

"—instead of rushing in and just furthering the divide—"

"Spoken like a true manipulator," Edric said.

"Sir Woods is not the only *manipulator* in the room," Ramsay said.

Tension quivered across the table. Ash's voice did, too. "If you're trying to avoid a civil war, then attacking the rebel base isn't the answer. You'll only spark a war between the Houses and alchemists instead.".

His heart fell when Callum responded. "Allowing the rebel alchemists freedom to attack as they wish isn't the answer, either." The older man only stared forward pointedly, his expression and tone now practiced. "We'll do our best to keep each member of the party alive," Callum said again. "They would be more useful that way, ultimately."

Ash didn't like Callum's choice of words. He didn't like the idea that Marlowe and Finley and Elena and Hendrix and even Riles were being *allowed* to live, only because Callum might find them useful.

Alexander spoke. "Useful for your next venture, perhaps."

Callum ducked his head and nodded briefly. "Yes, my lord."

Ash frowned, confusion tugging his brows.

"It's decided, then," Alexander said. "The attack on the base is approved. Next agenda point?"

※

When Ash returned to the comfort of his chambers, evening had already fallen. *Useful for your next venture, perhaps.* It seemed Ash wasn't the only one keeping secrets. It was ironic that he felt a pinch of hurt that Callum had kept something from him—ironic and pathetic, Ash decided, given just how much he'd betrayed Callum.

"You're usually better at noticing when someone's snuck up on you."

Ash jumped, heart thundering as he whirled around. Marlowe and Elena both stood in black shadows that fell from his wall. Cold crept toward him, a chill filling the air.

"Source," Ash said, breath caught in his chest. He should've felt relieved to realize it was only Marlowe and Elena; instead, the smallest fear pricked him. Had they figured out he was Alexander's spy? Had they come to kill him?

The moment wasn't lost on Elena, it seemed. "Do I frighten you that much, Ash?"

"Only when you've appeared in my room without any warning," he said. He lowered his voice, though he was almost certain no one lingered outside his door. "I guess I should count myself lucky that I wasn't in the middle of a bath. What're you doing here?"

"You wanted to join our group," Elena said, simply, as if this were explanation enough for why she was willing to break into the manor. She stepped to the side, gesturing to the shadow. "I'm here so that you can."

Ash's throat dried.

"Well?" Elena said. "Are you coming?"

Ash hesitated, glancing at Marlowe, who only looked back at him with raised brows. He took a breath, then stepped into the smoke and out the other side.

Ash assumed he would return to the safe house in Ironbound, but the space they walked into instead assaulted Ash's senses. It was a wide room, from what he could tell, big enough that Ash couldn't see the other end. It seemed to be perhaps the entire level of one building, though Ash had never seen a room as large as this. It felt like a field that stretched on into the horizon, though the floors and walls were concrete.

Ash looked left and right, but there was too much to see for his eyes to process all at once. A line of cots, some people asleep in them with bandages stained red around arms or legs—Source, one of them was Finley, but they were asleep. Ash stepped toward them, but Marlowe kept a firm hand on his arm, guiding him forward. "They're fine," she said. "We decided they'd get better care here instead."

"Where is 'here'?"

But she was interrupted by a laugh as they walked past a group of people, maybe as young as Ash, sparring one another with flashes of alchemy, an instructor stepping in with hands raised. There was a stall set up where fruit and a jug of water was handed over the counter, a line curving around—one person looked up and met Ash's stare. A tangle of laughter and shouts and the wails of a baby who cried. It smelled as if something burned while a spice of some kind itched his nose and a scent of sweet perfume made him want to sneeze. Someone passed with a basket, holding out bread to people who sat nearby. There were no windows. Dim lights that appeared to be powered by alchemy flickered on the walls. Ash looked up, and far above there were glass ceilings that showed a black sky.

"What is this place?" Ash asked, head turning right and left as he tried to take in everything he could.

"The head base," Marlowe said.

"We're only one chapter," Elena let him know. "There are seven total groups of the ALP that have broken off across New Anglia."

"The Alchemist Liberation Party," Marlowe explained. Ash realized it was lucky she assumed he would ask. He shouldn't have already known about the ALP.

"What're we doing here?" Ash asked, nerves building. This base was certainly something that Lord Alexander would want to hear about, something that would be helpful to Callum and his brother as well.

"I'd like to accept you as an official member," Elena said, "but the decision, ultimately, isn't up to only me. Come along."

There was a line of cots set up along the farthest wall, with piles of bedding and pillows, rugs and fabrics with colorful patterns laid out across the concrete floor. Orbs of light floated lazily around one young person as they read; another frowned in concentration as they held their hands up, bolts of electricity zapping back and forth.

Ash walked beside Elena and Marlowe, watching the people who glanced at him curiously, too. "Is everyone here a member of the party?" Ash asked.

"Not all," Elena answered. "Some opted to bring their families for safety." Ash watched as a child chased another in front of them with a squeal of laughter. "Others are registered alchemists who had received threats and were invited to seek refuge." Ash watched as an elderly woman hovered a hand over a pot, leaves unfurling. "Some were attacked and saved and brought here to recover."

"How many people are here?" Ash asked, forcing himself not to wince when he realized just how prying that sounded.

Elena didn't seem to notice. "Last I checked, there were about two hundred permanent refugees and over one hundred members who live here permanently. This is the largest base," she said when Ash's eyes widened in surprise. "It's the main head of operations, after all. There are also frequent visitors from other chapters across New Anglia."

Ash wanted to ask where, exactly, the base was physically located, but knew this would be one question too many, so he fell quiet as they continued on. There was one space that seemed just a little more isolated from all the rest. There was an oak table that might've been stolen from a manor office, paint faded and scratched, though there were no chairs. One man sat on its surface and spoke to another whose broad back faced them.

A younger woman, closer to Ash's age, seemed to have picked up on the group's energy and turned to face them as they approached. She had a larger body, similar to Callum's, with golden-brown hair and pale skin. Her waves of energy reached Ash, rolling over his skin and leaving a buzzing behind in their wake. The woman had reached out with her own energy to feel out Ash's vibrations, and though Ash wasn't sure of what she surmised, he was left knowing that she was, perhaps, one of the most powerful alchemists he'd come across. The energy he felt from her was overwhelming, the

sort that made his vision blur. She reminded Ash of his father—
was perhaps the kind of alchemist who could escape to other
dimensions on her own.

The two men looked up, noticing Ash and the others as well.

Marlowe whispered beside him. "ALP leaders."

"Elena," said the one seated on the table. He pushed off to
land on his feet. He was much thinner in comparison to the
woman beside him, with brown hair that seemed similar to hers
and ruddy cheeks. Siblings, perhaps. The man's gaze scanned
over Elena and Marlowe before it landed on and eyed Ash. "It's
been a while."

"Only a couple of weeks."

"A couple of weeks, when most chapters send an update at least
once every few days."

"Interesting," Elena said. "We fight for liberation and then
seek to control our own members."

"Asking for an *update* on your own organization is not *control*—"

"Is this *your* organization, Guthrie? I hadn't realized."

The man narrowed his eyes, but before he could speak, the one
whose back faced the rest spoke. "Enough."

His voice grumbled low enough that the air vibrated. He only
half turned, as if it would be too much effort to look fully at
them—but even with the man's face in profile, Ash recognized
him, along with the pink scar that traced across his cheek and the
corner of his mouth. The man's brow quirked as he looked at Ash,
as if he'd felt the vibration of Ash's surprise, the realization that
he'd been recognized. If this caused Baron any concern, he said
nothing about it.

"It's understandable, to want to know what is happening within
each chapter," Baron said. Ash had never met the man before, but
he'd heard plenty about him in Hedge and had seen him often
enough from afar. He'd been the leader of his own gang, though
Ash wasn't sure if it was still in operation after the attacks on
Kensington. It'd once felt like joining that gang and becoming

one of Baron's many errand boys was both Ash's and his former best friend Tobin's fate. There wasn't much other choice, for a life in Hedge.

Baron continued. "The attack on McKinley, for example. I assume that's your doing?"

"We have jurisdiction within Kensington, last I checked."

The woman raised her hands and shrugged. "A little warning for my group would've been nice, is all." Ash's brows rose in surprise, but maybe it shouldn't have been so shocking to find that there was a chapter of rebels in the city of Kensington, too. "Alchemists attack a Kendrick school, and suddenly my entire chapter is at risk for being blamed."

"I did send a notice," Elena said. "Through the network—"

"One week's time is not enough to prepare," the woman said. "We need one month, at least, to bolster our defenses and figure out an escape out of Kensington if necessary."

Elena nodded. "Fine. Understood." She took an impatient breath and gestured at the woman and the younger man who'd gotten up from the desk. "That is Gretchen and Guthrie," she said to Ash. She let her hand gesture at the final man. "And this is Baron Barrington." Ash swallowed as Elena continued speaking. "He's the *Lord Alexander* of the ALP, I suppose you could say."

Baron clearly didn't appreciate the comparison, which was perhaps why Elena had said it in the first place. His gaze narrowed as he inspected Ash without speaking, and Ash tried not to wither under his stare. But what was a gang leader doing in a place like this? Ash hadn't even thought Baron was a practicing alchemist, though if he was, it would make sense that no one knew. A man like Baron wouldn't have gone through the *proper* channels of learning alchemy and likely also didn't have a license; and wasn't it also true that many who sought power would seek to learn alchemy, too?

There was the other realization tingling over Ash as he tried to subdue the thought. Elena didn't know that Ash recognized

Baron; but if the man was here, the key leader of the ALP, then it was likely that the base of operations was also in Hedge.

Baron continued. "A lot was invested into this organization. It'd be a shame to let it all go to waste because of your poor leadership, wouldn't you say?"

"You personally made me the point in Ironbound," Elena said, "because you trusted me. We're busy with our own research, our own intel, our own battles. Stopping ourselves from moving forward just to provide *updates* would only get in the way of progress."

"One wrong move, and the Ironbound chapter could fall apart."

"One failed chapter would not mean the end of the ALP," Elena said. "You would simply send another out to replace me. Perhaps Guthrie here," she said, nodding at the younger man who glared at her still, "since he seems so eager. That's why we structured the organization the way we did, after all."

The woman named Gretchen had only watched the conversation unfold so far, but now she hopped onto the table's surface and swung her legs. "Well? Why have you graced us with your presence?"

Elena gestured at Ash. "I have a new member for your consideration."

All eyes turned to him. Baron narrowed his gaze, as if what he saw unimpressed him. "Name?" he said.

Ash swallowed. "Ashen Woods," he said, "but I go by Ash—"

Movement and breath stilled. There was only one reason for the tension that clenched in the air. Ash knew there were whispers about the boy who had been on the bridge with Gresham Hain, who had died and apparently come back to life, but he hadn't realized his name had traveled, too; but perhaps the rumors that circulated were different among the alchemists.

"Ash Woods?" Baron repeated, voice low.

Ash nodded.

"I knew your father," Baron said. "Not well," he added as he tilted his head to the side as he considered Ash.

Ash was surprised only because he knew his father to be an elitist; the man would have looked down on someone like Baron, but then again, maybe Gresham Hain would've been able to join forces with his *lessers* when it came to a cause like this.

"Your father wasn't interested in small talk nor sharing many details about his personal life when we were focused on our work," Baron explained. "He did mention you a few times, however."

Ash hadn't considered the possibility that the ALP hadn't been founded only since the attacks on Kensington. "My father never mentioned . . ."

"No, of course not," Baron said. "Why would he? We were in our early stages still, and he wouldn't have risked a leak for what we were building." Baron's gaze swept from Ash's shoes to the top of his head. "Hain seemed convinced that you would make the next leader of our organization," he said, "once you were properly trained."

Yes, Ash's father had said time and again that he wanted Ash to be his heir, his legacy—to lead the revolution of alchemists. This was what the man had meant, then. Hain had planned to destroy Kensington, the Houses, and see his son take over the rebellion, maybe foreseeing that Hain would be too overwhelmed by the Book of Source's energy to be grounded to earthly matters anymore. Things hadn't exactly gone to plan, luckily. Ash decided to keep to himself that he would never willingly take the role his father had expected him to.

"So, Ashen Woods himself wants to join the Ironbound chapter?" Gretchen asked. Her grin flashed. "He's a little scrawny, isn't he?"

"That doesn't have anything to do with his alchemic power," Elena said.

"No, but the ability to take a punch in the jaw does," Guthrie replied. "We can't accept him just because he's Gresham Hain's son."

"Yet you're the ones who've been hounding me to up the Ironbound numbers."

"You represent the second-largest city and yet have the second-smallest chapter."

"The number of members doesn't equate to success," Elena said, voice steady. "We've operated a number of missions and have contributed to the ALP more than any other."

"Why *have* you brought Ashen Woods to me, then," Baron said, "if it isn't only to raise your numbers, as you say?"

Elena took and held a breath. "He's powerful," she said, "and useful. He's currently stationed in House Alexander's manor. He has access to inside information that we don't, and he has ties to House Kendrick as well. He can warn us of any oncoming attacks."

"And you trust him?"

"I wouldn't have brought Ash to you if I didn't."

Baron seemed to consider this. "Gretchen."

The woman raised a palm at Ash. He took a step back, but Elena's look froze him in place. Gretchen smiled as she approached, her palm reaching for Ash's face. "Don't worry. It won't hurt." She shrugged. "Much."

Her hand stopped an inch away from Ash's nose. Heat emanated and grew. Vibrations wavered over Ash's skin, a dull ache starting in his neck and spreading to the back of his skull. He clenched his eyes and teeth. He *felt* her reaching through the caverns of his brain, like a worm inching through his cells—but Callum had trained him against this, back when Ash was still his prisoner many months ago, natural mind reader that he was; he had helped teach Ash to imagine the walls built around his thoughts, impenetrable and inaccessible—

"He's hiding *something*," Gretchen said. Her voice sounded far away as Ash gasped, her energy snatched from his skull, leaving behind pain that throbbed. "Something about alchemists, I mean. But the thoughts were cloudier than usual." She squinted, as if this alone were cause for suspicion. Ash could only assume Gretchen wasn't used to having her access to minds blocked.

Ash's audience turned to him. He couldn't hesitate. That, too, would be seen as suspicious. "Of course I'm hiding something about alchemists," he said. "I've joined a rebel group under Lord Alexander's nose while I've been hired as his personal advisor. I'm lying to everyone who trusts me."

"Are we supposed to feel sorry for the kid?" Guthrie asked. "That's not enough of a reason to let him in."

"I've given up a lot for this cause already," Ash said, ignoring him. "My peace of mind. My integrity. I can barely look the people I love in the eye." His voice grew louder as he spoke. Ash hadn't meant to be so honest in the moment. He swallowed, lowering his voice again. "So I would really, truly appreciate it if strangers stopped accusing me of betraying them," he said, "and started focusing on the traitor you already have hiding in your group."

The inspiration from such a speech must have been delivered by Source itself; it certainly hadn't felt like Ash's words, anyway. Either that, or it had come from desperation. His words lingered in the air as Baron and Elena exchanged glances, then looked to Gretchen.

Her face had soured. "He's telling the truth, as far as I can tell," she said.

"He may not look like it, but Ash is a powerful alchemist," Elena said. "He was a great help on our latest mission against McKinley. He'll be useful in the future, too."

Baron clenched his jaw so that a muscle jumped. "The boy will be your responsibility. If he turns—"

"I'll take full accountability," Elena said. Marlowe's breath caught beside Ash. To him, this could only mean one thing: If he was found to have betrayed the ALP, it wasn't only his life on the line now.

"Fine." The man nodded as he inspected Ash once more, as if searching for any evidence that this was truly Gresham Hain's son and might just be the one to save them all. But, then, without another word, Baron turned his back on them again, a simple dismissal. Before any of the three could leave, though, Baron spoke behind them.

"The leak," he said. "This has been a problem since before Woods even arrived, as he's so helpfully mentioned."

"We're doing what we can to suss the traitor out," Elena said. "But if even Gretchen's questioning showed no results . . ."

"We could just dismantle the Ironbound chapter," Guthrie offered with a straight face, though his energy vibrated with glee. "Get rid of the current members. Start again. That would take care of the traitor problem, wouldn't it?"

"There isn't any definitive proof that the leak is in Ironbound. Who's to say that the traitor isn't based in Glassport?" Elena said, eyes flashing. "It'd be easy enough to frame a chapter."

Baron held up a hand. "This discussion is pointless. I expect you to find your own leak, Elena, before you complete any other mission. Understood?"

Ash could better see why Elena was slow to return to the head of operations. She narrowed her eyes, but nodded. "Yes. Understood."

17

The return to the Ironbound safe house was quiet and inexplicably tense. Elena seemed to have a lot on her mind after the meeting with Baron; Ash did, too, now knowing that the man behind the largest gang in Hedge was the leader of the alchemist rebels. Source, this was precisely the sort of thing Ash would be expected to go running to tell Lord Alexander. Sharing this information could be the downfall of the entire movement. Surely the redguards would know how to have Baron traced, captured, perhaps executed, upending all the chapters.

"Marlowe will set you up in one of the spare rooms," Elena said once they'd stepped through the inky blackness and into the safe house again. "I know you won't be able to stay here permanently like the other members—your Lord Alexander would be suspicious, after all—but it'd be good for you, still, to have a space of your own, too."

Ash nodded his understanding and tried not to appear too eager to leave—he was exhausted, his body weak with the nervousness that had racked through him for hours—but before Marlowe could move to take him, Elena raised a hand. "Before you go, I need your help with another mission."

Elena stood in front of a wall and placed a palm against it. She gestured at Ash to join her. He frowned but walked to her side.

"Put your hand on the wall," she said.

He did. A cold sweat prickled over Ash's skin. He shivered, heart thumping harder, though he wasn't sure why. He jolted when black shadows began to curl from the panels. He looked down to see those shadows twisting around his legs, too. He'd thought them to be a substance closer to fog, but he could see the particles stretching and waving and tightening again, as if black molecules of steam.

"Don't panic," Elena said. "Stay still."

"What is it?" Ash whispered.

Marlowe watched from across the room and answered for Elena: "Chaos."

Ash yanked his hand back. The shadows withdrew. Elena only looked at him out of the corner of her eye, as if she'd expected this reaction from him.

"What do you mean 'chaos'?"

Chaos was the original spark, the energy that became aware of itself and exploded into Source—existence, the universe. Still, chaos also continued in its original form, theorized to remain as a layer beneath all that could be seen—an energy that alchemists could draw power from, though it was an uncontrollable and unpredictable force. The idea of chaos had always tempted Ash, but his own energy was wild enough; and besides that, he'd thought chaos was unseen, invisible. He'd never witnessed chaos like *this*.

"Something's happened," Elena said, as if hearing his thoughts aloud. "Chaos energy has never been this dense, not so much that we can perceive it even in our physical reality."

"But how is that possible?" Ash said, voice hushed.

Marlowe spoke. "Hain—he did something, I'm not sure what. But reading the Book of Source, gaining that much power . . ."

Ash frowned as he watched Elena hold her palm up. The black swirled around her skin, shadow flickering like smoke from a flame. Ash realized it wasn't only that the shadows blocked his view of her. As he stared into the inky darkness, he realized there simply wasn't anything there, as if pieces of her had vanished from his vision. As the chaos swirled, snaking around her hand, Elena's skin returned. Ash hated the curiosity that bubbled. He stepped closer, heat building in his chest. He wanted to know more. He wanted to touch it, to see what chaos felt like.

"But chaos—it's *nonexistence*," Ash said. "It's the original spark of Source. How could it be here, in our physical reality?"

"The fact that chaos *is*, that we can talk about it at all, means it does exist," Elena argued. "Chaos was the first beat of consciousness, aware of its own presence, before it organized into the physical realities and infinite dimensions of the universe. Even the idea of *nonexistence* suggests that there is something more, something for Source to expand into, to create."

She was right, Ash knew, but still: "How is it *here*?"

"I think it's a byproduct of Hain's attacks," Elena said. "He used so much energy that he ripped through Source, the very material of our universe, and now chaos is leaking through. That's my theory, at least."

Ash turned to Marlowe. "What do you think?"

She took a breath. "That this was exactly what Hain intended."

The moment she said those words, Ash knew it was true. His father had been filled with Source energy; he would've been able to see the past and future and present as one, would've been able to see through the threads of the universe and into parallel universes and their infinite realms. Other versions of Hain in other universes would have seen Ash's father, too, and they could have acted together, ripping apart the fabric of existence. If chaos was leaking into their physical reality, then it was because Gresham Hain had wished for it to happen. A final parting gift from his father, perhaps.

"But chaos is dangerous," Ash said. The words felt hollow, like something he was supposed to say as any responsible alchemist would, rather than something he truly felt.

"Yes, very," Elena agreed, "if not handled properly."

"How do you handle *chaos energy* properly?"

"The same as when using your alchemy," she said, as if this was simple enough. "Some can see Source energy. You can, too, can't you? The flickers of light that shine in the air, the energy that fills every existing creation. We can manipulate this energy with our alchemy—heal and create and transform objects in our reality. Though we haven't been able to see it like *this*, not until now, chaos energy isn't much different, really, at the heart of it all."

"Only that it's more difficult to control," Ash said.

"This energy is unfiltered, that is true. With this chaos, you'd have more energy than you've ever experienced fueling your alchemy. You use Source and chaos energy in exactly the same way: You imagine what you would like, and you keep your intention clear."

Elena held out her hand invitingly again; Ash hesitated, then reached a palm to hover over hers. The chaos immediately reached for him, like oil floating through water. A string of black snaked over his fingers. He turned his palm over, and the void pooled in his hand like ink. He stared into its depths and saw nothing, felt like he could look at the chaos with a microscope, and that through its lens, he would find an entirely different universe sitting in the palm of his hand.

Knowing what it was now, he understood the dread he'd felt every time he stepped through one of Elena's portals. It was the same one that filled him when he felt too close to chaos when performing alchemy: the fear that he would lose himself to it. But there was the other side of the chaos, too, that was just as familiar. His hand felt warm, then hot. He started to glow. The true power of existence rushed in his veins and drummed through his heart, the understanding that there was no Creator, for he *was* the Creator—

The chaos sank into him. Ash's hand throbbed for several heartbeats before the ache faded. He gaped at Elena and Marlowe both, but neither seemed concerned.

"Intention," she said. "That chaos is a part of the original fragment that I used to give everyone access to this space from anywhere they wish. I've now included you in this, too. If you ever want to return to this house, you only need to place a hand against any wall and think your desire to come. You'll be able to walk through and arrive in any of the rooms you imagine."

Using intention with the energy of Source would never have been powerful enough to bring Ash back to the safe house with his alchemy alone. He would've needed a portal door or would've had to learn how to materialize, like Marlowe. It felt almost like this chaos energy was a cheat of sorts, a wish granted for any alchemic intention. Ash's pride would've liked to have learned alchemy the true way, the hard way—but maybe this didn't matter much, with a state on the edge of war.

"Does Baron know about this?" Ash asked, though he assumed not. It seemed Baron Barrington's main motivator was to keep control over each chapter. Ash didn't think the gang leader would much like any person under him having access to so much power.

"No," Elena said. "And I don't mean for him to find out." She hesitated, maybe wanting to choose her words carefully, before she continued. "I'm sure you can understand that there are some who might claim they want freedom for all, without quite realizing they only want power for themselves. If Baron learned about this chaos, its properties and potential, I'm not convinced he would continue to focus on the ALP's mission. The rebellion would fall apart."

Even in Hedge, Baron Barrington had been known for creating the largest gang that reflected the Houses of New Anglia, with the supposed mission of allowing opportunity for its people that the elite did not provide; but Baron had taken advantage of people like Ash, in some ways further running the city into the ground while he lived like a king.

"You said that you found this chaos?" Ash asked, still staring at his now-empty palm.

"A small drop," Elena said. "Too small to do much damage, but it begs to suggest, doesn't it? If there is one fragment of chaos like this, then there are probably more."

The black orb, as large as the moon itself, crashing into the earth.

Elena continued. "These fragments are pieces of the chaos leaking into our reality. They've manifested into what look like

miniature globes or a child's marbles. I've consumed two orbs."
She swallowed. A pulse of curiosity made Ash's mouth water.
He wondered what consuming a fragment of chaos would be
like, *feel* like, but Elena said nothing about this as she continued. "One has been used for the portals I create and the access I
give to others. The chaos still shows itself, whenever those portals are in use. The other orb I consumed helped me better my
illusion alchemy."

"What is it like?" Ash asked. "When you consume a fragment,
what happens?"

Elena hesitated. "The power when you consume these fragments, Ash—the rush is intoxicating, I can't deny that. It can be
addicting, if you're not careful."

He had the feeling there was more Elena could share, but she
chose not to in that moment. Ash bit his lip. "Even the strongest
alchemist could lose themselves to the chaos, if they use too much
of it. That's what every text on chaos energy has said, anyway."

"You would know about feeling uncontainable, I suppose."

Ash closed his mouth for a moment, then took a breath. "You
said you wanted my help."

"Yes," Elena replied. "These fragments have been scattered
across the state. From what I can see, the origin point is a tear
in the fabric of physical reality above Kensington, where chaos
energy has been seeping through."

Ash thought of his father, flickering in and out of reality as
he'd hovered above the city, moments before the firestorm.

"This leak will eventually become a flood," Elena said. "That
much chaos energy? It could tear this physical reality apart, starting with New Anglia. We need to find as many fragments as possible. I want your help to find them."

Ash shook his head. "How would I be able to help with that?"

"I'm certain Alexander is aware of these fragments, too."

Ash blinked at this; the lord had never mentioned the possibility of chaos to him.

"He may well already be on the search for fragments himself. We need to find as many as we can before Alexander does, before Baron becomes aware of chaos, too, along with every other alchemist in New Anglia."

"What will you do when you've found them?" Ash asked.

"We'll use the chaos energy to organize a new intention," Elena said. "We'll stitch the tear left by your father. We'll save New Anglia—potentially our entire physical reality."

Ash was certain there was more that Elena didn't say. He didn't believe she only wanted the fragments for unselfish reasons; he wouldn't have been surprised to find that, after saving their physical reality, there would also happen to be a few extra fragments just for Elena's personal use.

She didn't seem to notice Ash's doubt. "Do you understand your mission, Ash?"

He nodded. What other choice did he have? "Yes."

"Good." She gave him a soft smile. "You should get back, before anyone realizes you're gone."

※

Marlowe walked Ash to one of the rooms on the second floor, empty except for an old mattress pushed into the corner and a dresser splintering against the wall. The space reminded Ash of his old Hedge apartment. It gave him more comfort than the numerous House chambers he'd been forced to live in, at least.

Ash had hesitated to speak as he followed her up the stairs and down the creaking hall, but once the two were alone in the room, he said what had been building in his throat. "I never thanked you," he said. "For defending me, I mean, after . . ." He had a hard time saying the name of the school that'd brought so much pain in recent days.

Marlowe kept her back to him. "I almost didn't," she said, voice clipped with anger. "I felt the same way as Riles. You shouldn't have argued for the reds' lives."

"You promised there wouldn't be any fighting. That was the only reason I went at all."

"You stopped me from killing the student who first saw us," Marlowe said, spinning to him again. "That student alerted others. You saved a person who would not save us in turn. Fine, I suppose, if you'd like to risk your life—but mine was on the line, too. Finley's. All of ours."

Ash couldn't meet her eye. "Why bother to defend me at all, then?"

"Because I also believe everything I told Elena, against my better judgment," Marlowe muttered. "I believe you really do want to make up for what your father's done."

Ash hesitated. "You know that this isn't a good idea," he said. "Finding chaos—trying to contain it, to use it, no matter if it's for a good reason or not. It won't go well, Marlowe."

"What other choice do we have?" she asked. "Either we allow things to stay as they are, doing nothing to stop the tear in the fabric, or . . ."

Ash didn't need her to finish that sentence. "Do you really think it'll work?" His father had been powerful when he created the tear, as powerful as Source itself. It would take an equal amount of power to repair the damage Hain had done.

"With enough chaos energy, yes," Marlowe said. "It'll be difficult, of course, but not impossible." She sighed. "Sometimes I think the only way to fix everything that's happened would be to start over. Begin again. We've tangled ourselves into such a mess that the knot can't be undone."

"Anything can be untangled."

"Not everything." Marlowe placed a hand to the wall.

18

Ash had been up all night, with only hours until dawn by the time he returned to his chambers in House Alexander. He twisted and turned in bed, thoughts of his father and images of a pale Finley in a cot and memories of inky chaos flickering through him.

He knew he needed to sleep. He would need his energy in the coming days, if he was really going to help Elena with his new mission, but fear filled his lungs. His nightmare was real. The orb in the sky, crashing to earth—

And how long would they have? Elena estimated months, but if he and the rebels couldn't find enough pieces of chaos . . . What if her theory was wrong, and there was no possible way to undo what his father had done? Ash would've preferred to stay in blissful ignorance than learn he was witnessing the end of the world.

Even worse, Ash couldn't go to the people he most wanted to seek for comfort. He couldn't tell Ramsay and Callum, couldn't risk either of them spilling the secrets of the ALP to Edric and destroying everything Elena planned, couldn't risk giving up his role as Alexander's spy—and anyway, maybe he didn't deserve their energy, their time and love. Perhaps it would've been better, now, to go to Alexander about the rebels with everything he knew, but even lying in bed, staring up at the ceiling, Ash shook his head to himself. Regardless of which side Ash was on, he knew without any doubt that a man like Easton Alexander could not get his hands on fragments of chaos. He was exactly the type to be enticed by so much power. Lord Alexander, and any secret plan he hid from Ash, would become unstoppable.

※

The black orb had spread like ink staining across paper. It filled the sky, chunks of the earth crumbling and breaking apart, shaking beneath Ash's feet. The ground cracked down into the earth's embers, an explosion of heat searing through the wind that carried his mother's scream—

The ropes bit into her wrists, the fire burning her eyes—

The boy had been alive for three years, but his mother wouldn't stop insisting he wasn't her child, he was a trick of alchemy and her real baby had been *stolen*—

A man was made to kneel. He grunted as the backs of his legs were kicked. He refused to show his fear. He wouldn't give them the pleasure.

"Why do you keep books on alchemy at all?" one said.

The man looked up into the eyes of his accuser. They'd lived down the road from each other for nearly ten years now. He remembered when the person in front of him had been a child with a missing-tooth smile, covered in mud. "I'm a member of House Alder," he said, voice unshaken. "It's my duty to be a keeper of literature. That can, at times, include texts on alchemy."

"Even when it's texts that help manipulators kill?" another in the crowd demanded.

"I only see one group of killers before me," Mr. Brown replied. He received a boot to the cheek, laughter and shouts of approval rising.

He grunted as he struggled back onto his knees. His glasses were shattered on the ground. He released a heavy sigh and looked to the sky. This was it, then. "There's something I've realized over the years," he said, though no one was listening. "The language of hate is always the same, no matter the side one believes they're on."

Mr. Brown was yanked to his feet and dragged across dirt. He heard someone crying for him, asking that the others stop. He would hold on to that bit of mercy. A rope was slung over a tree branch. He didn't fight. He knew there wasn't any point. "And even this is Source," he said.

White ash rained from the sky, drifting across the city's remains. Wind whipped around his feet, and in the sky, the black sun fell toward him—

His mother's hands were warm. A palm pressed against his cheek. "Find me," she said.

Ash's eyes blinked opened. Sunlight poured through his balcony windows. He raised fingers to his face, where tears had fallen in his sleep. His mother's hand had felt so real, so tangible, that his skin still hummed with her energy.

A knock on the door made Ash wipe his cheeks with the heels of his palms. "Sir Woods?" a muffled voice called. "Lord Alexander has requested a meeting with you."

The clock on the wall read ten minutes after one. Ash forced himself to his feet. He pulled on his binder, lacing up the sides, and yanked on a fresh shirt and pair of slacks, the most effort he was willing to show the Head of New Anglia.

He was led to the dining room, a wide space with white paneled walls and golden tile. The glass table spanned the length of the room, long enough for more than twenty people to sit, though when Ash entered, it was only him and Lord Alexander inside. The attendant who escorted him slammed shut the doors behind him.

Alexander sipped tea at the head of the table. "Would you like anything to eat? You're looking thinner than usual."

It was lunchtime, and Ash hadn't even had breakfast yet, but he shook his head. The sooner he could get away from Alexander, the better.

The lord shrugged, as if to say, *Suit yourself.* "What's your update?" he asked. "You were at the school, I suppose?"

Ash ignored the fear that stabbed his chest. "Yes, of course I was—it was a chance to risk my life by 'proving my loyalty,' as you said," Ash said. He hadn't meant to sound so bitter.

"And did you? Prove your loyalty, I mean."

Ash chewed the inside of his cheek. "For most," he said. "There's one in particular who still doesn't trust me."

"But the others in the group do?" Alexander said. "That's quite the feat."

Shame licked Ash's insides. "I don't consider lying and betraying trust to be a feat."

"Hm," Alexander said. "You haven't been a part of this society long enough, then." He offered Ash a smile before asking, "Did you learn anything new?"

Telling Alexander that Baron was the head of the Alchemist Liberation Party would mean the end of the rebels, Ash was almost certain of it. Yet when he opened his mouth to speak, he couldn't force the words out.

"You're hesitating," Alexander noted. "Not something I would expect for a hired spy."

It was his duty, his responsibility, to betray the rebels.

"What is it, Sir Woods?" he asked. "Surely you've learned something useful."

Elena had said Alexander was aware of the chaos and was searching for it just the same as her. Ash wondered if Alexander had already been successful in finding orbs, if he'd already consumed a fragment himself, and used it for his own purposes. What would the lord's intention be?

"The attack on McKinley," Ash said. "We were expected. The redguard students already knew we were coming. Someone leaked that information to House Kendrick or the school itself."

Whose hands were more dangerous when fueled by chaos? Elena claimed to work for the benefit of alchemists, but Ash realized he didn't know Alexander's motivations at all. Why would the man desire the energy of chaos when he couldn't even practice alchemy himself?

"I'm surprised you didn't inform me of the attack," Alexander said, "or at least attempt to send a warning. It's a good thing the students were aware and prepared."

Ash opened his mouth and hesitated, then said, "I couldn't. If I raised the alarm, the radicals would've known I betrayed them."

Alexander simply hummed.

"Is there another spy?" Ash outright asked. "Do you have someone else working for you besides me? I think I deserve to know."

"Why would I need two spies?" Alexander asked lightly. "Maybe a redguard managed to learn that information themselves."

Ash gripped his hands into fists on his lap. "It was a fight that could've been avoided. The student who died—"

"Sophie Galahad," Alexander said. "A shame, truly. I heard she had a lot of promise."

"And now Callum is searching for whoever was behind the attack."

"Is that what you're afraid of?" Alexander asked. "That Commander Kendrick will learn the truth about you?"

Ash hated admitting his vulnerability. "Will immunity be given to me if he does?" Though he asked this, Ash knew there were too many blurred lines. Even if Alexander defended him and said Ash had only acted on his orders, Ash had still played a hand in Sophie Galahad's death. Callum's forgiveness was his alone to give.

"Timing," Alexander said. "It will matter when the truth is revealed, ultimately. Too soon, and certain members of the Houses would be displeased to learn I'd employed you as a spy, working alone. That would cause more conflict between the Houses than is worth at such a fragile time."

"You'd let the reds lock me away?" he said.

"Yes, if necessary," Alexander said. "And I would ask that you also keep the knowledge that you worked under my orders to yourself." He tilted his head. "It'd be for the best, then, if you aren't caught as my informant at all. Wouldn't you agree?"

Ash couldn't answer the man, not with the anger that gripped his throat. It'd never been clearer than now that this man was not Ash's ally, and even worse, Ash felt trapped. He'd gone too far along with Alexander's play to pull out now.

"Is there anything else to report?" Alexander asked.

"No. There's nothing else."

Lord Alexander was silent long enough that Ash was certain the man didn't believe his lie; but still, he said nothing about it.

19

The best part of having access to the Ironbound base, Ash decided, was no longer feeling trapped and forced into doing nothing but stare at a blank wall for hours on end. He brought a couple of books to help fill his time and placed a palm against his chamber's wallpaper panel. He thought on his intention to access his room in Ironbound and stepped through the cold smoke.

Marlowe sat cross-legged on her mattress, reading, when he poked his head through the threshold. "Wasn't expecting to see you so soon," she said as she turned a page.

He flopped onto the floor in front of her, dropping the books beside him. "How is Finley?"

Marlowe reached for the copy on the history of early alchemy, flipping it open and skimming a page. "They're still resting at the main base," Marlowe said. "Elena didn't ask you to come, did she?" She put the book down again.

"No. I just don't have anything else to do."

"You're only here because there's nothing else to do? I feel so special." She sighed and folded a page of her own book to bookmark her spot, hurting Ash's heart—he hated to see pages folded and spines cracked. "Why don't you go bother your partners instead?"

Callum had been pulled away in his investigation; he spent most of his days at McKinley now, gathering evidence and interviewing students. Ramsay still had classes to teach. "They're busy," Ash said, sitting forward and playing with his boot's shoelaces. "They usually are."

"Paradise isn't so perfect after all?"

Ash didn't think Callum or Ramsay especially would much appreciate it if he complained to Marlowe of all people about how lonely he was in their relationship; and besides, though the three were partners, that didn't mean it was Callum and Ramsay's responsibility to entertain him daily. "It doesn't matter."

"And how do you know *I'm* not busy?" Marlowe asked, though her slow smile suggested otherwise.

"Are you?"

"There haven't been any new orders from Elena, though I have the feeling she's planning something. She just won't share what that is with the rest of us yet."

It went unspoken, the reason why she kept this information to herself. Ash lowered his voice. "You haven't had any luck in finding the traitor, then?"

"Elena is certain it's not actually anyone from our base," Marlowe said, "but that it's a member of another chapter trying to sink us. So much for being united in our cause."

Ash frowned. His father had wanted Ash to be the one to unite a rebellion of alchemists. The thought seemed impossible, when most didn't even trust Ash, and with reason. "I've been thinking about the McKinley attack," Ash said. "You used illusion alchemy, right?"

Marlowe nodded. "Elena taught me. I'm nowhere near as good as her, of course."

Ash bit his lip. "Do you think you could teach me, too?"

"It isn't easy, and I'm not the best at it."

"That's okay. Knowing even a little might be helpful. Better than not knowing any at all."

Marlowe stood, shaking out her hands. "All right. Illusion alchemy is tier four. It's actually similar to creation, when I think about it, so you might have an easier time with it."

"You're pretty good at creation alchemy, too," Ash noted.

"It never came to me easily, though. I think of illusion as a mixture of creation and alteration. You first have to think of the makeup of the light and air itself in front of what it is you'd like to create an illusion of—that's all it is, really, the altering of the light in front of another's eye. But to succeed at that, you need creation: to think of the image you'd like to transcribe, altering the light to change what the viewer sees. Like this."

Marlowe took a breath, and a mirage shimmered in front of her—the altering of the air and light, Ash realized, along with a heating of alchemy. Sparks of golden light danced along her skin as her face seemed to change into his own. A near-perfect image stared back at him, brows raised expectantly.

"You try," Marlowe said.

Ash stood, took a breath, and focused on the air and light in front of his face. It was more difficult than he realized, to imagine the makeup and existence of each molecule and particle he could not see in front of him—harder still to then imagine the shifting of each into the image he had in mind.

Marlowe, still with Ash's face, laughed. "It's a good effort."

Ash looked in a mirror hanging from her door and saw a skewed version of Marlowe. One eye was significantly lower than the other, and a nostril was missing. He dropped the heaviness and heat, then watched as the air in front of his face shimmered and his own image appeared again. "That's harder than it looks."

"For a first time, it's a pretty good job," Marlowe said, dropping her own illusion. She sat back onto the mattress. Ash sat, too.

"Source," Marlowe said, lying down and staring up at the ceiling. There was more than one kind of leak at the base, apparently; mold had started to spread. "I'm looking forward to a day when I can just rest. When I don't have to fight anymore."

She'd been fighting her entire life, Ash realized. He didn't know what her childhood had been like at the Lune estate, but he could only assume it wasn't exactly peaceful. He was curious, and not only for Marlowe's experiences; his mother had never described her early life as an orphan in Lune, before Hain came and forced her to work for him, too.

"What was it like?" he asked. "At the Lune estate, I mean."

Marlowe released a great sigh.

Ash put up his hands. "I'm sorry. It's okay if you don't want to—"

"It's fine," she said shortly. "Life in Lune was like what anyone might expect. I was yelled at, beaten. Other kids were . . ." She swallowed, still staring up at the ceiling. "It was amusing to me then, though looking back on it, it's not so funny now—but I would be forced to stand on my feet for hours at a time and listen to Head Peterson Lune's teachings on love. He'd profess that we are all worthy of love in the eyes of Sinclair Lune and the Creator, but then would turn around and pass judgment on anyone he decided was not as worthy as him."

"The Lune teachings have always seemed hypocritical to me."

"Oh, no," Marlowe said, shaking her head. "The teachings are clear. They're actually beautiful, I think—the real teachings, I mean, and not just Lune followers' sermons."

Ash was surprised to hear these words come from Marlowe's mouth. He hugged his knees to his chest and listened.

"Sinclair Lune apparently left behind scripts that described energy as being made of love," she said, "and that we in this physical realm have the ability and choice to act with love toward others. When we don't, we ultimately create a realm of fire, burning ourselves in a self-made hell."

Ash rested a cheek against one of his knees.

"See, it's a common misinterpretation," Marlowe said. "I would know, because I had to read those forsaken scripts more times than I can count—but the original teachings foretold of a world burned by fire not because of our sins, but because we did not act with love toward one another. I look at Peterson Lune and the other Lune followers and see how they treated others with hate. I think about how they're creating that very same hell on Earth now. But aren't I doing the same?" she asked Ash. "I don't look to Lune followers with love. I hate them," she said. "I hate what they've done to alchemists. I hate how they would treat me—beat me, kill me—if given the chance. It's almost like a riddle, the scripts Sinclair Lune left behind. How do we figure out how to love someone who hates us? How do we learn to stop our world from burning in a self-made hell?"

Ash sat back, considering. "I don't know what the answer is," he eventually admitted.

"I don't, either," Marlowe said.

Both were quiet for some time. Marlowe eventually offered Ash one of her books from her stack. He hesitated, then picked up his father's, though he'd already read it several times, and sat with his back against the wall, both reading in silence.

"The man—the one claiming he's Sinclair Lune," Ash said. Marlowe glanced up. "He doesn't really seem to be the type to follow those scriptures."

"Yeah," Marlowe said. "I didn't think so, either."

※

It was evening by the time Ash returned. He sorely hoped no one had come knocking, but if he was questioned by a redguard or visitor or Alexander himself, he figured he could simply say he'd been wandering the halls. *You must've just missed me.* He'd eaten at the base with Marlowe, so he didn't go to dinner before he washed and changed into his sleeping clothes. Ash wasn't particularly tired, not yet, but he still had his own goal, after all.

He lay on his back and closed his eyes. He was more tired than he'd thought. He already started to feel himself drift—but there was something different, this time. The heaviness felt like a weighted blanket, pushing him down into the mattress. As he continued to breathe and think his intention again and again, he started to see patterns. Source geometry filtered behind his lids, complex structures he could make no sense of, a group of beings made of light, turning—

He was in a room. It was all white, with only a single bed.

The room itself was familiar, Ash thought. One from his night-mares.

"Do you remember?"

Ash turned. Behind him was not his mother, as he had hoped so desperately to see.

Gresham Hain was dressed in all white, too. His shoulders and back were straight, familiar unimpressed scowl on his face. "Well?" he said.

Ash frowned. "Do I remember what?"

"That this is only a dream."

The colors that exploded around Ash raced around him, a flood of light that was too vibrant for the physical realm, a rush of energy that reminded him that he was but a fragment of the energetic existence that was Source—

He blinked.

He was in an endless field. Grass swayed. White flowers bloomed. The blue sky above wavered like a mirage, and just be-yond that he could see the blackness of space and its infinite stars. Ash's father stood only several feet away in front of him, arms behind his back as he peered up at the sky, too.

"Are you surprised?" Hain said without looking at his son.

Surprised wasn't the word, quite. Numb, perhaps—disgusted. Disappointed. Enraged. "Why're you here? I didn't ask to see you."

Hain glanced at him. "Have you considered the possibility that you're lying to yourself?"

Ash shook his head. "I'm pretty sure I wanted to see my mother, not the man responsible for the deaths of hundreds of thousands of people."

"You spoke your intention to see your mother," Hain said. "But you know it well, don't you? Energy doesn't lie. You can tell your-self of a desire all you like, but if beneath those words there is another truth . . ."

But it was impossible. Ash couldn't have preferred to meet with

Hain over his mother, not when he detested the man who had caused so much devastation; not when he'd missed his mother so desperately, had ached to see her and speak with her and hear her comforting words again. But even as Ash thought this, the truth settled, souring his tongue. He didn't miss his father, at least that much was true; but Ash also wanted answers from him.

He couldn't admit this. He looked around at the peace of the fields. "I would've thought you'd been chained up and tortured by the people who died in your massacre."

Hain puffed a smile. "Most of the people who died by my hand have already chosen the peace of Source. Others linger out of curiosity to see what happens next. Some have already returned to Earth with new lives. Very few choose to be tethered to the energy of hate once they've left their physical bodies. It all feels a little pointless, you see."

"And you?" Ash said. "You were the most hateful man I'd ever met."

"I never hated anyone nor anything, Ash," Hain said. It struck Ash then: This was his father's first time saying his correct name. "I made choices that I thought were best for the evolution of our human species. Right or wrong, it doesn't quite matter now."

Ash gestured at the fields. "So you wreak havoc and cause suffering, then get to spend eternity in peace?"

"It isn't my place to explain why I might deserve peace and love as much as anyone else in the eyes of Source. But then again, you would remember that, too, wouldn't you?"

Ash's bubbling frustration faded. Yes, he remembered well what it was like to have returned to Source. It was uncomplicated, there: no anger and hatred and judgment and fear, only endless love for himself and the others who had played a part in his life. Perhaps it wasn't Ash's place, either, to decide whether another deserved that same love or not.

"Why am I here?" he asked. "Why *you*, and not—"

"Samantha is with you constantly; I'm sure some part of you is already aware that she watches you, guides you, assists where she can. She asked you to find her."

"Then why isn't she here? Why won't she come to me when I look for her in the higher realms?"

"The decision is her own," Hain said simply. "Maybe it was only a prompt that would lead you to where you are now. Maybe she knew you needed to meet with me one day, but that you would never willingly reach out to me on your own."

Ash didn't want to believe it was true. The number of dreams his mother had appeared in, screaming his name, couldn't have been only a ploy to force him to meet with his father instead. "She wouldn't have tricked me like that."

"I'm not sure she would ever mean to trick you. But she has been dead for some time now. The longer an energy is untethered from the physical, the more symbolic their communication becomes. For them, life and death—it's all the same dream."

Ash's hands rose to his face, wiping the tears that'd built in frustration. It was humiliating, that he should begin to cry in front of his father. "I have nothing to say to you."

"Don't you?" Hain asked. "Not even questions about the dreams you've received?"

Ash dropped his hands.

"It was me," Hain said, "who sent you those dreams. The dreams of chaos, the black orb falling from the sky, that was your mother—but I wanted you to see what was happening to other alchemists around you, too. You were protected in your bubble, trying to ignore the very despair you hate me for causing—"

"Stop it."

"You're happy to turn an eye away from the suffering happening around you—"

"I said to *stop*—"

"—because you're too afraid to do what your soul longs for: To create change. To fight back."

"Most of the suffering in this state was caused by you!" Ash yelled, voice tearing. "And even after you were killed, you ripped a hole in our physical reality. You've allowed chaos energy in."

"I don't deny it," Hain said.

"Why?" Ash said, voice hoarse. "You knew what it would do. Our reality will fall apart. It's already unweaving."

"And as a result, so much change has sparked," Hain replied. "So many who would have been perfectly content with their lives, with the oppression alchemists faced—they are now fueled to fight, to create the world they wish to see instead. Can't you see that, Ash? Can't you see the good in my actions, too?"

"You killed me."

"I thought I had no other choice, at the time. I was wrong."

Ash turned away in frustration. There was no reasoning with a man who was bent on lying to himself—allowing himself to feel righteous for the hell he brought onto the world.

He was surprised when Hain whispered, "Perhaps my main regret now is not seeing that there is more than one way to create change." Ash paused, hating the warmth that spread through him at his father's words. "When I died, Source showed me other possible lives I could have had, if I'd made other choices. I could have raised you. I could have instilled love and empowerment in you. I could have died knowing I had created a true legacy—a son who would lead change in New Anglia."

Ash faced his father in silence, the only sound now the whistle of a breeze that felt so real against his skin; but then, he would think that in the physical realm as well. "Why did you want to see me?" he asked. "Why did you come?"

"I regret not showing you that you are worthy of more than this world has given you," Hain told him. "Maybe then, you wouldn't have fought for their acceptance. You would've spent your energy changing this world into the one you deserved instead."

"Did you see that version of another universe yourself?" Ash asked. He'd meant to ask the question coldly, but curiosity had leaked into his voice. "After you read the Book . . ."

"I was overwhelmed with more power than my mind and body could take," Hain said. "There was a part of me that was relieved when you pulled its power from me."

The wind was growing stronger, howling over the plains. Colors started to morph and swirl above the blue sky. It was time for Ash to wake up, he realized. He jolted with surprise when he saw his father watching him with tears in his eyes.

"So many regrets," the man said. "I couldn't figure out how to create that change, how to bring alchemists freedom—but perhaps you can."

"How?" Ash said, but already his voice felt whipped away by the wind.

The wind became black. It rushed around his father like streams of smoke, until only his eyes were visible. "Would you like to know where to find the pieces of chaos?" he asked.

Ash sat up with a gasp. He wheezed, heart pounding, as he looked about his room. Nothing had changed, yet somehow, the chambers didn't feel real—not as real as the fields or the white flowers at his feet. Ash closed his eyes and fell back to the sheets. The last image his father had shown him lingered in his mind. A crowd, people standing in lines, all wearing robes of white.

He realized what had woken him: Energy buzzed over his skin, a ringing in his ears and a weight on his skull.

Ash.

He groaned, palms digging into his eyes. "I'm here, Marlowe."

Her voice whispered, even as the words seemed to echo. *Come to Ironbound tonight. Elena is ready to share the details of your new mission.*

20

Ash planned to stay hidden away in his room until night fell, but as the day wore on and his stomach grumbled with hunger, he had no choice but to get dressed for lunch. He was just buttoning the collar of his shirt when there was a knock on his door. He swung it open, already buzzing at the familiar energy that waited.

"Source, Ash," Ramsay said, eyeing his tangled curls and rumpled shirt. She wore her usual corset vest and slacks, making Ash think she'd just arrived from Lancaster. "You look like you haven't slept in days."

That was more accurate than she knew. "I was just about to head to lunch."

"Perfect. I was just about to invite you to join me."

Ash closed the door behind him as he followed Ramsay down the hall. It'd been over a week since they'd spent any real time together, and Ash was surprised to find words clogged in his throat, unsure of what to say. He missed the ease they'd once had, the bickering and laughter and even Ramsay's condescending lectures.

Even worse, Ramsay was quiet, too, a pinch between her brows. It seemed she struggled to fill the silence, too.

"Don't you have class?" Ash finally asked as they turned one hall.

"The first years have their mid-fall exams for the rest of the week," she said.

Ash hesitated. "More time for yourself, then."

"Hardly. Lord Val is even more demanding now, with the attacks on McKinley." Ramsay's mouth and shoulders tightened.

Ash looked to her out of the corner of his eye. He sorely wanted to ask Ramsay about her weapons. Why would she invent the fire-lock, knowing how much damage it could do? He wondered what Ramsay would say, if he told her that one of the prototypes had been used to blow a hole in the stomach of a child. She couldn't have really believed that the firelock would be used to help alche-mists, too. Or was she so blinded by her desire to bring House Thorne back that she was willing to look away, to ignore the fact that she'd created something so harmful? Maybe she was lying to herself, as so many humans were prone to do.

They arrived at the dining room. Ash usually came only at the tail end of a meal, when the table was nearly empty, but he'd ar-rived earlier than usual today, stragglers still filling some seats. At the far end, Ash noticed Callum eating with Charlotte. He immediately looked up, sensing his partners' energies. His eyes widened, a wave of embarrassment clouding the air. Ash paused, but only for a moment, before he ducked his head and turned for the other end of the table.

Ramsay followed closely behind, humor in her tone. "Ash?" she said. "What in the name of Source was that?"

Ash shrugged, pulling out a chair and plopping in front of an empty plate and glass. "I didn't want to interrupt their date."

"Date?" Ramsay's head swung to inspect Callum and Char-lotte on the other end of the table. "Is that what you think they're doing? Really?"

Ash shrugged. "They're eating lunch alone, aren't they?" Not only that, but the energy between the two—leaning into each other, Callum blushing like a schoolboy . . . Anger pinched Ash. Callum hadn't thought to invite him to lunch, even though he knew Ash was locked up in Alexander's manor. He'd chosen to ask Charlotte Adelaide instead.

"Huh. I think you might be right." Ramsay scratched a cheek. "I'm not sure how I feel about that."

"I thought it 'wouldn't be fair' of us to limit Callum's love, too."

"Yes, well," Ramsay said, "I'd like to think he would at least speak to us about it first."

Maybe Ash didn't have the right to make demands of Ramsay or especially Callum. He wasn't much of a partner to them, with the number of lies he kept. An attendant appeared at Ash's side then, asking if he would like the steak or lamb course. It was another reason Ash avoided the dining hall. He hated the feeling of being waited on, like he was some high-society snot. "Lamb, please."

Ramsay ordered the same. As the attendant left, Ramsay eyed Ash quietly for a moment, then asked, "Is everything all right?"

He nodded quickly. "Yes—yeah, I'm fine. Why?"

But he could feel her concerned vibration in the silence that followed. Energy never lied. "How've you been filling your days?" she asked. "At least before, you had your garden and walks through the woods . . ."

Ash pushed down the welling grief at the reminder of losing his home. "There's plenty to read," he said. "And I take walks around the manor. I'm fine," he said again.

Ramsay squinted as she nodded slowly. He remembered what Charlotte had said, the night she'd visited. She hadn't believed him when Ash had insisted he was fine, either.

At the other end of the table, Charlotte's smile lit her face. Her hand touched Callum's, lingering long enough that Ash would have liked to ask that she oh-so-kindly *remove it*.

The older boy must have sensed Ash's pointed energy. He looked across the table to Ash and Ramsay again, hesitant. Ash glared at the empty plate in front of him while Ramsay shifted in her seat with a sigh. "Is it time for another argument already?" she asked. "I feel like we just had one last week."

Callum leaned into Charlotte and spoke lowly before he pushed back his chair and stood, her following. The two began to make their way over.

"Does he really have to bring her, too?" Ash muttered.

Callum and Charlotte stopped only a few feet away. They looked like the picture-perfect couple of Kensington, Callum in his red uniform and Charlotte in her pale blue blouse.

"Uh—hi," Callum said.

Ramsay looked up at him with the touch of a bemused smile. "Hi, Callum. Hi, Charlotte."

Charlotte beamed, as if completely ignorant to the tension. "It's good to see you two."

Ash stared blankly at her.

"It isn't—this—" Callum gestured behind him, where he and Charlotte had been sitting. He gave up with a sigh. "I didn't think either of you would be eating."

"No?" Ramsay said, looking to Ash with a smirk. "Isn't that usually what a person does approximately three times a day?"

Callum frowned. "Don't do that."

"Don't do what?"

Charlotte's smile fell slightly as she looked between the three. She looked at Callum, concerned. "Should I leave?"

Callum shook his head. "No, it's okay—"

"Actually, Charlotte," Ramsay said with a wide smile, "we would like a chance to speak to Callum. Just the three of us. Please."

She seemed surprised by the request, even if she'd just suggested the same herself. "Yes, of course." With a polite curtsy, she turned on her heel and left, looking over her shoulder only once as she disappeared through the doors.

"Take a seat, Kendrick," Ramsay said, brow raised.

Callum stayed standing. "That was really rude."

"Why?" Ash said. "Because we didn't want to have lunch with your girlfriend, too?"

"I didn't know you were going to have lunch here," Callum said. "If I did, I would've asked you to come also."

"I think you've had the wrong response to that one," Ramsay pointed out. "Shouldn't you be insisting that Charlotte isn't your girlfriend instead?"

Callum worked his lower jaw back and forth. "She isn't my girl-friend."

Ramsay only gazed up at him with a quirked brow.

Others around the table had turned to look. Callum dragged out a chair opposite Ash and leaned forward, voice low. "Even if she were, would that be a problem? We never discussed . . . *rules* for other relationships, outside the three of us."

"So, that gives you free rein to do whatever you like without talking to me or Ash about it first?"

"I haven't done *anything*. Having lunch with a friend isn't a be-trayal."

No, Ash didn't feel particularly good at all, making any de-mands of Callum. "It feels like one," he muttered. "Knowing you chose to ask Charlotte first, when I'm stuck in this manor—"

Callum sighed, falling back in his seat. "Fine," he said. "I'm sorry. I'll *get permission* before having lunch with a friend in the future."

Ramsay's humor had left her expression. "I know things are difficult, with the McKinley investigation and the loss of Sophie Galahad," she said, "but that doesn't mean you get to meet my and Ash's real and valid concerns with *sarcasm*."

Callum swallowed. He nodded, then said, "Sorry."

An attendant returned with Ash's and Ramsay's meals, though neither moved to start eating. Callum took another deep breath, then said, "Charlotte's just been helping me through it all. Giving me support, helping me heal my stress. My grief."

Ramsay's expression softened. Ash bit his lip, guilt piercing him.

"I . . ." Callum swallowed, then said, "I won't lie and pretend I don't have feelings for her. I've always had a crush on Charlotte. But that's all it is. Feelings. I haven't acted on them. I wouldn't, not without talking to you both first."

"And now?" Ramsay asked. "Is this you, talking to us about it first?"

Callum looked from Ramsay to Ash. He hated it, the jealousy

that seared inside him. He wanted to have Ramsay's view, to see that Callum shouldn't be limited by the two of them. Callum deserved all the love anyone in the world wanted to give him, to show him; and Charlotte was good for Callum, too, Ash could see that. And still he felt a selfish spark, wanting to keep Callum to just Ramsay and himself. Wasn't it already hard enough, feeling like Callum and Ramsay shared something Ash didn't have? He didn't need to see the perfect, beautiful Charlotte Adelaide added into the mix, too.

But Callum shook his head. "No. Not right now. Not—not yet, anyway," he added, glancing up at both to see their expressions. He must have been able to feel Ash's muddled jealousy. Ash did nothing to hide it. "I think . . . we can all just settle into the idea. See how we all feel, before I consider asking Charlotte for more."

It was a space where all three could find an agreement, at least.

Callum moved to stand. "I'll let you both finish eating. I need to get back to McKinley."

Ramsay nodded. "I can't stay long, either. I need to return to Lancaster for a meeting with Lord Val."

Callum made an attempt at friendliness. "What will you do with the rest of your day, Ash?"

He ducked his head, lie sour on his tongue. "I'm not sure."

※

Elena sat alone in the safe house's sitting room with her legs and arms crossed. She waited as the smoke uncurled, returning to the shadows. Ash took a sharp breath as he slowed to a stop in front of her. He wasn't sure he'd ever be used to the icy dread of chaos.

"Where're Marlowe and the others?" he asked, glancing around at the empty torn and scuffed furniture scattered around the room. Ash hadn't expected to be alone with her.

"Why don't you sit?" Elena said, nodding to the sofa waiting opposite.

Ash hesitated, then did as suggested, fear threading through his vibrations. Had Elena learned the truth? Had she somehow found out that Alexander had sent him?

"Is something wrong?" Ash asked, forcing his fingers still so that he wouldn't fidget.

"Why would anything be wrong?" she asked with the smallest of smiles.

He shook his head. "No reason."

She hadn't taken her eyes off Ash, not once. "I have a new mission that I could use your help with. We've found the location of another fragment."

Ash thought of the image his father had showed him, the followers in robes of white. He already had some idea of what that location might be, but he waited for Elena to speak.

"But before we discuss the mission," she said, "I have something to share."

He swallowed, heart pumping, and waited.

Elena paused. Her silence was unnerving as she seemed to consider her words carefully. "I have to admit, Ash—I haven't been completely honest with you."

Ash frowned, quite certain he wouldn't much like what Elena was about to tell him. "What is it?"

She stood from the sofa, pacing away from Ash, her back to him. "I've consumed two orbs now, as you know," she told him. "My power has grown stronger with each fragment," she said, "but my body has suffered the consequences."

The air in front of Elena shimmered with heat. Her hair, which had only shown streaks of gray before, had become a stark white. Deep lines creased her eyes. She was thin, skeleton pushing against her skin. Elena was only in her thirties, but the woman in front of Ash looked closer to eighty. He sucked in a sharp breath, muscles clenching.

"I'm not vain," Elena said. "I don't care that this is now my true image—only that anyone else might take one look at me and decide I'm too weak to lead—decide to take my Ironbound chapter from me."

"The chaos is killing you."

"My body can't handle the raw energy of the fragments," she admitted. "It's deteriorating. If I consume another orb, I believe my organs will begin to fail. Some have already begun."

Ash stared at her, unable to look away. Elena had worked hard to keep up her act—to pretend she wasn't dying—but looking at the state of her, he couldn't see how much longer that would last.

"My plan was to find as many fragments as possible," she said. "I wanted to consume enough orbs that I would be put into a better position to find more. I'd originally thought I could simply take one with the intention of stitching the tear in the fabric of Source, until finally the hole was patched completely.

"The problem," Elena continued, "is that your father's manifestation was powerful. One fragment wouldn't be enough to stitch the tear."

Ash hesitated. He wasn't sure he wanted to know the answer to his next question. "How many would it take?"

Elena swallowed. "I now estimate it would take consuming at least five fragments, each with the intention of closing the tear your father created, to be successful."

"Five fragments?" Ash echoed. "Your body is already failing with only two. Five would be overwhelming—fatal . . ."

And he understood it, then, in the silence. This was how he could atone for his father's mistakes. This was how he could truly prove his loyalty to alchemists—potentially save all of New Anglia and the people he cared for with it. "You want me to consume the orbs instead."

Elena's mouth pressed into a line, a crease in her brow. She was ashamed, at least, for suggesting that Ash potentially allow himself to die, even if it was for the sake of the world. "You are your father's son, after all. There's something about you—your physical makeup and design, in particular—that can withstand more energy than the average person at a time."

Ash had often wondered why his body could hold so much more alchemic power than others. There'd been enough theories about people whose energies had returned time and time again, had experienced so many lives that their energy remembered existing in different forms.

"Some train their bodies for years to store so much energy," Elena said, "but you—you're a natural. Your body was even able to bear the energy of the Book of Source, according to Marlowe's telling of what happened that day on the bridge. Anyone else might've been blown to bits."

Ash clenched his jaw. It felt like a small betrayal, that Marlowe had shared what'd happened between him, her, and his father. Did this mean Marlowe had talked about him with Elena—that they'd discussed his life and decided it was worth sacrificing?

Ash shook his head slowly as he considered this. It was true that even his father had needed to train to allow his body to contain so much energy, and Ramsay herself had told Ash, once, that the raw power his body held was remarkable, even if he didn't have the technique to use it at the time.

"Couldn't someone consume the fragments more slowly?" Ash asked. "Let their bodies get used to—"

"There isn't enough time," Elena said. "We can't trust that anyone in the ALP would be able to train to handle so much chaos energy, only to fail. We need you, Ash."

Ash almost asked the likelihood that he would even survive, but he already suspected the answer. Perhaps just one or two fragments' worth of energy was what the average alchemist could handle, when calling on chaos to practice alchemy. Three fragments were likely the limit, before the alchemist's body began to fail. Four? Ash assumed the alchemist would undoubtedly break—a heart attack, perhaps, unable to handle so much energy forced into their body at once. And five?

Ash shook his head, breathless fear prickling his throat. After consuming five orbs total, if he at all managed to survive, Ash assumed he would feel similarly to how his father had, flickering in and out of reality, with only seconds to hold any intention to patch the tear in his world's physical reality. His body would strain before it broke apart. Some alchemists had theorized a body under too much alchemic pressure would simply implode, shattered to the molecular level.

"I have to warn you," Elena added.

"There's more? Please, do tell."

"There were the physical changes," she said. "But even consuming the first orb, already I started to feel . . . side effects, I suppose you could say."

"What do you mean?"

"Consequences. My body longs for the chaos's power now—its rush when first swallowed, it's hard to describe. I can only assume this desire will grow with the more fragments that are consumed. I tell you all this, Ash, because I want you to fully understand what you would agree to."

"And if I don't agree?" he asked. "How long before physical reality begins to unravel completely?"

"I estimate a few months," Elena said. "Not much time, in the grand scheme of things."

A few months to find as many fragments as possible, to consume them and stop the unraveling of physical reality.

The two shared quiet for some time while Ash mulled over the possibility of his future. "I guess I don't have much of a choice, huh?"

Elena sighed, mirage of heat wavering in front of her before she returned to the version Ash was used to seeing. "I've found the location of another fragment," she said. "Unfortunately, it's in the hands of someone we'd rather not have it."

"Who is that?" Ash said. His voice sounded hollow even to his own ears.

"The man who claims to be the reincarnation of Sinclair Lune."

Ash's head snapped up. He'd suspected House Lune to be part of this. It was as his father had shown him, the lines of followers in their robes of white. But for Sinclair Lune himself to have a fragment? "How do you know he found one?"

"You aren't my only set of eyes and ears," Elena told him. "Marlowe has done excellent work keeping tabs on the man, and was able to see that a fragment was in his possession. House Lune was decimated by your father, but Lune followers have started to gather to the west. Join us," Elena said. "Help us attack Sinclair Lune's base."

"You'll start a war."

"I know you aren't so ignorant, Sir Woods, that you don't see we're already in one." Elena's gaze hadn't left Ash, her unblinking stare unnerving. "The choice is yours, as always."

Yet Ash couldn't see how he could refuse. Maybe it wasn't his right to say no. Maybe this was his atonement for his father's mistakes. Still, he couldn't help but think, for that moment, how upset Ramsay and Callum would be with him.

He nodded his response.

"Good. We leave tonight."

21

The group stepped into a room dark enough that Ash, at first, thought the smoke of the chaos energy had simply filled the space. There were no windows. Ash's palms glowed, allowing him to see that the walls and floors were made of what looked like red clay. The others stepped into the darkness around him, still wearing their masks.

There hadn't been much information for Elena to share. "Our attempts to scout were ended before we could gather enough intel." The group was left to gather information about the base while searching for the fragments simultaneously. Riskier, of course, but they had no other choice.

Ash was relieved that Finley, at least, had been left at the main base. Hendrix had been left behind in the safe house, too. Even with the healer's help, one of the firelock projectiles had shattered his bone, which had been slower to heal. It didn't seem like he would be able to join missions for a long while.

Ash could reach out both arms and simultaneously touch the opposite hallway walls, the texture rough and hardened. The air was dusty. Ash felt caged in. Elena put a finger to her mouth, then pointed at Ash and Marlowe to go in one direction and at Riles to follow her. There was no need for hesitation. They went down opposite ends, Elena and Riles disappearing around the corner. Ash's breath echoed in his gas mask, the goggles fogging despite the heat. He was sweating beneath his cotton coveralls, the fabric sticking to his skin. Ash couldn't shake the feeling that he was being watched.

He and Marlowe walked for several minutes without speaking,

footfalls muffled. They were likely underground, Ash thought. The halls seemed like a maze, all with the same curved ceiling. There were no patterns, no indication that he and Marlowe weren't simply walking in circles, down one hall and then another before starting at the beginning again. After another several minutes of walking in silence, Ash was convinced this was exactly what'd happened. Marlowe moved slowly ahead, Ash unable to stop glancing over his shoulder, waiting for the moment someone jumped out of the shadows.

The walls were all the same red clay. Ash could reach out both arms and simultaneously touch the opposite hallway walls. The air was dusty. Ash felt caged in. His breath echoed in his gas mask, the goggles fogging despite the air's heaviness. He was sweating beneath his coveralls, the fabric sticking to his skin.

The halls—they were like a maze. Ash slowed to a pause. There was no indication that they weren't simply walking in circles, down one hall and then another, right back to the beginning again. He squinted, a tightening in his chest. He was too hot. "Marlowe."

"What?"

"I feel like this has happened before."

She didn't pause. "Yes, you have indeed already told me that."

Ash frowned, heart pounding harder. "Something's wrong."

She sighed in frustration, pausing and turning to him. "Are you playing a joke on me, Ash? You just said the same thing not a minute ago."

He squinted at the air around him—usually whenever alchemy was performed, he could see the aftereffects as color shimmering in the air—but there was nothing.

"Now isn't the time for games."

"What did you say?"

"I said to stop playing games—"

"No, I mean—when I said something was wrong, how did you respond?"

Marlowe opened her mouth to answer, then hesitated. She frowned. "I don't . . ."

"You don't remember?" Dread was heavy in Ash's chest.

Marlowe pointed behind her. "Go that way."

"We shouldn't split up, should we?"

"Source, just listen for once in your life."

Ash did what he was told, though reluctantly; and behind him, Marlowe walked to the other end of the hall. "Shit."

Marlowe's voice came from ahead. He turned and saw her behind him—looked in front again, and saw not only Marlowe far down the hall, but another person. Another *Ash*. The other pair came around the corner, backs to Ash as they made a turn, oblivious to the fact that they were watched.

"It's a protection barrier," Marlowe said. "A powerful one. I've never seen this manifested. I've only ever heard about it in theory."

"What is it?" Ash said, lowering his voice though he couldn't be sure if the other Ash and Marlowe could even hear him.

"A loop of sorts—both in physical reality and in time. Each hall represents another section of the timeline. Turn a corner, and we could end up having this exact conversation. Source, another two of us might have already."

It was difficult to breathe. "We'd be trapped."

"The other pairs of us—they're just aftereffects, memories stuck in the barrier. The barrier isn't meant for anyone to realize what's happened. We could've continued on for hours, days." Ash imagined they could've starved or died of thirst, neither noticing what'd happened until it was too late. Marlowe continued. "It takes particular talent to even remember we've experienced this before."

Ash warmed, but this wasn't the time to be embarrassed by compliments—and besides, Marlowe had been the one to recognize they'd had the same conversation at least once already, too. It unsettled Ash, the fact that they could've been in the hall for hours already, and it'd only felt like minutes. "Elena and Riles—do you think they've been caught in the same trap?"

"If they were, I'm sure Elena would've figured it out by now. They'll be all right. We need to focus on making sure we can get out of here."

"How do we do that?"

"We need to break out of the barrier. Quite literally break out of the halls."

Marlowe placed a hand to the rough wall. Ash's goggles warmed and glowed brighter as heat emitted from Marlowe's chest and down her arm. The wall began to tremble and shake until clumps of it fell and broke apart. It didn't surprise Ash, that Marlowe would be adept in demolition alchemy, too.

Another identical hall waited before them. Ash wondered how many walls Marlowe would have to break for them to escape the barrier completely. "Let's go."

※

Marlowe broke through six walls before chunks of clay fell to reveal a grand hall, streaks of light falling through cracks in the ceiling. The floors were mosaic tiles now, rather than loose dirt; the walls, red tile. The space almost seemed to be an enclosed courtyard, an empty water fountain of white stone standing in the center. It was suspect to Ash that the hall was empty, no one waiting for them. It was too quiet. Thoughts filled his head. What if the members of the base knew they were coming and were only waiting for the two to walk into another trap? Surely if there was a security measure as powerful as a time loop, the members of the base also would've been notified of intruders.

Movement from the other side of the hall—Ash fell into a stance, fists heating, but it was only Elena, walking through an archway. A red line of blood leaked from her temple and into her goggles. Riles was beside her, a tear in the fabric around his arm and a long red line wrapping around it. Riles didn't lower his own fists.

"Names," Elena said.

Marlowe took a step back. "Elena, it's us."

Riles took three steps forward. "The other pair that looked like you two said just the same thing."

"*Names*," Elena said. "Now."

"Ash."

"Marlowe."

Riles murmured to her. "It'd be easy enough for them to figure that out. Another fucking leak—"

Annoyance prickled Ash's chest. "How do we know you aren't fake?" he asked. "You could be another trap thrown at us, couldn't you?"

"Another?" Elena said.

Marlowe stepped in front of Ash. "Questions," she said. "Let's ask questions, to be sure we're each who we say we are."

Riles interrupted. "Anyone could've done research—"

Elena stepped forward. "What did I tell you, the night I found you?"

Marlowe didn't hesitate. "The change we seek in others must first come from within ourselves."

Elena's tension faded, though she still turned her head, looking one way and then another. "They know we're here. We need to tread carefully."

Ash was surprised to see the quiver of fear in Riles's cheek. "Should we leave? We could take more time to study the base— try again, when we're better prepared—"

"No. Now that we're here, we won't have another chance. We move together."

There was an archway that led to another set of halls Ash didn't want to enter, not when he didn't know what could be waiting inside, but he made himself follow Elena while Marlowe and Riles took up the back end, footsteps tapping. As they went on, it became clearer that they were in an underground maze of sorts, tunnels burrowed through red dirt. There wasn't any way to see how far the tunnels went. For a moment, Ash worried that they had been caught in another trap—until finally, Elena paused.

They'd come to a larger opening. The room itself looked as if it'd been carved out by bare hands. It was a hollow, a crude pocket where dust fell from the ceilings and walls with every breath. Standing in wait were dozens—Source, it might have been nearly one hundred people standing in lines, cramped into the small room, their backs all to Ash and the rest.

At the opposite end of the room was a man. He had pale hair and skin, linen robes threadbare. It was all the more disconcerting that the man felt empty. It was as if Ash might as well have been looking at a doll of a man, a statue that breathed. Instead of the glow of light shining around his being, Ash saw a shadow emitting from his skin, as if his aura was black.

"You who are the chosen," the man said, and though he whispered, his voice somehow managed to echo in Ash's ears. "You who are the worthy—hear me now."

An alchemic force began to vibrate from the stranger's hands as he stood over another who knelt as if in prayer. The force was a pressure that filled the air and stifled Ash's breath. It was heavy, thick. Ash took a step back. This energy suggested he fall to his knees, too.

Ash wasn't the only one affected. Marlowe stiffened beside him. Riles sagged, hand against the wall. Only Elena stood straight, unmoving, as they watched this man press a hand against the cheek of his follower.

"Accept my gift of love, this purification from the sin of your world."

The shadow drifted from the man's hand and gathered, smoke clouding the air. It shot forward, filling the follower's mouth and nose and eyes and ears—she shook. Ash swallowed a gasp, certain that the energy would make the woman implode—

Until she stilled. She stood, slowly, and walked to join the line. The people who faced their leader were rimmed with black shadow, too, Ash realized, even if it wasn't as strong as the chaos energy that spewed from the man who called himself Sinclair Lune.

"Visitors," the man said, though he hadn't looked their way once. "Welcome."

The lines of people in front of the group turned as one, facing them now. Ash sucked in a quick breath. He tightened his trembling fists, heat growing—but the people didn't move. They weren't even blinking, Ash realized. He wasn't sure if they were breathing.

Sinclair Lune's quiet voice echoed against the walls as he spread his hands as if in greeting. "We've been expecting you for some time now. I foresaw your visit in a dream."

"Look," Marlowe whispered. "Behind him."

There was a table, small and the sort meant for kneeling, and on top was what appeared to be an offering. A candle flickered. A dish was set. Above it hovered the fragment.

"I'm sorry to say," Lune said, "that I also foresaw each of your deaths."

Elena raised a hand, palm pointed at the earth. The ground beneath Ash's feet trembled, then shook, rocking violently. Cracks split through the dirt and webbed over the walls. The cracks raced forward, earth falling. The ground sank, lines of people with it, but there were dozens still—they raced forward, leaped into the air over the fallen, scrambling over the crumbling dirt as they rushed at the four.

Marlowe shouted with effort as she threw up her arms, needles of light shooting forward and through skin and bone. Holes of red bled, but the mass of bodies crushed forward as if they felt nothing. Ash gritted his teeth as he raised his hands, too, a shield of fire along with it, heat searing the air. Skin melted and charred as faces twisted in pain, though no screams left their lips—and still the people threw themselves at him. The pale man had appeared in the fire that surrounded them, so colorless that some parts of him appeared translucent, organs beating beneath his skin. He stood in the flames that licked his legs and his hands, still raised.

The hordes of people left standing—dozens still—had stopped moving. They stood frozen, eyes focused on the crew, as if waiting for the order to tear them all apart.

"It's him," Elena said, gaze stuck on Sinclair Lune. "He's their puppeteer."

"I think it was the ceremony," Ash said. "When he touched the follower, energy flowed from him and into her. That's how he's controlling them."

Elena nodded her acknowledgment. "Whatever you do, don't let him touch you."

Riles raised crossed fists. "Should we just kill him first?"

Time seemed to slow, then. Ash blinked. The man had vanished from the flames. A heartbeat, and he reappeared inches away from Elena's face.

Ash opened his eyes. One moment he was in the cavernous room of dirt, and the next he was on a cliffside. An ocean that stretched on as far as the eye could see crashed into the rocks below, the scent of salt floating on the breeze and sticking to his skin. He spun around, but there was no sign of Marlowe and the rest—only the pale man, white hair glinting like spiderwebs caught in the light.

Lune smiled at Ash when the smaller man threw up his hands, heat glowing. "Where are the others?" he shouted, hoarse with fear. His pulse raced in his neck. "What've you done with them?"

"Calm yourself," the man said. His voice sounded genteel, peaceful. "Your friends are exactly where you've left them—and so are you."

Ash blinked. He was in the shadowed room of red dirt, Marlowe screaming for everyone to get back—

He stumbled backward. Rocks from the edge of the cliff tumbled over the side. "What—How're you—"

"I wanted only a chance to speak with you alone," Lune said. "You can understand that curiosity, too, can't you?"

Ash held a shaking breath. "Why me?"

"I see through the fabric of existence," Lune told him. "I see the infinite lives you live now as we speak."

Ash thought of the other lives he had seen, shown to him by his father at the Lune estate—a life as Hain's claimed son, living among the elite as Ash had always thought he'd wanted, and the death he'd experienced, too, killed by Callum. His breath staggered. A hand gripped his elbow—Marlowe's, he realized, as she screamed at him to run—

"In many of them," Lune said, "you're quite infamous. Ash Woods, the boy who unites an alchemist rebellion against the state of New Anglia—the boy who kills the Head of the Houses, Lord Alexander himself, along with the Head of House Kendrick. You're in all the history books," Lune said, eyes shining. "It intrigues me, to meet that boy face-to-face now."

Ash didn't disbelieve Lune's abilities; his own father had been able to send Ash's mind into parallel realms, and though an ability to see all the parallel worlds at once would require even greater power, Ash was also well aware of the waves of energy that threatened to knock him into the ocean below. Whether the man in front of him was really Sinclair Lune or not, it was clear that he was powerful.

Ash didn't see Marlowe's hand, but he felt her fingers tighten against his elbow, the panicked energy hitting him as she screamed. The heat of alchemy seared Ash's skin.

"Why're you doing this?" Ash said. He couldn't quite make himself ask the question he really wanted to—was too afraid of the answer, the possibility that this man really was—

"Why?" Lune asked. He seemed to consider for a moment. "How am I ever meant to save the worthy, if there isn't first a hell on Earth?"

Marlowe's scream echoed in Ash's ear. "No—Elena—"

Ash's fists tightened. "Why am I here? What do you want with me?"

"What do I want?" the man asked. Lune raised a hand. It wasn't there before, Ash was certain of it, but now, floating above his palm, was a black orb. Shadow fell from the chaos, emitting inverse light. "Aren't you the one who seeks something from me?"

"*Ash!*"

He opened his eyes. He knelt before Sinclair Lune in the room of dirt floors and clay walls. The man's pale palm extended, reaching for Ash's forehead. Before Ash could jerk away, fingers lightly tapped Ash's skin. A force pushed through him, vibrations humming so achingly deep that Ash couldn't see anything but a haze that drifted in front of his eyes. He moved his arm, though he hadn't meant to—got to his feet, though he hadn't wanted to. He turned to face Marlowe, Elena, and Riles. He tried to open his mouth, to shout no, to tell them all to run, but the sound was trapped in his throat, a nightmare where he could not scream—

They'd been cornered against the wall, nowhere to escape—he raised his own palm, fire blazing through the air—

"*Wake up!*"

He gasped, air sucked from his lungs.

Marlowe's fingers dug into his bicep. "It's Elena—he touched her, he's controlling her—"

Elena stood in the center of the room, eyes rolled and hands raised to the ceiling, black smoke shrouding her. An illusion. Ash hadn't considered just how powerful illusion alchemy could become, to alter not just the eye's perception but the mind's, too. For every aspect of alchemic science, there was an opposite effect: materialization and dematerialization; creation and demolition. Ash had never practiced disillusion, but he took a deep breath—focused on the dirt beneath his feet, his knees, the palms of his hands, and imagined waves of grounding energy spilling from his core and into the air. Riles had fallen back against the wall, eyes wide with terror at the illusion Elena had forced on him. Marlowe's glazed expression furrowed with pain—she'd managed to fight off her own illusion without any help. And Elena—as the haze dissipated like fog rolling away, her gaze became clearer. Her hands dropped and she stilled, confused—

"Elena," Marlowe called, hoarse. The throngs of people under Lune's control lay on the ground in heaps. Ash couldn't tell if they were breathing.

Sinclair Lune stood on top of the bodies. He pinched his fingers together.

Elena gasped. A trickle of blood fell from her neck. A line glinted—a string. His fingers twitched. Red sprayed. Marlowe screamed Elena's name as the woman's body fell, her head falling beside it. Riles roared.

Marlowe gasped. "No—wait, Riles—"

He threw out an arm toward Lune as a line of white glinted. Riles's arm flew as he screamed. Marlowe sobbed as she clenched her hands into fists, glass springing from the earth and cutting straight into the ceiling. Lune stood on the other side of the glass, staring in. Marlowe dropped to one knee, arm around Riles as he curled in on himself in pain. She was too weak to materialize. They wouldn't make it back to the safe house alive if she attempted to take them all, and there was no wall close enough, no time to drag Riles and Marlowe to one and place a hand and wait for the chaos to open a path to the safe house. They needed to get out *now*. Ash tightened his fingers into fists. He would die, he realized. This man was too powerful. Ash wouldn't survive a battle against him, but he wouldn't allow himself to die without trying to fight.

"This is why you came, isn't it?"

Sinclair Lune vanished and reappeared in front of him. He offered a hand, shadow wrapped around his pale skin. It sucked into one point—an orb, hovering over the palm. "Is this what you were looking for?"

Ash almost fell back, but Lune snatched his neck—held him in place and yanked him forward. The orb rose. Ash scratched at

Lune's wrist, his arms and fingers, but Lune's hand gripped Ash's throat so tightly that his skin burned.

"Can you feel it?" Lune asked. "The way the chaos calls for you. It longs to be a part of you—to be a part of your energy, to be under your command."

Ash tried to shake his head. It was in vain. Lune squeezed Ash's mouth. The orb floated.

"And you," Lune said quietly, for just Ash to hear. "You have longed for this, too. It's why this moment has come, you see—a manifestation of desire, finally coming into existence."

Ash tried to pull back, but Lune's grip tightened. The orb entered Ash's mouth. Pain spiked through his teeth and jaw like ice, his tongue numb and his ears ringing.

"You're ashamed of it, this desire for power," Lune told him. "And so you try desperately to hide it from yourself and others, to tell yourself that you are different from your father—that you will prove you are better by atoning for his sins."

The sharp pain dulled into an ache. The throb matched the pulse of his heartbeat, and with it a fog that seemed to rise from Ash's skin.

"But is that not only shame, created by humans in this dream?"

The heat that grew inside Ash's chest had spread to his lungs. It was clear, then—the connection he had to Source and chaos; energy rising as colors fogged his vision, lightning sparking through the haze, and in the sparks of light, he saw the threads of the physical, and through those threads, the slivers of images of infinite physical realities, the flickering visions of the higher realms, patterns of energy that were among the first of consciousness, the whole of the universe expanding with every realization that it *exists*—

"Yes," Lune said. "That power. It's unlike anything you've ever experienced."

Ash saw it, too—the flow of light that streamed, the consciousness at the root of the universe, the original spark of chaos that turned into Source. He wanted to cry with the unadulterated love that his human body couldn't contain; the energy was too power-ful, too *much*—

"What will you do?" Lune whispered. "How will you use this fragment of chaos?"

Ash could do anything at all, if he held all of chaos at his fin-gertips. He could create a new universe. He could kill Sinclair Lune. He could bring his mother back from the dead.

Riles was unconscious, only the whites of his eyes showing as a sticky red pooled around him, staining Marlowe's hands. Her breath shuddered, cheeks wet. Elena's body was several feet away.

Ash took a slow breath.

Give me the ability.

Ash's vision grew hazy, his limbs weak. Lune released him. He fell to the ground.

Let me materialize at will.

He reached for Marlowe and Riles.

22

Ash landed hard on his back, cold burning his skin. He rolled, slamming into ice, and groaned. Wind whistled. He shivered, teeth clenched, as snow whipped into his eyes and cheeks. The thin gray trees were familiar, at least.

"Ash?"

Marlowe's voice echoed. He followed it until he found her standing in a clearing, snow almost to her knees. Riles was at her feet, eyes rolled back. Blood gushed from the severed arm, freezing into red ice around him.

"He doesn't have long." She knelt. "Help me."

Ash heaved Riles up, arm around the boy's waist, while Marlowe put his unharmed arm over her shoulders. Ash looked up, a path leading to the manor he knew would be waiting at the top of the hill. "I tried to get us inside," Ash gasped as the three stumbled forward. "It was the only place I could think of, in the moment."

It was the second time, now, that the group's plans had been breached, enemies waiting for them. The safe house was compromised; it had to be. Finley was at the main base, at least, but Hendrix and all the others in Ironbound could be in danger.

Riles groaned. Marlowe panted. "Ramsay won't be home, will she? I don't think she'd be too happy to see me."

"Hard to say," Ash replied, though he silently agreed it'd be best if the manor was empty.

They made it to the front gardens of dead gray brush. Ash stumbled forward and slammed a hand to the door, palm spread. Ramsay had placed an energetic lock on the premises, allowing only herself, Ash, and Callum entry. The doors clicked as they unlocked. He shoved them open, the three staggering through the familiar stone corridors. "Ramsay?" Ash called, but there was no response.

"Here—take him here." Ash opened the doors to the sitting room. Ash was certain Ramsay wouldn't appreciate it if Riles bled all over the sofa, but they needed to get him down and heal him. Before they could make it to the couch, Ash stumbled under Riles's weight. Riles fell to the floor with a thud. His breath wheezed, and he stared forward at nothing.

"We're losing him," Marlowe said. "We have to stop the bleeding."

Healing alchemy wouldn't bring his arm back. Healing was a form of alteration, of mending wounds and broken bones—not creation. Ash couldn't simply grow Riles a new arm, certainly not without understanding Riles's physical makeup first.

Ash took a deep breath. Source knew he had little skill in the medical sciences, but anything would help. Marlowe seemed to sense what he planned. She whipped a hand, a strip of leather appearing. She rolled Riles onto his back and tugged the strip between his teeth and tongue. She nodded to Ash.

Ash closed his eyes. A crackle of heat sparked into flame. Riles screamed. He thrashed his legs, his other hand tearing at Marlowe. "It's almost over," she said. "Riles—please, it's almost done."

The fire died, Riles's screams replaced by moans. The smell of burnt flesh turned Ash's stomach. Marlowe raised both hands, white light glinting as she reached for the blistering skin. She breathed long and slow. The bubbles melted, new skin patching over the burns—

"What—"

Ash spun. Ramsay stood behind them, snow clinging to her hair and shoulders as she stared down at the scene. Ash hadn't even heard her come in. "What the hell is this?"

Ash looked to Marlowe, who glanced up at him with a clenched jaw but hadn't paused in her work. He stood and went to Ramsay, hand on her elbow. "I didn't know you were home."

"Is that *Marlowe?*" Ramsay breathed, anger blazing in her eyes now as Ash tried to turn her away. "What the fuck is she doing here?"

"I can explain everything—"

"Yes, you sure as hell will—"

Marlowe called. "I need your help, Ash."

He held his breath, then spun around to kneel beside Riles again. He closed his eyes, and for someone like Riles, it was difficult, the reminder that, in the eyes of Source, every human being was worthy of love, indeed *created* by the energy of love—but still Ash managed to pull that energy from his core, to envision the healing that washed over Riles's burns.

Ramsay's voice was softer behind him now. "What happened?"

Ash dropped his hands. Riles's brows were tugged together, but his breathing was even now, at least. "I'm sorry," Ash began, unable to even look at Ramsay. "I should've said—"

"Be careful," Marlowe murmured—a warning.

Ramsay was still behind Ash. "You're a part of it, aren't you?" she said. "You pretended they captured you against your will, but you've been with them all along."

"No—no, it isn't as simple as that."

"They're the ones who attacked the gala—who tried to *kill* me—"

"They've promised not to harm you again," Ash said. He stood and faced her, a hand gesturing weakly at Marlowe. "As long as I joined, they said you'd no longer be a target."

"You lied to me." The hurt in Ramsay's eyes made Ash's chest ache.

There wasn't much Ash could say to explain why he was with the rebels—not with Marlowe there, listening; and besides that, Ash wasn't sure how much of that excuse would be a lie. Could he really say, without any doubt, that he only worked now for

Lord Alexander, doing the man's bidding? His own feelings on the matter were so tangled that he wasn't sure.

The only words he could manage to say were "I'm sorry."

Ramsay swallowed. She looked from Marlowe to Riles. "Are you also the ones who attacked McKinley?"

Breathlessness leaked from Ash's chest and into his stomach. Marlowe was silent. Ramsay stared hard enough at Ash that he knew she wouldn't let the question go unanswered. "Yes," Ash said, "but—"

Ramsay turned away. "That—Source, I don't know what to say to that."

"It was an accident," Ash said. "The student who died—there wasn't supposed to be a fight at all. They shouldn't have even known we were there—"

"Yet she did die," Ramsay said. "And Callum mourned her, and you—you looked him in the eye, Ash, and you offered your condolences."

"You're being too harsh on him," Marlowe said.

Ash knew it wouldn't help. Ramsay clenched her fists as if stopping herself from throwing fire at Marlowe. "What did you say to persuade Ash to join your group?" she said. "It was you who did, wasn't it? It could've only been you."

"It's only because of me that Ash is even alive. The group wanted to assassinate him. I convinced them otherwise."

"It's true," Ash offered, though he'd barely managed a whisper.

"And now you work with the people who wanted you dead?"

"They're not bad people, Ramsay."

Ramsay raked her fingers through her black strands. She seemed at a loss for words.

Marlowe stood now, too. "We request sanctuary."

Ramsay outright laughed. "You're delusional if you think I would ever help you."

"This is Riles," Marlowe said. "He's just been gravely injured, as you can see. He needs shelter or he will die."

"Why not just take him back to your base of operations?" Ramsay asked. "I can only assume that's where you've been, Ash, each time you ignore your in-shelter order. Truly outrageous, to think that Edric's suspicions about you were right all along."

"He isn't *right*—"

"Do you even know how much time and energy Callum has spent arguing on your behalf?"

"He's the one who had me locked away in the first place," Ash said, quiet anger now heating his words. "And you're the one who allowed him to without a single word in my defense."

Marlowe held up a hand. "Please," she said when both Ash and Ramsay looked at her. "We only need a room for the night. There's no question now that the safe house has been compromised. I want to return after I've searched the area with a remote viewing. I promise to leave with Riles as soon as I know it's safe to do so."

Ash stared hard at his boots, shame and anger mingling. Ramsay took a long moment to answer. When she did, her voice was tight. "Ash, you can take them to the west chambers."

"Thank you," Marlowe said, reaching down for Riles.

"You won't tell Callum," Ash whispered, "will you?"

Ramsay had already turned to leave. She paused in the threshold. "I don't know." She continued forward, leaving the three behind.

※

A sweat broke on Riles's skin. Marlowe and Ash had done their best, but there was still the possibility, after all, that Riles might not make it. Marlowe sat at the edge of the bed with a damp cloth that Ash had wet in the sink. She'd spent too much energy healing Riles and needed to rest before she could attempt something as draining as a remote viewing.

"I'll be ready in another hour or so," she said. Anyone else, and they might've needed a full night's sleep and a meal to feel replenished; but then, Marlowe was hardly like anyone else. Ash sat on the floor at her feet, back against the bed frame and palms pressed into his eyes.

"Source," Ash said. "How did everything get so fucked?"

He hadn't meant only with Callum and Ramsay, though that was certainly reason enough for the ache that started to grow behind his eyes.

"Are you sure you're not overreacting?" Marlowe asked. "I'd assumed you and Thorne and Kendrick were the type to swear loyalty to one another, no matter what."

"Only if the loyalty is returned first," Ash murmured. And it was true, wasn't it? He'd betrayed Callum and Ramsay. It would be entirely fair if Ramsay went to Callum and told him the truth. Ash had to face the fact that he'd hurt the people he loved.

Ash sighed. "Will Riles be all right?"

"It's hard to say. He keeps teetering back and forth."

There was the subject Ash had been afraid to broach since they'd reached the Downs, but he knew it couldn't be avoided forever—yet, before he could open his mouth, Marlowe spoke for him, as if she could hear his thoughts. "Elena wouldn't want us to waste time mourning her."

"Do you want to mourn her?"

Marlowe stared forward at the paneled wall. "I've never had anyone in my life who cared for me," she said. "Growing up on the Lune estate, I was tormented; and then I was adopted by your father. I was only ever a tool—a spy, a weapon. It used to upset me, to see others receive love and feel belonging, knowing I'd never experience that; but as I grew older, I eventually learned to accept my circumstances. There was no point in wishing for anything different. That was simply my lot in life. But Elena . . ."

Ash stared hard at the ground and swallowed as he felt the heartache emanating from Marlowe's skin.

"She found me fighting off Lune followers. She helped me—offered me a home. I knew better than to let myself feel too attached to anyone in that house, but for the first time, I started to believe that maybe I could find a family, too."

Ash was quiet. He surprised himself with the words that next came out of his mouth. "You know, technically, you're my sister."

Marlowe raised a brow at him.

He shrugged one shoulder, more embarrassed now. "My father adopted you."

Marlowe's smile quirked. "You have a morbid sense of humor, Woods."

Riles groaned in his sleep, teeth clenched, before he fell silent again. Both Marlowe and Ash still watched him when Marlowe spoke again. "Someone's betrayed us. I know it isn't you," she said, before Ash could interrupt. "But someone at the base is leaking information—to Lord Alexander and Lune followers both. They're responsible for Elena's death now, whoever they are; I will find them, and I will kill them for what they've done."

"Who do you think it is?" Ash asked.

"Honestly? I thought it was this one," Marlowe said, gesturing at Riles. "I wasn't buying the *constantly enraged* act. It'd always seemed to me that he was only trying to cover up something, to distract us from a truth."

Yes, Ash saw how that might make someone like Riles appear suspect. He didn't know anyone else among the group well enough to think who might've betrayed them. He couldn't begin to imagine how Hendrix would've gotten away with it without any of the others knowing, and Finley seemed too young, too innocent, to be so callous.

"What will you do?" Ash said.

"I'll complete my remote viewing, take Riles back if it's safe, and act as if I don't believe we were betrayed. It was only bad luck. We'll all be focused on regrouping—making new plans, now that Elena is gone." She swallowed the swell of energy that prickled Ash's skin. "Meanwhile, I'll gather what information I can until I've found the traitor."

With Marlowe's particular skill set, growing up as his father's spy, Ash was certain she'd be successful. He hoped to Source she wouldn't turn those skills against him. It was enough to deal with the consequences now of having betrayed the two people he loved; he wasn't sure if he could bear the weight of shame if Marlowe learned he'd betrayed her, too.

"Do you need to be alone?" he asked.

"No," she said with a small shy smile. Ash was used to seeing the gleaming, overconfident smirk she'd shown when hunting him just a year before; this softer smile was more genuine. It was a nice change. "You can stay, if you like."

✳

After Marlowe meditated, she opened her eyes. She said she'd seen the safe house and saw no evidence of attack nor that anyone else was watching, too. "Only Hendrix was awake, still waiting for us to come back." Her gaze fell. She must have thought of the fact she would have to be the one to break the news of Elena's passing.

"Would you like me to come?" Ash said.

"It's all right. Now that Thorne knows the truth, you might be better off here, convincing her that it's for the best you're working with *extremist rebels*."

Marlowe gave a smile that seemed to say, *Good luck*, as she helped Riles to his feet, slouched with his arm over her shoulders. She touched the wall, black threads uncurling, and stepped into the void with one last glance at Ash, shadows sucked away as the two went.

Ash wondered if he should hide in the room or leave immediately himself, returning to House Alexander, where he was expected anyway—but Marlowe did have a point. He wandered the corridors, sticking his head into the kitchen and office until finally he found Ramsay sitting in a chair in the library, book facedown and tented in his lap as his chin rested on his fingers and he stared at nothing.

He sighed and slipped his spectacles on when Ash stepped inside. Ash leaned against the wall, hands behind his back. "I'm sorry," he said, because he realized there wasn't anything else to say.

"Those words feel particularly meaningless right now," Ramsay let him know.

"But it's true. I'm sorry I've kept things from you and Callum. I'm sorry I've lied."

"I'm not sure if you understand the full implications of what you've done," Ramsay said, voice quiet. "You've lied to me and Callum, yes—but you've betrayed the state. You're a traitor, Ash. You could be executed for this."

Ash sorely wanted to explain that Alexander had sent him on this mission, but he realized it would only be an excuse; he would be lying to Ramsay again, to pretend he was only working on behalf of New Anglia. Maybe it was fair to admit to himself, finally, that he was also a radical alchemist rebel.

"You've seen how alchemists are treated," Ash said. "You must feel the same way—"

"Feel what, exactly? That we should burn down Kensington? Kill every Head?"

"We have no one on our side within the Houses. No one fights for us, Ramsay, except maybe Alder, but they can't help. Even House Adelaide just follows orders blindly—"

"*Callum* is on our side."

"Do you really think that's enough?" Ash demanded. "The reds are under Edric's control. Edric's looking for any reason to get rid of Callum. We can't depend on him to save us, no matter how much he wants to try."

"So you'll have me betray Callum and the state, too?" Ramsay asked. "That's what I'd be doing, if I kept your secret." When Ash didn't respond, he continued. "The reds are under Edric's control, but he ultimately answers to Lord Alexander."

"And you trust Alexander, do you?" Ash asked.

Ramsay stared at him for one long moment, brows furrowed. "Lord Alexander believes in alchemist rights," he finally said, when he apparently decided that Ash had been entirely serious. "He's considering loosening the license requirements—doing away with the tier laws altogether."

"He just wants to control us, Ramsay. Isn't it obvious?"

"How is *freeing* us *controlling* us?"

"Having a patron hand us our rights whenever he feels like it isn't true freedom," Ash said. "Better that we take our rights ourselves than be tied to Alexander, kissing his feet for his generosity for a natural right that was owed to us in the first place."

A muscle in Ramsay's cheek jumped. "Do you agree with the rebels, then?" he asked.

"What?"

"Do you think the way to create change is blowing a hole in a building?" He paused. "Trying to kill me?"

"Source, Ramsay, of course I don't."

"You say that as if it's obvious. I'm not so sure it is."

Ash wasn't the only one who'd made mistakes, who had hurt others. "Your inventions . . ." Ash said, before he could stop himself.

Ramsay frowned. "What about them?" he asked, voice dangerously cold.

"You invented a weapon with the sole purpose to kill."

"That is generally what weapons are meant for."

"New Anglia has seen enough death without your help."

"And do you think the killings would stop if my invention were to disappear, too?" Ramsay asked, and continued before Ash could interrupt. "The firelocks are meant to *help* alchemists," he said. "The average practicing alchemist who is innocent in all this. The firelock can be used for protection: to stop the Lune extremists, to assist House Kendrick in putting order to New Anglia and ending the murders of innocent people."

"I've only ever seen your firelocks used against alchemists," Ash said. "A man can barely walk. A child nearly *died*."

Silence followed. For a heartbeat, Ash worried Ramsay would say that, perhaps, the rebel alchemists didn't deserve to live.

"And you're not worried about those weapons being used to kill alchemists?" Ash asked.

"Not the particularly violent ones who have a tendency for murder, no," Ramsay said. He continued before Ash could speak. "You have to admit, Ash, your words sound dangerously close to extremist rhetoric."

Ash shook his head. "I can agree that Alexander can't be trusted and disagree with extremist methods."

"Like you did with your father, you mean?"

Ash's head jerked backward. Ramsay's stare was unmoving, though his hands tightened around his crossed arms.

"What does Hain have to do with any of this?" Ash said.

"My parents were extremist in their methods, too," Ramsay reminded him. "It's what drove me to atone for their killings in the first place."

"And I don't want to atone?" Ash said. "I'm burdened by what my father did every day!"

"I know. I thought we had that in common," Ramsay said. "It's why I'm surprised that you'd speak like you're following in his footsteps instead."

"Hain asked your parents for help, too," Ash said, "and they ended up using an invention that killed hundreds. Maybe you're more like your parents than you think."

He'd gone too far. Ash realized it the moment the words slipped from his tongue. Ramsay's face and body were both perfectly still, but Ash could practically feel the coldness that washed over him in waves.

Ash listened to Ramsay breathe for a long moment, expected Ramsay would look at him again, that he could apologize and they would make up as they always did—

"Maybe you should go," Ramsay said.

Ash's heart fell. "Ramsay, I'm sorry—I shouldn't have said—"

"Please." He still wouldn't look at Ash.

He stayed where he was for a moment more as he hoped, waited, for Ramsay to change his mind. When he didn't, Ash did as he was asked and turned for the door.

23

It was odd to return to the manor of House Alexander, where the attendants who bustled past were blithely unaware of the hell Ash had just survived. It likely would take some time for anyone to even learn what had happened, if knowledge of the attack on the Lune base spread at all. And wasn't this dangerous, too? The Houses knew the growing number of Lune followers could be a threat, but they had no idea about the level of danger that waited in Sinclair Lune.

Ash knew he'd be expected to go to Lord Alexander and tell the man what had happened; he'd want a report that the leader of the Ironbound faction of the ALP had been killed and that they'd attempted to attack Sinclair Lune himself. If Alexander learned that Ash had not come to him with the truth, Ash would only be questioned. And the fragment Ash had consumed . . .

His breath shuddered at the very memory of the rush that had filled him. The chaos had taken over all his senses, and for a moment, he forgot that he was alive in a physical body at all. He'd released all the pain and fear that had stalked him relentlessly for months on end. He lost his breath at the thought of finding another fragment—letting go and being lost in the chaos again.

Source knew Alexander would want to know that Ash had found and consumed a fragment, would expect a report on the battle of the Lune base. But Ash only felt a tug pulling him to his chambers, away from the lord and all other responsibility he faced.

He closed the door behind him with a click and stood in the center of the room, unable to move. He wondered if Ramsay and Callum had met, if Ramsay had told the older boy the truth.

What would Callum say to Ash? He didn't want to think of the possibility. He'd made so many mistakes, and Ash was certain not all could be forgiven.

✳

Ash saw Elena's head on the ground every time he closed his eyes. He heard Riles's screams. His heart thudded as he remembered Lune's grip on his neck. Ash checked the mirror and saw that fingerprints had left bruises. He didn't know if it was true, that this man was truly the reincarnation of Sinclair Lune—now, it felt more plausible than ever.

A second day had passed when Ash decided he couldn't take being trapped in his room another second. He wandered the halls until he came to the dining hall. It was a slower day, it seemed. There were only scattered visitors, chatting amicably among themselves. Lord Alexander himself was not there, but Ash spotted a cousin of Val and Lady Alder herself.

Ash noticed Charlotte just as she glanced up and saw him, too. She offered a smile, and especially after their last awkward encounter in this very room, Ash felt he had little choice but to take the empty seat beside her. And besides, Ash wouldn't have easily admitted it, but he was lonely, too, and at least he knew Charlotte wouldn't hide sharp insults behind pretty words.

"It's nice to see you, Sir Woods."

"And you, Lady Adelaide."

Ash had arrived just in time for appetizers; attendants came forward with plates of breads and salads.

"How have you been?" Charlotte asked him. "Have you managed to fill your days, serving Lord Alexander as advisor?"

Ash remembered well that Charlotte would likely be able to see through any lie he told. Healers who worked with energy tended to be much more in tune to emotion, to the point where those feelings could translate into words. Ash shrugged, imagining a wall between them. "Lord Alexander doesn't call on me as much as I would've expected him to."

"Count your blessings, then, that you're able to spend your days at leisure while reaping the reward." Charlotte gave a pleasant smile.

The reward, Ash supposed, was living in the manor. He didn't have the heart to tell Charlotte that it felt much more like a prison. He picked up his fork and shoveled lettuce into his mouth. He felt the stares of others at the table.

Charlotte didn't seem to mind his ungraceful manners. "I had the chance to speak with Callum last evening," she said. Ash was surprised she hadn't avoided the topic of Callum altogether. "He seemed tired. Understandable, I suppose, for a commander of the redguards." She paused. "Is he doing better today?" she asked.

Ash didn't know, and it embarrassed him to say. "I haven't seen nor spoken to Callum for the past few days."

Charlotte hesitated, maybe realizing she'd overstepped. "I see." She sipped water. "Well, perhaps to be expected. He's been so busy recently, much more than before. I honestly worry if he's able to handle the stress of it all."

"It's kind of you to care," Ash mumbled.

"I know it can seem like all of Kensington is swept away in falsities, but Callum is a close friend of mine," Charlotte said.

Ash couldn't bite back his curiosity. "You attended Pembroke with him, didn't you? What was he like?"

An attendant arrived with another course—stuffed chicken with creamed mushrooms and a bowl of soup for Charlotte. "He was much more of a troublemaker than you'd expect," she said once the attendant left.

Ash's brows rose as he quirked a smile of disbelief. "Really?"

She nodded. "At Pembroke, we were expected to take what we were taught as fact, but Callum constantly questioned everything. I was in the year above him, but even I heard about the debate he'd gotten into with a professor, once, about the *point* of war. Apparently, the professor had claimed that the Great War brought peace to New Anglia, but Callum insisted that war would never be a tool of peace—that war would only ever bring more war. I decided I rather liked him then." Charlotte's smile at the memory faded. "Well, that was all before secondary. Callum became more interested in his loyalty to his family name, as the years passed."

That would've been around the time Callum had met Ramsay. "I heard that was a difficult time for him."

She sipped her clam chowder from a spoon before she responded. "Callum tried his best then. Just as he's trying his best now. His new responsibilities will be especially taxing, I think."

"New responsibilities?"

"Callum might not have had the chance to tell you yet," she said, uncertain, as if afraid there was a chance she'd said too much again. "Lord Alexander has given Callum an opportunity to form his own House."

A pang vibrated through Ash's lungs, taking his breath away. "What?"

"It's a chance, apparently, to branch off from House Kendrick." He put the fork down beside his plate. "He hadn't said."

"I hope I haven't overstepped."

"Not at all." Ash swallowed. "What's the purpose of the House?"

It was lucky that Charlotte didn't seem to consider the possibility that Callum didn't want Ash to know. "From what Callum told me, he wants to blend the redguards and alchemists."

Ash stilled. He wasn't sure what to say to that, and he was also aware of his expression—he wiped his face clean, though from Charlotte's tugged brow, he was sure she'd sensed the tangle of energy. The hurt, the disgust, the anger. "Redguards and alchemists?" he echoed.

"He wants to recruit alchemists, apparently, to fight as redguards and train any redguard who wishes to learn alchemy. I think it's a wonderful idea," she said. "It could mend alchemist relations with the Houses that are more—ah—*conservative* in their beliefs."

But Ash had stopped listening. It occurred to him, then—the reason Callum had been so insistent on not killing the rebel alchemists, the *new venture* Lord Alexander had mentioned. Callum would claim it was for the best, that he was only trying to find compromise; but Ash could easily see how Callum would request that this be the punishment of Marlowe and Finley and the rest: to be forced into his House as alchemist redguards, perhaps made to fight against their will. That was certainly one way to be rid of the rebel problem, wasn't it? To coerce them into fighting for the Houses instead.

"And it would only make the Houses more powerful, in the end," Charlotte added.

And Lord Alexander—yes, of course the man would've been glad for this idea, if it wasn't his to begin with. It suited his goals of controlling alchemists while pretending to be on their side. Horror, Ash realized at the end of it all: That's what he felt most.

"I have to go," he said, pushing out his chair.

"But you haven't finished your course yet—"

"I'm not hungry," Ash said over his shoulder, leaving the room as quickly as he could, ignoring the stares that followed.

※

A voice whispered to Ash that going to Callum would not help, but still he couldn't stop himself from entering the Kendrick town house through the manor's portal door. The portal wasn't linked to Callum's office, like it had been at the cottage; instead, Ash stepped into what appeared to be a meeting room of sorts, with cherrywood paneled walls and gold marbled floors. A smaller mahogany table took up the length of the room, though the space was now empty.

The town house wasn't the same as the one where he'd been kept prisoner, Callum his personal guard (it'd been close to the initial blast and had probably disintegrated along with everyone else

inside; the people probably hadn't even had a chance to scream),
but it had been modeled to look similar enough, with the dark
mahogany panels and red hues throughout. The halls were much
busier than Ash expected; a mix of attendants and redguards
and scribes hurried back and forth, most not even noting Ash at
all, though a few did seem to recognize him, double glances lingering.

Ash strode forward with purpose. There was little chance that
someone would stop him and question him if it seemed like he
belonged. He turned one corner and then the next. It was just a
little harder for him to breathe as he leaped up the stairs two at
a time, turning a sharp corner to where he knew Callum's office
waited—

He knocked into a solid body, stumbling back. Ash looked up,
for a split second thinking he'd accidentally run into Callum, but
his stomach fell when he saw Edric instead. Edric paused. Two
reds stood tall on either side of him as the man stared Ash down.
Ash's fingers dug into his palms. Edric didn't practice alchemy,
as far as Ash knew—wouldn't have been able to read his mind—
but still, Ash feared that at any moment the man would be able
to realize Ash had betrayed all of New Anglia with just a single
glance.

"Sir Woods," Edric said. There was no expression in his tone
nor face, but Ash recognized his vibrations all the same—and
could Ash truly blame him? Edric was only a few years older than
Callum. He hadn't really had the chance to take his time growing
up, like all his older brothers, before this role was thrust into his
hands; and not only that, but he had lost his family: his older
brothers, his mother and father. Ash would look for someone to
blame, too, if he had survived so much tragedy. Maybe Ash could
understand Edric Kendrick, even with hatred burning in the
man's eyes. It was even worse, Ash realized, that the man's hatred
wasn't entirely misplaced. He hadn't been wrong to distrust Ash,
to want him locked away and killed.

Ash ducked his head. "I'm sorry," he said, as much as he hated apologizing—it was better to avoid a potential conflict with Edric now. "I was looking for Callum."

"Did Commander Kendrick give you the password to our portal door?"

"Yes."

"I'm sure you can understand how that might be a risk to New Anglia's security."

"Callum trusts me," Ash said.

"Yes. I'm aware." Edric turned to one of the reds standing at his side and asked that he make note to have the password changed. Edric pushed past Ash, the others filing by as well. Ash listened as the thud of boots slowed to a pause behind him. "I'm not sure what alchemy you've performed on my brother," Edric said, "nor how, exactly, you got into his head that night, to make him betray his family . . ."

Ash's memory took him to the night Edric described: Callum, running away with Ash so they could save Ramsay. Edric had been the one to find them, to try and stop them. Even then, he'd tried to protect his youngest brother in the only way he knew how.

Edric continued. "But you're fighting against lineage, Sir Woods. Blood is design. You must know that you cannot win."

Ash turned to look at Edric's back, a frustrated tangle of words stuck on his tongue.

※

Callum's office was empty when Ash found it. A heavy desk had neatly stacked papers that seemed to be awaiting signature, and the shelves lining the walls held tomes of history and politics and law. Ash could feel Callum's lingering energy, as if maybe the boy had been here just moments before. Flickers of pale blue light faded in and out of the air. That light would've been comforting, once. Now, it only reminded Ash of how much had changed.

Ash very much felt that he was intruding, arms tightly held as he stood at the window. Would Callum think it strange to come to his office and find that Ash had appeared uninvited? The clock on the wall said only five minutes had passed, though it felt closer to an hour by the time the door opened and a familiar energy marched into the room.

"Ash," Callum said. Ash took a breath and turned. Callum closed the door behind him slowly, staring at Ash in surprise. He scanned Callum's expression for any hint of anger or betrayal. It seemed Ramsay hadn't told him the truth yet, Ash thought with a flicker of gratitude. "I thought I sensed your energy in the hall," Callum said.

Ash didn't know where to start. He swallowed, hands still gripping his arms as he scuffed the floor with a boot.

Callum hesitated by the door with a frown. "Is everything all right?"

"No," Ash admitted. "It's not. I heard from Charlotte Adelaide that you're forming your own House."

Callum's expression faded. "I'd have preferred for her to keep that to herself," he eventually admitted. "It was only a proposal from Lord Alexander—an idea, that's all."

"You would force alchemists to train as redguards, Callum?"

"I wouldn't force anyone to do anything," Callum said, and sounded offended by the implication.

"Only the rebel alchemists, if you find them."

Ash realized there was something in his tone that made Callum pause, but only for a moment. "They would be test subjects, yes," Callum said. "An opportunity for them to earn their freedom, instead of being locked away and executed. A mercy, I'd say."

"That isn't true freedom."

"Why're you so upset about this?"

"Because you know that this isn't where the House would stop," Ash said, voice louder now. "You force the rebels to fight for you— and if it does well? You'd need more alchemists. Who would you turn to next?"

"Why're you assuming no one would volunteer?"

"Which alchemist would ever want to fight for House Kendrick?"

Callum's eyes narrowed. "It wouldn't be House Kendrick."

"The roots are the same. The history of people who don't believe alchemists deserve the right to exist—that's all the same."

"That's why I'm here, Ash," Callum said. His usual patience was pulled tight, threatening to snap. "What the hell do you think I've been doing all these months? Why do you think I rejoined House Kendrick at all?"

"To follow your brother's orders, apparently."

Ash might as well have spat in Callum's face. His head rocked back, before he turned away. "Why does it seem like you're more concerned with the well-being of alchemists than the state of New Anglia?" he asked. Paused, then added, "Than me?"

Ash swallowed. "I care about you—of course I do."

"We've drifted," Callum said. "I know I've played a part in that. I've been too busy. I've hardly seen you. But you've played a role in this, too."

"Me?" Ash said. "I haven't done shit, Callum," he said, even as his energy screamed otherwise.

"You've fought me at every turn, whenever I make any request—"

"Because your requests always sound like orders," Ash said. "You act like just because you're a commander now, I have no choice."

"Technically, you don't." Callum's words vibrated in the air, lingering on his tongue. He swallowed, then dropped his head. "I didn't mean that."

"Right."

"I'm sorry, Ash. Truly, I—Creator."

Ash wanted to believe him. "You've changed—or changed back to who you always were, I don't know which."

"My position isn't easy. I've been given a chance to transform New Anglia, handed enough power that I could help alchemists.

What would you rather I do?" Callum said. "Should I turn the opportunity away? Do nothing to help alchemists—to help you?"

"You could stop playing the middle ground," Ash said. "Trying to appease your brother and Lord Alexander—"

"That's how politics *work*, Ash," Callum said. "If I didn't try to appease them, I would lose my position, and I'd have no way to help anyone at all."

"Then lose it," Ash said. "Don't be a commander anymore. It'd be a better help to have you on the side of alchemists, fighting for us, than helping Alexander to control us."

Callum worked his jaw back and forth, perhaps struggling to find the right words. "Working with the redguards—it'd be a fine opportunity, Ash, a job that pays well and offers housing in the barracks. I don't see how joining a House would be oppressing anyone."

"Then I'm not sure you understand what freedom means to begin with." And with a man like Winslow Kendrick for a father, Ash couldn't blame Callum, not entirely. How could Callum have ever learned what freedom meant for himself? He'd been taught from birth that his only role in this universe was to be controlled, disciplined, punished, and eventually inherit the role of doing the same to others.

Callum gave a heavy sigh, arms crossed. "There isn't any point to fighting like this. We're supposed to be on the same side. I thought we were."

Ash didn't reply. He'd thought so once, too.

24

An attendant knocked on Ash's door the next morning with the message that Lord Alexander expected Ash to join for that afternoon's meeting with all the Heads of the Houses. Ash had hoped he could spend the day locked away in his chambers; he was exhausted, emotionally and physically, and the thought of seeing Ramsay at the table and Callum seated behind his brother made his shoulders ache.

His relationship with Ramsay and Callum was the only good he'd experienced since he lost his best friend and his mother. The thought of returning to a life alone wilted Ash from the inside. Well, maybe he needed to get used to the idea—it was a strong possibility, now, if Ramsay's reaction to him joining the rebels, and the last argument Ash and Callum had, was anything to go by; maybe he needed to learn that he could stand on his own, too, without them by his side.

He bathed and dressed and walked down the marble halls to the conference room. He was late, of course, though only by a few minutes. Glances slid to him as an attendant opened the doors and he slipped inside. The conversation had already begun, Charlotte giving an update on her House numbers.

"—risen since the attacks," she said as Ash ducked his head and found his seat behind Lord Alexander. He received a couple of dirty looks from Head Val and Edric.

Callum stared at the back of his brother's head, though gentle blue energy reached for Ash all the same. He couldn't have been told the truth by Ramsay yet, then. Ramsay herself stared hard at the table's surface, as if the mere sight of Ash were too painful to bear.

Charlotte continued. "I think there's a growing sentiment that more healers may be needed, in the coming months."

"And rightfully so," Lady Alder said. "There have been a number of attacks against members of my House, regardless of whether they practice alchemy or not. We were promised advanced security measures. Where are Thorne's prototypes?"

"The supply chain has become more limited in recent days," Head Galahad explained. "It's difficult to access the materials needed for Head Thorne's newest development."

"How vital is the assembling of the newest prototype?" Alexander asked.

"Well, Head Thorne has done remarkable work," Lord Val said, "but a report from Head Kendrick described a number of issues—"

The firelocks hadn't been as successful in killing as they'd hoped. Ramsay blinked at the opposite wall. Ash wasn't sure if she was hesitant to provide a detailed report knowing a rebel was in the room or if she was simply ashamed, knowing her invention had been used against him. "The recoil gets stuck," she murmured, then cleared her throat and spoke more loudly. "And it takes too long to reload, apparently."

"We need the continued production of the firelocks for protection against the ALP," Edric said. "The Alchemist Liberation Party grows more brazen. We've received reports of attacks against the base of the reincarnated Sinclair Lune." Ash sucked in a breath. "The man who calls himself Sinclair Lune has not been seen since the attack."

Charlotte frowned. "Did Sir Lune not accept the luncheon invitation?"

Edric's glare slid to her, and Ash realized she had spoken out of place. Maybe it wasn't meant to be shared knowledge outside the Great Houses that Lune had been asked to tea.

Alexander said, "Lune was invited to meet with me before the attack on his base. He politely declined."

Edric continued as if there'd been no interruption. "His followers call for justice. There's to be an expected rise in the number of attacks against manipulators in retribution."

"Maybe it would help," Ramsay said, voice rough, "to begin by not using that word to describe alchemists."

Edric ignored her. "If the ALP attacks in turn, we will see the beginnings of the cracking of New Anglia." *The cracking*—another way to describe civil war, perhaps. "My suggestion is to instate a new Head of Lune immediately to quell the growing anger of the Lune followers. Sinclair Lune would be the perfect candidate." There were outraged murmurs around the table, but Edric continued. "I recommend that squadrons locate Lune and bring him to safety so that he may take his title as Head."

Ash tightened his hands into fists, nails digging into his palms. He wished he could've spoken then, described to them all the danger he'd witnessed for himself. The man would be able to touch whoever he wanted, spreading his control over each of the Heads of Houses. He could take control of Lord Alexander himself and order the execution of any and every alchemist. Inviting Sinclair Lune into the manor could only mean the end of New Anglia.

Lady Alder spoke. "That man was the one who initially called for the attacks against alchemists. To invite him into the manor of House Alexander—"

Edric spoke over her. "I also request more funds in the fight against manipulators. We've gathered evidence that the ALP has grown in both resources and numbers, in part due to Commander Kendrick's investigation."

Ash stiffened as Callum stood, hands behind his back. The stance reminded Ash a little too much of Callum's late father. "The investigation has brought me to two possible bases within the Alchemist Liberation Party." Ash's gaze snapped to Callum and then Ramsay, only to find her already staring at him out of the corner of her eye. "One base is on the outskirts of Glassport," Callum said. "They have been responsible for the attacks against several redguard stations in the area. Another, which House Kendrick will prioritize, has been found in Ironbound."

Ash's skin burned under her gaze as he blinked, eyes drying.

"There's conclusive evidence that the base in Ironbound is responsible for the attacks against McKinley College and the gala honoring Sir Woods. Witnesses of both claim seeing a smoke-like substance at the scenes of the attacks; data collected with the help of House Val traced this substance's energetic pattern's origin point to the suspected base."

Ash stilled. Source energy could be traced, energetic patterns of alchemy recognized with different tools, such as a meter that sensed alchemic properties in the air once alchemy of certain tiers was performed. It hadn't quite occurred to him that the same could be said for chaos energy, too. And if a meter was used within Alexander's manor, it could take its tracker directly to Ash's room.

Lord Alexander sat back in his seat. Though Ash could only see the back of the man's head, he felt the lord's energy focus on him all the same. "That's excellent work, Commander Kendrick."

"Thank you." Callum swallowed, his only sign of emotion. "My main goal is to bring Sophie Galahad justice."

Ash's stomach twisted. He stared hard at his hands.

"I assume you will be heading the attack against the base?"

"Yes, my lord," Callum said. "Head Kendrick has given his approval for the operation to begin this evening, once the sun has set."

Ash jolted. "What?"

Everyone turned to look at Ash, Alexander included. The man's eyes narrowed, cold—a silent warning for Ash to be silent. Callum frowned.

"So soon?" Alexander asked, turning to face Callum again.

He hesitated. "Yes, my lord. It's my belief that the alchemists have a line of communication within one of the Houses, and I don't want to give them enough time to prepare for the attack."

Ash couldn't stay silent. He didn't even know what to say, only that he had to try to say something, *anything*, that could stop Callum. "Don't—"

He cut himself off, freezing under the glares sent to him around the table. It was now his second time interrupting the meeting. Edric's glare suggested he was moments from asking that Ash be told to leave. Ramsay didn't look away from a point on the wall. Callum's brows tugged. "Don't what?" he asked.

Ash swallowed and ignored Alexander's glare. "Don't attack tonight," he said. Even buying himself an extra few hours to go to Marlowe and warn her and the others would be better than leaving them all to be captured or killed. "To move so quickly—I doubt you and the reds would be prepared. We don't know what's waiting at the base. It could be dangerous."

Callum's expression softened. "Thank you for your concern, Sir Woods," Callum said, "but we're trained redguards. We'll be fine."

He thought Ash was only worried for his safety, and wasn't that a betrayal as well? Ash had worried for Marlowe and Hendrix and even Riles, but Callum was risking his own life by going to the base, too. Maybe Ramsay had a point after all. Maybe Ash didn't even realize he'd stepped onto the path his father had laid for him. Ash's energetic wall trembled against Callum's energy. One crack, one simple thought could have Callum suspect—

It was small, almost unnoticeable, but it was there all the same. Callum frowned for the briefest moment, the slightest tinge of confusion. Ash focused on the wall between them.

"I agree," Alexander said to Callum. "I wish you success and look forward to hearing an update once your mission is complete." Callum nodded his thanks and returned to his seat. "Next agenda point," Alexander said with just one more chilled glance at Ash, a warning to keep his mouth shut.

Ash stopped listening. The pale sky outside the window suggested the sun was close to setting. He didn't have long to warn

the others and help them escape the base unharmed. He itched
to get out of his seat and run to his chambers, to warn Marlowe
and the rest. When finally Lord Alexander dismissed the meeting, Ash was among the first to his feet, headed for the door even
as Callum's energy reached for him, curious if something was
wrong—

"Sir Woods," the lord's voice called. Ash paused. Alexander
still sat at the head of the table with a wide smile. "A moment of
your time, please."

Ash couldn't refuse the lord's order, not in front of all the Heads
who still filed out the door, Ramsay nodding as she listened to
Head Val's urgent whispers. Callum lingered with raised brows
at Ash. If Ash hadn't warned the rebels to leave in time, there was
a chance, wasn't there? That Callum could battle against Marlowe
and Riles and the rest—that he could be injured, left to die without Ramsay or Ash there to help—

The door snapped shut. Ash stood at the other end of the table. It struck him that Alexander must've been able to see how
anxious he was to leave, and Ash forced himself to take a breath
and approach the lord. He pulled out a chair.

"A pity, about your new friends," Alexander said, his stare bur-
rowing into Ash.

"I hope Commander Kendrick and his squadron will be all
right," Ash said. There was something particularly sick about his
words, Ash thought.

"I was surprised when you spoke."

"The rebels are stronger than Callum might anticipate."

"I'm sure Commander Kendrick will be fine. The redguards
have trained to battle against alchemists, after all." Lord Alexander tilted his head. "We'll have to find a new role for you, once
the safe house is destroyed. There won't be any extremists left for
you to watch."

Ash swallowed the urge to scream. The safe house wasn't filled
with extremists—only the injured, people who wanted a better

New Anglia. "An attack on the base will only do more harm than good," Ash said. "You must be able to see that."

"I don't think I do. Though I will always remain on the side of alchemists, there was a reason I asked you to join the party in the first place. If they become too dangerous—attack and kill innocents—then negative views of alchemists will only grow." Alexander peered at Ash. "I can't help but wonder if you've become too invested."

Ash didn't blink. "You asked me to infiltrate, to share information with you. I've worked hard to do so. Of course I'm invested."

"Not because you've grown to care for the rebels you've worked with?" Alexander prompted. "Fought alongside? Maybe it was too much of a risk after all," he said, "asking you to join them."

Ash clenched his fingers to stop them from shaking. Alexander wasn't hiding his distrust. Ash needed to offer information—anything, even if it was only a lie, to help him get back into the lord's good graces.

"What happened, with the attacks on Lune?" Alexander asked.

"It must've been another chapter of the ALP," Ash whispered.

Alexander didn't believe him—he couldn't have, the way he watched Ash as if frozen without even the hint of a smile. "It interests me, that in all your time with the Ironbound base, you haven't learned any information about the other base locations."

There was a hidden threat in the man's words. Ash hid his hands in his lap. "The main base of operations is in Kensington," Ash said. Close enough to the truth to seem realistic; far away enough that the reds could be sent on a chase for weeks, hopefully, long enough that Ash could warn them that the redguards were close to finding the other bases. His gaze flicked up to Alexander, to see if the man bought his lie; it was a gamble, a risk, to assume Lord Alexander hadn't already learned that the base was actually in Hedge.

Alexander didn't speak for a long moment, until finally he asked, "How do you know?"

"I overheard a conversation between Marlowe and another rebel."

Alexander stared blankly at Ash for one long moment. It was impossible for Ash to know what the man thought or felt, impossible to sense if Alexander believed Ash.

Alexander hummed. "Fine," he said. "Thank you for that information. I'll have Edric increase the number of patrols around Kensington."

※

Ash raced through the halls, almost slipping as he turned a sharp corner. He reached out to Marlowe through the energetic web, calling her name, but got no response as he leaped up the stairs. He slowed as he reached the hall of his chambers. Ramsay waited outside, arms crossed as she leaned against the wall beside his door. She didn't look up nor move as Ash slowed to a stop beside her.

"Callum's already left," she said. "His brother needed him back at the town house. Last-minute preparations."

"You haven't told him yet?"

"No." She scuffed a boot against the marble tile. "It isn't exactly an easy task, telling the person you love that he's been betrayed by the other person you both love, too."

Ash swallowed the pressure growing in his throat. "I have to go."

"Stay, Ash—please," she said, pushing from the wall finally. She stood in front of Ash, blocking him from the door. "I don't know the particulars—why you're doing this, nor how you got so tangled in it all, but it isn't too late. We can go to Callum together, explain what happened—he'll be angry, of course he will, but he's always been forgiving—"

Ramsay suddenly closed her mouth and clenched her jaw. "Please," she said again.

"I'm sorry," Ash told her. That was all he could think to say as he called on the chaos beating through his veins. He saw the pale barriers of protection around the manor—imagined shattering through them, his body appearing in the safe house he had come to love, and he lurched.

25

The air around Ash heated and expanded as he stumbled into the room that had been given to him. The mattress was still bare, pushed into its corner, the shelves still empty—but, somehow, the space felt like the only home he had left. He raced down the hall to Marlowe's room, sliding to a stop at her threshold. The door was already open. Marlowe sat at her desk as she read. She turned with a smile that faded when she saw Ash's face. She closed the book in her lap. "What's wrong?"

"They're coming," Ash breathed.

"Who is?" Marlowe said, though her expression suggested she already knew the answer.

"The reds. They're coming here. They're planning to attack tonight."

Marlowe cursed beneath her breath. She called Hendrix's and Riles's names.

"I was just in a meeting with all the Heads. Callum—" Ash swallowed, then tried again. "Commander Kendrick plans to lead a regiment here once the sun's gone down."

There was a thud of footsteps before Hendrix stood in the threshold, shoulders slumped and bruises beneath his eyes. Riles pushed past to stand in the center of the room, too. The stump of his arm was wrapped in bandage. Even if Ash disliked the boy, he was glad to see Riles on his feet.

Marlowe looked at a boarded window, cracks showing the red light of a setting sun. "Not much time, then. Redguards are probably already in the area scoping out the house."

Hendrix cursed beneath his breath and stuck his head out into the hall, shouting to the other occupants of the safe house. "We've got reds incoming!"

An echo of startled calls and questions replied. Otto appeared at his door's threshold at the far end of the hall. Ash wondered who else was there—how many people could be killed by Callum and his guards. Finley, at least, was still recovering at the main base in Hedge.

Riles clutched the bandaged arm to his side as if it still pained him. "What should we do? Should we fight?"

Ash looked to Marlowe, just the same as the other two. He wondered if they all agreed that she would take control of the Ironbound base in Elena's place. Marlowe sucked in a quick breath. "No," Marlowe said. "Too many of us are injured. We need to evacuate."

Hendrix crossed his arms over his chest. Ash wondered if possibly, just maybe, Hendrix might have been the one who betrayed them all. "That's a weak position," he said. "We can't just give up this base. It's in a prime location for the Liberation Party."

"The base location has already been revealed to the reds. We can't stay here anyway, whether we decide to fight or not."

"This could be a strategic opportunity," Hendrix argued. "The reds don't expect us to know they're here. We could get the upper hand."

"Do you really think we're prepared to take on the redguards right now?"

"I agree with Hendrix," Riles said, hoarse. "We should stay. Fight."

"We're in no state to—"

A thud shook the walls. Dust fell. The floors trembled. Everyone froze. Another thud, vibrations running up Ash's shins. Their gazes fell to the creaking floorboards beneath them.

"They're already here," Ash whispered.

Marlowe ran to a boarded-up window and stared through a crack, a spotlight on her cheek. "There's a line of them—maybe twenty. They've surrounded the town house. They're trying to blast the door open."

"We're out of time," Ash said, voice rough. "There isn't any point in fighting just to die. We have to go—*now*."

"What if they find something that points to Hedge?" Riles demanded.

"At least we'll be better prepared to fight in Hedge!" Ash argued.

"We can't leave without getting rid of evidence—"

Another explosion almost threw Ash off his feet. Marlowe stumbled back, while Riles gripped the doorway for balance. It was the hardest blast yet. Hendrix stared up at the ceiling as the walls groaned, and Ash wasn't sure if he imagined the floors beneath him sway.

Marlowe pushed away from the window and stormed past. "Riles, you and I have thirty seconds to clear as much as we can. Hendrix, lead the evacuation of the others out the back and into the alleys. I'll meet you there to get us all to Hedge. If we don't make it, travel to the Hedge base without us."

She knew there was a chance they didn't have thirty seconds. She didn't want to risk the lives of everyone in the safe house. Riles raced from the room, too, as Ash watched Marlowe throw open her desk drawer, rummaging through papers—a glimpse of a map of McKinley, scratched notes. She set it all on fire with a spark of alchemy.

"It's no use," he whispered. A storm of voices and heavy footsteps thumped in the hall. Hendrix and Otto and the others were running down the stairs. "There isn't enough time. You'll *die*, Marlowe—"

"Either leave, or shut up and help me."

He swallowed, then followed Marlowe as she raced down the empty hall and into another room—Elena's old room, he realized. He grabbed books from shelves as Marlowe threw stacks of paper into a pile on the floor. Ten seconds.

Marlowe threw a flame at the pile and sprinted out into the hall. "There's a desk on the first floor with—"

The final blast hadn't been as powerful as the rest, but it was enough. Its echo ricocheted through the halls. Debris flew up from the staircase and into the hall. Ash ducked as Marlowe stumbled to a stop. A plume of smoke filled the air, darkening the hall. Ash's eyes stung. A scream echoed. Hendrix, Otto and the others— they'd run down the stairs. Had they made it outside yet? Shouts, thundering footsteps—the reds were in—

There was a roar from below—Hendrix's yell—and a familiar series of *pops*. Riles staggered down the hall covered in gray dust, but he didn't look injured, didn't look like he was bleeding—

"First floor," he gasped. "They're on the first floor. Hendrix and the others—"

Marlowe hurried to a wall and pressed a palm against it, black tendrils flowing. "Go. Now."

Riles gasped. "What about—"

Footsteps below were the only sounds. The reds were trying to be quiet. Marlowe shook her head. If Hendrix and the others hadn't been killed in the blast, Ash doubted they would've survived the weapon fire that followed—and if the three didn't move now, they would be next.

Marlowe grabbed Riles, pushing him into the chaos. Ash ran after, just as he saw the flash of red—a uniform, a guard at Marlowe's threshold, raising a firelock—

Marlowe leaped into the chaos after Ash, both stumbling out the other side.

※

Ash hardly had a chance to take in his new surroundings of a wide room; everything had blurred, and the darkness of his new setting did little to help.

Riles let out a heavy breath and fell to the floor, head hidden

between his knees as his shoulders began to shake. "Creator—
fucking hell—"

Hendrix and the others were likely dead; if they weren't, they'd
been taken prisoner by Callum. The other boy had said, promised, that he wouldn't kill any of the alchemist rebels. Ash wasn't
the only liar, it seemed, though this did little to comfort him.

Ash squinted up at Marlowe, who stood unmoving. She shook
her head. "I—I meant to send us to Hedge," she said.

As much as Ash had considered the safe house to be his home,
he could only imagine how much more that was the case for Marlowe. It'd been the only safe space she had found, her first and
only sanctuary. Ash knew what it was like to lose a home he'd
loved, but at least he had other rooms, other beds, other places
where he'd found comfort, too. Ash put a wall up around his
emotions, to be dealt with on his own.

He stood, a hand on Marlowe's shoulder. "You're in shock.
Both of you are."

At his words Marlowe blinked, nodding as she wiped her eyes
with her shoulders. "We'll mourn later."

The three appeared to be inside an abandoned warehouse. The
walls were brick, some crumbling to chunks on the stone floor.
Glass windows had shattered above, though the remaining pieces
tinted the moonlight green. Marlowe got to work starting a fire in
the center of the room, smoke gushing.

"I guess the energy of my intention mattered more than what I
said to myself in the moment," Marlowe murmured. "I'd wanted
safety. This was a hideaway I often used, before Elena found me."
She stood, inspecting her work as the fire sparked embers.

Riles had also gotten to his feet, wiping his face. "Is it secure?"

"For now. I'd put barriers up, but I don't know how strong
they are still. We have a few hours, at most, before anyone truly
searching will find us."

Ash's heart thundered at the thought of Callum storming

through the warehouse doors with orders to arrest, maybe kill, everyone hiding inside.

"What now?" Riles said.

"We rest," Marlowe said. "We need to move on within the hour."

"Where do we go?" Ash asked.

"Hedge," Marlowe said. "It's the only place for us left."

Ash had wanted to travel with the two to the Hedge base and help them resettle however he could, but he worried that he would only be in the way. That worry was only reinforced when Marlowe insisted that he go back to the safety of Alexander's manor.

"We'll be all right," she said. "You should go back to Kensington, before anyone realizes you're gone."

Though it was her suggestion, guilt pierced Ash at the thought of his friends begging for refuge, finding thin cots to sleep on, and bargaining for food and water. And Hendrix, Otto . . . Ash felt that he should've been there, too, to grieve the loss.

When he stepped through the shadow that engulfed his Kensington chamber's walls, he stood frozen in the center of the room. The weight of emotion that he'd tried to hold above his head with trembling arms began to sink. His shoulders shook, tears falling. Maybe he'd been in shock, too. There was so much he'd tried to push away, to put aside, but it'd become too much now, the attack and the feeling that he constantly fought for his life without rest and the knowing that he'd deceived the two people he loved and that they had both betrayed him, too—

Ash lay curled in his bed, though he couldn't sleep. Pressure swelled in his chest. A second heartbeat reminded him of the peace, the bliss, of the chaos streaming under his skin. He could find more chaos—let it take over his body so that he wouldn't have to think nor feel. He focused on his breath: out and in and out again.

Whispers of the redguard attack on an Ironbound rebel base spread through the halls. Ash heard an attendant tell another that a majority of the alchemists had just managed to escape, apparently, though two had been killed. A red standing guard beside another at the back doors to the gardens muttered that Head Kendrick was furious at his younger brother for botching the ambush. "Sounds like the manipulators had been pre-warned. There might just be a traitor among the ranks after all."

Ash walked the garden path. As long as the reds and Callum thought the traitor was coming from within, there was a chance they wouldn't look his way. Maybe he felt a little too confident as he returned to his room. He opened the door, stumbling to a stop when he saw Callum inside.

"Hey," Ash said, slowing as he pulled the door shut behind him.

Callum sat on the sofa in the sitting area, leaned forward with his elbows on his knees. He was still in his commander uniform. Ash wondered if he hadn't had a chance to change from the night before. Emotion tumbled through Ash—anger, mainly, as he shuffled inside. He focused on holding a wall against Callum, imagining steel, Callum unable to feel or sense the heat swelling in Ash's lungs at the thought that Hendrix and Otto could be dead—

"What brings you here?" Ash asked, back to Callum. He yanked off his sweater, feeling too hot, and adjusted his binder beneath as he opened a dresser drawer, searching for a shirt.

It took another moment for Ash to realize that Callum hadn't responded. He turned, brows raised, then paused. He didn't know how he hadn't seen it, the book in Callum's hands. Ash's breath shuddered to a stop.

Callum stared only at the book he held, brow furrowed. He flipped open the cover, rustling through the pages, and then snapped it shut again.

Ash didn't know what to say.

Callum sat straighter, placing the book on the sofa beside him. It was the same he had gifted Ash after their last visit to Riverside. "I'd thought there was a chance," he said, voice hoarse. He cleared his throat and tried again. "I thought maybe it wasn't yours—that it was only a coincidence. Even the note," he said, laughing to himself. "Creator, I told myself that there might be another Callum living in Ironbound, another Callum who happens to have my handwriting." He swallowed, smile dropping. "I waited to see your reaction."

And now he'd seen it. Ash clamped down on the waves of shock he knew surged from his skin. "I don't know what you mean—"

"Please, Ash," Callum said, voice softer now. "Don't make this more difficult than it already is."

The lump in Ash's throat grew.

"You're one of them," Callum said. He nodded to himself. Maybe it was a fact he'd held on to all night, turning it over and over in his head, trying to convince himself that it couldn't be true and searching for reasons why it wasn't, but it was a fact Callum had to accept now. "You're one of the radicals."

Panic tore through Ash, pulse racing. The fear that drowned Ash sucked his breath away. He shook his head. He'd tell the truth—he'd tell Callum that he was only a spy, that Alexander had hired him, fuck the man's request to keep it from House Kendrick—

"Were you there?" Callum asked.

Ash could hardly hear himself speak. "What?"

"When the rebels killed Sophie," Callum said, eyes meeting Ash's now. Even when Ash had been Callum's prisoner, before they'd come to know and respect each other—love each other—Ash had never witnessed the sort of fury burning in Callum's gaze. The force of Callum's rage made pale blue light glow from his shoulders, but it didn't remind Ash of clear skies. The color was an ice tinted blue, cold enough to burn Ash's skin. Callum's narrowed gaze looked like the sort he would save for someone he hated. It seemed like an impossible thought, one that Ash questioned even then—but at that moment, Ash wondered if Callum hated him.

Ash was speechless. He shook his head, mouth open.

"Did you see it happen?" Callum said, standing from the sofa. "Did you do it yourself?"

Callum usually held curiosity. He'd ask questions. He'd say that he knew Ash, loved him, and so would ask why Ash's book would be at a rebel base, rather than conclude that Ash was a murderer. Salt burned Ash's eyes. He blinked, tears falling.

"Tell me why," Callum said quietly, walking closer now.

"I—" Ash shook his head. He couldn't speak.

"Why the hell would you do this?" Callum shouted, voice ricocheting through the room.

No—Ash didn't *want* to speak. Ash's own anger snuck up on him. Callum hadn't been interested in hearing the truth, and right then, Ash didn't have any interest in telling him.

Ash steeled his expression. He raised his chin and blinked his tears away. "You've completed your investigation, haven't you?" he said. "You should be able to figure out why on you own."

"Are you mocking me?"

"I'm sure you'd be able to figure that one out, too, if you tried hard enough."

And there was the other simple fact, too, the one that wasn't as easy for Ash to look at now: He could insist that he'd only been working with the radicals as a spy as much as he liked, but he knew that the energy behind his words would speak the truth. He was as much of a rebel as Marlowe and Riles were, too.

Callum's balled fists shook at his side. Ash's memory showed an image of Callum's late father, moments before Winslow Kendrick had slammed his fist into Ash's gut. Would it have been so surprising if Callum did the same now? Ash wouldn't have thought Callum would be willing to become a commander of House Kendrick, once; wouldn't have thought he'd try to form his own House to keep alchemists as his prisoners, forcing them to fight as reds. Ash hadn't thought Callum would become his father nor start to look like the nightmare Ash had seen in a parallel realm. Why wouldn't Callum hit Ash now, too?

Callum took a slow breath, but his gaze remained cold. "I should have you arrested."

"Yes, maybe you should."

Callum swallowed hard. "If I arrest you, my brother will order your execution," he said. "He'd likely have you killed by tomorrow's end, before anyone could interfere."

"But I'm just an alchemist rebel," Ash said. He'd meant for the words to be taunting, but his voice was softer now. "Isn't that what I deserve?"

Callum squeezed shut his eyes, brows pinched together. Ash thought maybe the older boy was trying not to cry. "I don't understand," he said, words tumbling out now. "I don't—Creator, Ash, we were fine. You, Ramsay—we were happy. We'd figured out a way to make it all work, and you—"

"Do you really think that?" Ash said. "I was lucky if I saw you and Ramsay at all for weeks, and when I did see you, it was only for you to yell at me, berate me like I was a child—"

"I was trying to keep you *safe*."

"And then you have me *locked away*—"

"What do you expect me to do?" Callum said, voice louder. "Now that I've learned the truth, now that I know you're one of them—what am I supposed to do?"

Ash realized then that Callum had found himself in another similar situation just half a year before. Callum had needed to choose between Ramsay and his family. He'd chosen Ramsay then. He'd told Ash that he couldn't stand by and watch Ramsay's execution. But Ramsay and Callum—their relationship had been different. They'd had each other for years, had built a tender love that ached. Ash and Callum's love was new. Maybe it wasn't enough for Callum to risk saving Ash's life, too.

"You've already left your family once before," Ash whispered.

"The rebels will tear New Anglia apart."

"The *Houses* are already doing that," Ash said. "House Kendrick, the Lune followers—"

"You're asking me to choose between you and the lives of innocents."

"Innocent alchemists are dying, too."

Callum seemed to have run out of words to speak. He sat heavily on the sofa, staring at nothing. "I was doing everything I could to mend . . ."

"Your idea of mending was our sacrifice. It wasn't enough."

"What should I do?" Callum said. Ash thought he was only speaking to himself but was surprised when he looked up and met Ash's gaze. "Tell me what you want me to do."

Quit the redguards. Leave House Kendrick. Practice healing, as he'd always wanted. Become the man Ash knew Callum could be, if only he'd let himself try. "I can't tell you that," Ash said. He sounded strangled. "You have to decide for yourself."

Callum nodded, hands gripped together. They shared silence for a moment, before he asked, "Does Ramsay know?"

Ash hated that he would be a point of hurt between Callum and Ramsay now, too. "He just found out," he whispered. "He was trying to decide if he would tell you."

"Betray your trust or mine," Callum said. "A difficult choice."

He stood suddenly then. Ash took a step back. His body was tired now, weak from the emotion that had coursed through him. "I won't let Edric kill you," Callum said, voice tight. "Of course I won't. But I need time to decide what I'll do next."

Callum always had been the type to want time, to consider his thoughts and feelings before acting. Ash wondered if what Callum truly needed was a little more impulsiveness. Maybe then he would be more willing to choose what his heart wanted instead.

26

Word had spread: A boy who had lived in the cottage had not only been a practicing alchemist, but had been related to the killer Gresham Hain, the man behind the massacre of Kensington. That boy—Ashen Woods was his name—had played a role in the killings as well.

"He's been titled a hero by Lord Alexander himself," one man told another as they sat together in the pub of the town's inn.

"More evidence the bastard elite can't be trusted," another replied.

Several miles away, in the heart of Hedge, a boy rolled out of bed before the sun had a chance to rise. The scar across his palm was light and thin, but it still ached from time to time—a painful reminder of the friendship he'd lost. Well, perhaps it was for the best. He'd already worried that he and Ash hadn't been as close as they'd once been; and now he had no way of knowing whether his friend was even alive or not.

He dressed in overalls and boots fit for the docks and slammed his way down into the Hedge streets, dodging puddles of muck, the stench of garbage and piss clogging the air. He had a brown envelope folded in his pocket still. He couldn't be sure what was inside it; since the day he had officially joined Baron's lower ranks, he'd been given envelopes and brown paper bags with instructions to hand the merchandise off to someone who would be waiting at such-and-such pub, and to not, under any circumstances, look inside. That's what it was always called: *the merchandise*. Tobin was not by any means curious and had never peeked inside once.

He might not have been as quick-witted as some, but he certainly didn't have a death wish.

He'd grown up in Hedge, so it was odd to see how much the city had changed in the past months, though he could understand why so many were uncomfortable returning. The streets were emptier now, with more people sitting in the alleyway shadows. Tobin had heard rumors that a boy had been involved in stopping the man who had destroyed so much in just the blink of an eye and that he now lived in the manor of House Alexander among the elite. It didn't matter. Tobin never had cared much for the happenings of the upper classes.

Tobin didn't think much of it when he heard a rise of shouts. Fights often broke out in Hedge, especially now when so many had lost so much. It was only the flash of white that caught his eye and made him pause. Dozens—Creator, close to one hundred people—wearing the robes of Lune marched through the gray streets. Tobin had always preferred the words of Lune and the Creator rather than the words of alchemists and Source, but even he had to admit that recently it often felt like the remnants of House Lune were only finding opportunity in the fear of others. Maybe that was what anyone who sought power was prone to do.

A man walking before the group had his arms spread wide to the sky. "Repent now, for he has returned! Sinclair Lune will look upon us and see our sins." Cheers rang from those who followed, marching in lines. Others stopped on the side to watch, too. "He knows who manipulates, who steals the energy of the Creator. He will save only the worthy: the true followers."

It seemed to Tobin that, no matter what side anyone was on, someone was always trying to tell everyone else what was right and what was wrong. He hated that he thought of Ash then. His former best friend had been headstrong. He'd always decided what was best for himself, no matter what anyone else thought— even Tobin.

One of the followers near the end of the march slowed to a

stop. Maybe it was something in Tobin's expression. Maybe it was the fists curled at his sides. The follower raised a hand to him. "Do you believe in the power of the Creator, young man?"

Tobin might not have been as quick-witted as Ash had been, but he'd always had a pretty good sense of self-preservation. "Yes," he said. "Of course I do."

The follower smiled. "Then join us, won't you?"

※

A young boy sat cross-legged on a wooden floor. The smell of mold choked him. The walls were stained black. Flies buzzed in his ears. Lines of laundry hung across the kitchen and the living room, where they'd shared the mattress, his mother and his baby sister and the boy who would one day claim the name *Sinclair*. His mother hadn't moved from her bed in three days. A fly landed on her open eye. His sister wouldn't stop crying.

Her body was found, Sinclair and his sister taken to the estate of Lune. He didn't have a name then, since he would not speak; and because no one had any record of what the dead woman had called him, he was simply called *boy*. His sister died after two weeks. The boy stood on the patch of dirt where her small body had been buried, staring at the stone that had been used to mark her grave. The Lune attendants who saw him whispered the boy was mad. He hadn't cried when his mother died either, apparently. He'd been found sitting beside her, refusing to speak.

As the months passed, he blended into the estate. He took well to his lessons. A teacher murmured that the boy had a mind that would've suited House Alder, had he been born into better circumstances. He'd learned to read in only seven months. When he spoke again for the first time in two years, it was lines he had memorized from Sinclair Lune's teachings. "We are each made of the love of the Creator," he recited, "and so we are each a fragment of the Creator, too."

It wasn't a particularly popular teaching, and the timing of this recital had been less than ideal. A girl had been beaten for dropping a dish that'd shattered. The children had been lined up to watch her punishment, and while she sat crying on the floor, the boy chose his moment to speak; he was beaten next, his words considered insolence.

The boy had often witnessed those who spoke of love choose to act with hate. He had seen the beatings and whippings of other children around him and had watched neglect lead to their deaths. As the years passed, the boy recognized a simple truth: Each human was a reflection of the Creator, yes; but in that case, the Creator was nothing more than a hypocrite. The Creator had given life and death, happiness and pain, creation and destruction.

The boy watched the Lune followers around him preach of heaven as they created the very hell they feared, listened to them speak of love for their enemies while they planned to hang their enemies by their necks. And wasn't the boy nothing more than a hypocrite, too? He hated the Lune followers for their hatred. He wanted them to burn for the suffering they caused. He was willing to light the flame himself.

When the boy survived his childhood, he was given a name, now forgotten; and when he was a man, he left the Elder lands to spread the teachings of Lune, wearing his robes of white. It was all he had been trained to do. He preached as the hypocrite he was and knew each human to be, too.

He had been in Hedge, the day the man called Gresham Hain appeared in the sky. Firestorms raged. Smoke billowed and white ash rained. The nameless man wasn't afraid of death. He stood and watched while people around him screamed, crowds jostling around him as they ran. The nameless man saw when a white stream of light shot into the heavens; and he saw, too, a rip in the sky, a black line tear above the clouds of smoke, before that line faded.

The man crawled over the carnage and wreckage. The city ruins were silent. Night was falling. He stood on a pile of crumbled white stone, below where he thought he had seen the rip above the clouds, and he stared up. There was nothing but smoke. He looked down and saw a black pearl floating at his feet. It seemed to glow darkness as he reached for it—watched as it hovered over his palm. Tendrils of smoke curled toward his mouth. He swallowed the orb. He didn't think to himself what he wanted, not consciously—but alchemy was the language of energy, after all, and the fragment of chaos knew the intention that was in the man's heart.

Ash opened his eyes. Gray fog drifted, so thick that he could hardly see his hand in front of his face. When he looked down, he saw clear water. Ripples spread from his bare feet. The fog dissipated, showing the outline of a person who stood across the lake. His father's voice whispered, *Would you like to know where to look next?*

Ash gasped. He shot up in bed, hands grasping at the sheets. His breathing slowed, and he clenched his eyes shut. The last images he'd been shown faded: a manor of gray stone, halls of white and shelves of vials, one holding a black orb that seemed to swallow the room's light.

*

The Hedge base seemed to have only grown in numbers since Ash last visited. More people milled about, heads turning to watch him pass. It seemed word about him had spread. A child chased another while a baby's wail bounced off the walls. Ash wove between people standing about until he saw them: Marlowe and Riles had been given cots near Finley.

The last Ash had seen the child, Finley was pale and teetering on the edge between life and death. Now, they had some color in their cheeks, at least, and their eyes were bright. Finley jumped from their cot with a gasp and threw themselves at Ash hard enough that air got knocked out of his gut. He stumbled back a few steps and grinned as he patted Finley's shoulder. "It's good to see you, too."

Riles gave Ash a nod in greeting from his cot. It was much more than he would've gotten just a few weeks before.

"You didn't have to come," Marlowe told him as he sat with her on the ground in front of her cot.

"How could I not?"

"The more you come here, the more of a chance that you could be caught."

"Ash!" Finley said as they hopped back onto their cot. "Look at this." They pulled up their shirt enough to show a fleshy scar that webbed beneath their ribs. It had Ash believing, for a moment, in the miracles of the Creator.

"Does it still hurt?" Ash asked with a wince.

Finley dropped their shirt with a shrug. "Sometimes. But I can handle it."

Fury flashed inside Ash for a moment—fury at the redguards who had done this to Finley, at Commander Rake for attempting to have a child killed. Fury, for just a second, at the hands that had created these weapons.

He swallowed and smiled at Marlowe, who watched him closely. "How has the relocation been?"

"It isn't the safe house we'd all made a home, but it offers protection, at least, and a warm place to put our heads."

Finley and Riles had been in the middle of a game. Ash and Marlowe watched as the other two sat opposite each other. Finley held up two fists, and Riles pointed at the left; Finley grinned and opened an empty palm, and then their right, a gold orb floating, Riles expression falling into devastation.

"We'll be all right for now," Marlowe added.

Ash knew he would need to tell Marlowe, at least, that Callum had learned the truth about him, knew he was a radical—but it felt like she already had more than enough to handle. Well, maybe that was only an excuse, and Ash wanted to put off telling her for as long as possible.

Riles sighed as he hunched forward. "We'll be all right for as long as Baron lets us stay here, anyway."

Ash frowned. "He wouldn't ask you to leave, would he?"

"Some are still convinced that our base is the source of the leak, even though they have no evidence," Marlowe said. She sighed, rubbing the back of her neck. "Pretty sure it's just an excuse to destroy the Ironbound chapter while they still have the chance—replace us with their allies and friends. Whoever Baron chooses might just have some say in reshaping New Anglia," she said. "If we win the war, anyway."

Maybe it shouldn't have surprised Ash, that even within a rebellion for freedom, there were vies for control and power within. Humans certainly had a way of repeating the same cycles, again and again.

Marlowe nodded over her shoulder at Ash. "Come on. Baron wants to speak with you. You should see him before you go."

Ash fell into step beside her, Riles following as he pointed at Finley and said to stay put. People bustled back and forth across the floor, but the base was quieter than Ash had remembered. Most relaxed in their cots, sleeping. A group of teens laughed as they played a game of cards that floated between them, sitting cross-legged on the concrete floor. The three turned one way and the other, until they slowed to a stop. Baron stood over the oak table that was covered in scattered papers. Ash was relieved to see that Gretchen wasn't there, nor the Glassport leader, Guthrie. One man's animosity would be enough.

Though Baron didn't look up from the mess of papers, he somehow knew Ash and the others had come. "Sir Woods," he said without looking up. "How kind of you to visit."

Ash's fingers fidgeted behind his back. "Marlowe said you wanted to speak with me."

Baron ignored this with a heavy sigh. "Pity, about the Ironbound base," he said, eyes still fastened to the papers in front of him. "It's lucky that you were able to learn about the attack and warn the group in time."

Baron stood tall, finally meeting Ash's stare. "Maybe I shouldn't be surprised you've been so helpful, even as Alexander's lapdog."

Ash glanced uncertainly at Marlowe and Riles. It'd been a seed of thought, but Ash remembered how Baron's eyes had narrowed on him, once, as he'd mentioned Gresham Hain's plans for his son to inherit the revolution.

"Elena had insisted you were particularly useful for the information you could provide," Baron continued. "It appears she was right."

But Baron must've been able to see that this had only been Hain's dream. Ash had no desire to take control of the ALP. He wasn't a threat at all to Baron's title—yet the man's gaze chilled as he inspected Ash. Maybe Baron was concerned that Ash had gained too much of a foothold within the group, or he'd had too much time to consider that, perhaps, it would be better to get rid of the boy before he had the chance to become a leader in the revolution.

Ash forced himself to stand still as Baron approached him slowly, gaze stuck on Ash as if he'd secretly been a mind reader all along. "Perhaps you'd like to find a way to be even more *useful*," Baron said, voice low.

Ash's heart thudded. He had to find a way out of this. "I'm not sure how much more helpful I can be. I'm giving you information directly from the manor of Alexander—"

"If you truly were your father's son," Baron interrupted, "you would've offered Alexander's head on a platter by now."

Ash glared as the man towered over him. An impossible request, one that would only end with Ash's death, though he was sure Baron already knew that. "I can't do that."

"You still won't do what you can to win this war for the ALP."

Marlowe spoke up. "It wouldn't be any help for an alchemist

group to be responsible for the death of Alexander. The Houses would only have the lord replaced. They would target alchemists more than they already do."

"It's not only the Houses we have to worry about."

Ash froze, air caught in his chest at the memories that swarmed him. "Lune's base was attacked, weakened, thanks to us."

"Yet you can't confirm if the man lives. He's vanished, seemingly into thin air."

Marlowe narrowed her eyes. "He's probably hiding in a hole somewhere, licking his wounds."

But even Ash heard the quiver of uncertainty in her tone. It was strange that the man had disappeared, no sign of him since the attack.

"But you're right," Baron said, waving a hand about. "We also have to keep the Houses in mind. They have a plan to attack alchemists and imprison us—to follow Sir Woods's lead, and make us all into their lapdogs."

Baron's gaze flitted to Ash. How could the rebellion leader already know about Callum's new House? Ash hadn't warned Marlowe yet. Ash narrowed his eyes as he wondered if the man had another insider within the Houses, too.

"Ash has already done more than enough." Ash blinked in surprise and turned to see Riles clutching his shoulder as if it'd started to pain him. He glared at his boots. "He's saved all of us twice over. You should be thanking him."

Baron stood taller, arms spread. "Thank you, Sir Woods, for everything you've done for the ALP, as well as alchemists across New Anglia. But it's worth questioning, isn't it? If you truly were a fighter for this cause, you would offer to handle Alexander personally—perhaps Head Kendrick and his younger brother, too."

Ash never had been good at controlling his temper. "Watch what you say."

"What?" Baron said, smile quirking, as if this was exactly the reaction he'd hoped to see. "It's true, isn't it? You aren't the only eyes we have within House Alexander. The reports that you are partners not only with Commander Kendrick but with Head Thorne—"

"They have nothing to do with this."

"No?" Baron scoffed. "Thorne is the creator of the weapons used against alchemists. Kendrick killed your ally." Ash tried to interrupt, but Baron spoke over him. "Though, to be fair, you wouldn't have been able to warn the Ironbound base at all without sharing Kendrick's bed. Tell me, how does that all work, exactly?" Baron asked, sarcasm dripping.

Ash's skin was hot. He felt on display, everyone watching. "How does what work?"

"Being with a person who believes you are his to control."

Ash took in a breath to speak, but he couldn't force out the words. He wanted to argue that Callum didn't believe this at all, but the truth tangled the words in his throat.

"So," Baron said, "Callum Kendrick is only managing to oppress every single practicing alchemist in the state of New Anglia except, somehow, you."

"Callum—he's only trying to do what he thinks is best, even if he's wrong." Ash's words were quiet and rushed. "He's trying to help."

"Trying to help by—what, killing us? Imprisoning us?" Baron outright laughed. "You're delusional, *Sir Woods*," he said. "You live inside House Alexander's manor. You're better positioned than anyone else here. If you were really on the side of alchemists, you would kill Lord Alexander, Head Kendrick, and Commander Kendrick yourself."

Ash's vision narrowed. Baron's voice sounded far away.

"Elena never wanted so much bloodshed," Marlowe said.

"Elena is *dead*," Baron said. Marlowe flinched. "She died because she was too weak. She still clung to the hope of *peace*." He eyed Ash. Ash wished sorely that he had not come. "It's time to try something new."

Ash shook his head. "I'm not killing anyone. I refuse."

Baron took a short breath. "Then I'm not sure you're as necessary to this cause as you seem to think you are."

Baron's words felt like a threat. He glanced at Marlowe, who met his eye with a clenched jaw. If he left then, Ash wondered how long before Baron sent his own after Ash, claiming he was nothing more than a liability, a potential leak within House Alexander itself.

He swallowed. Elena hadn't wanted it, had thought it was too much of a risk, but it was the only game piece Ash could think of, the only leverage that might convince Baron—

"Well?" Baron said.

Ash opened his mouth to speak. "Elena kept something from you, before she died."

This piqued the man's interest, at least. He raised a brow, head tilted. "And what is that?" he asked, tone suggesting he knew this was Ash's last attempted scramble.

Marlowe seemed to have caught on to his plan. Her eyes widened, energy screaming that he stop. He released a shaky breath. Ash could tell Baron about the chaos. He could use the fragments as a bargaining chip, something that might extend Ash's life, if even just for a few days more.

"Did you wonder—" Ash swallowed, mouth dry.

"*Ash*," Marlowe said, breathless.

Ash struggled to speak. Just the idea of potentially finding a fragment of chaos only to turn it over to Baron instead of consuming it himself made Ash's skin sweat, his throat dry. Ash tried again. "Elena suddenly became a much more powerful alchemist after my father's massacre," he said. "Right?"

Light faded from Baron's eye, a flinch of annoyance in his jaw. Yes, the man had clearly noticed this, too. "Go on."

Marlowe outright shook her head. "It was nothing," she said, speaking over Ash. "It was a dangerous experiment, one that weakened her, ultimately—"

Baron's eyes hadn't left Ash. "Chaos," Ash said.

Riles hadn't caught on to what Ash meant to say, but at this, he spoke up. "Ash—"

"Chaos has been leaking into New Anglia because of my father's attacks," Ash continued. "It's energy that can be used, very similar to Source energy—but much more powerful."

Baron sat back on his table, hands clenching the edge. His surprise seemed to silence him for a long moment. Ash's heartbeat thudded in his ears. Beside and behind him, Marlowe and Riles held their breath. "That would explain a few things," the man eventually said.

"Elena wanted my help to find the fragments," Ash told him, "and I know where one is now." Marlowe's head swung to him, surprised, but he ignored her. "You don't trust me. I understand that. But maybe I could earn your trust. I can bring you a fragment of chaos." He shrugged a shoulder. "Maybe you could get a taste of power for yourself."

It was too tempting. Ash could see it in the man's face. Baron pretended to consider, but the vibrations that flowed from him in waves were more than obvious: His answer was yes.

"Let me find the fragment for you."

It was only once the three were out of earshot of Baron that Marlowe turned on Ash, walking backward, her eyes burning with anger. "What're you doing?" she hissed. "Why would you tell him about chaos? After everything Elena warned—"

"He doesn't think I'm useful anymore," Ash said, not meeting her eyes. "So I had to make myself useful."

Riles marched beside Ash. "He's right. You sensed Baron's energy. He doesn't trust Ash. He's jealous as all hell, too, like a fucking child—thinks Ash is going to replace him. That's a dangerous combination."

Marlowe released a defeated breath, turning back around and walking alongside Ash again. "But you can't seriously be planning on giving him a fragment—"

Ash bit his lip. He wasn't sure what his plan was, to be perfectly honest. He'd only done what he could to buy himself more time. At least now he wouldn't have to go to sleep at the manor, uncertain if he would wake up with a knife at his throat. But the next day, and the day after that?

Marlowe took hold of Ash's elbow, and the three slowed to a stop. "You know that I wouldn't let Baron do anything to you," she said. "Don't you?"

Ash hesitated. What could she do to protect him?

"Do you really know where a fragment is hidden?" Marlowe whispered.

He hesitated. He trusted Marlowe, of course he did—but even then, a pinch of uncertainty flickered. "My father showed me in a vision."

Marlowe and Riles exchanged quick looks. "Then let me come with you," Marlowe said. "We'll find the fragment together."

It could have been possible, couldn't it? That Marlowe, in the end, only wanted the chaos fragment for herself.

27

It was easier than Ash expected, to slip from the Alexander manor later that night. Few people wandered the streets outside. Understandable, really. Ash had done his best to avoid the Kensington streets, too. The intricate buildings of white that curved along the road had been razed in an instant. Empty lots of dirt remained where town houses had once stood. Ash's heart started to beat slow and hard, fighting to pump blood. Screams echoed in his ears. A heaviness sank into his skin and weighed down his bones. House Lune followers would say that the energy of the dead were souls that rightfully belonged to the Creator—that upon death, they would each return to His waiting arms. This did nothing to explain what felt like the whispers of hundreds of thousands of people, lost, waiting to be told that they had passed on.

Patches of the neighborhood of Wynnesgrove had been flattened by fire, too. The homes that still stood were abandoned now, windows black and gardens dead. Only the college loomed in the distance, the main hall standing over an empty campus. Ash hadn't come back to Lancaster once, not since his own explosion tore through the college. It was odd to return to the place where he'd worked every day for nearly a year. He'd had a different life then; been a different person, impatient for the chance to prove himself. It seemed so obvious now, in retrospect, how much the energy of his desperation for his father's approval had transferred into nearly every other facet of his life. Returning to Lancaster felt like stepping back into a painful dream that he'd rather have left behind.

Baxter Hall had been rubble and smoke the last Ash had seen, but it was rebuilt now, newer stones of white shining against the older gray bricks that remained. Marlowe had warned that there could be new security measures with the growing resentment toward alchemists, but Lancaster College was a lot like the elite of Kensington: comfortable in its power, too arrogant to believe it could be touched. Ash tapped up the familiar front steps and placed his palms on the heavy front doors, a push of alchemic energy forcing open the locks.

The marble floors and paneled walls were familiar. Ash hurried through the corridors, past closed office doors, until he slowed to a stop outside one. A plaque read RAMSAY THORNE. Ramsay's office was in the same location as in the old building, luckily, even if the doors were new. Ash hesitated, a hand on the knob. Even if the college itself was too overconfident to put protections into place, he was certain Ramsay would think better. He took a breath and remembered what Marlowe had taught him. He focused on the energy of the space around him, more than himself—his own vibrational field heating, melting as the air shimmered.

Ash pushed open the door just enough to slip inside. He lit his hand so that to any watching eye it would only see a ball of light, Ash himself invisible. He shined the light across the familiar mess of papers and texts atop Ramsay's desk, then to the shelves—

"Took you long enough," Marlowe's voice whispered.

Ash clicked the door shut, hand still on the knob. She was invisible to his eye, too. "How'd you get here? Materialization?"

"Too many barriers preventing that," Marlowe said. "I walked in through the front doors, same as you. Let's get moving," she added. "No point in waiting around."

The less time they spent in Ramsay's office, the better. Ramsay could've created another barrier that could attack or read energetic signatures in a way that'd let her see who, exactly, had entered her space without her permission.

Ash took a breath. "And you're sure of the password?"

Marlowe had made it her business, once, to know each of the

passwords for the House manors, when she still worked for Ash's father. "It's possible Head Val changed it in the past year, though I don't know why he would," she whispered. "House Val has enemies, yes, but not many with access to portal doors."

Marlowe had already given Ash the description of the manor itself: House Val was located along the southern border of the state of Washington. She'd warned the manor had strong alchemic protections against materialization and remote viewings. "But I often joined Hain on visits," she said.

Ash remembered well that Sir Pentridge Val, cousin of Head Val, had been found dead with flowers in his throat a year before. Gresham Hain had been meeting with Pentridge, trying to discover the location of the Book of Source. It made sense that Marlowe had visited House Val alongside Hain, too.

"The top floors are all living quarters, parlors," Marlowe said, "but below, top Val members and Head Val himself conduct alchemic experiments, perform tests . . . If Hain showed you House Val in your dream, then I'm willing to bet the chaos fragment is being kept there, in the workrooms."

They'd need to make this a quick mission. Ash couldn't afford to be caught. He spoke the password Marlowe had given him. "Blue iris."

The door clicked open to dim halls. The Val manor was minimally decorated, as far as Ash could see. There were no paintings on the bare walls, which were the dark indigo of House Val, faint silver floral patterns glinting in the moonlight. Ash narrowed his eyes. There was a deep vibration humming in the air. Usually, Ash only saw light and color in the aftereffects of alchemy. This? He wasn't sure what the sound was.

Marlowe tapped in behind Ash, a glimmer of light the only proof that she was with him at all. The door shut behind her. "Do you hear that?" he whispered.

"Hear what?" Marlowe said.

Ash hesitated, then shook his head. "Never mind."

Neither moved as they breathed, both taking in their new surroundings. Marlowe had already warned Ash not to take another step once they entered. Each hall would have its own security measures, some potentially fatal. Ash focused his gaze, and there—right there, he could see the glimmers of energy shining like threads across the floor.

Marlowe took a deep breath beside Ash and held up her palm. Her energy sparked in front of them. Golden light unfurled, flattening into a disc. This should have been easy for Ash to replicate, but his breath was already shaky from upholding the illusion alchemy around him. Still, Ash closed his eyes, took a deeper breath, and envisioned the same, a red stepping stone appearing in front of him. Both looked at each other, nodded, and leaped onto the floating discs in front of them as one before jumping onto the next, running down the hall as each disc disappeared with a burst of sparks. Marlowe was faster. Her last disc at the end of the hall exploded into light and disappeared. Ash's breath trembled. He could make it to the end of the hall with just three more—

His foot sank through the last. He staggered. Purple lights flashed along with the piercing scream of a siren. The low hum grew louder, a bass that he could feel in his bones. His shoulder stung. He looked up to see a golden box had caught him a foot in the air. Spears of light had shot from the walls, the box protecting him from most, though three spears had cracked through, shattering the glass. Marlowe's illusion was down. She stood in front of Ash, fists outstretched as she grimaced with the effort. One of the spears had caught her forearm, too, a deep red gash bleeding. Ash crawled to the end of the box's opening, hand clutching the cut on his shoulder. It didn't seem deep. He'd survived worse.

He jumped to the ground. "You saved my life," he shouted over the siren.

Marlowe dropped her fists with a relieved breath and clutched one hand over the wound. The box disappeared behind Ash, too. "Making up for all the times I tried to kill you, I guess."

They stood at the opening to another hall, both ends going in separate directions. Ash was certain guards would come running at any moment. He swallowed the panic that rose. It wouldn't do any good to let his senses be overrun by fear now. "Do you really not hear that?"

Marlowe glanced at him, worried now. "I don't hear anything."

"I feel like I'm going insane."

"Just because I can't hear it, too, doesn't mean it's not there."

Ash swallowed. "What now?"

Marlowe knelt. She placed her palms on the floor, both heating with energy. "No point in trying to sneak around. Unless the manor's blueprints have changed, the laboratory will be beneath us—and I don't think House Val has a habit of redecorating."

He didn't need to tell her to hurry. She already moved swiftly. The tiles beneath her palms turned red as they began to melt. Source knew how long that would take. Something flashed in the corner of Ash's eye. He stood tall, brows raised. A figure stood at the far end of the hall. It appeared to be nothing more than a black shadow, but the longer Ash stared, the more the figure seemed to materialize.

"Uh—Marlowe?" he said.

"I know."

Ash looked at an exact copy of himself, clothes and all. The other Ash had no pupils, only the whites of his eyes, yet he was certain his copy was looking directly at him. The copy lifted a palm, a spear appearing. Ash looked over his shoulder to see, at the end of the other hall, a second Marlowe had appeared, too.

"Marlowe!"

"I'm going as fast as I can."

Ash squeezed shut his eyes and threw all his energy into two shields of light—

A sound whizzed as his shield snapped shut into place. Ash opened his eyes to see the shield had caught the spear, its tip inches from his nose. His copy stood straight and, without warning, raced forward, appearing feet away, as he leaped into the air and kicked the end of the spear, whipping it forward. Ash threw himself at Marlowe, the spear landing with a *thunk* into the melted tile where she'd been seconds before. The spear vibrated to a stop. Ash breathed hard and stood, helping Marlowe to her feet—froze when he saw Marlowe's copy standing against the other side of the shield. Her palm was pressed to the glass, skin glowing red.

"Fuck!" Marlowe grabbed the spear, yanked it out, and drove it down into the half-melted hole beneath their feet with a burst of energy that shot down. The floor cracked and crumbled, the only warning before Ash fell, air rushing through his ears. They landed hard. Light flashed in Ash's vision before he blinked it away. He'd hardly taken in the hall he and Marlowe had landed into. Glass walls held rooms, each brightly lit by bulbs that hung from the ceilings. The vibrations were louder here, a droning buzz that shook his insides and matched the beat of his heart. It was driving him insane, the sound.

Ash looked up to see his leftover shield shatter above, bits of glass scattering and raining down on them as he and Marlowe covered their heads with their arms. He glanced up in time to see the copies of himself and Marlowe stare down, directly at them.

The back of his shirt was yanked as Ash's copy lifted a hand, a burst of energy pulling him out of the way as Marlowe rolled backward in the opposite direction. The ground where they had been seconds before exploded into bits of stone, a piece slicing into Ash's cheek.

"What the hell are they?" Ash yelled, scrambling to his feet. He brushed away the trickle of blood as he ran.

Marlowe raced after him, head swinging as she searched—maybe for a sign of the fragment, maybe for a place to hide. "Creation alchemy—shadows, empty husks designed to kill, probably created using our blood when we were cut. But that's all they are: shadows."

There were two echoing thuds behind them. Ash glanced over

his shoulder. The shadows had jumped down the hole after them. "They don't look like empty husks to me."

It was surreal, for Ash to watch himself walk slowly and then begin to run—rush forward with such speed that, suddenly, he was feet away from Ash himself. He barely had enough time to turn around. The copy threw out a leg, kicking the arms Ash threw up, the only thing he could think to do—

Ash flung sideways, into one of the glass walls that shattered, and slumped to the floor. He gasped, looking up, as his copy stepped over the wall's remains, crunching closer. A burst of light flashed behind in the hall, Marlowe fighting her own battle.

Ash scrambled to his feet, just in time to throw up a red shield to block the blaze that seared the air around him. His copy materialized through the flame, inches away. Ash ducked and sidestepped the knife his shadow created and slashed at him. Ash tried to roll to the side, to get out of the room he was trapped in, but it was as if his copy knew what he would do, leaping to block his exit. Ash threw up his hands, fire sparking—his shadow's hand blew ice into the air with a hiss of steam. Ash gasped for air, sweating. He wouldn't win, not at this rate. Behind his shadow he saw Marlowe's step into view. Marlowe was on one knee, bleeding from her brow.

He couldn't defeat himself, not when his shadow seemed to know what Ash would do before he'd moved. He watched Marlowe slowly stand—watched as she looked his way, eyes wide. Her gaze flicked to Ash's shadow and then to her own, and even without her speaking, Ash understood her plan. He nodded.

A heartbeat's pause, and they ran toward each other, clapping hands as they passed. Marlowe's shadow only stared after her target, unmoving until Ash had slammed a rock he'd envisioned into her cheek. She flew into the far wall hard enough that her head cracked the glass. Ash saw Marlowe rush his own shadow in the corner of his eye, a spear of light driving through his chest— Source, it was odd to watch himself dying—

Marlowe's shadow raced at him. Ash sidestepped and envisioned a glass box surrounding her. She ran into the glass, then pounded a fist against it, white eyes wide. Ash winced, hesitant. It wasn't really Marlowe, he knew, but just the thought of killing her, even a fake version of her—

Tapping footsteps. Marlowe got to the glass first, eyes closed. A blade of light sliced through the box and the shadow's neck. Ash grimaced, looking away. By the time he'd opened his eyes again, the only sign of the shadow at all were bits of black light, drifting up like rising snow. He panted, breathing hard. The vibration hummed in his bones and beneath his skin.

"You were right," Marlowe said, watching closely. "They weren't only husks. Looks like Lord Val's decided to use a sampling of chaos, too."

Ash looked to where his own shadow's body had disintegrated in a corner of the room, black rising. He looked at his palms. His fingers shook in tune to the drumming hum, too. "Do you think Val consumed any?"

"Not likely," she said. "The Head Val I knew was always too cautious a man. But I wouldn't be surprised if he found a way to extract the chaos energy and turn it into something like—well, something like *that*."

Ash hadn't considered the possibility, extracting chaos—giving that chaos an intention outside the body, allowing it to become its own power. As Ash watched the last of the black wisps of light fade, he thought of Ramsay—remembered how closely she worked with Head Val, too. She could've been aware of the chaos fragments all along. He swallowed thickly. She could have decided to use the chaos energy, too.

"Come on," Marlowe said, footsteps tapping away. "Head Val will already know there are intruders by now. We won't have much time to find the fragment."

She walked in one direction, and Ash followed for two steps before he paused. He looked over his shoulder at the very last room in the hall. It was dark as night, no bulb lit inside. He moved toward the room, crunching through the crumbled stone and shattered glass. He ignored Marlowe when she called his name. He put a hand on the glass door and pushed it open, one palm lit. The room had a table, papers of notes spread across the surface—and on the table was a rack of vials. All were empty but one.

The hum matched Ash's heartbeat now. His mouth was dry, pain running beneath his skin. He watched himself move to the table, hold up the vial, and look at the chaos fragment within. What would his intention be? Ash didn't know. It didn't matter, not really. He only knew the hum that filled him, the buzz that ached for the fragment to join what he had already consumed—

"Ash, stop!"

He emptied the vial into his mouth. The power that surged through him splintered pain in his core, ripping through his stomach. He doubled over and grasped the edge of the table, almost falling—heard Marlowe's call, felt her hands on his arm, but it was like his skin had been burned; he yanked away, gasping in pain—

There was a click. Ash looked up to see the door to the room had been closed, and on the other side of the wall stood Head Val.

28

"Sir Woods," Val said, head tilted. His skin seemed yellow in the harsh light. "Source knows I shouldn't be surprised—you *do* have a habit of stealing from Houses, after all."

Ash couldn't speak. He was choking, the chaos fragment tangling in his throat, weaving into his body. *What is your intention?*

"And Marlowe, wasn't it?" the man said as he eyed Marlowe as well. She stiffened beside Ash. "I would've thought you'd died in Hain's attacks, since you always followed after him like a dog. Pity you survived so much, just to die like this now."

The hum vibrated, demanding an answer from Ash. He fell to a knee. He was going to be sick. Holes in the ceiling that Ash hadn't noticed emitted a steam-like substance. Marlowe began to cough, elbow over her mouth. She sagged, falling to the floor beside him.

"Though," Val said, "I must admit, I am saddened for Head Thorne. She's already lost so much. I suppose she won't be able to focus on her work for some time, after this. The energy you just stole from me—no one is supposed to know it exists. I can't allow you to go to Lord Alexander nor Kendrick nor even Thorne, telling them all that I have chaos."

You will die. The steam stung Ash's nose and the corners of his eyes. Ash realized the simple truth. Val would kill him. Ash would die if he didn't figure a way out. *Power*, he thought. He only wanted enough power to live—to survive.

Val raised a finger. Fire sparked the gas that filled the room. In one universe, an explosion had already started and was over, Ash screaming in a flash of pain before his body shriveled, organs no longer beating, skin's cells charring, his energy rushing through the dimensions as he left physical reality with the joy of realizing he could return to Source. Yet in this universe, Ash could see the explosion as if in slow motion. He watched the crackle of flame. He saw Marlowe at his feet. She couldn't die, not like this. He touched her, and he imagined her in the safety of Hedge, resting on her cot, perhaps, laughing at Finley and Riles as they played another game. He watched her dematerialize, slowly, cell by cell. The flame burst like bubbles, larger and larger, heat coming toward him. He met Head Val's eye. The man had not even realized Marlowe was gone. It would be easy, Ash thought, to appear outside the glass—to take a blade of light, and slit the damned man's throat—

Ash was in front of Val. The older man's head was turning to Ash slowly, eyes blinking closed and opening again with surprise. It'd be fitting, wouldn't it? His father had killed a Val, too, after all. Ash held the blade of light, arm pulled back, fist moving forward.

No. No, he didn't want to kill the man. That wasn't right. That wasn't *him*.

And who, exactly, was he? If Ash was only his body, then he was also the empty husk of shadow he'd left behind. Was that not Ash's body, too? Was it not true that Ash was a piece of Source itself, which was also an infinite number of fractals of energy? Didn't that mean Ash was also chaos?

Ash fell into a bed and curled in on himself. He shivered, pulling the covers over him. He didn't know which bed, nor where he was, nor what had happened. There'd been a time, once, when Ash had rocketed through the higher realms with only Ramsay as a lifeline. She would've reminded Ash to ground himself— reminded him of their intention, their mission.

A boy screamed as he ran through the fields.

A woman sobbed as she held her cold son.

"Stop," Ash said with gritted teeth.

A man roared that his father wasn't an alchemist—

A girl younger than Ash asked her killers, "Why doesn't my life matter? Why do you choose who gets to exist?"

Fire burned through Ash's mind. The back of his skull splintered in pain. He curled in on himself tighter.

A crowd of people wearing robes of white knelt. There were hundreds. They had each been named the most loyal of followers— those who were willing to sacrifice their own lives for their lord, with the faith that their souls would be gathered by Sinclair Lune and ushered to paradise after they left the physical realm.

A door shuddered. Callum raised a hand. "Again."

"Those who declare that you will fight on my behalf," Lune said. "You are the chosen ones."

The door splintered and fell. Redguards rushed into the creaking house. A man turned, raising his hands. Callum recognized the energy of a healer. It was the same energy that called to him, too.

"It's time."

Callum had tried to stop the red at his side—had shouted and raised a hand at the firelock that shot a hole through the healer's skull.

"Time to create the world that we envision."

They marched. Villagers stood at their windows and doors and watched as the followers shouted. Tobin yelled his praise of the Creator.

Ash clutched the sheets. Focusing on his intention, his *mission*, would ground him. *Close the tear in the fabric of our universe.* He repeated this again and again, focused on his intention as if this thought were his only anchor—

But you chose power, did you not?

Ash sat with his father. A white table spread with small cakes was between them. A porcelain cup of tea on a round saucer was in front of both. Ash frowned and looked down to see Earth was below, white clouds casting shadows on the sea. They were on the edge of the atmosphere, blue light dancing at their feet.

His father sipped from his cup. "You don't even realize it, do you? Just how close the chaos was to killing you."

Ash had nearly died. He looked at his hands. They were transparent, the green of the planet below. "I didn't have any choice. Val would've killed me instead."

"Then maybe you should've died," his father said with a shrug.

"If I'd died, how would I have *led your revolution?*" Ash asked, unable to keep back the bitterness.

His father put the mug onto the table with a delicate *clink*. "It's only after death that human matters can feel trivial. If you want freedom for alchemists, then the goal is your own—not mine."

"You're the one who—"

"And am I forcing you to act as you do now?" Hain asked. He smiled, hands folded on crossed knees. The smile seemed out of place on his father's face, when Ash was used to seeing it lined by cruelty. "I only showed you where the fragment was; I didn't ask you to find it."

"How else am I supposed to defeat Lune?"

"That's impossible," his father let Ash know simply. "You cannot, and will not, defeat the man who calls himself Sinclair Lune."

Ash paused—shook his head, a tug between his brows. "If I find enough chaos—I can stitch the tear you left behind, and—"

"Sinclair Lune is not only a man who consumed chaos," Hain said. "He is also a manifestation of desires, a human sent by Source, born to fulfill the role he does now. Hundreds of thousands of people have waited for hell on Earth and for their savior, too. That is all any of this is, Ash—a manifestation, a play, acting out what so many have requested."

"Then I'll manifest defeating him."

Hain laughed to himself as if Ash were only a child who had said something amusing. "Sinclair Lune's rise to power, and the death of New Anglia as you know it, is inevitable," Hain told him. "It is stitched into the fabric of the universe." He looked down at

Earth with some regret pulling at his brows. "Though I suppose threads can always be unwoven again."

Ash blinked open his eyes. An invisible weight pressed down on his lungs as he wheezed. The bedsheets stuck to his skin with sweat. He stared up at the ceiling. It was familiar, he realized. He turned his head. The balcony doors were shut, but he could see the mountain ranges in the distance.

"Finally awake?"

Ash looked up to see Ramsay pushing open the door and walking inside, balancing a tray that held a damp cloth and a steaming bowl of what appeared to be broth. He placed the tray on a table near the bed and sat on the edge of the mattress, the back of his hand against Ash's forehead. "The fever's broken now, at least."

Ash struggled to sit up, but Ramsay only impatiently pushed his shoulder back down.

"You still need to rest. You look like death."

His voice cracked. "How did I get here?"

Ramsay reached for the cloth and pressed it against Ash's forehead. It was cold enough that Ash flinched. "You don't remember?"

He shook his head.

"You materialized into the middle of my office—scared the hell out of me." He frowned as if considering a calculation. "I didn't even know you could materialize."

Ash hesitated. His throat was sore. It hurt to speak. "I learned recently."

Ramsay patted the cloth against Ash's cheek. "Not to mention, my manor has protections against materialization, too. It'd take a particularly powerful alchemist to break through."

Ash's voice rasped. "Maybe you subconsciously allowed me access."

Ramsay didn't reply. He put the cloth down, then reached for the broth. "You were screaming," he said. "About what, I still don't know."

Ash's memory flickered. He'd asked the chaos for power in House Val—enough to survive. And then? It'd been like his energy was stretched across dimensions, as if he'd viewed parallel worlds and multiple scenes of his own reality happening as one. Had that been an effect of the intention, the power that'd streamed through him; or had it only been the chaos, too much for his body? Elena had theorized that Ash could handle more chaos energy than most, but maybe that's all it'd been, in the end: a theory.

Ramsay fed Ash broth. The liquid was savory and warm. It shamed Ash to be fed like a child, yet when he tried to raise a hand to take the spoon himself, it only shook and fell to his side. Ash swallowed three more spoonfuls before his stomach turned. His neck heated as a memory flashed—he'd been sick all over the bathroom floor, the tub, as Ramsay rubbed his back, trying to tell him to breathe—

Ash turned his face away from the spoon Ramsay raised. Ramsay put it back onto the tray and sat silently for several heartbeats. Ash's eyelids were heavy.

"You scared me, Ash," Ramsay said. "I thought you were going to—" He paused, then cleared his throat. "Never mind. I'll let you sleep."

Ramsay took the tray and closed the door behind him. Had the intention for power saved Ash only once, then? Or had the chaos sunk into him, making his alchemy more powerful than ever?

Ash tried to remind himself of the true definition of power. Wasn't that what he had learned? This chaos energy fueling his alchemy would not help him feel empowered in the face of those who deigned him unworthy. Yet he couldn't ignore, too, the buzzing that grew in his chest and sped through his veins, the desire for *more*.

✳

Ash woke. A cold wind whistled through his doors. He shivered, pulling the blankets up over his shoulders.

He padded out into the hall, looking one way and then the other. It was empty. He paused in the dining room, the kitchen. It was possible Ramsay had returned to Lancaster or maybe had gone to a House meeting where Val would be, too. Ash had been ill, on the edge of death, and hadn't thought to tell Ramsay the truth about breaking into the man's manor. How long before Val told Ramsay the truth?

Ash walked into the empty parlor and to the window, looking down at the dead gardens. Ramsay wasn't outside, either. He turned to leave when something on the desk, on top of a mass of papers, caught his eye. This time, it wasn't a hastily scribbled note about the Book of Source; it was a sketched illustration of a tube with a handle. It reminded Ash of the firelocks that had been fired at him, that had blasted holes through Finley and Hendrix both. This firelock was larger, with notes on the use of alchemy to allow the weapon to send multiple projectiles at its victim at once.

He swallowed the impulse to set the papers on fire. It felt impossible, that such a destructive weapon could have come from Ramsay's mind and hands, the hands that had made tea and touched Ash so carefully. Ash couldn't stay. He needed to get back to Alexander's manor, before the lord began to question where he'd gone; needed to check in on Marlowe, to be sure she'd made it back to the Hedge base safely. He returned to his room and dressed in slacks he'd left in his room's closet, tied on his binder and pulled on a sweater.

The door clicked open, and Ramsay stood at the threshold, surprised. "I didn't realize you were awake."

Ash turned away, picking up his boots. "I was just heading out."

"Already? You could barely keep food down two days ago."

Two days? "How long have I been here?"

"A week," Ramsay said.

Ash slumped to the edge of his mattress. Shit. "Lord Alexander hasn't been looking for me, has he?"

Ramsay crossed her arms, leaning against the doorway. "Yes," she said. "I let him know you'd fallen ill. He asked that you meet with him once you're on your feet again."

"Then I should get back—"

"What happened, Ash?"

Ash paused. He couldn't outright ignore the question, but he didn't know what to say. What lie could possibly explain everything? "It doesn't matter."

"What do you mean?" Ramsay asked, annoyance trickling through. "How could you almost dying *not matter?*"

"That's a little dramatic, isn't it?"

Ramsay stood taller, a vibration of anger turning her cheeks red.

Ash shook his head, yanking on one boot and then the other. He couldn't afford to waste time on an argument. "Source, forget it—I have to go."

He pushed past Ramsay, out into the hall—then froze. Callum leaned against the wall outside the door, arms crossed, glaring at the floor. Ash should've recognized the boy's energy, but the sharper vibrations, heavier in anger, were different from the soft waves Ash was so used to.

"What're you doing here?" Ash whispered. He looked behind him to Ramsay, who still stood in the room. "What is this?"

"Come back inside," Ramsay said. "We only want to talk to you."

"Ganging up on me again?" Ash asked. "At least you're not trying to hide it this time."

"Don't be such a *child*," Callum said, voice rough. It was like he couldn't even bear to look at Ash.

Ash ignored Callum, storming past him down the hall. He needed to get to Ramsay's office, to the portal door—needed to get away from them both. Callum's thudding footsteps followed, Ramsay striding past and coming to a stop in front of Ash. She spoke fast. "Head Val believes you broke into his manor and stole something from him. Is that true?"

Ash stepped around her, snatching his hand away when Ramsay pulled at his wrist. Maybe Ash should've told Ramsay that her dear mentor had tried to *kill* Ash and Marlowe.

"I've convinced Val not to have you arrested," Ramsay called after him. "Callum's had to bargain on your behalf—"

"Thank you," Ash threw over his shoulder. "I'm ever so grateful."

He'd made it to Ramsay's office. He hurried his pace, nearly running for the door—but Ramsay got there first. She stepped in front of Ash once more, blocking the threshold.

"Move," Ash said.

"No," Ramsay replied.

Ash listened to Callum's slower footsteps entering the office behind him, taking his time as he walked to one of the chesterfield seats and fell into it, elbow on an armrest and face hidden by his hand. Ash clenched shut his eyes, trying to imagine his body dematerializing—but even with the chaos powering his energy, Ash was still weak, and Ramsay still had her barriers in place.

"You're going to keep me hostage?" Ash demanded, looking between the two of them. "Now who's the child?"

"Your illness," Ramsay said, ignoring Ash. She was more businesslike now, chin tilted up as she stared down at Ash. "I'm not much of a healer, but it seemed to me that your body was breaking down from an overuse of chemical alteration."

"What?"

"It's as if you'd taken multiple kilograms of powder from the streets of Hedge."

"You think I was *high*?"

"Yes," Ramsay said without hesitation. "I know that you were.

It explains so much, Ash—your sudden changes in behavior, in mood—"

"I wasn't on *drugs*, Ramsay—"

"What did you take?" Ramsay asked. "Is it because of your anxiety?"

"You must think everyone from Hedge is on drugs, but I—"

Callum spoke even with his eyes still closed. "I asked Charlotte to tell me the symptoms of an overdose. She described your illness perfectly."

"Right, yes, because Charlotte knows everything about me and my circumstances, whether I want her to or not."

"Don't do that," Ramsay said. "Callum has been doing everything he can to protect you, to help you—he's been here with me, healing you—"

Ash heard the venom in his words, and even then he couldn't stop. "At least he's finally doing what he really wants and not just following in his father's footsteps."

"Source, Ash, don't be ridiculous!" Ramsay yelled, anger cracking through. "We spent days cleaning up your vomit, spoon-feeding you and bathing you so that you wouldn't be questioned by House Adelaide if you were dropped off to some healer, which would have been a lot easier, mind you."

Ash rubbed a thumb between his brows. He should've thanked Ramsay and Callum, but anger bristled beneath his skin. He turned away, vision blurred.

"Even now," Ramsay whispered. "Your energy is different. This isn't you."

"So, powder from Hedge is the only possible answer?"

"If it isn't, give me one."

Ash's tongue was heavy in his mouth. He couldn't speak.

"Is that why you're with the rebels now?" Callum asked, his eyes open now as he glared at Ramsay's fireplace. "Are they supplying you?"

Ash laughed, hands leaning on Ramsay's desk for support. He

wondered which of the two had broken first, whispering to the other that Ash was a traitor. "Yes, of course, I'm with the rebels for *drugs*—not because you've been allowing the deaths of alchemists, nor because we're losing our freedom thanks to you and your forsaken family. We're being *killed*—"

"Don't speak to Callum that way—"

Ash whirled on Ramsay. "Killed by *your* weapons, designed to target people like me—"

"People like you?" Ramsay repeated, incredulous. "I practice alchemy, too, in case you've forgotten!"

"And you're perfectly fine getting into line, doing as you're told like the good little alchemist you are—"

"You've lost your mind—"

"—desperate to prove you're nothing like your parents, even if it means kissing Alexander's ass—"

"That's the only explanation—"

"—and creating weapons to kill every other alchemist in the world but yourself."

The air Ash breathed felt like ice. Hurt shined in Ramsay's eyes, but only for a moment. She blinked, walls up once again. It reminded Ash of the days before he and Ramsay sat together and breathed in harmony. Ash hadn't been sure he could trust Ramsay at all, then. It was painful to admit that he felt the same way again.

"I don't know how to reconcile the person you are now with who I knew then," Ash whispered. "You wouldn't have ignored what I'm saying. You would've looked at the truth yourself."

Ramsay swallowed, throat moving up and down again. "I—"

Ash waited, heartbeat pulsing in his ears. Callum watched Ramsay with a softness in his gaze that stung Ash to see, knowing Callum would likely never look at him that way again.

"Source, of course I've had my hesitations," Ramsay whispered. "I don't want to hurt anyone. That was never my intention. I was asked to design a weapon, to hand the blueprint to Head Val—and it'd been my first assignment as Head of my family's House. I wanted to do well, to meet any expectations others had of me."

Ash could have some understanding for Ramsay, too, couldn't he? Ramsay had so much to prove after her own parents' mistakes, and it'd been her goal and dream for so long, to restore House Thorne. It must've been difficult, to realize that her dream of rejoining the Houses and inheriting her title had been unfulfilling.

"It isn't too late," Ash whispered. "Cancel its production. Tell Val—"

Ramsay shook her head once, with enough finality that Ash stopped speaking. "He'd only want to know why. I can't risk . . ."

Ramsay's words were unspoken, but Ash understood anyway. "What? Can't risk anyone thinking you're a rebel, too?"

"I dedicated my life to atoning for my parents and clearing the Thorne name. You can't expect me to throw all that work away."

Ash rubbed a palm over his face. "Did you know that Callum's creating a new House?" Ash asked. Callum didn't move nor speak, but Ash knew he was listening. "Forcing alchemists to work under him?"

"Yes," Ramsay said without pause, though she couldn't hide the uncertain frown. "It'll help to mend fences between alchemists and redguards."

"You can't honestly believe that." Ash gestured at Callum. "That's the lie he tells himself, but I know you don't think it's true."

Callum couldn't resist looking at Ramsay for her response, it seemed. Ramsay stared forward, swallowing hard, and for a moment, Ash thought—hoped—that maybe Ramsay would admit she didn't.

"Does it matter, Ash?" Ramsay only said. Ash's heart fell. "We're happy, aren't we? We have everything we need. We have one another. You, me, Callum—we've fought to be together, and now you're willing to throw it all away. For what?"

"Maybe you're happy, but I'm not."

Ramsay stood frozen still, as if the words had sent ice over her skin. She appeared speechless before she blinked, her wounded expression wiped clean. Callum had listened patiently, quietly, but he spoke now.

"Is this how you've felt about us all along?" Callum asked, tone even. "This disgust for me and my family, this anger you have toward Ramsay—why bother to pretend you love either of us, then?"

His words, usually so comforting, cut at Ash's heart now.

"I would've preferred to know sooner," Callum said. "It would've been easier to handle your betrayals, if I didn't think you were willing to hurt me so much while claiming to love me, too."

It was the risk of loving someone who had held Ash's heart so preciously, carefully, that Ash had come to trust that he would always be safe in Callum's hands. Ash blinked the tears away. "And what about you?"

Callum looked at him now, at least. "What about me?"

"You and Ramsay couldn't wait to be rid of me. You're both in love, and I've just been in the way—"

"You sound paranoid, Ash," Ramsay let him know. "We both still love you." Ash didn't miss Callum's clenched jaw, looking to the crackling fire once more. "I still love you," Ramsay continued, "even knowing . . ."

"Even knowing what?" Ash said. "Go on. Even knowing I'm a radical?"

Ramsay worked her jaw back and forth. "Stay. We can help you through the withdrawals."

Ash shook his head, turning away. He didn't want to leave, not like this—there was still too much discuss, still too much that went unanswered—but he supposed, too, that working for the freedom of alchemists meant sacrificing his own desires. It would've felt selfish, to think that his love for Ramsay and Callum was just as important as the lives of alchemists across New Anglia.

"I have to go," Ash said. "Please, let me go."

Ramsay seemed to understand that Ash hadn't only meant to let him leave the room. She didn't look away from Ash for one long breath—before finally she sighed and stepped aside.

29

Ash wished he could have time to rest, but he needed to see Marlowe. His last memory of her had been grabbing her arm, watching her dematerialize. The surge in power from the chaos must've been strong enough to tear through even the barriers of House Val; but Ash had also been out of his mind. He needed to know with certainty that he'd sent Marlowe to safety.

He hurried through the halls as quickly as he could without outright running. He took the stairs two at a time, making it to the third floor, and turned down the hall to his chambers—

"Sir Woods."

Ash paused and immediately regretted it. A white-haired scribe with his pointed beard approached. "Lord Alexander has requested your presence at once."

Ash was amazed at how fast word of his return had spread. "I'm a little tired," Ash tried with a sheepish grin. "If Lord Alexander doesn't mind—"

"Excuse me," the scribe said with a jovial smile. "It was my mistake, using the word 'request.'"

What other choice did Ash have? "Lead the way."

※

Ash expected to be taken to Alexander's office and was surprised to find himself brought to the archives instead. Alexander stood in front of the shelves as if only idly browsing. Ash waited, looking over his shoulder as the scribe snapped the door shut behind him.

"Welcome back," Alexander said without a glance.

Ash hesitated. He wasn't sure why his hairs stood on end. "Thank you."

"I hope you're well. Head Thorne described your illness as quite serious."

"I'm better now."

Alexander pulled out a text. It was one Ash recognized, a book about the theory of manifestation. It was curious, that Lord Alexander would have so many texts on a science he didn't practice himself.

The man flipped open the book, skimming the introduction.

"Did you want to see me?" Ash asked after another moment. He wondered if Alexander meant for the silence to stretch on so long that Ash began to sweat.

"The Ironbound base was nearly empty when Commander Kendrick ambushed the house," Alexander finally said. "Two alchemists died, unfortunately. Many more were expected to be found inside."

Ash's eyes were dry, no matter how much he blinked.

Alexander turned the page, though Ash wasn't convinced he was reading. "You wouldn't have anything to do with that, would you?"

"Are you asking if I warned the rebels?"

"I find it odd that I haven't heard an update from you since the attack on the base."

"I'm sorry. I would've come sooner—"

"Yes, of course. You were ill."

Lord Alexander slipped the book back into its place. He faced Ash, staring him down. "It was a disappointment, to not capture any alchemists alive. We hoped to have a trial run of sorts, for the new division of House Kendrick."

Ash's breath was too shallow. "It'd be difficult to force imprisoned rebels to fight for the redguards, wouldn't it?"

"We have our methods," Alexander said. "And anyone who chooses not to fight under Commander Kendrick will face execution. The choice will be theirs, ultimately."

Ash couldn't stop himself from speaking. "Fight or die. It doesn't sound like much of a choice." Alexander inspected him. Ash needed to be more careful with his words, he knew. He ducked his head. "I plan to meet with ALP members shortly," he said. That wasn't a lie, at least. "I'll bring another update when I can."

"Very well."

Ash turned to leave, taking a few hurried steps forward. He was eager to get away from Lord Alexander, to go back to Marlowe in Hedge—but the curiosity bubbled, words rising before he could think better. He slowed to a stop. "What are the methods?"

"Pardon?"

Ash faced Alexander once more. "How do you plan to force rebels to fight for House Kendrick?"

Alexander's brows rose. "I'm sure you're aware of Kendrick's means."

Ash swallowed the nausea that churned at the thought of Marlowe—of Finley and all the rest—being tortured by redguards. "But the rebels—they can't be trusted. They'll only fight back. They *hate* the Houses and what they stand for—"

"Then each member will be executed until they comply," Alexander replied, as if it were truly as simple as that.

But Alexander said this so dismissively that Ash wasn't sure he believed the lord. Callum had been so insistent that the new House needed the rebels to begin its trial. It hadn't quite occurred to Ash, the question of why the redguards wouldn't have simply asked for alchemist volunteers from the start.

"House Kendrick decided to use the rebels specifically," Ash said, thinking aloud, speaking more to himself than to Alexander.

Alexander tilted his head as he examined Ash. "Beginning with the rebel alchemists was Commander Kendrick's initial idea," he said. "An offer of mercy."

But maybe it wasn't only that warm bodies were needed to fill positions of the new House; maybe Alexander and Edric both had been more concerned with what it might take to force an alchemist to fight as a redguard.

A thought sent a spike of light behind Ash's eyes. His vision blurred as the heat of realization tingled over Ash's skin. "The new House has been called a trial," Ash said, "as if House Kendrick would need to do the same again."

Ash, for a moment, thought—hoped—that he was wrong. But Lord Alexander watched him for a long moment before he finally released a puff of a smile. He shook his head, brows raised. "I shouldn't be surprised," the lord said. "You are your father's son, after all, and many always did remark that Gresham Hain was too clever for his own good."

"It wouldn't be possible," Ash said, perhaps only hoping to convince himself.

"It's a difficult decision, as I'm sure you can imagine—but alchemists are dangerous, Sir Woods. You of all people should understand that."

"So you'll have us all killed instead," Ash said. His voice sounded hollow.

"Only the ones who fight," Alexander said, hesitating for just a moment before he added, "and the ones who are too powerful to control."

Ash couldn't stop the sinking feeling in his chest, the pressure growing in his neck. Callum couldn't have known about this; he would've refused to help create this new horror.

"Not everyone will be made to fight, of course," Alexander continued. "Redguard healers will be a part of the new House, too."

"What about House Thorne? Houses Val and Adelaide?"

"Each will be summarily disbanded," Alexander said. "Alchemists with the ability will continue to develop New Anglia's science and technology, but will answer to Head Kendrick instead. Better to keep an eye on the particularly talented, wouldn't you agree?"

Ash's heart ached for Ramsay. She'd dedicated her life to restoring House Thorne, only to have it stripped away from her. "But we're all alchemists," Ash said, voice soft. "You can't force so many people—"

"The licenses will be useful to find those who practice," Alexander let him know. "Anyone found practicing illegally without a license will be executed by House Kendrick."

Ash imagined himself studying quietly by candlelight. He would've been one of the few arrested by Edric's order, hung in Hedge. He took in a slower breath, holding Alexander's gaze. "Thousands will die."

"Yes," Alexander agreed. "Better thousands now than entire cities later."

Ash didn't speak—he couldn't, not with the fury tangled in his throat and spreading through his lungs. He wanted to scream. Alexander had lied to him, and Ash had been foolish enough to believe him. And hadn't Ash always been warned? He really had been nothing but the man's toy, used against alchemists across New Anglia.

Alexander had continued speaking, voice muffled by the pulse echoing in Ash's ears. "Head Kendrick has already begun preparations to enact the arrest of the first round of alchemists, starting tomorrow night. Once under proper control, they'll join the redguards and be most helpful in capturing the next group of alchemists."

An image filtered through Ash's mind: redguards marching the streets, arresting people across the state with a license, along with anyone even accused of practicing alchemy, killing those who didn't surrender—

"Does Callum know about this?" Ash whispered.

Alexander eyed him. "I believe Head Kendrick worried his younger brother would make too much of a fuss. He's decided to wait until the first arrests are made."

Ash's heart flared. If Callum hadn't been told yet, he'd fight his older brother once he found out—and Edric never had wanted

Callum as a commander of House Kendrick. It was too possible that, in the end, Edric would only have his brother arrested and killed, too.

The lord's silent stare cut into Ash for a heartbeat, before he spoke. "Exceptions will be made, of course. You will report to the new House and, ultimately, Head Kendrick as a practicing alchemist, but you can stay on as my advisor, as you like—a liaison of sorts between the alchemists and House Alexander."

The man's gaze was careful, watching for any twitch of disloyalty. Ash's breath was tight as he nodded. "Thank you, my lord."

"I trust this is something you'll be able to keep to yourself, Sir Woods."

Ash nodded once, shakily. "Yes—of course."

"Very good," Alexander said, gleaming smile in place once more. "You're dismissed."

Ash turned on his heel and tried to take his time crossing the room for the door. He didn't want to appear to be running away. His hand trembled to a stop when Alexander called after him.

"Another thing," the lord said. Ash didn't turn, his hand still hovering over the knob. "Head Val came to me, concerned. He seems to think you've stolen something from him."

Ash looked over his shoulder at Alexander. The man watched Ash carefully with hooded eyes. Ash shook his head, furrowing his brows with confusion. "I couldn't have. I was sick in bed."

"Yes, that's what I let him know, too," Alexander said with the briefest of smiles. "I'll look forward to your return."

※

Ash was numb as he pressed a hand to his bedroom wall and walked into the dark. He stepped out onto concrete. The sun was close to beginning its descent, light dim as it filtered through the ceiling's glass. His body felt like it was underwater as he made his way past cots of crying children, people on their knees scrubbing clothes in buckets. Heads turned. Quiet spread, whispers following as Ash approached the end of the hall.

Baron sat in his chair like it was a throne. It appeared Ash had interrupted a meeting with the ALP members: The siblings Guthrie and Gretchen stood nearby. Marlowe was there, too, well enough to stand on her own feet, at least. She nodded at Ash, though her eyes burned with a silent warning. Ash forced himself to continue forward even as the alchemists turned to stare Ash down, until he came to a stop in front of Baron.

"Sir Woods," Baron said. Ash knew by now that this was not a sign of respect. "Good of you to join us. We hadn't heard from you in so long that I was afraid you were dead."

Ash decided it was better to keep the fact that he almost had died to himself. "I'm here with news from Kensington."

Baron smiled. "I worried that, once you'd consumed the fragment of chaos for yourself, you decided you didn't have any more need for the ALP."

Marlowe's stare screamed at Ash to be careful with his words. Source, there wasn't any time for this. "Alexander plans to announce a new law."

Guthrie spoke. "He tries to distract from the topic."

"Why did you take the chaos energy yourself when you'd promised it to me?" Baron asked him.

Ash kept his eyes on Baron's narrowed gaze. "I didn't have any choice."

"Is that so?"

"Marlowe and I would've been captured or killed," Ash said, "and you would've been down your Ironbound leader. You wouldn't have gotten the fragment anyway."

"What did you use the chaos for?" Baron asked, leaning forward with a false curiosity, elbows on his knees.

Something whispered to Ash that it was better to keep the truth to himself. "To send Marlowe and myself to safety."

Gretchen's gaze burrowed into Ash, her energy sliding through his ear and behind his eyes. "He's lying," she said. "Something is wrong about the chaos energy he stole."

Guthrie tilted his head as he inspected Ash. "Maybe he's taken the chaos energy for himself because he plans to use it against you."

"If I'd done that, I wouldn't have bothered to return to Hedge at all," Ash said. "Listen to me. I've learned that Alexander plans to have Edric Kendrick arrest all alchemists. We're to be forced under House Kendrick's control. Anyone who refuses will be killed," Ash said above the murmurs that erupted, "along with anyone found practicing alchemy illegally."

If Ash thought he'd be met with interested ears, he'd assumed wrong. Glances were exchanged, distrust souring the air. Guthrie sneered. "The boy clearly wants to distract from the fact that he hasn't come back with the chaos fragment, as he promised he would."

"Edric Kendrick plans to begin arrests tomorrow night."

Baron held up a hand, a silent signal for the discussion to end. Ash held his breath. He wouldn't simply stand by as the man ordered his death, but he was worried for Marlowe, too. Baron seemed the sort who would be willing to brand all of Ash's friends traitors and have them punished in his place.

Finally, the man spoke. "I don't trust you," Baron let Ash know, "but I know a way you can earn that trust. Edric Kendrick."

Ash's heart hammered. He was certain he wouldn't like where this was going.

"If what you've said is true, then he's become a top priority of the ALP." Baron's eyes flashed. "I need you to kill him."

Ash forced himself to breathe slow and steady. "I'd thought the ALP decided killing Edric was too big a move so early in the rebellion."

"Redguard bases have been attacked and weakened throughout New Anglia," Baron said. "Now is the time to start making those big moves."

Ash's chest flooded with buzzing energy. He remembered Sinclair Lune's words, whispered in his ear. He was the boy who had killed the Head of House Kendrick across the realms.

"Losing Edric Kendrick would throw the Great Houses into disarray," Baron continued, voice muffled through the heartbeat echoing in Ash's ears.

And if Edric was killed, Callum would become the Head of Kendrick. Callum would only be targeted next.

"It'd give us an opening to attack the manor and take Alexander hostage—to make our demands, and give alchemists the protections and rights we deserve."

Baron had to know it wouldn't work. "We won't win."

The man only leaned back in his seat, eyes fastened on Ash as if he hadn't spoken. "You're sitting pretty in the Alexander manor. You have access to the Kendrick homes, their manor and town house in Kensington. You are best positioned to handle the job."

Ash felt the silent threat: If he refused, Baron would only use that as the final proof he needed that Ash could not be trusted, and he'd have Ash killed instead. Ash's fingers twitched. Edric and Callum weren't close, not when Edric still blamed his younger brother for his family's deaths; but for Callum, Edric was the only family he had left, the brother he still clung to, following the man's orders even if Callum disagreed. To lose his brother—to potentially learn that Ash was the cause of that . . .

"We need an answer, Sir Woods."

Yet Ash couldn't see another choice. Edric would kill thousands if he was allowed to live. If alchemists were to have any chance at all against the Houses, then weakening the redguards would be an important step. Ash only had to decide if he was willing to sacrifice his relationship with Callum; because there was no question, in Ash's mind: If Ash killed his brother, Callum would never forgive him for it.

"Fine," Ash said. "I'll do it."

He hadn't made it far before Marlowe caught up with him,

walking in stride. "Are you sure about this? You won't be able to take it back, once you—"

"I'm not sure about it at all," Ash murmured. It wasn't his place, his right, to decide that one life was less worthy, even the life of a man like Edric. He remembered the conversation he'd had with Marlowe, once, about the teachings of Lune and the question neither could answer. "Edric hates alchemists—hates me. I don't know if that means he deserves to die."

"Then don't do it," she said. "Someone else can handle Edric Kendrick." She lowered her voice. "You're not a killer, Ash. That's the one thing that's always separated you and me."

Ash thought of the pale-haired girl in Riverside, sitting at a table. She'd called Ash a killer. He hated the fact that he considered proving her right.

※

Ash was silent during the meeting of the Heads of Houses the next day, glad that Alexander didn't ask him to speak. He wasn't sure he'd be able to, with the pressure of energy that filled the room. Head Val openly watched him, jaw clenched, as if at any moment, he would declare Ash a thief, demanding he be arrested at once; but if Val did that, the man would also need to admit to what Ash had stolen, and Ash was at least confident that the man wanted to keep the secret of chaos to himself for as long as possible.

"Would you be able to share an update on the number of shipments from Caledonia, Sir Galahad?"

Ash stared hard at his lap, ignoring the energy he felt pulsing from Ramsay. They were both aware of each other's every little movement and breath along with the silent agreement to not so much as even look at each other.

"The number of attacks against our bases across New Anglia has grown substantially in the last week. There was another on a base near Glassport early this morning."

Callum sat motionless, staring forward as well. Usually, Callum would reach for Ash with his soft energy, whether he was consciously aware of it or not. His blue light would soothe Ash, the image of blue skies and still water. Ash wondered if Callum purposefully held a wall between them now.

"We believe the ALP rebels are orchestrating a large-scale attack, targeting the Heads of Houses."

And there was Edric. Ash made a point not to look in the man's direction, too, as he spoke his update. Ash knew he would only lose his nerve as he imagined Edric motionless, unblinking and unbreathing. "Potential targets are the House Alexander manor and the House Kendrick town house, as well as the House Adelaide town house here in Kensington. I believe their goal is to weaken the Great Houses."

Ash stood the moment the meeting ended, sweeping past Ramsay and Callum. It was easier than he'd thought it would be, to push down the emotions that threatened to drown him, easier to ignore them both, when it was clear they'd decided the best course of action was to ignore Ash, too.

He took a deep breath as he turned the corner, knowing it was the direction Edric usually took as he headed for his own private meeting with Lord Alexander.

". . . business in Claremont," Edric said as the two men passed. "I'll leave a team of guards in my absence." His gaze slid to Ash, who only ducked his head as he hurried down the hall in the opposite direction.

⁎

Ash had only ever seen the manor where Callum had grown up in the other boy's memories. Even after Hain's massacre, Ash had no desire to visit Callum's childhood home, not when the energy felt ripe with nightmares. Still, Callum had always given Ash and Ramsay access, letting them know the password for the door linked to the Alexander manor—hopeful, maybe, that the two might be willing to visit him on the days he had to return. Ash's heart crumpled with guilt at the realization that he had never been willing to visit the manor to support Callum, but went now when willing to hurt him instead.

The manor's portal door opened to an office that was similar to Callum's in the Kendrick town house: cherrywood panels, a mahogany desk cleared of clutter. The air around Ash heated, and he disappeared as he swept out into the corridor, with its dark mahogany-paneled walls and hardwood floors. The manor had been spared from Hain's razing, and the original intricate stone and gardens still stood. It was strange, that such a place could feel so familiar to Ash when he'd never been there himself. His palms were clammy, and it was becoming more difficult to breathe.

Could he really do this? No matter the reasons he told himself Edric needed to die, it'd always been the line Ash had said he would never cross. He wouldn't be so much different from his father, in the end, if he was willing to kill for his beliefs.

Ash moved down one hall and another, looking for a sign of the older Kendrick brother. A low rumble of voices made Ash pause. He pressed his back against the wall, breath held, as two figures turned the corner in front of him, a pale man wearing an eye patch and a darker-skinned man wearing the uniform of the Head of Kendrick.

"Just kill him. Don't bother with a public execution."

"Understood, sir."

Edric paused. He turned his head, and he looked directly at Ash. The air around Ash glimmered with heat. In his peripheral vision, Ash saw only the wall behind him where his shoulders should have been, the ground where his boots stood. Edric hesitated, eyes squinted—then turned, continuing his orders to the guard that followed.

Ash waited for a heartbeat, then slipped down the hall after them, boots lightly tapping the hardwood. Streams of thought tangled in his mind. He wasn't his father—but he would do what he could to protect innocent alchemists from Edric Kendrick. He wasn't a killer—but if Edric didn't die, others would. He couldn't take a life, but he would need to, if it meant saving other lives instead.

The men opened the door to a parlor and stepped inside. It was minimally decorated, heavy drapes blocking the red of the sunset bleeding through the glass. Edric had given the guard who accompanied him one last order, to which the red bowed, fist to chest. He marched from the room. Ash slipped inside before the door could click shut behind him.

Ash had planned to wait until Edric was alone—to strike then, if he was truly able to, without speaking to Edric nor even having to look at him. It was the coward's way. A blade of light to the throat, or perhaps to the heart—it would be quick, without any evidence left behind, except that an alchemist had done the killing.

He couldn't let himself think, if he really meant to go through with it. Ash's breath was slow, his steps shaky, muffled on the rug. Edric stood over a desk of papers in the corner of the room. He leaned forward, hands on the surface.

"If you're going to try to kill me," the man said, "you should at least show your face."

Ash froze. His heart stuttered in his chest.

Edric turned. His eyes swept the room. "I don't need alchemy to sense you." Edric placed his hand on the hilt of his sword, Ash's only warning before it was yanked from its sheath. Edric stared around the room with a narrowed gaze. "I've been trained all my life for battles where I'm disadvantaged—outnumbered or facing an enemy I can't see."

Ash hardly had a chance to jump back, out of the way—Edric swung his sword in a wide arc as it hissed through the air, inches from where Ash had been only moments before. His focus had been on retreating, the air around him flickering—

Edric's eyes narrowed on Ash, leaping forward. A gust of wind

Ash threw knocked Edric off course, but he planted a boot to the ground, straining against the wind and slashing forward. Ash winced, throwing up his hands. The tip of the sword cut through Ash's arm—the sharp sting, followed by a burn, drops of blood falling to the hardwood. He clapped a hand over the gash—realized a second too late that his illusion had dropped entirely—

"Sir Woods," Edric said, standing straight. "Why am I not surprised?"

The pain had become a dull throb. Ash threw up a shield of stone as Edric slashed at his neck, the bits of rock crumbling to the floor.

"I heard a nasty rumor," Edric told him. "A mole let me know that I've become a target of the Alchemist Liberation Party."

Ash's breath shook as he stumbled back.

"Apparently, I'm to be assassinated," Edric whispered. "Are you here to assassinate me, Sir Woods?"

Edric stabbed for his stomach. Ash imagined gnarled, twisted bark growing from the floorboards. The sword stuck into the wood as Ash scrambled from the corner, turning to face Edric once more as he yanked the sword out.

"Does my brother know that you're here to kill me?" Edric asked, turning to Ash once more. "Did he send you here himself?"

"No," Ash said, breath ragged. He looked wildly around the room—he was certain Edric would only dodge anything he attempted to throw at him. He needed a new plan. "Callum has nothing to do with this."

"Is that so?" Edric said, seeming to consider as he stalked closer. "Well, it'll be an easy enough claim anyway. The commander's partner, an attempted assassin? Callum will be deemed suspect, too—arrested, perhaps executed before there's any protest."

"He's your brother," Ash said, voice strangled.

"Yes," Edric agreed. "And he's a fucking traitor."

Ash was trapped. His back against the wall, the door on the other end of the room—and he'd spent too much power now, too much energy defending himself already. A familiar buzzing hummed in his blood, vibrating through his bones. *Fight.* If he didn't, Ash would die.

He threw out a palm and released a pulse of energy that flung Edric back. Edric landed on his feet, sliding into position as he threw a dagger Ash hadn't seen—he ducked, the tip cutting the top of his ear. Edric didn't allow a moment's pause. He raced forward, cutting the air with his sword where Ash's throat had been moments before—Ash fell to the floor, but before he could roll away, a boot caught his side. Ash gasped and gagged, crawling to his knees—another boot, this time to his cheek. Ash's ears rang. The chaos energy pulsed inside him. It was woven into his skin. *Fight. Survive.*

Energy sizzled inside Ash—heating, expanding, a spark of flame that could become an explosion, except that this time, he saw the black orbs of chaos raining, the seams of reality splitting—

A thud hit the back of his head, where his skull met his neck. His hair was yanked back, scalp screaming, as a cloth with powder pressed over Ash's mouth and nose. He breathed it in, eyes rolling. Ash's vision dimmed into nothingness.

30

The warehouse didn't offer easy entry. The iron doors had been sealed shut with alchemy. The reds needed to scale the red-brick walls to the glass roof above; they moved in the darkness, on a night with only a sliver of a moon, their shadows unseen. Ropes unraveled to the floor below like hanging vines. A child lay awake in a nearby cot; they couldn't sleep as they bounced a ball of light back and forth between their palms.

They heard the thump of boots and sat up in bed. They squinted at the dark, turning their palm over as the ball of light hovered. A redguard aimed. The child screamed Marlowe's name as the first rounds exploded into the bodies that slept.

A man stood in the shadow of the hall, listening to the shots, the screams and cries and pleas. *"There are children here—not everyone is an alchemist!"*

He grimaced but did nothing else. Beside him waited a guard with an eye patch. "Kendrick didn't say anything about a massacre," he said.

Another voice spoke behind him. "I only need fifty," the man said, stepping to the open doors and looking within. A second rapid burst of explosions, screams—a blast of alchemic light brightened the room, before that, too, died. "There isn't any need to take everyone here prisoner."

The man eyed Kendrick warily. "Don't know why I still need to be here."

Head Kendrick raised a curious brow. "These are your people, Baron," he said. "They're dying for you. It's only fitting that you would die here, too."

Baron's eyes widened. He took a step back, raising his hands—

The red behind him stabbed a sword through his back and out of Baron's chest. He sputtered, specks of blood flying. His expression faded. "Why—"

"I don't negotiate with extremists," Kendrick said simply. The sword was yanked from Baron's back, and the man fell to the ground, dead.

The shooting had stopped; only the sounds of thudding boots and soft cries remained. A young woman with red hair screamed a child's name, clutching their still body.

Across a bridge, a mansion stood tall in its city. The white walls gleamed like marble, halls filled with bustling attendants and scribes. There was a room, unknown to most—a shelf that Ash had overlooked. The glass container held an orb, a miniature black moon, that hummed a vibration.

✳

Ash gasped awake. He coughed—he couldn't breathe—but strings of air made it to his lungs. He gulped, chest rising and falling hard. His gaze flitted, taking a moment to adjust to the dark shadow that filled the room. Stone walls with white mold leaked down the sides, chains dangling on the opposite wall.

He was in the dungeons. His arms were chained above him, shoulders already sore. There was no way for him to tell how long he'd been like that. He brought his wrists down hard, but they only clanged with the effort.

Ash sucked in a breath and closed his eyes, trying to concentrate on the chain's properties—it should have been easy to force the chains to unlock or become undone, but it wasn't any use. Either Ash was too weak, even with the chaos energy streaming through his body, or an alchemic block had been placed. He tried to call, but his voice scratched his throat. He tried again. "Is anyone there?"

There was no response.

＊

Ash had no sense of time, no way to know if hours or days or only minutes passed. He fell asleep, jerking awake the moment he leaned on the chains too heavily. His skin was rubbed raw, and the gash on his arm burned. His throat was cracked dry, his stomach churning with hunger and nausea. He thought he might be sick. It was easier to let himself fall asleep again.

＊

His vision blurred. Voices murmured in his ear. He couldn't make any sense of them. *"Prisoner—base—"*

Footsteps, clinking. Ash heard what might have been crying before he drifted again.

＊

Ash's groans of pain were the sound that woke him next.

"Finally back to the world of the living?"

Ash lifted his heavy head to see that Marlowe stood against the opposite wall of the dungeon's cell. She was also chained, arms above her.

He wondered for a moment if she was only a trick of alchemy or perhaps a phantom of his mind. "Marlowe—Source, what happened?" His voice was strained, rough with dryness.

A cut was above her eye, dried blood cracked along her skin. "An attack on the Hedge base," she said. She sounded drained. Even in the dim light, Ash could see her eyes had welled.

Ash's heart sank. "Where's Finley? Riles?"

"Riles was taken prisoner also. I don't know where they're keeping him. Finley . . ."

Ash felt Marlowe's waves of grief; they became his own, too. Heat welled from his stomach and to his eyes. He swallowed bile, but couldn't stop the sob that broke through.

Before either could speak again, the dungeon cell door banged open. Footsteps echoed in the hall. Ash's fingers twitched above him as Edric strode into the cell, two reds standing guard by the doors. Edric stopped halfway. He knew better than to get too close to an alchemist. No one besides the guards were with him. That worried Ash most of all.

"I shouldn't be at all surprised to find you here, Sir Woods—yet, somehow, you managed to convince even me that perhaps I was too distrusting."

Ash swallowed. Finley was dead because of the man in front of him—because Ash couldn't kill him. "Did you come here just to gloat?"

"Not at all. I've come to ask questions."

"Where's Callum?" Ash asked. He hated himself for it, the hope that Callum would come to his rescue.

"Do you believe that Commander Kendrick will save you?"

Callum must've heard by now that Ash had tried to kill his brother. Ash tried to imagine the other boy's reaction: Disbelief, perhaps; shock, before a slow acceptance. A realization that Ash had now changed into someone unrecognizable.

"Commander Kendrick won't be joining us," Edric said when Ash didn't respond. "Not for the interrogation."

House Kendrick was well-known for its interrogation methods. Ash did his best to suppress his energy's quiver of fear. He wouldn't give Edric the satisfaction. "I don't have anything to say to you."

"Good," Edric said, holding out a hand. "That'll make this much more satisfying."

One of the reds stepped forward and handed Edric a dagger. It was small, the type more used for carving into skin. Ash tensed, breath hitched. He had one more option. He could request that Edric find Lord Alexander, explain that he'd been acting on the lord's orders, even if that was now a lie—but with Marlowe there, listening, he couldn't bear letting her think that he'd deceived her.

His vision turned when Edric took a step not toward him, but to Marlowe instead. "As much as I would like to begin with Sir Woods," Edric said, "it's my understanding that this one was a key leader in the rebellion."

Marlowe raised her chin, but she didn't argue nor attempt to persuade Edric any differently. Ash's hands clinked above him. "No—don't touch her—"

Edric stopped in front of Marlowe, dagger raised. "I have some questions for you. For every answer you refuse to give, this is the pain I will administer," he said, then pressed the point of the dagger into Marlowe's shoulder—she grimaced with clenched teeth for as long as she could, before Edric began to twist the blade in her skin. Ash squeezed shut his eyes as Marlowe's scream filled the cell. "Do you understand?"

Marlowe gasped with a broken sob. She pulled her head back for a moment, then spat in Edric's face. The fist around the dagger's handle tensed, shaking. "You fucking—"

There was a clang. Ash looked up to see the guards had stepped away from the cell's door, bowing their heads. Edric gritted his teeth for a moment before he did the same. "Lord Alexander."

The lord took his time walking into the cell, observing the scene. His gaze landed on Ash, then Marlowe, before it ended with Edric. "I don't remember giving an order to interrogate the rebels," Alexander said.

Edric kept his head bowed. "I deemed it necessary to learn the locations of the other bases, my lord."

"So necessary that you would even act without my command? Some might see that as treasonous, Head Kendrick."

"I apologize," Edric said, biting the words out. "That wasn't my intent."

The lord sighed, standing in the center of the dank cell. A spotlight managed to shine through a crack and onto him even then. "I would've preferred to avoid this," Alexander said, and seemed truly frustrated for it as he raised a hand to his temple. "Sir Woods has been beneficial, and your thirst for petty revenge has led me to losing a key informant."

Silence followed Alexander's words. Ash was too afraid to look at Marlowe, but he felt the loose vibrations of confusion, before the intensity of her stare burned his neck. "Ash," she said weakly, voice cracked. "You . . ."

Ash's gaze dropped to the floor. Source, he hadn't wanted her to find out like this—hadn't wanted her to learn the truth at all. He wished he could explain. Yes, it had been true once, but Ash had realized working for Alexander—betraying Marlowe and all the rest—had been a mistake.

"Informant?" Edric said, voice like ice. "Informants, spies—that's under the Kendrick jurisdiction."

"I decided it was for the best to keep Ash's secret to myself."

Ash forced himself to look at Marlowe. The expression on her face—the denial, brows creased in disbelief, eyes shining with tears—

"He could've gotten in the way of my plans against the rebels."

"Are you questioning my judgment, Head Kendrick?"

Edric's eyes cut into Ash. "No, my lord—though you may want to question your informant more carefully. He tried to kill me before he was brought here."

"A misunderstanding, I'm sure." Alexander raised his brows at Ash. "Did Sir Woods use a weapon, or alchemy, against you?"

"He tried to, once I—"

"Oh—did he not attack first, Lord Kendrick?"

Edric was silent for a heartbeat, and another, before he managed to spit out, "No."

"It sounds to me, then, that the boy acted in self-defense."

"He had no reason to be in Claremont—"

"Except perhaps doing as I'd ordered, gathering information that could be helpful to the safety of New Anglia."

"By spying on me?" Edric demanded.

"Are you exempt from the possibility of betraying New Anglia?" When Edric didn't respond, Alexander smiled. "Head Kendrick," Alexander said, "release Sir Woods, please."

Edric glared before nodding at one of the guards. The man stepped forward, hands reaching for the chains locked around Ash's wrists. Ash fell forward to the ground.

"Take him to his chambers," Alexander said to the guard. "Let him rest. I'll let Head Kendrick have a talk with the rebel."

Marlowe's disbelief had shifted. Truth settled. Her expression melted into a blank stare with the barest quiver of rage.

"Please," Ash said. The red had dragged Ash to his feet, but he pushed the man away. "Let Marlowe go."

All movement in the cell stopped. Lord Alexander's eyes dangerously narrowed.

Ash knew what he risked now, but still he couldn't make himself stop. "She was only doing what she thought was right—"

Alexander didn't move nor speak. His eyes glinted with a familiar coldness, but it was the calm energy surrounding him that scared Ash most.

"You must be tired," Alexander said. "Confused." He spoke to the guard. "Please, ensure that Sir Woods settles into his chambers for the rest he needs."

The red bowed and grasped Ash's shoulder. He dragged Ash out of the cell, up the stairs, and into the golden halls. The door opened and shut again, a panel blending into the wall. Ash wondered who else knew that the manor kept dungeons below. Though Ash had been released, he still felt a prisoner as the red's grip tightened. Attendants who passed stopped and stared at Ash and the state of his clothes, his gaunt face, as he was taken up the flights of stairs.

The door to Ash's room was opened, Ash flung inside. He stumbled, weak, as the door snapped shut. The lights were off, room in shadow. Ash grabbed and tried to turn the knob. It rattled. He'd been locked inside. He closed his eyes and tried to take a breath, to feel the grooves and imagine a key—but he hadn't eaten nor had any water in some time. He pressed a palm against the wall, intention bringing the familiar uncurling of smoke, but he paused.

The safe house was gone, as was the base in Hedge. Ash wouldn't be welcome in the Downs nor the Kendrick town house. He didn't have the cottage. The streams of black smoke sucked back into the wall's shadows. Ash didn't have anywhere else to go—nowhere else to run.

He trembled. Finley was dead, along with the dozens of people he had seen in his dream—their screams and cries over the rapid shots turned his stomach. The shock in Marlowe's gaze, the hurt that shined—Callum's disgust, Ramsay's disappointment—

A buzz beneath his skin itched. It whispered promises: *If you consume more chaos, the power you feel will make every other emotion disappear. You won't have to deal with such painful memories.* Ash had no one, and wasn't that what he deserved? He'd betrayed every person he loved. Bile rose. He turned and stumbled to the bed, falling to the floor before he could reach the mattress. He didn't have enough strength to pull himself to his feet as his vision faded to black.

※

Ash blinked open his eyes to bright yellow light. He heard a humming and felt a soft hand against his cheek. He turned his head. The pale wallpaper was familiar. Yes, that was right. He was back in the manor of Alexander. He squinted at a figure across the room, surprised when Charlotte turned. Her brows raised with a smile when she saw him.

"You're awake." She approached and pressed the back of her hand against his forehead. "How do you feel?"

"Like shit."

She nodded empathetically. "You've had a rough go. The broths and tonics seem to be helping, at least."

Ash winced as he sat up. He held up his arm. The gash that had been there was gone, a thin, faint cream scar remaining against his brown skin. "How long have I been out?"

"You've been in and out of consciousness for about a day. It's afternoon now." She smiled as if sharing a secret between them. "Callum and Ramsay came by, worried out of their minds, of course. I had to insist that they leave to let you sleep."

"Callum and Ramsay were here?" Ash couldn't quite believe it.

"Yes, of course they were," Charlotte said, as if confused by Ash's surprise. "We all heard what you've done for Kensington, Ash. It was brave of you to risk your life for the Houses."

Ash's skin was cold. "What did Lord Alexander say?"

"The truth," Charlotte said. "That you were a spy among the rebels. Thanks to you, the leader has been killed, most of the extremists captured. You truly are the Hero of Kensington."

Ash's memories trickled back. Marlowe, left in the dungeons with Edric. His breath quickened. He tried to push back his sheets, to get to his feet, but his body felt as if it were weighed down by stones. Charlotte put a hand on his shoulder with a gentle push of energy.

"You still need to rest," she said. "You could make yourself ill, if you exert yourself."

He wanted to argue, but even then his tongue was heavy, his eyelids falling shut. He shook his head, a sound of protest bubbling to his mouth as the weight of sleep blanketed him.

✳

He'd fallen in and out of sleep, images of patterns blooming behind his eyelids. He heard voices as he entered his dreams. Callum and Ramsay, he realized, murmuring.

"He's going to need time," Callum said.

"There's something else," Ramsay whispered. "Something we're not seeing."

Ash tried to drag himself from the hole of sleep, but fog settled across his mind.

✳

Ash opened his eyes. The bright white light and crisp air was familiar. He frowned, sitting up in bed. There was a mug on his bedside table with a rusted spoon. The old canopy bed creaked, emerald-green wallpaper faded. He was in his room in the Downs. Ash thought he would never see this home again, the way he and Ramsay and Callum had left things.

He rubbed his temple with a palm. His head pounded. He vaguely remembered Callum helping him to his feet—Ramsay leading the way, down the halls, but it'd all felt like the faint memories of a dream.

Ash couldn't even be sure he wanted to see them—not now, not after the fight they'd had and especially not after he'd tried to kill Callum's brother. Shame wrapped around his lungs, heating his chest. He pushed from his bed and stuck his head out into the hall. There was no sign of either Ramsay or Callum, he thought, until he heard muffled clinking dishes. He followed the sound to the kitchens, breath tight in his chest. He didn't know what he would say.

Ash paused in the threshold, expecting to see Ramsay and surprised instead to see Callum standing at the sink. Callum must've sensed Ash's presence. He looked over his shoulder with a smile that seemed hesitant, wiping away soapy water that'd somehow gotten on his cheek.

"Glad to see you're on your feet," Callum said. "You look rested."

Ash shuffled into the kitchen. Source, he could hardly look at Callum now. The Callum Ash had last seen was burned into his memory: the disgust, the suppressed rage. The coldness in Callum's eyes had reminded Ash of Edric, of their father. Ash wondered which was closer to the true Callum: the icy expression worthy of the Kendrick name or the uncertain pull at Callum's brows, the softness in his gaze.

"I'm surprised you're here," Ash said.

Callum's smile became more worried. "Is it all right that I am?"

"Yeah—of course." Ash sat on the edge of the table where he'd shared tea with Ramsay many afternoons before. "It isn't my home. It isn't my place to say if it's all right or not."

"I suppose that's true."

They fell into quiet. Tension felt like humid air, heat bogging Ash down and making his skin prickle with sweat. Usually, Callum would find just the right thing to say. It was rare to see the other boy just as hesitant.

Ash rubbed an arm uncomfortably. "Where's Ramsay?"

"Working in his office," Callum said. "He'll be happy to see you're awake."

Ash nodded, but the thought of seeing him frightened Ash more than he would've liked to admit. "Did you two take care of me?"

"Yes," Callum said, back to Ash again. "I asked Lord Alexander for permission to bring you to the Downs. Charlotte agreed that getting out of the manor and the city might do you some good."

"How long have I been here?"

"A day and a night."

Ash bit his lip. There was a question that tried to force itself to the forefront of his mind.

Callum placed the last dish in the sink and finally turned to face him fully, arms crossed. "I should apologize, Ash. If I'd known you were only acting as Alexander's spy—"

Ash couldn't bear to listen to the end of that sentence. He pushed away from the table. "It's fine. I'll let Ramsay know I'm all right." He hurried from the kitchen, eyes downcast—then lost the battle he'd fought with himself and stopped at the threshold. "Do you know what happened to Marlowe?"

Callum paused. He grabbed a hand towel, drying his fingers. "She's still in the dungeons, I believe."

Ash nodded. "I should get back to House Alexander."

"What? You're still recovering, Ash."

"I'm feeling better now," Ash said, an old annoyance rising. He turned on his heel and headed out into the halls.

Callum followed. "But you should be in bed, resting—"

"Source, Callum," Ash said, spinning to him. "I'm tired of you telling me what to do. I can decide for myself."

Callum blinked for a moment, then nodded. "I know that— yes, of course you can."

Ash felt rooted to the stone floor. He'd prepared himself for another argument, so was wordless now that Callum had agreed.

"I've tried to control you too much," Callum said, nodding as he spoke. "I didn't trust that you could take care of yourself, I'll admit to that. But you'd secretly been fighting battles for Lord Alexander all along. You've proven ten times over that you really don't need me by your side, protecting you." Callum took a short breath and released it slowly. Wind rattled the windows they stood beside, cold leaking through the cracks. "It was a little harder for me to see, I think—that this was just the role I gave myself to play," Callum told him. "If I wasn't by your side, protecting you from everyone and everything that wanted to hurt you, then what would keep us connected?"

"What do you mean?" Ash said. "We were connected because we loved each other, Callum." But the words felt automatic, like something Ash was supposed to say.

"I've always been self-conscious with you," Callum murmured. "You and Ramsay—you laugh more, bicker more, are more passionate than she and I are, sometimes. I was afraid you'd both decide you loved each other enough without me in the way. I didn't want to lose you."

It was the same fear Ash had for so many months now. There was something amusing about the fact that they'd been afraid of the same thing—devastating, to realize things might have turned out differently, had either been brave enough to say it.

"Loved?" Callum said quietly. He hadn't missed Ash's choice of words, then. "Not love?"

Yes, of course Ash still loved Callum—the Callum he recognized, anyway, the Callum he'd grown to know. He wasn't sure how he felt when he saw the echoes of Edric and Winslow Kendrick in Callum's expression instead. And there was the other thought, too—the realization that Ash's feelings might not matter anymore, in the end.

"I have to debrief with Lord Alexander," Ash said. He ignored the haze that seemed to cover his vision as he hurried down the hall. He listened to Callum's hesitant footsteps follow.

"Are you sure Lord Alexander will want to meet with you now?" Callum said.

"Why wouldn't he? I'm still his advisor."

"He made it clear that he would call for you when he was ready to speak—"

Ash had turned down the hall and into Ramsay's office. He came to a stop, surprised to see Ramsay sitting at his desk, feet up in the corner as he spun a pen around in his hand. "Up on your feet already?" he said. The words didn't quite match his watchful gaze.

Ash paused under Ramsay's scrutiny, hesitant. "I was just going back to House Alexander."

Ramsay dropped his feet from the corner of his desk. "Looking like that?"

Ash hadn't even considered that he was still in his sleeping things. He blushed faintly. Maybe he was more out of it than he thought.

"Ramsay," Callum said, "help me convince him to get back into bed."

"Ash," Ramsay said with a sarcastically loving tone, "please get back into bed before our darling Callum has a heart attack. I'm not ready to lose him just yet."

"I'm not tired," Ash said, even as he tried to blink away the haze. Ramsay snorted.

"How could you not be?" Callum said with his usual gentle

tone. It was comforting in its familiarity. Ash pushed that comfort away. "You've been through so much—the act you put on, your battles—"

Ash didn't mean to say it, hadn't considered the words before they were already on his tongue—but was it really so surprising that he would say the truth now? He was tired of the lies, the web he'd tangled himself in. "It wasn't an act."

Callum stilled. Ramsay's gaze flitted up to Ash, unsurprised.

"What do you mean?" Callum asked.

Ash turned to face him and Ramsay both. "It started as one," he admitted with a nod. "I was only following Lord Alexander's orders, to spy on the ALP members. But the more time I spent with Marlowe and the rest . . ."

The lightness that had filled Callum's eyes at the possibility that Ash had not betrayed them all dimmed. Ash could see the shard of pain that filled Callum with every heartbeat.

"They're right," Ash said. He swallowed and looked from Callum to Ramsay. "The ALP. They're right about everything. We shouldn't have to fear for our lives for being alchemists. We should have the freedom to practice alchemy. There shouldn't be any licenses nor tier laws."

"Bullshit," Ramsay said lightly. "The world is already dangerous enough with those protections in place."

"Anyone who wants to cause damage will do that whether they have a license or not," Ash argued. "Besides, these days I'm pretty sure the people who're causing the most damage are the House members."

Ramsay took an impatient breath. Callum seemed to have abandoned hope for disbelief now. He shook his head, then settled into one of the chairs along the wall. Ash finally gave in to the weariness that clouded his vision and sat in another chair along the opposite wall. It was almost amusing, this polite sit-down to discuss their futures; for this was what Ash knew the conversation would turn to. He had tried to ignore what he could for as long as possible, but it felt impossible after all, to be an alchemist rebel with the Head of a House and a redguard commander for his partners.

"Why?" Callum eventually settled on.

"Why what?"

Callum closed his eyes as if seeking patience. "Help me understand why you've chosen this path."

"Why did you choose yours?"

"Me?" Callum said, eyes snapping open as he stared Ash down. "I inherited my role, and I'm using it to do what I can to create peace."

"Peace for whom? You? Other House members?"

"Meanwhile, you've made the choice to destroy our society."

"There isn't any peace for people like me," Ash said.

Callum shook his head. "This isn't you, Ash."

"Your father, maybe," Ramsay murmured.

"You're one to talk," Ash snapped.

Ramsay sighed, head falling back as he stared up at the ceiling. "It's so obvious, Ash. You're just following in your father's footsteps, exactly like Hain wanted."

"And aren't you doing the same?" Ash demanded, voice rising. "Creating inventions that kill, no matter the cost. Becoming a redguard commander, hunting down alchemists. If I'm continuing my father's legacy, then both of you are, too!"

They were silent for a while, each examining the truth they'd laid out for one another. Callum's heaviness forced his shoulders to round forward, elbows on his knees as he gripped his hands together. "I'd been glad—so happy, Ash, to find out that you hadn't betrayed all of New Anglia. Even after the last argument we had, I realized I didn't want to lose you. I still want this to work. I still care about you. If you agree to leave the rebels, then—"

"I'll never do that." Ash sighed and rested his palms into his eyes, wiping away the tension. "I refuse."

"Callum argues to keep us together while you argue to keep us apart," Ramsay noted.

Ash fought to keep the annoyance out of his tone now. "While I fight for alchemist liberation, Callum will be hunting me down. What? Do we decide to be in love only after working hours?"

Ramsay raised a brow. "No need to get testy with me. I'm only making an observation."

"I wouldn't arrest you," Callum said.

"Not even when it's your duty?"

He hesitated. "I wouldn't let any harm come to you. I'd refuse to let Edric or Lord Alexander have you executed. I can't stand by and allow that to happen."

Ash snorted, though there was nothing funny about the matter. "Edric wouldn't listen to you. Your brother planned to have you executed, too—planned to claim you were helping me, just because you and I—"

Callum's face twisted. It was another shard that it seemed he'd done his best to ignore, the fact Ash had not been acting on orders when he attempted to assassinate Edric. "Do you think I'm not aware that my brother wants me dead?" Callum said, voice heavy. "I fight every day to make him see that I'm on New Anglia's side, that he can trust me."

"And you'd have me locked away in a cage just to convince him."

"Is that what you think of me?"

"You were willing to denounce your own family for Ramsay," Ash said, "but for me? You become a commander."

"Don't be so *selfish*, Ash," Callum said. "Creator, you can be so self-centered sometimes. I'm a commander now because my father is *dead*," he said, "and because I saw this as a chance to make change—to House Kendrick, to New Anglia."

Ash took a breath before he said what he most feared aloud. "Maybe it would be easier for you two to be together without me."

Callum shook his head, quieter now. "You see? I speak of my

father—my responsibilities—but you somehow find a way to twist it all back to you."

"I'm allowed to have feelings," Ash argued, even as Callum's stinging words rang true. "Isn't that what you always say?"

Callum took a sharp breath. He seemed unable to look at Ash. "You're right. Maybe it would be easier."

Callum might as well have reached into Ash's lungs and snatched the breath out himself. Salt stung his eyes as he blinked them away.

"Don't be cruel," Ramsay said softly.

"How could he not?" Ash asked. "He's a Kendrick, after all."

Callum stood abruptly, icy-blue energy shining from his skin, but he didn't move to leave. Silence followed as Callum breathed, chest rising and falling. Ramsay watched Callum for one long moment before speaking again.

"Yes," he said, "maybe Callum and I would be better off without you, Ash." Ash's head hung low, eyes burning. "We have that history. We know each other, certainly more than we know you. And we're both members of the Houses. Callum may one day become the Head of his own House, too."

Ash swallowed. He waited for Ramsay to say that it was over, to ask that he leave.

"But there's a reason Callum and I didn't work before," Ramsay said. "Callum is about *communication* and *feelings* and whatnot," he added, twirling a hand around. "And I—well, I admittedly forget where I am half the time, I'm so invested in my work. Callum's often felt . . . neglected by me, I suppose."

The icy blue that shimmered around Callum began to fade. Callum still stood, blinking rapidly at the floor. His throat bobbed, maybe swallowing back words he would've regretted.

"You're the right balance of energy," Ramsay continued, and though the words were directed at Ash, Ramsay looked at Callum now, too, as if wanting to remind the older boy of this as well. "The—ah—*heat* that welds us together. It would be easier without you, sure, maybe for the first few months—but Callum and

I didn't work before. We wouldn't work without you this time, either."

It took a moment, but Callum finally sat heavily back into his seat. He wouldn't look at Ash as he cleared his throat. "I'm sorry," he said.

"I am, too," Ash mumbled.

"Do you feel the pressure?" Ramsay asked with the smallest smirk. "Break up with us, Ash, and you're forcing Callum and I to break up, too."

"Don't tease him like that," Callum said. Even with the lingering anger and hurt, it seemed he felt the need to defend Ash.

"I can't help it," Ramsay said. "It's so easy."

Ash wiped his eyes with the heels of his palms with the smallest smile. He knew Ramsay was only trying to make him laugh, and it was working, whether he wanted it to or not.

"I'm surprised, honestly," Ramsay confessed. "Here you were, worried that Callum and I would run off into the sunset together, but that's what I'd worried about most of all with you two."

Ash's brows rose. "What? Why?"

"Because you two balance each other out so perfectly," Ramsay said. "Fire and water: Ash's outbursts tamed by Callum's calm. It's a perfect match."

"Creator," Callum said, "I always worried you two would get bored of me and I'd be left in the dust." Callum scratched his cheek. "I've feared you two are more . . . *passionate*."

Ash and Ramsay looked at each other with mirrored cringing expressions. "Passionate?" Ramsay repeated. "Really, Callum?"

"How else am I supposed to describe it?"

"Besides," Ramsay said, "I think we all have more than enough evidence for how *passionate* we can be."

Callum blushed as he turned his face away for a moment. "So?" he finally said. "We can talk like nothing is wrong, treat one another like nothing's happened." Ash's gaze dropped. The echoes of the harsh words they'd shared still hung in the air. "We obviously care for one another. We've made that clear. Can we figure out this relationship of ours?"

Ash wished the answer were easy. "I don't know," he admitted. "It almost feels like the paths we're on are predestined. Manifestations of Source that we have no choice but to take."

"We always have a choice," Ramsay said. "We're just fragments of Source, too, after all. We get to decide what we want and how our lives will play out."

"I love you," Callum told Ash. "Despite everything that's happened, despite all that we've said, I still do. Isn't that enough?" And, when Ash didn't answer, Callum shook his head. "So, what? Are you leaving us?"

Ash still wasn't sure what to say.

"I think it's possible this is just another programmed state," Ramsay murmured. "Think about it, Ash. Isn't it possible you're just repeating another cycle, too? One where you feel more comfortable alone, because that's all you've ever known."

Ash hated that he paused, considered, for a moment, if Ramsay had a point. "I would rather be with you—Source, of course I would prefer to stay here with you both."

"Then stay," Callum said.

Stay. Callum wasn't only asking Ash to stay there in the Downs. He wanted Ash to stay in the relationship the three shared, too. Ash shook his head before he could even form the words. Maybe Callum had a point after all: Ash was self-centered, selfish, always putting himself and his wants before others. This time, he couldn't—not when he thought of the thousands who would suffer if he did.

How could he say goodbye? There was no way, Ash realized, to capture all the words he could possibly want to say in this last moment. The three breathed together in silence, Ramsay frowning in thought as if he was still searching for the right mix of words to convince Ash not to go.

"At least stay the night," Callum said. "One more time. We can pretend there's no war, no rebels nor redguards. It's just the three of us, living together happily, exactly as we always wanted."

Ash needed to return to Kensington, but at Callum's words, he decided he could be selfish just one more time.

✳

Ramsay had finally begun to stock his kitchen with food, so Callum made the three pancakes for lunch. Ramsay "helped" by taste testing while Ash helped to set the table. They sat, and they laughed, and they ate.

Ash pretended it was just another day, one out of thousands they would have together; and when his mind lingered closer to the truth, a frown on his face, Callum reached for his hand and touched his fingers. Callum suggested a walk, so they roamed the wintery grounds, Ash bundled in a coat Callum had wrapped over his shoulders. They talked, shared memories, and laughed some more.

The sun began to fall. It was too early, but the three went to bed without speaking, Ash listening to their heartbeats while Callum and Ramsay listened to his. None could sleep. They held each other, breathing. Callum might've started to cry, if his shaking shoulders were anything to go by, which only made tears prick Ash's eyes. Ramsay kissed both their cheeks with a sigh.

Ash waited as long as he could, watching the sky lighten, before slipping out of the bedsheets.

31

Ash assumed it was one last farewell gift on Callum's part, to give him the head start he needed. He hurried through the Alexander manor's halls and down the stone steps, toward the redguards who stood outside the dungeon cell. Ash didn't bother to speak to the two. He supposed, if he was to do the work of a rebel, he might as well act like one.

Two clumps of fabric materialized and shot forward, tying around the reds' mouths. They let out muffled yells, hands rising to tear the fabric away. Ash envisioned rope twisting around their arms and legs so that both fell over, unbalanced and wriggling in indignation. Ash ignored the muffled shouts as he jumped over one and reached into the pocket of the other for the set of keys, pressed one hand to the door's knob, and heard a click as it unlocked.

Marlowe's face was a patchwork of bruises and cuts. One gash across her cheek had turned yellow with infection. Marlowe's head barely rose as he stepped in, until her purple swollen eyes widened. Ash put a finger to his mouth and worked quickly, unlocking one manacle around Marlowe's hand and then the other. She fell forward. Ash caught her, laying her on the floor gently as she rubbed her wrists, red lines carved into her skin.

"We don't have much time—"

Marlowe shoved Ash's chest weakly. "Get away from me."

"Marlowe—"

She slapped him. It felt like she'd put most of her energy into it, judging by the sting. Ash grabbed her wrists. How long before more reds came running? "Listen to me, Marlowe. Everything Alexander said—it was true, at first."

She grunted, eyes pinched together in pain, perhaps both physical and emotional, as she tried to pull out of Ash's grasp.

"But I realized that I was wrong," Ash said. "Speaking to you, spending time with you . . . I realized what side of this I want to be on." His grip tightened, and Marlowe's eyes widened as she met his stare. "Please," he said. "Trust me."

A muscle in Marlowe's jaw jumped. Maybe she realized she didn't have much of any choice, if she wanted to survive. "What's the plan?" she said, voice rough.

Relief spread through Ash's chest, but not much—he still needed to worry about getting Marlowe out. "I can't materialize us away," Ash said, knowing Marlowe would be too weak to make the attempt herself. "House Alexander has defensive barriers against materialization."

"You materialized through the barriers at House Val."

"I'd just consumed the chaos fragment. The energy was more powerful then, more volatile. It's settled now, weaker than before— and besides, I can't handle us both." The last time Ash had tried and failed to attempt a materialization, he'd created an explosion strong enough to destroy a section of the railways and bury Marlowe under rubble. He didn't want to risk a similar result.

Marlowe stumbled to her feet, Ash's hands out and ready to catch her. She pressed a hand to the wall. Ash expected to see black tendrils snake from her hands, to spread across the wall like ink—but there was nothing. Marlowe only stared forward blankly, her palm curling until it closed into a fist. The chaos only linked them to the Ironbound safe house, now overrun with reds. They had nowhere to go.

Ash was in a similar predicament. "We just have to make a run for it," he said.

Neither looked up for it, but what other choice did they have?

Marlowe had the back as Ash took the front when they passed the guards who were still tied and on the floor, trying to wriggle themselves free. Ash saw that one of them had managed to use his shoulder to pull down the gag, and it was as they rounded the corner that the red's echoing shouts followed. "Escaped—they've escaped, the prisoners—"

Ash and Marlowe made it to the first floor. It'd be a straight run through the front doors and out into the Kensington streets, but they'd be within full view of every red on duty as they ran down the manor's front steps, and Ash was willing to bet they wouldn't make it far. "Brilliant plan, this," Marlowe remarked.

"I was low on time, all right?" Ash said, spinning around as he took in the hall, thoughts formulating, an idea coming—

Footsteps. Reds raced down the hall and the stairs, slowing to a stop. The guards at the front must have received the message. They paused, too, fingers wrapped around the handles of their swords. The reds surrounded Ash and Marlowe. Surprise crossed faces as gazes swept over Ash, confused glances exchanged. Breaking out prisoners was hardly behavior expected of the *Hero of Kensington*.

Marlowe panted as she held up an arm, face gray. "Would've preferred to die in the dungeons," she said beneath her breath. "At least I would've had a few more hours to live."

"Sir Woods," one red said, stepping forward through the line of guards and into the center of the hall. Ash's heart fell. Callum didn't seem any happier to be there, chin raised. Ash wondered if he'd been called in from the Downs to report for duty that morning or if he'd come to the manor on his own. "You have one chance to step away from the prisoner. If you do so now, punishment will be lenient."

Even these words seemed to confuse the reds under Callum's command, brows raised. House Kendrick didn't believe in second chances and lenient punishments. Ash had been caught betraying New Anglia by releasing a rebel leader of the ALP. Anyone else, and their execution would have been ordered on the spot.

Marlowe murmured behind him. "Sometimes we have to make our own doors, right?"

Ash took a breath and grinned. "Thank you, Commander Kendrick," he said, "but I'm afraid I'm going to have to pass on your offer." He raised both hands. The reds around him instinctively ducked, but they weren't the target. He imagined a flint of fire. The last time he'd done something like this, desperate to escape, the outcome had been catastrophic. It was a sign of his growth, he thought rather proudly, just how easily he could manage the fireball and its explosion.

The hallway blew out into dust and a stream of light. There was silence, coughing, and the thud of rubble falling to the ground. Callum stood straight, seeming to survey the reds—and when he saw no one was injured, he raised a hand and shouted, "Search the premises. They couldn't have gotten far."

Ash knelt beside Marlowe as she stood, palm face up, air shimmering in front of them. They waited as they listened to the clack of footsteps pass and disappear. Marlowe muttered, "Your boyfriend's kind of an asshole."

It hadn't really sunk in fully. It was odd saying the words aloud. "He isn't my boyfriend."

Marlowe looked at him with a raised brow.

"We broke up," Ash said, and tried to sound apathetic about it, though he was sure he couldn't hide the wave of grief that leaked into the air.

A crunch of footsteps silenced them. Marlowe put up her other palm, too, face scrunched in concentration as Callum stepped out of the hole of rubble and debris. He paused, seeming to look out at the courtyard and the reds that shouted as they searched the wall and the open gates. He took a breath. "You're here, aren't you?"

Ash stilled. Marlowe sucked in a breath.

"I can't see you, but your energy—it's here, I know it is." Callum hesitated, brows scrunched. "I'll try to buy you enough time to escape. I think I'll have another twenty minutes before I'll be forced to order a citywide search. Make sure you're not in Kensington by then. Stay away as long as you can."

He turned on his heel then, crunching back into the manor. Marlowe stared at Ash for one long moment. "You two have a really strange relationship," she finally said.

"Yeah. I know."

＊

As long as the two didn't bump into a person or knock a piece of trash across the cobblestone with their feet, no one was any the wiser that they were around as they maneuvered past patrolling reds. When Marlowe was drained, she traded off with Ash, breathing slowly with each step, the mirage that concealed them shimmering.

"Could just take the train out of Kensington," Marlowe whispered.

"And keep the illusion up for the entire ride?" Ash said. "No. Go to Hedge. You can hide out there, at least—recover, then materialize the hell out."

They crossed the familiar iron bridge. Ash stiffened and felt Marlowe do the same beside him. "Is this your first time back?" Ash said. "Since . . ."

She nodded. That seemed to be all she was willing to do or say on the topic. They slowed to a stop. There was a shadow burned into the stone, where Ash had been filled with the light of Source—where Marlowe had come and stabbed his father through the heart.

Ash's sigh was heavy. He wasn't fond of the idea, and he knew Marlowe wouldn't take to it well, either.

"What is it?" she said.

"You and I need to part ways here."

Marlowe's hands slowly dropped. The illusion faded, and anyone looking would have seen the two suddenly appear.

"You want to part ways?" Marlowe said. "But why?"

"You're safer without me. I'm more of a hindrance than a help, at this point."

"And if I'm caught anyway?" Marlowe asked. "I'd have a better chance if you're with me. We could fight together."

Ash hesitated, looking out at the gray sea. "I have more work to do in Kensington still, and you—alchemists need you, Marlowe. Hain wanted me to be the leader of the revolution, when he couldn't see the real leader right in front of him."

Marlowe shook her head. "No. I'm not a leader, not like you. Your energy—it draws people to you, whether you know it or not."

"It's only because I'm Gresham Hain's son," Ash told her. "You're the type of person who follows through, takes action, and makes change. I'm just a symbol."

"A symbol is necessary sometimes, too."

They stood in silence for a moment more, looking out at the gray sea that matched the sky above. It was fitting, that they'd returned to the place where both had survived Hain, after surviving so much more together.

"Are you going to look for chaos fragments?" Marlowe asked and, without waiting for an answer, "Are you going to do it? Are you going to stitch the tear?"

He needed to at least try. That, and the fact Ash would now have to survive alone, scared him more than he wanted to admit. But he hadn't always been an elite advisor and spy of Kensington. He'd survived on his own before; he would make it on his own again.

Marlowe nodded as if she understood everything that had gone unspoken in the silence. "You know how to reach out if you need me."

"Thank you," Ash said, knowing his energy shared just how genuinely he meant that.

He'd never been good at goodbyes. He turned, walking across the bridge and the fog that had started to drift, pausing once he'd returned to the Kensington side to see that Marlowe was already gone.

※

Ash placed a hand to an alleyway wall and stepped through the ink, into his chambers in the Alexander manor. The Val meter tracking the use of chaos would undoubtedly lead reds to his room, but Ash would be long gone by then. The room was blue in shadow. Ash crossed to his wardrobe. He'd change into something that was easier to run in, to fight in—he'd use illusion alchemy for as long as he could to escape, but inevitably—

He paused. Ash turned. He didn't know how he'd missed Lord Alexander. The man leaned against Ash's closed door, watching with eyes that appeared to glow in the dim light. "Sir Woods," Alexander said with the twitch of a smile. "It's good to see you. I assumed you'd sneak your way back into my manor again eventually."

Ash didn't respond. He deepened his breaths, heat growing in his palms.

Alexander didn't seem to mind as he pushed off from the door and strolled across the room to the balcony, footsteps tapping the tile. He paused and inspected the courtyard below.

"You've disappointed me, Sir Woods," Alexander said.

Anger clogged Ash's throat. "Why? Because I'm not your perfect little pet anymore?"

"I'd thought our agreement was mutually beneficial."

Ash pressed his tongue into his teeth. "You promised to give alchemists freedom. You said you would do away with the tier laws, the licenses. But you haven't done shit for us."

"You speak as if you think you're still just a Hedge boy, illegally practicing alchemy. You have your license now, Sir Woods. You're a member of House Alexander. You're among the elite. Why argue for the side of the extremists?"

His words twisted Ash's stomach. Haze covered his vision. "I don't think freedom should end with me."

Alexander's eyes narrowed, though his smile was still planted on his face. "Head Kendrick was right. You do sound like a rebel more and more every time you speak."

The lord tilted his head, and as he watched Ash, an invisible energy seemed to suddenly press on the younger man's shoulders. He swayed on his feet, knees almost buckling. Something was wrong.

"You asked me, once, how I would control alchemists," Alexander whispered.

Ash wavered, legs weak, and stumbled to the sofa in the center of his room. He fell before he could reach it. It was hard to breathe.

"What you stole from House Val, Sir Woods—apparently it has intriguing properties," Alexander said. "I have no talent for alchemy, yet this particular energy would give me the ability to do anything I like, with just one thought alone." Alexander faced Ash. "It's been most helpful, as of late."

Ash had gripped the sofa's arm, struggling to push himself to his feet, but at this, Ash's brows tugged down. He watched Alexander approach him. The energy surrounding the man had been suppressed, but Alexander allowed Ash to see it now: The outline of black glowed faintly from the man's skin, embers of darkness falling to his feet.

"You're working with him," Ash whispered. "You've been working with Lune all along."

Alexander smiled. "You're almost there," he said. "Come now— you're supposed to be clever. Think, Sir Woods."

Ash shook his head, breath stuck, but the answer came to him even then. Realization sank into Ash's skin, dread souring his tongue. Lune's intention had been to control anyone he touched. Sinclair Lune must have touched Alexander and spread his energy into the lord. How long had Alexander been controlled? Source, maybe Lune had been in Kensington all along.

Alexander—no, Lune—stopped in front of Ash. His smile glimmered. "Yes," he said. "You've got it now."

Ash's heart hammered. He had to get out.

"Taking the body of the leader of New Anglia has certainly been helpful," Lune said. "It's been an easier position, to create the changes I've needed to make New Anglia my own."

"How long?" Ash asked, voice rough. He tried to force himself to his feet, but the weight of Sinclair Lune's energy made his legs buckle beneath him.

"Easton Alexander met with me in private, after you and your friends attacked my home," Lune told him. "He wanted to consider me for the Head of Lune." That very meeting following the attack on the base, Alexander had already been dead.

"You might be right, *Sir Woods*," the man said. "Perhaps your lord truly had great ambitions for manipulators in this state. You understand, then, why I couldn't allow it."

"You say that while using alchemy yourself."

"This is not *alchemy*," the man said, disgust riddling his tone. "This is a gift of the Creator." He held up Alexander's palm and watched as shadow swirled into an orb. "I was chosen. I am the vessel for the Creator's judgment upon this earth."

What Lune had accomplished was tier-six alchemy: to leave one's own body in a state of rest, an unconscious husk waiting for consciousness to return, and take over another body instead was no easy feat; and for that to have happened, Alexander's consciousness had likely been pushed out, too. Once Lune left the lord's body, there'd be nothing but a breathing shell.

There was no space to mourn, even if Ash wanted to. "Why not just kill Alexander, then?" Ash said. He was breathless. His eyes flitted around the room. He was only stalling, looking for a way out. "Why not just take control of the Houses, if that's what you wanted?"

"I couldn't simply kill Easton Alexander and declare myself the ruler of New Anglia. I would never be respected as the rightful ruler of this state. No," Sinclair Lune said through his puppet. "Better to put new laws into place now, to destroy the enemies of Lune from within and build my throne. Alexander can hand his rulership to me: declare Sinclair Lune the new Head of the Houses. Then I will be ready to step forward as the rightful ruler."

Ash could hardly move, let alone fight.

Lune seemed to notice Ash's struggle with a soft laugh. "What?" he asked. "Do you think I plan to kill you now? Rest easy. You still have a role to finish playing, Sir Woods, son of Gresham Hain."

"Are you going to have me executed?"

"When the time is right," Lune said. "The people will want to see a symbol of a new era. Your death—your public execution, the killing of an infamous manipulator—will be that symbol."

Ash's breath was short, anger growing. "I won't be sacrificed."

Lune smiled. "I'm not sure you have a choice."

As Lune reached for Ash with a spread palm, embers of black falling from his fingers, Ash threw up his own with a slash of light. Lune's roar filled the room, echoing as Ash stumbled into the hall. The farther he got away from Lune, the less pressure pulled him to the ground. He ran, racing down one corridor and toward the stairs—guards were near, heads whipping up with surprise as Ash rushed past them, startled when they saw the bloodied body part that Ash clutched with a fist.

Alexander's voice yelled after him. "Get him—catch him, don't let him get away—"

Ash glanced over his shoulder at the reds who followed now, too; Alexander was at the top of the staircase, clutching his bloodied wrist and its missing hand. Ash ran through the empty conference room and to the far end—pressed the hand he'd caught against the wall. It slid open, crunching as it moved. Ash flung himself inside just as he heard the echoes of boots behind him. Reds gushed into the conference room. All raised their firelocks, pointed at Ash. He held up his hands and a barrier rose. Shots rang out, projectiles exploding against Ash's shield and the door of Alexander's hidden room as it slowly closed. Finally it shut with a thud, throwing Ash into pitch darkness. He held up an orb of light as he turned, taking in the room—the chairs, the shelves—

Another set of bangs against the closed door. A muffled shout. *"Open the door!"*

There on the top shelf was a glass container. The glass warped Ash's view of what was inside, but it was unquestionable: A black orb floated within.

Ash grabbed the glass just as he heard the familiar crunch of the door. Lune must have caught up, pressed Alexander's other hand to the door—Source, Ash should've taken both—

He pulled his arm back and threw the glass to the floor. It shattered, glass shards flying. Among the pieces of glass scattered across the stone, the round fragment lifted into the air. Ash snatched it. Its hum vibrated through his skin and into his bones like needles, each prick screaming that he consume the chaos.

He put it into his mouth with a shaking hand and swallowed. Relief flowed, water touching a parched throat. Fire licked beneath his skin, images rushing beneath his eyelids. He blinked, and Ash was no longer inside the chamber of House Alexander. Blackness—chaos, Ash realized—and light. Source loomed. A thread stretched across the darkness, comprised of an infinite number of particles of light, each particle a universe containing an infinite number of particles of light, each of those particles a universe containing an infinite number of particles of light—

Consciousness. The Creator. Existence. The stillness in being. Silence. Life.

What is your intention?

Ash was on the floor. He must have collapsed. The door was open, Alexander stepping inside.

Ash squeezed shut his eyes. *Stitch the tear. Close the tear above Kensington.*

Ash's muscles twisted. His organs squeezed. He screamed. The black tear above Kensington had widened. More orbs fell from the sky like blackened snow. An older man with a bent back picked up an orb—held it, inspected it. A child near the docks played with another she had found, laughing as it floated through the air. "What do you think it is?" Lady Alder asked an assistant, who only frowned as he shook his head, both peering at the orb that hovered above her desk.

The tear trembled, opposite ends stitching—but they would not meet. Maybe once, the tear would have stitched, but the two sides had since stretched too far apart. Ash gasped as bile rose. Vomit splashed on the floor. Edric stood over him. The man made his orders, voice muffled. Ash's eyes rolled back, body slumping to the floor.

※

Ash watched his body. He watched Edric kick his body's side, then order reds to handle him. Ash saw his body dragged from the floor and across the hall. People had gathered, watching with hands rising to cover open mouths that gasped, whispers following. A healer clutched Lord Alexander's wrist, yellow energy glowing as she stopped the bleeding, but not much else could be done now.

Word had spread. Sir Ashen Woods, the Hero of Kensington, had tried and failed to assassinate Head Alexander.

"Can you really be surprised?" Lady Galahad whispered to Lord Malone. "He is the son of Gresham Hain, after all."

Ash stood over the city, beside the tear in the fabric of the universe.

"Do you see how fickle these humans are?" his father asked.

The tear reminded Ash of the streams of light that filled the northern skies at night. There were multiple light streams of different colors, flowing across one another like waves—and in between those waves, the small particles of black fell through.

"One moment they praise you, and the next they want your head," Hain said. He scoffed. "Hypocrites, all of them."

Ash leaned forward to inspect the tear. "It didn't close."

"I've already warned you a number of times that your plan

would not work," Hain let him know. "The tear has only grown. Chaos energy is powerful once consumed, yes—but you would need to consume another fifty fragments to heal a tear like this."

Ash wouldn't survive another fifty fragments. His body was already breaking down; he was caught between life and death, even then. He looked down at the newly built Kensington Square, directly below. The Square was made of white quartz. It was where Hain had begun his attack on the city. Fitting, that Ash's body was dragged into its center now. His head lolled, unconscious, as redguards pulled him onto a wooden platform, swaying beneath their feet. The guards tied Ash's arms behind his back and around a wooden pole so tightly that he was forced to stand even asleep.

Hain watched his son's physical body as well. "It seems they're preparing for a public execution," he said.

Ash nodded. It was strange. Standing above the city like this, he felt removed from the grief he might've felt at the loss of his own life. Instead, he only felt disappointment—guilt. "I failed," he said. "I wanted to save the city—New Anglia."

"Hm," Hain replied.

They stood in silence for a moment more, looking down at Ash's unconscious body. Crowds had started to gather. Onlookers read the sign that had been placed on the edge of the platform, announcing his crimes. *Rebel alchemist. Traitor to the state of New Anglia. Attempted assassination of Lord Alexander.*

"You can stay here, if you like," Hain said. "You're still between two dimensions. You can wait here until they kill you, so that you won't have to feel your physical body's pain. It'll be like the blink of an eye, death," his father told him.

Ash had trouble looking away from his body. People in the crowd had begun to yell. "*Kill the manipulator!*" A stranger threw garbage at him. Another threw a stone.

"Are you trying to comfort me?"

"Is it so wrong that I am?"

"It's a little too late to act like my father, isn't it?" Ash asked.

Hain considered this. "I wasn't the best father to you. I can see that now."

Ash snorted. "That might be an understatement."

"But I can still try to do what I can for you now, can't I?"

Another rock hit Ash's head below. A cut at his temple bled. The reds guarding him stepped forward then, shouting at the crowd to disperse. It wouldn't do any good to see Ash die before his execution.

"Thank you," Ash said, "but I'd rather live."

✳

Pain brought Ash back. It was everywhere: His stomach cramped with nausea, his skin riddled with embers despite the cold. A cloth had been tied around his mouth and nose, covered in the powder that made Ash choke. Any and all chaos energy left in his body had been spent trying to stitch the tear. The effort had taken most of his energy from Source, too. The cells in his body had been overpowered. It was a wonder that his heart was still beating.

Guards stood motionless in front of the platform below him. The pole and rope he was tied with scratched his hands, his back. People walked past, slowing to look at the spectacle that was Ash Woods. Their hatred, their disgust, burned him. Source, maybe Ash should've accepted his father's offer. But if there was even the smallest chance that he could survive, then Ash would do what he could to fight.

Ash tried to pull at the rope, but the muscles in his arms strained and grew numb, skin scratched raw. He tried to breathe to grow more energy, but the white powder itched his lungs and he coughed. He felt like he was slowly drowning.

The night was long. Ash wheezed, tears rising, though he tried to blink them away. He considered himself lucky, that the physical distracted from the emotional pain that swelled in his chest again and again, every time he allowed himself to think of Ramsay and Callum. Would they come to his execution? He hoped to Source that they wouldn't and, in the same breath, hoped to Source that they would. At least then, he could see their faces one more time, if he didn't manage to get out of this alive.

The dark faded into light on the horizon. The sky pinkened before it turned a pale blue. Ash's eyes burned as he watched crowds begin to gather once more, this time for the show. It seemed to be the one uniting factor of all people in Kensington, this temporary peace between classes where everyone gathered to witness Ash's death. People glared, whispering to one another. Children stared with wide, curious eyes.

An echo of boots thudded across the Square. Ash twisted his head to see a line of redguards. Edric marched in front, striding toward the platform, thumping up the creaking steps as a line of reds followed him. Ash's heart clenched. Callum took up the rear. His face was frozen, stricken—he stared at the ground, straight ahead at the crowd, anywhere but at Ash himself. Source, it was particularly cruel of Edric, to force his brother to witness Ash's execution.

Edric stopped in front of Ash and stared down at him, as if savoring the fact that he was finally able to see Ash killed. Edric turned his back on Ash and stepped to the edge of the stage, addressing the crowd. His voice boomed. "The accused is guilty of treason, conspiring with extremists, and the attempted assassination of Lord Easton Alexander."

Murmurs spilled through the crowd. Callum didn't move from the front of the platform. Edric faced Ash once more. His quick smile was the only sign he was greatly enjoying this moment. He nodded to the red who stood on the other end of the platform. The red didn't hesitate. He raised a firelock. Ash wondered how much it would hurt, if it would happen as quickly as his father had said. He squeezed his eyes shut.

He expected an explosion, a sharp pain. Instead, there was a shout. Ash squinted at the figure who had appeared on the platform. Callum, shoving past Edric and throwing the guard and his weapon to the ground. There were screams—a flash of purple light, Ash would recognize Ramsay's energy anywhere—

Callum ripped the cloth from Ash's face. He sucked in a rasping breath as Callum's fingers worked at the rope. "Are you all right?" Callum grumbled.

Ash's throat was so sore that it hurt to speak. "Didn't see that coming."

"You didn't really believe I'd stand by and watch you get killed, did you?"

Ramsay had rushed from the crowd, a shield up as a gust of wind pushed him into the air, helping him to leap onto the platform. He grasped Ash just as the ropes slid from his hands, falling forward. Ramsay was pale, trembling. "Source, Ash—"

The shield Ramsay surrounded them with tinted the world purple. Edric roared. He pointed at the three, yelling his muffled commands. "Don't let them get away! Kill all three if you have to!"

Callum stood tall. "We'll need to fight our way out."

The arms that wrapped around Ash reminded him of resting in bed in between Ramsay and Callum, with soft sheets and gentle fingers and whispered promises. When Ash closed his eyes, it was easy to pretend that they were nestled together.

"He's losing consciousness," Ramsay said. His voice was high, panicked.

The red raised the firelock that had been meant for Ash. It was what would have killed him. Ramsay's hands were on Ash's shoulders, trying to help him to his feet. Callum's hand was on the hilt of his sword, pulling it from its sheath. Ash watched the blast, as if slowed—watched as it cut through the air, coming toward him. He hadn't realized Ramsay saw it, too. Ramsay stood instinctively, it seemed, and pushed Ash aside. The bullet pierced through Ramsay's shield, shattering it. Ramsay looked down, as if surprised. Red started to seep. Ramsay's knees buckled, and he fell.

Silence followed, but only for a moment. Ash's scream tore his throat before he realized it was his own. He dropped to his knees, turning Ramsay onto his back. Ramsay gulped air, staring at Ash with panicked eyes.

"No," Ash said, hand reaching for the wound. "No, no, no—"

Callum shouted at Ash, but nothing he said made sense. Ash looked up to see the red reloading his firelock. *I want to live.* Chaos energy exploded in Ash's veins. Ash reached for Callum's hand, clutching Ramsay's shoulder—didn't realize what he'd done, yet, until all three had appeared on a cold stone floor. Ash's vision spun as Callum dropped beside Ramsay, hands hesitant, hovering over the wound. Blood gushed. It pooled around Ramsay now, sticking to his hair.

"We have to heal him," Ash said, voice high with desperation. He put his hand to Ramsay's chest and thought of the love they shared—it should've been easy enough, to draw on that love—

Callum sat back. His eyes were wide, tears building.

"What're you doing?" Ash said. He grabbed Callum's hand and put it to Ramsay's chest, too. "Help me heal him!"

They'd done it before, once, when the two found Ramsay wounded in the Derry Hills. It'd worked then, and it'd work now, too. Callum slipped his hand into Ash's, tears falling.

Ash yanked away. "I'll—I'll find Charlotte," he said, hoarse. He stumbled to his feet, still weak. "She'll know how to—"

"Ash," Callum whispered. "He's gone."

Ash hadn't let himself look at Ramsay's face. It was pale. His mouth was parted, blood still spilling from his lips. His eyes stared blankly, pupils wide. He wasn't breathing. Ash shook his head. "It hasn't been long," he said.

"Ash," Callum pleaded.

"There's enough time," Ash said. "As long as I bring his energy back within a few minutes—we can heal him, and—"

Callum grabbed Ash's hands. He was crying now, shoulders shaking. Ash tried to pull away; there wasn't enough time to explain, he needed to get his copy of *Communicating with Plasma Particles* and read its instructions to bring Ramsay back. "Let me go," Ash said, voice scratching his throat. "Please—I have to . . ."

A sob broke from Ash's mouth, and once it did, he couldn't stop. He body wracked as he heard himself gasp and heave, tears squeezed from his eyes, grasping Callum's arm and hand, holding on to him, Callum's softer cries mingling with Ash's screams.

※

Ash couldn't look at Ramsay's body without feeling sick, but he couldn't look away, either. He and Callum sat against opposite walls, Ramsay lying between them. The sun was going down now, the sky red. Edric and the reds didn't have the password to the Downs. That was the only explanation Ash could think of, for why they hadn't been followed yet—but he knew it was inevitable that they would come.

"We should move him," Callum said, the first words either had spoken to each other in hours.

Ash only shook his head. He wasn't ready to stop looking at Ramsay.

"We need to wash him," Callum said. "Bury him."

"No," Ash said softly.

"He can't be left like this—"

"Why did you save me?" Ash asked.

"What?"

"Why didn't you both just stay away?"

Callum seemed speechless for a moment, as if he didn't know how to respond. He got to his feet shakily. He fell to one knee beside Ramsay and reached for him. Pressure swelled inside of Ash's chest, a protest rising to his lips—he almost demanded it, that Callum leave Ramsay alone—but the pressure burst as Ash watched Callum pick up Ramsay gently, carefully.

"It's okay," Callum whispered. "It's all right if you can't . . ."

Ash raised his hands and looked at his palms. They were covered in Ramsay's blood, he realized. He sat where he was as Callum walked past, carrying Ramsay down the hall.

※

Ash walked into his chambers. The balcony doors were open, showing the green of mountainsides that promised spring. Ramsay sat on the edge of the bed, his back to Ash. His head turned ever so slightly, the only sign he'd heard Ash come in. Ramsay smiled. His hair had grown longer. Ash had meant to ask if Ramsay wanted to cut it again.

Ash woke up slowly, blinking open his eyes. He was still in the hall, dark with shadow. Ramsay's blood had sunk into the stone. It would stain, a permanent mark. Maybe it didn't matter. The Thorne lineage had ended with Ramsay, and Ash couldn't imagine ever returning to the Downs.

The sky outside was still black, but birds had begun to sing. The sun would soon rise again. It felt offensive, an insult to Ramsay's memory, for the world to continue on as if nothing had happened. Ash knew he needed to move. He needed to eat, to drink water. He was still in a physical body. He regretted returning now, regretted turning down his father's offer. He should have waited to die instead.

Ash got to his feet weakly. He walked the corridors to Ramsay's chambers. He stood frozen in the threshold. Ramsay lay on top of the sheets. He'd been washed and dressed in a loose black shirt and slacks. His eyes were shut, lashes against his cheeks. It was odd to see Ramsay's still face, when usually his expression was cracked into a smirk or grin, cutting words or laughter coming from his lips. Ash swallowed the bile that threatened to rise. Tears swelled and fell.

Callum sat so still in a chair against the far wall that Ash thought he'd fallen asleep, too. But he looked up then, heavy bags beneath his eyes.

"He looks beautiful," Ash said.

Callum didn't respond. It hadn't been fair of Ash, he realized, to leave Callum with the task of taking care of Ramsay on his own.

Ash forced himself to shuffle into the room. He couldn't face Ramsay fully. He stopped in front of Callum. "Have you eaten?"

Callum only shook his head. "Not hungry."

Ash wasn't, either. "We should eat something."

Callum didn't move. He stared at his hands, fingers spread. "I wanted to blame you, at first," he said. "It was only misplaced anger, I know. Anger at my brother. Anger at myself." He held in a breath, as if struggling not to let himself cry again. "I didn't want to see it, but you were right. I was too worried about appeasing both sides, looking for Edric's approval, wanting his forgiveness. Ramsay's dead because I was a coward."

"That isn't true," Ash said softly. He regretted the things he'd said to Callum in anger now. "If you're to blame, then I am, too. But we aren't the ones who killed Ramsay."

Callum nodded slowly. He pushed himself to his feet, wavering for a moment. "What will you do now?" he asked, hoarse. "My brother will have reds search our town house, Claremont, and the Downs first. We might only have a few hours before they come."

Ash wasn't ready yet—his body still felt too heavy with grief and exhaustion to move, to run—but what other choice did he have? "Then we should hurry." The next words he tried to speak were stuck in his throat, but he forced them out. "We should bury Ramsay, and—"

Callum shook his head once. "No," he said. "I'll stay. I'll bury him. You need to go."

"What?" Ash said, frown pinching his brows. "But your brother—he'll arrest you, *kill you*—"

"I can handle my brother," Callum said. "I know what to say, what he wants to hear. Edric just wants my complete submission. He wants me to become a mindless red and follow his every order.

I'll tell him that I realized you were the monster he's said you were all along, that you manipulated me into loving you, but that I don't love you anymore."

Ash didn't have the heart to ask Callum if these words were closer to the truth than he wanted to admit.

"I'll say that my loyalty is only to my family now. But I won't be able to protect you if I do that," Callum said. "If you don't stay away from Kensington, I'll be forced to fight you."

Callum's gaze was fastened on Ramsay's body. Ash forced himself to look at Ramsay now, too. "Where are you going to bury him?" he asked.

"In the garden, I think."

Ash nodded. It was a nice place, with a view of the mountains. The two stood still for a long moment, until Ash walked to Ramsay's side. He made himself look at Ramsay's unbreathing body, which belonged to the earth and would soon crumble into dirt. The body was only a husk, a beautiful shell. Ash knew that Ramsay wasn't dead, not truly; he wasn't in the physical realm anymore, but his energy was still a part of Source, a thread in the fabric of the universe. Once he existed, he could never stop existing again. Ramsay could have been watching Ash and Callum even then, looking down from another dimension; he could have felt the joy that Ash had experienced once, too, and returned to the endless warmth and safety and love of Source, where he would wait for Ash and Callum to join him. This did nothing to comfort the deep ache that spread from Ash's chest.

Ash reached for Ramsay's cheek—paused, afraid to feel the skin's cold. His fingers curled back. "There might be a way, still," he said.

He turned on his heel and passed Callum. Ash paused at the threshold, wishing the right words would come to mind; the words that would encompass the love and anger and grief. He felt the soft brush of Callum's energy. Maybe that was Callum's way of saying, too, that he couldn't bear to say goodbye. Ash kept walking.

He stopped outside the gray manor. He stared at the dead gardens. Ash wasn't sure where he would end up, eventually; but he did know of a particular cabin, hidden away in the mountains, near a deserted village. It'd been stocked with enough supplies to last him at least a month, the last he'd been there. He closed his eyes and took a breath.

32

The crack had split across the sky. Black orbs fell like dust, raining down onto Kensington Square. The people were told not to touch the fragments; that they were poisonous, an aftereffect of the alchemy used in New Anglia and created by sin.

"Is this not the evidence you need?" one Lune follower shouted to the crowd that had gathered. The streets were clogged with followers who wore their robes of white. Wind whipped. "The end is near, and only Sinclair Lune can save the worthy!"

A body lay on its back upon a stone platform. The man's hair was so pale, it shone like spiderwebs. His eyes were closed. Attendants wiped down his skin and put water to his lips.

"Has it been tried before?" Ash asked. He stood on the edge of a sea, water gray and waves frothing around his feet.

"Yes," Hain replied. He watched as ripples in the water trembled. The ground shook. "Each life stream is a thread upon itself. The infinite variations weave together."

Sharp edges of land rose from the ocean. Mountains grew. "There are streams where you were not born," Hain said. "Streams where your mother is not dead. Streams where I raised you as my son."

It was possible, then, wasn't it? There might've even been a stream where Ramsay was still alive, too.

*

It was easier than Ash expected, to slip through the solid stone wall. It was a new ability, one he hadn't tested yet. Maybe it would've been better to at least *try* the ability before attempting a life-threatening mission, but, well, Ash always had been the sort to throw himself into situations without thinking them through. The manor reminded him of the Downs, he thought with a pang, one he swallowed as he moved swiftly through the blue shadow, avoiding the light of the ceiling-tall windows that showed the expanse of forest below. The floors were lined with rugs that Ash was grateful for, softening his footsteps, as he made his way down one corridor and the next. He slowed as he reached a grand doorway.

He slid through these doors, too, and almost took a step. He sensed it—the vibrational waves emitting from the floors were some sort of protective barrier, one that Ash didn't know the outcome of if he were to move. Ash's stare slid from one corner of the room to the next. It was more like a gallery, a museum exhibit with artifacts on display. The home belonged to a wealthy minister of the Union, to the far south of the continent. It hadn't been an easy journey, by any means, since he could not simply materialize to the location without knowing where he was going. He had followed the hum for a month, traveling by a combination of foot and train, for which Ash had to hold up illusion alchemy comparable to only what Elena's talent had been, a mirage masked in front of his face for hours at a time. The fragment Ash had found weeks before had helped.

Ash had a particular idea for what this new fragment would do, once he consumed it. His eyes scanned the artifacts, the collection of paintings and carvings and jewels; and there, in the center and on display, the newest piece that had been sold at an underground auction, from what Ash had heard: The vial held the black orb that floated in its center, emitting the dark particles of energy. The barrier waves zigzagged about a foot from the ground. It would take more energy than Ash had planned to use for the night, but he'd come all that way; he wouldn't leave now without the chaos.

He took a deep breath, then released it slowly—envisioned himself rising, the air beneath his boots expanding and solidifying. To any other eye, Ash would be floating two feet in the air. He took one gingerly step, testing the weight of his alchemy—then dashed forward, even as he felt his feet sinking with every step—

He snatched the vial before he could sense the invisible ball of energy that engulfed the display. His hand seared, blisters erupting over his palm, pain tearing over his skin—he gritted his teeth against the scream and grabbed the vial just as his feet hit the ground, a siren piercing the air. Ash closed his eyes, took a breath, and lurched.

He opened his eyes. He was in the forest outside the castle. He fell to one knee, holding out his hand—the palm's skin was peeling from the burn. He swallowed a sob, bent in half, and tried to slow his breaths as he reflected on the love he had for himself. He'd had such difficulty with healing, once. One of the first of the twelve fragments he'd found had helped with this. Taking the orb with the intention of mastering healing had allowed a simple truth to rise: His block in healing had come from believing he was only worthy of love if others loved him; he hadn't been able to heal because he hadn't loved himself.

Having the ability to heal himself had become a priority, when surviving the wilds and the reds and the Lune followers, too. He was the most wanted man in New Anglia, considered to be as dangerous, if not more so, than Gresham Hain. Lord Alexander himself had ordered that Ash be killed on sight, offering a healthy reward of one million sterling to whoever managed to bring the boy's head.

Well, Ash couldn't say that he had learned to love himself as unconditionally as Source itself, but the orb had allowed a path through that block, at least. He watched as the blisters sank into his skin, which became pockmarked with scars as the pain faded, too. Ash didn't mind. It was just another set added to his growing collection. The purple scar running from his shoulder and down to his elbow was his largest now; it'd been where a red had knifed Ash just before he managed to dematerialize and escape a trap that had been laid for him. His day's return to Kensington, curious about a rumored truce between reds and alchemists, had been particularly reckless, even Ash had to admit.

The pain was gone now, his hand healed. Ash sighed as he sat, back against the trunk of a tree, rough bark digging into his thin shirt. He clutched the vial and held it up, inspecting the orb inside. This would be the thirteenth orb he would consume. His body ached for it, the surge of power that would tingle over his skin. His breath shook as he closed his eyes. He'd made the mistake, once, of letting this desire for the chaos consume him. His intention had been forgotten, his goal—to gain more physical strength— lost with it.

He trained his mind on why he'd come for the fragment. It was the final ability Ash needed, what would fit in with his plan—as long as all the other pieces came together, too.

※

Ash materialized into the center of the creaking cabin. Wind bit through the gaps in the logs. He shivered, sweat cooling on his skin, and fell into the pile of blankets. He curled into himself. The chaos energy still racked through his body whenever he consumed it, but he'd gotten more used to the fragments, over the past six months. He didn't lose himself to the chaos, at least, flickering images and visions and dreams. Instead, stabbing pains riddled his core, his chest. He wasn't sure how much more his body could take. But, if all went to plan, Ash would need only one more fragment. Just one more.

"Source," Ash muttered. "You'd call me a fool, wouldn't you?"

There was no response but the wind.

※

Ash's axe thudded as it cut another log in half. He stood straight, wiping his brow with the back of his hand, and looked up at the blue skies. Even from where he stood in the mountains, Ash could see the split. The tear was a black line that cracked for miles, interrupted only by clouds. It looked like an eye that had started to blink open, the largest orb of chaos preparing to fall through. It wouldn't be long, now. The black moon, falling to the earth—its gravitational pull tearing apart everything in its path. Already a wind had started to form, storm clouds perpetually gathered in the distance.

Ash picked up an armful of logs and carried them to the door that he pushed open with a boot. He tossed the wood to the side of the fireplace and added one log to the dying embers, poking at the fire with an iron stick. "So," he said, "how long are you planning on standing there?"

Marlowe stepped from the corner's shadows and into the light. Her hair was longer now, pulled back into one braid that hung over her shoulder. "How'd you know I was here?"

"You're not as sneaky as you think," Ash let her know with a tired smile.

She had a new scar on her cheek, and she'd put on more muscle, too, shown by the black top and pants she wore, reminiscent of their Ironbound days. She stepped forward, hesitant. "You look good, Ash."

Ash had developed a more muscular frame also. He hadn't come to the mountains only for solitude. He'd worked to build his body and its capacity for storing energy. He'd lifted rocks and carried them up the mountain slopes each morning. He hunted his own meat and collected water from snow. He'd sat in silence for hours every day, focused on controlling the chaos energy that twisted through him, the beating drum that demanded more.

"You, too," Ash said, falling into a chair with a sigh. There was a breath of silence, snarled with memories.

Marlowe hesitated. "I heard about Ramsay," she said.

"I don't want to talk about Ramsay."

She winced. "Understood."

Ash flexed his hand. It'd pained him for the past week since he found the latest orb, a deeper ache in the bone. "I'm guessing you're not just here for a wellness check."

"Have you heard?"

He nodded. Ash had spent every night remote viewing, watching Kensington and the redguards who patrolled with their firelocks. Change had escalated quickly in New Anglia. Lord Alexander's new anti-alchemist policies had taken root. Dozens were rounded up daily, accused of practicing alchemy whether they really had or not. Hundreds had already been lined up and shot.

"The banquet is tomorrow night," Marlowe said. "Alexander plans to announce that his House will step down from the leadership role and hand that position to Sinclair Lune instead."

Ash stared hard at the ground. Only he knew that Sinclair Lune used Alexander like a costume. Tomorrow, it was likely that Lune would shed Alexander's skin and return to his real body, declared the Head of New Anglia.

"There's a small faction I've been working with," Marlowe said. "We've been keeping an eye out for you for months now. You're a hard person to find, Ash."

Marlowe was the first person he'd spoken to in just as much time. He rubbed a hand through his curls. Ash hadn't wanted to move for weeks, when he first arrived; he was isolated, alone in the cabin, buried in grief. He didn't mind the idea of dying, then. He slept most of the day and night, hoping for a chance to dream of Ramsay, though he never came.

And then a month had passed. Ash knew that he would never stop grieving, not truly; but if he was going to die because of his father's choices anyway, then he would dedicate the rest of his life to trying to save the world—even if that meant he had only a few more months to live, in the end. He'd started his work.

"My group and I will be going to the banquet tomorrow night," Marlowe said. "We were hoping you might join us."

Ash already had his plan. He didn't need potential distractions getting in the way now. "I'm going to stop Lune alone."

Marlowe's brows rose. "Is that so? He won't be an easy man to kill."

"I'm aware of that," Ash said. It didn't matter. He didn't have any other choice, if he wanted any chance at all for his plan to work.

"Well, why not use me and my friends, at least?" Marlowe asked. "We can help defend you at the banquet. We're willing to fight for you, Ash. We're willing to die, if it means helping you kill Lune."

Ash recalled the lines of redguards he'd seen in his remote viewings. The numbers had tripled since the creation of the subdivision Callum oversaw. Alchemist prisoners, lined with Lune's black energy, acted like hollow shells as they captured, even killed, fellow alchemists in the name of House Kendrick. Any fight would become an all-out battle.

"We'll be there," Marlowe said, "whether you agree to work with us or not. It's the only opportunity we have to strike Lune, and if you fail, we need to be there, ready to make our attempt, too."

Ash hesitated. Would it hurt to have allies fighting alongside him? Maybe he'd been isolated for too long. "As long as you leave Lune to me first," he said.

Marlowe nodded her understanding. It hadn't been much of a reunion, but Ash knew she was likely busy with her own preparations for the battle, too. She turned to the wall she'd entered from, then paused. "Do you have a plan?" she asked. "For the chaos, I mean."

No amount of fragments Ash consumed would undo the black moon that had begun to push itself through. It was already too late for this world, this universe and all its threads. Too many mistakes had already been made.

It wouldn't help to scare Marlowe. "Yes," Ash told her with a small smile. "I have a plan."

That, at least, was true. Marlowe frowned as if she'd recognized there was a lie, hidden somewhere in Ash's energy, but she said nothing more as she pressed a palm to the wall.

"We'll meet in Hedge at the old warehouse," Marlowe said. "Prepare yourself, Ash. This won't be an easy battle."

※

He lay awake for hours that night, until the black sky began to pale. The nightmares had become too stressful. It wasn't worth it, to rack his body with panic each time he went to sleep. He stared at the flickering embers instead.

His father stood on the still gray lake before Ash, ripples circling his feet. His back was unmoving as he watched something Ash could not see.

"Are you happy?" Ash asked him. Fog drifted on a chilled breeze. "This is what you wanted, isn't it?"

Hain didn't respond. Ash's father had been quiet, the last few times Ash had seen him.

33

Marlowe had been busy in the half a year that'd passed, it seemed. The people who stood in the shadow of the warehouse weren't all strangers; Ash recognized the Glassport siblings, Guthrie and Gretchen, though the ten or so others weren't as familiar. Guthrie had been less than amicable in the past, but he offered a hand to Ash now. "It's good to see you."

The others Marlowe had found and gathered nodded to Ash as she made introductions. Ash listened to each name, though mostly out of respect; it felt important, to know the names of people who would likely soon be dead. It was silent, unspoken, but the vibration of resolution in the clenched jaws and gray faces showed it to be a truth all had accepted. The chances of surviving the night were slim, if not nonexistent. Ash supposed the others agreed with him when he thought it was better to die in a way he chose—giving his life for something he believed in—rather than to be killed pointlessly by hands that hated him.

Ash stood before the group. He didn't have time nor energy to be self-conscious nor nervous. He spoke what he planned plainly, describing the layout of the manor and where the banquet would be held. Orders were given, questions asked. The days of fighting for power within the rebellion were long past.

"It's a good plan," Guthrie said, others murmuring that they agreed.

The others spoke in low voices as they fitted themselves with old gas masks, some glass cracked. Ash wondered where the masks had been hidden away all this time. "I wish we had time to celebrate," Marlowe said, once the debrief was complete and she'd walked away from the group with Ash for a moment of privacy.

When Ash only frowned in confusion, she said, "It's your birthday, isn't it?"

That was right. It'd been a year exactly from Ash's honoring. "Celebrating my birthday doesn't exactly feel appropriate right now."

She grinned. "Multiple things can be true at once, can't they? Today is your birthday. You're twenty years old. That's a big deal, in my book."

"And it's also the night I'll most likely be killed," he told her, "along with everyone else in this room."

She lifted both palms with a shrug. "Multiple truths exist at once. Our dying doesn't take away from the fact that it's a special day for you, too." Marlowe smiled. "Happy birthday, Ash."

He remembered with a sinking heart how Ramsay had said the same exactly one year ago now, a finger lifting Ash's chin. It didn't matter. It wouldn't help, to lose himself in the past. "Thank you."

※

The banquet celebrating Sinclair Lune was to be held in the gardens of House Alexander's manor. It was a message, Ash assumed: a declaration that the Houses had nothing to fear from anyone who might attack them. Maybe they were right.

Ash held his breath as he stepped out of one shadow and into another. His old chambers hadn't been given away, it seemed. It was abandoned, dust gathered. Ash supposed no one wanted to sleep in the previous living quarters of a traitor.

The air around him heated, and he faded away as he took his time crossing to the balcony, where he looked down at the courtyard. Lights had been strung through the fall leaves and bushes, some floating in the air, glowing like miniature stars. An invisible barrier had been placed around the courtyard—the entire manor itself, Ash realized as he squinted. It was night, but Ash looked up to see the split, the black tear that was darker than the sky itself. Muffled wind howled. Laughter and glasses clinked, and stringed music flowed through the air. House members wore gowns and suits of their lineage's color. They were all so comfortable, as if they thought their wealth meant they could not be touched, even by a universe being ripped apart.

Lines of alchemists wearing white uniforms stood against the courtyard's walls, as still as stone, faces empty. Ash narrowed his eyes and saw that most were rimmed with black energy. Ash's throat stuck. Riles stood against the wall, unmoving, the sleeve of his missing arm rolled to his shoulder.

Ash waited until he saw an ember spark and rise from the far corner of the garden—the signal that the others were in position. He slipped from the room, into the too-familiar marbled corridors. It was odd to have returned to a space that seemed to not have changed at all, when Ash himself was now a completely different person. He sped down one hall and then another, past attendants who did not see him, and to the steps that would take him to the doors—

A redguard turned the corner. Ash stuttered to a stop and backed away, pressed against the wall as he breathed slowly. He had hoped he could avoid this particular scene. It'd been the scenario he'd dreaded, the possibility that had kept him awake all night—the idea that he might see Callum Kendrick again.

Callum's brother marched beside him. Edric seemed to have grown years older in the past months, bags beneath his eyes and skin lined, but Ash supposed that's what could happen to the Head of a House. ". . . thinks he's immortal," Edric muttered to his brother.

"The event is well guarded."

"Yes," Edric agreed. "You've made sure of that. You've done a fine job training the alchemists, Commander."

Both brothers stopped. Edric seemed to inspect Callum for a

moment, eyeing from the top of his head down to his boots. "It took you some time, with many errors on your part," Edric said, "but I think I can say now that you've finally grown into a Kendrick who would have made our father proud."

Callum's chin rose slightly. "I don't have any more distractions to pull me away from who I was meant to be," he said, "and I also have you to thank for guiding me."

Distractions. It was hard to think that this was all that Ash had been to Callum now—the way he remembered Ramsay. Edric nodded, eyes narrowed, then clapped a hand on Callum's arm—the most brotherly affection Ash had ever witnessed between the two. "I'll return to the banquet. Complete inspections before you return as well."

"Yes, sir."

Edric continued, footsteps fading. Callum stood where he was, watching his brother leave. Ash was alone with him in the hall.

Ash hesitated, but only for a moment, before he hurried past Callum, only a few feet away. He kept his illusion up, energy glimmering around him, and imagined a wall of steel around his emotions, too—yet there was a mixture of fear and relief when Ash heard Callum speak behind him.

"It's you," Callum said lowly. "Isn't it?"

Ash didn't respond. He could barely breathe.

Callum turned. His eyes searched the air until they landed on Ash, the mirage of heat surrounding him. "It's okay," Callum said. "I understand if you don't want to talk."

Ash couldn't move. Callum would've attacked Ash without hesitation, if he really had fallen into line and acted as a true son of Kendrick.

"I thought you might come tonight," Callum whispered.

Something about Callum had changed. He looked the same, but his expression—his energy—once so open, was now clouded, his own walls up. It was what Ash had found most beautiful about him, that Callum couldn't keep his love for others to himself.

"I—Creator, Ash, there's so much to say and not enough time."

But Ash couldn't blame Callum, could he? He had changed so much, too.

"You're here for Alexander," Callum murmured. It wasn't a question.

Neither spoke. Ash listened to Callum breathe, while Callum listened to him. There were pops—Ash flinched but saw from a near window that they were only fireworks, illuminating the sky. He saw the eye of the orb above before the glow faded.

"It's okay," Callum said. "I know that you need to go."

Ash forced himself to move. He couldn't linger, or he'd only want to stay by Callum's side. He hurried away from the older boy, fingers clenched into fists to fight the urge to touch Callum's hand as he passed. Still, words came from Ash's mouth. "Please stay away from the courtyard."

"I can't do that," Callum said, hoarse. "But I'll give you a head start."

❋

Ash stepped out onto the cobblestone. Crowds laughed and whispered. He wondered if the people were all truly that comfortable; maybe it was closer to say that they were in denial about their fates. At the end of the path, a table had been set. Lord Alexander himself sat on a high-backed gilded chair. The hand Ash had lobbed off was replaced by a glove; it seemed to be an alchemic invention of sorts, mechanical fingers moving like any other.

As Ash walked, he allowed his illusion to slip away. He noticed the glances of surprise, the double takes and whispers that followed. "That boy—is that—"

"But that's Woods—"

Yells of alarm and shouts followed. People took steps back even as their gazes were stuck on Ash. He paid them no mind as he approached the head table. Alexander—*Lune*—only steepled his hands and smiled, as if he'd expected Ash to come.

"There you are, Sir Woods," he said. "I was afraid your invitation had been lost."

Ash hadn't come to banter with Lune. He gestured at the crowds of guests. They'd pushed back into one another, giving Ash a wide berth. "Are you going to tell them the truth?"

Lune tilted his head to the side. "And what truth is that?" he asked.

"The fact that you're Sinclair Lune."

Ash's words were met with a high-pitched laugh, but he recognized the other energy, too. There was a sway in the crowd, crumpled eyebrows.

The man's smile widened. "I knew you were ill-minded, to have betrayed New Anglia as you did," he said. "But I suppose I underestimated just how sick. Redguards," the man said, gesturing lazily at Ash.

Ash didn't move. "Has no one questioned you?" he asked, his voice echoing. "You say that Sinclair Lune is controlling House Lune from the shadows, not willing to risk being killed by alchemists—but no one has seen Lune except, somehow, you."

He heard whispers, murmurs—yes, he knew it was a point of gossip and concern. It was strange, that the House members would not have met the man themselves.

"Lord Alexander is dead," Ash continued. "You are Sinclair Lune. You've taken over his body."

The murmurs quieted to silence. Alexander's gaze only watched Ash with a growing smile. He laughed, hand smacking the table in front of him. "Is this what you planned?" he asked. "Was this the grand reveal? Declaring me to be Sinclair Lune, thinking, maybe, that everyone gathered would *gasp* and realize their faults in following me."

Ash frowned. Something was wrong—something he hadn't planned on.

"Take a look around, Sir Woods."

He didn't want to take his eyes off Lune, but his curiosity

turned his head. He glanced at the crowd. The people in the audience stood still. Their energy glowed black, too. Some twisted and turned in confusion. Another guest held onto the arm of her friend, shaking her hand and asking why she'd stopped speaking.

"You came here, hoping to reveal the truth," Lune said as he stood. "But so many already know that I'm Sinclair Lune. What now?" he asked Ash. "Did you think my own House members would rebel against me?"

Ash had known the man had touched and controlled each alchemist forced into Callum's House. He hadn't quite considered the possibility that Lune would stretch his ability to so many others across the Houses, too. Ash had hoped that announcing the truth about Lune might create enough confusion—

"Guards," Lune said. "Take care of him."

Ash clapped once. Light echoed from his palms, a flash that split the air. A crack followed, a thunderous boom. The people around Ash screamed and covered their eyes, momentarily blinded. Marlowe and the rest jumped out of the shadows. Yells sounded, the rebels cutting into the lines of redguards and alchemists.

Ash's ears rang as he exploded forward. Alexander grinned. Ash stopped in the air, frozen, and landed hard on the table—looked behind him to see that alchemists against the nearest wall had raised their hands, strings of light tied around Ash's legs. He closed his eyes, snapped the threads with a breath, and rolled out of the way of a blast that blew a chunk of stone from the table's surface, where Ash had been moments before. He threw up a shield that shattered with another blast, dove behind the table as guards in red uniform reloaded. He was feet away from Alexander now—

Edric threw himself in front of the lord, firelock raised. Ash managed to duck to one side, blast ripping shrapnel into the air. He grimaced but bit back the pain, hand flying to his cut shoulder. He tried to roll, but realized he was stuck to the earth. He was sinking, a nearby alchemist holding two fists at him. Edric took one step and towered over him. He pressed the firelock to Ash's forehead.

"I can't tell you how long I've waited for this," he said.

A blast echoed. Ash winced—realized he felt no new pain. He looked up to see a hole had appeared in Edric's cheek. Blood dripped before it gushed, a river running down his chin. Edric fell, eyes empty. Ash turned to see Callum. His gaze was focused, unflinching. His hand dropped.

Ash hadn't fully believed Marlowe, when she told him that Callum had reached out to the rebels. He had helped them as much as he could, passing information on to them while playing the role of commander. It was because of Callum they'd even known of the banquet.

"Difficult to trust a red," Marlowe had admitted.

But Ash had seen Callum mourn Ramsay's death. Callum had recognized the mistakes he'd made, too. Ash understood his desire for atonement.

Lune stepped back, eyes wide—turned and ran. Ash whipped out a hand. The blade of light caught Lune in Alexander's back. The man stumbled amidst the screams. Ash clenched his fist and twisted it. The blade turned, piercing Alexander's heart. The man's body fell.

Ash got to one knee, breathing hard, still clutching his shoulder. There were shouts, confusion as House members ran, pushing toward the doors. Ash wanted to call a warning—he knew it wasn't over, not yet—

The doors exploded forward. White light blasted from the windows and cracks in the walls. The pillars of the manor crumbled with thuds, and the House itself fell. Silence, but only for a moment, before screams and cries rose. Dust settled on skin. Flashes of light echoed in Ash's vision. Alchemists battled alchemists. Callum shouted in pain, red leaking from his side.

Ash stood and approached the rubble. He took a breath, skin and flesh and bone moving through stone of crumpled halls as he walked. Pockets still existed, air filled with particles of haze. Bodies were caught beneath marble. He passed, ignoring the cries for help. He only stopped when he reached the door of the stone wall that still stood.

It was open. Sinclair Lune—the real Sinclair Lune, risen from his sleep—waited for him.

"I have to admit," Lune said, as Ash stepped forward. His voice was softer than Alexander's had been, but it was the same man still. "I never anticipated that you'd manage to interfere so much."

Ash flashed forward. Lune smacked away the hand clenched around a blade. He reached out, fingers inches from Ash's forehead—his hand passed through Ash's skin, illusion faltering—

Lune gasped. Blood sprayed from his mouth. He turned, rage burning his eyes. "Fucking—little—"

Ash didn't hear what Lune thought of him. The man stumbled, then fell. His breath was harsh, chest rising and falling quickly. Ash grimaced and staggered, too. He leaned against a wall that still stood. Stone and dust fell around him. His hand was pressed into his side, where shrapnel had cut through his stomach. His hand came back away red, vision blurring in and out and in again.

Lune laughed. "Looks like—you and I—don't have—"

Ash whipped out a hand. Lune's throat cut open. He gagged, blood pouring from his neck. Ash waited, until he saw that the black pupils had widened, empty. He waited until he knew, without any doubt, that Lune was dead.

He gasped. He fell to one knee, red hand leaving a smear against the wall. Lune had been right. Ash would soon follow right behind. He clenched shut his eyes and reached for the glass container he'd kept around his neck. He popped it open with trembling fingers. The chaos fragment thrummed. Ash put it to his mouth and swallowed.

What is your intention, dear boy?

34

Ash opened his eyes. He stared up at a familiar ceiling. The pain was gone, from his side and his shoulder and his mouth. He sat up. He'd forgotten what his old apartment looked like. The wallpaper was torn and stained. The space smelled like dust. The mattress was pushed into the corner. Papers of notes hung on the walls. He stood slowly, gingerly. He walked to a nearby wall, fingers tracing lines about electro dynamics and parallel realms.

Unweave the threads.

Ash couldn't have done it, not until Lune was dead. The man was too much of a manifestation of energy, of the years of hatred and fear built against alchemists. Lune was the result that had bloomed from the thoughts and actions of hundreds of thousands of people, a knot in the threads that had woven together. But even once Ash killed Lune, the chaos seeping through the tear in the fabric of the universe wouldn't have changed. Ash had wondered, considered, the possibility: What would've happened if one life-changing thread hadn't crossed with another?

Light spilled across the sky. There was no sign of the crack nor the chaos. The wind wasn't the storm of blackened energy that he had left behind. Now it was only a salty breeze. Ash realized he'd be late. He pulled on his overalls and boots and stomped down the stairs. Tobin leaned against the brick wall, arms crossed. "Late again, like always," he muttered.

Ash forced a shaking grin. "Sorry."

The two walked together in silence through the gray streets of Hedge and toward the docks for their morning job. Once, Ash had felt uncomfortable with Tobin because of the night they had

shared; now Ash was quiet because he knew and accepted that
their friendship was already over.

Ash glanced around the twisting roads and tenements. Somewhere in these streets, Baron's rebels were already gathering. Elena,
Hendrix, Riles, and Finley might have already met. There wasn't
much Ash would be able to do to stop the oncoming war between
alchemists and Lune followers. Ash wondered where Marlowe
was and if she was all right. He hadn't known much about her life
during this time, except that his father had given her a town house
in Kensington and that she waited for his orders. This version
of Marlowe wouldn't have been told to kill Ash yet; she would
be confused, wary, if he came knocking with the suggestion that
she leave Gresham Hain and New Anglia behind. He wasn't sure
how he would be able to save her from his father, but Ash would
at least try.

✳

Ash knelt in the dirt. The air hadn't quite chilled yet, and it was
hot enough for sweat to prickle his brow. He patted the dirt with
his gloved hands, then sighed as he stood, wiping his face with the
back of his arm. He breathed. The college campus was exactly as
he'd remembered it. Lancaster College's buildings of gray stone
stood scattered, students walking the path, ignoring Ash altogether as they chatted about electrodynamic equations and the
exam they had surely failed. That had upset him so much, once—
being ignored, feeling the arrogance of the students who looked
down on him. Now, he wondered why he'd needed their acceptance so much. Ash pushed the wheelbarrow across the path and
in the opposite direction.

He'd already decided to leave his job. He would give his notice
later that day. Ash didn't know what he would do next, but he
knew he couldn't stay here—not when Ramsay was still on campus as a graduate apprentice, and not when his father still roamed
the halls. Ash had done his best to avoid the corridor where he

was sure his father would later walk past, and he'd stayed out of Baxter Hall entirely, knowing what waited inside Ramsay's office.

The path had been set the day Ash met Ramsay. Together, they searched for the Book of Source, leading Ash's father to it. Hain read the Book and, with its power, ripped open the fabric of the universe, releasing chaos. An unknown man, who would come to call himself Sinclair Lune, had consumed it.

Again. Ash only wanted to try again, to untwist the threads and see if reality could turn out differently this time.

He pushed the wheelbarrow into the greenhouse and sighed. Yanking off his gloves, he stepped back outside into the sunlight. Ash's body had returned to what it had been once before—fingers calloused, shoulders sore from bending over gardens day after day—but he was still the same person as when he had confronted Sinclair Lune. He had the same memories. Source knew he'd wanted to race to Ramsay's office, to open the door and see that he was still alive—but the risk was too great. He couldn't connect their threads again, knowing it might only lead to the same ending. He'd survived in the wilds on his own, had lived for years in his apartment without anyone else to call family. He would make do alone again.

He was just crossing the front lawn when Ash saw him. The other boy looked exactly the same as when the two had first met. Ramsay strode forward without looking up, muttering something to himself, probably a formula he went over in his head. In another life, Ash was already inside Ramsay's office, practicing alchemy. In another life, he was only moments from being caught, one life tangling with another.

Ash took a shaky breath, forcing back the tears that welled. Again.

Ash knew it was the only way, to bring Ramsay back to life, for him to live without the trail of mistakes that would end with his death.

Ash thought of Callum as he watched Ramsay pass. The other

boy was likely in either Claremont or the town house in Kensington, still thinking of his love for Ramsay, unsure of whether he should reach out to the other boy and afraid to disappoint his family. Ash had been the one to push Callum into action. Callum had decided he wanted to apologize to Ramsay and admit that he was still in love with him. Without Ash's arrest—without them ever having met at all, Ash thought with a sharp pang in his chest—Callum would likely stay the path he was on. He would marry Charlotte Adelaide. He and Ramsay would likely never reunite.

But Ramsay would still have his life.

Ash wiped his eyes with an arm, furiously. Source, of course Ash was relieved to see the other alive, happiness expanding in his chest. Yet it was unbearable, too, to know that he could never speak to Ramsay again. He turned, making his way across the lawn. It would have to be enough, to know that Ramsay Thorne lived, even if the version Ash had grown with, fallen in love with, only existed in a future that would never come.

"Excuse me."

Ash spun. Ramsay had crossed the lawn without Ash's notice. He stood in front of Ash now, with the same bitter scowl that'd intimidated him, once. Ash took a step back for another reason now.

"You dropped this."

Ash looked at the palm Ramsay had extended to him. One of his gloves.

"You should do better not to litter on this campus," Ramsay said, brow raised. "Well? Aren't you going to take it?"

Ash hesitated. He almost laughed at the look on Ramsay's face, the annoyance and condescension and the glimmer that had taken Ash some time to recognize, the touch of humor, too. Source always did have a way of pulling its threads together.

His hand quivered as he reached for the glove. He tried to blink away the wetness in his eyes. "Thank you," he said.

Ramsay raised a brow at Ash in surprise. "Source, I wasn't that harsh, was I?"

Ash laughed. He was certain Ramsay would only think he'd lost his mind, but he supposed it didn't matter much, this time. "No," he said. "You weren't."

There was so much more he wanted to say, so much more that he couldn't. It didn't matter, really. Ramsay didn't have the same memories that the two shared. They hadn't gone to the higher realms together, connecting their energies and learning to love each other. This Ramsay hadn't fallen in love with Ash, hadn't even known Ash existed until a minute ago.

Ash tossed the glove into the wheelbarrow and kept pushing it along, back onto the path. He thought he felt Ramsay's curious gaze following, but by the time Ash had turned, the other was already gone.

ACKNOWLEDGMENTS

Thank you to everyone who helped *Chaos King* come to life:

Beth Phelan, Marietta Zacker, Nancy Gallt, Ellen Greenberg, and the entire team of Gallt and Zacker.

Ali Fisher and the rest of the Tor Teen team: Dianna Vega, Saraciea Fennell, Isa Caban, Anthony Parisi, Esther Kim, Heather Saunders, Dakota Griffin, William Hinton, and Devi Pillai.

You're all rock stars! Thank you for helping my dream become a reality.

BELLA PORTER

Kacen Callender is the bestselling and award-winning author of multiple novels for children, teens and adults, including the Stonewall Honor Book *Felix Ever After, Lark & Kasim Start a Revolution* and the National Book Award for Young People's Literature winner *King and the Dragonflies*. Their adult fantasy, *Queen of the Conquered*, was a World Fantasy Award 2020 winner for Best Novel and was named one of the hundred best fantasy novels of all time by *Time* and one of the fifty best fantasy novels of all time by *Esquire*.